Promises

—of the—
HEART

OTHER BOOKS AND BOOKS ON CASSETTE
BY JOANN JOLLEY:

Secrets of the Heart

Promises

—of the—
HEART

a novel

JoANN
JOLLEY

Covenant Communications, Inc.

Cover painting "Little Stone Bridge" © Carol Harding

Cover and book design © 2000 by Covenant Communications, Inc.

Published by Covenant Communications, Inc.
American Fork, Utah

Printed in the United States of America
First Printing: September 2000

07 06 05 04 03 02 01 00   10 9 8 7 6 5 4 3 2 1

ISBN 1-57734-716-1

Library of Congress Cataloging-in-Publication Data

Jolley, JoAnn, 1945-
    Promises of the heart / JoAnn Jolley.
      p. cm.
    ISBN 1-57734-716-1
     1. Mothers and sons--Fiction. 2.Birthmothers--Fiction. 3. Mormon women--Fiction. 4.
    Adoptees--Fiction I. Title

    PS3560.O436 P76 2000
    813'.54--dc21   00-043057

To my mother, Rae Jolley, for a lifetime of love and caring.
It took a while, but I finally grew up . . . Thanks, Mom, for seeing
me through.

PROLOGUE

"You're thinking about him, aren't you?"

Paula Donroe winced as her son's deep voice pulled her back to the present. "Hmm? I suppose," she murmured, setting the bulky Sunbeam iron on its heel. It teetered for a second at one end of the long, fabric-covered ironing board, then settled into a statue-like stillness.

"Figures," Scott muttered as he slouched against the door frame of his mother's bedroom.

Paula took a deep breath before turning to face her tall, sullen, sixteen-year-old son. *Easy does it,* she silently cautioned herself. *We've all been through an emotional wringer lately, and he's probably hurting just as much as the rest of us. Maybe more . . . he was there when the shot was fired, after all.* An achingly familiar surge of grief rippled through her chest at the thought, and a moment later she felt an empathetic smile rise to her lips. "What do you mean, sweetie?"

"Nuthin'. It's all you ever think about." He stretched out one leg, dug the heel of his sneaker into the carpet, and dragged his foot slowly backward to make a long, wide furrow in the deep pile.

"Well, Scotty," she said, moving close enough to see the sparse patches of adolescent stubble on his chin, "it's only been a few weeks. We all need a little time, don't you think?" She reached out to touch his shoulder and felt the lean, hard muscles tense beneath his over-sized yellow T-shirt.

"Yeah." He set his jaw in a rigid line and stared at the floor.

"You know, honey," she ventured, "if you'd like to talk about it, we could always—"

"Nuthin' to talk about." He shrugged away her hand and smoothed the carpet with a circular motion of his foot. "I gotta go."

Paula sighed. *Maybe next week . . . next month . . . next year.* "Okay . . . mind if I ask where you're off to so early on a Saturday morning?" She steeled herself for the all-too-familiar response.

"The clubhouse."

"I see." Her voice was deliberately pleasant, even though she wanted to lash out at him, tell him he should find better things to do with his life than spend every waking moment with that useless gang of his. *But you can't risk driving him even further away,* she reminded herself. *Just love him and be patient—remember the eternal perspective. Let him know you care, and eventually he might return the favor.* "And how are the Crawlers doing these days?"

"Cool."

"That's nice, dear." *Patience—that's the key. Perhaps one day he'll actually speak to you in sentences of more than three words.* "Try to be home at a reasonable hour, will you?"

"Right," he growled, disappearing quickly into the hall. A few seconds later, she heard the front door slam.

Shaking her head, Paula turned back to the ironing board. She carefully smoothed the crinkled front panel of a pale blue oxford shirt, dampened it with a spray bottle, and lowered the iron to the fabric. A slow hissing sound accompanied a few light bursts of steam as the rumpled cotton cloth yielded to the hot metal and tightened, then relaxed into a polished, wrinkle-free surface.

For some unexplained reason, this simple act of ironing had, over the last month or so, become a comfortable and comforting routine for Paula. She had moved the ironing board upstairs to her bedroom, where she now stood facing the open window overlooking the front yard of her suburban home in Woodland Hills, California. In this peaceful setting, she would sometimes spend hours banishing the wrinkles from a large assortment of shirts, blouses, and slacks. Her favorite was 100% cotton. None of the permanent-press garments would rumple enough to give her the satisfaction of restoring their original crispness. But cotton—there was a fabric she could really work with. Its wrinkles were so deep and defined that by the time she had sprayed and ironed and smoothed and creased, she was in absolute control. Maybe that was it—the sense of control. It was what she needed most in her life at the moment. If she couldn't quite get the wrinkles in her mind and heart straightened out, at least she could take care of the wrinkles in her laundry.

On this Saturday morning in mid-January, Paula now returned to the thoughts that had absorbed her before Scott's interruption. Yes, she'd been thinking about him—about *both* of them. Her mind roamed over the details of her life since the bleak day in early November when her world had changed forever. TJ, her bright, funny, basketball-crazy twelve-year-old son, had been shot in a random act of violence as he and Scott and some friends had cruised the streets of downtown Los Angeles. He had lived less than a day, and in many ways Paula had felt that his senseless death was her fault. They had argued that morning because he wanted to join the Mormon Church. Paula had flatly refused to give her permission, and TJ, in his frustration, had taken off with Scott. Hours later, the final moments of his life had played themselves out in a cold, indifferent hospital room.

But it hasn't been all bad, Paula reminded herself as she nudged the tip of the iron into a v-shaped pleat on the back of the shirt. *There have been miracles, too.* She smiled, relaxing a little as the warmer memories took hold. After TJ's death, the Mormon missionaries, Elders Richland and Stucki, had taught her the gospel, and she had finally come to understand why her young son had been so determined to join the Church: it was *true.* On a golden morning just before Thanksgiving, she and Millie, her housekeeper and friend, had been baptized. TJ had been there, too, dressed in white, a joyful grin illuminating his freckled face. Paula had seen him.

Then had come the greatest miracle of all. "I still can't believe it," Paula whispered softly as she pressed the hot iron against the shirt's collar. For the thousandth time, she relived the heart-stopping moment when she had realized that Elder Mark Richland, the tall, clear-eyed, earnest young missionary who had agonized over TJ's death and moved Paula to tears with his testimony, was her son. Her *son!* Her heart had told her it was true the moment she'd seen a distinctive bumble bee-shaped birthmark on the inside of his elbow when he removed his suit jacket during Thanksgiving dinner. Twenty-two years earlier, in the wake of the tragic death of her young husband and estrangement from her parents, she had pressed trembling lips to that birthmark just moments before giving up her day-old baby for adoption. Unknown to her, a Mormon family in Idaho had raised him to be an extraordinary young man; and then some divine force beyond any human comprehension had brought him to California and back into Paula's life. "Thank you, Father," she breathed.

As quickly as it had come, her expression of gratitude was submerged in a wave of doubt, even despair. *But where is he now?* she questioned silently. She knew where he was, of course—home on a farm just outside Roberts, Idaho, where he'd been since the first of December, the final day of his mission. They had stood together in the Los Angeles airport saying their good-byes, she knowing the marvelous secret of his parentage, wondering when and how she would ever be able to tell him. Then, placing his lips close to her ear, he had whispered that *he knew.* He had seen the look in her eyes that Thanksgiving Day, had discerned the meaning in her subtle questions about his family, and now confirmed the joyful truth at their moment of parting. When she'd caught her breath, they had embraced, wept, promised to stay in touch. Knowing he was on his way to a long-awaited family reunion, she would stand back and let him make the first contact. "Call . . . write . . . whatever," she had whispered. "Whenever you're ready. I'll be waiting."

"I will," he had promised.

Paula's brow furrowed, and the iron stopped its rhythmic back-and-forth motion. *That was six weeks ago,* she mused. *Christmas, New Year's . . . times I would have expected a call, or at least a card. What's going on?* She plunged deeper into thought, considering all the troubling possibilities. *Is he ill? Has he decided he doesn't want me in his life after all? Has he told his parents, and have they forbidden him to contact me? Do I mean anything at all to him, or am I just another notch on his missionary name tag? Will I ever see or hear—*

"Ow-w-w!" Paula smelled the seared flesh on one side of her finger almost at the same instant she felt the white-hot pain. "Nice move, Donroe," she sputtered as a fiery red welt erupted and spread itself alongside her knuckle. "What were you thinking? That's your problem, you know—you were *thinking* too much." Her reflexes took over, and she raised the finger to her lips and sucked hard. With her other hand, she yanked on the iron's garish blue cord until the socket gave up and let go. Lifting the iron, she saw an angry brown scorch mark on the shirt's pale blue sleeve. "So much for being in control," she muttered.

With her throbbing finger still pressed to her lips, she set the iron on its heel and moved a few steps to her bed. Sinking onto the polished cotton comforter, she began to rock back and forth, her eyes closed tightly in an effort to shut out the pain. *Get a grip, girl,* she chided. *It's only a little burn.* But somehow this minor insult to her flesh was the last straw, and a suffocating wave of grief and helplessness washed over her. Hot tears coursed down her cheeks as she thought of her three sons—TJ, who now lay beneath a mound of cold earth in the Rolling Hills Cemetery; Scott, who seemed to be moving further away from her by the minute; and Mark Richland, the precious child she had found but now seemed to have lost again. "What's it all for, Heavenly Father?" she sobbed. "What's it all for?"

Falling back against the pillows, Paula yielded to the emotion of the moment. She wept until exhaustion stilled her slender body and she fell into a heavy, dreamless sleep.

CHAPTER 1

"You look tired, dear," Millie said as she refilled Paula's cup of hot chocolate. "Are you feeling all right?"

"What? Oh, I suppose I'm doing okay." Paula had been staring out the kitchen window, her thoughts far away as she absently pushed a morsel of scrambled egg around her plate. Now she picked up a piece of crisp bacon and slowly lifted it to her lips. "I just had kind of a rough time . . . earlier." She glanced at the clock above the stove: ten A.M. She'd slept for over an hour after the wall of emotion had come crashing down on her.

"Ironing again, were you?" Millie's voice held a touch of gentle humor.

Paula's mouth curved into a barely perceptible smile as she looked up at the older woman, who stood with her hands on her ample hips. "I can't put anything over on you, can I?"

"Not likely," Millie chuckled. She moved closer and laid a kind hand on Paula's shoulder. "I wish things were different, though. Happier."

Paula reached up to pat the sturdy hand. "I know—and they will be," she promised, resolving to believe her own words. "Just as soon as we all get a handle on . . . well, on everything. I can't believe how our lives have changed in a just a matter of weeks. Trying to cope with the hole TJ left . . . getting into the Church . . . Scotty's declaration of war on family life as we know it. And Mark . . . finding Mark. Then waiting to hear something—*anything* from him." She sighed deeply. "It's more than overwhelming. It's . . . it's . . ."

"Faith-promoting," Millie prompted.

"Excuse me?" Paula's jaw dropped a little as she watched Millie settle into a chair across the table.

"I said faith-promoting," Millie repeated. "You know . . . like the song we sing in Sunday School: 'Trials make our faith grow stronger.'" She tried to hum a few bars, but her voice trailed off when she couldn't quite remember the tune.

"Uh-huh," Paula responded, smiling faintly. "That's one way of looking at it."

Millie looked at her benignly. "You've got to admit that finding the gospel gave us all a boost—well, except maybe for Scotty. And you never know; he might just come around one of these days."

Paula's jaw tightened. *When the sun rises in the west.*

"And finding your boy . . . Elder Richland. That was a happy miracle if ever there was one. Such a fine young man." She laughed softly. "Scotty and I thought you'd gone completely looney when you came home that day and told us about it."

"Yes, and he's hardly spoken to me since," Paula said gloomily.

"Well, it was quite a shock for the boy, finding out he's had a half-brother all these years. It's like you've got a whole new family in Idaho."

"I suppose," Paula admitted. *But that's the best case scenario; Mark could have already erased me from his mind and life. What if I never see him again?*

"And your mother—the two of you finally making your peace after more than twenty-three years. There's another wonder for you."

"You're right about that," Paula agreed. *But at what cost? It took TJ's death to bring us back together. A son for a mother . . . doesn't exactly seem like a fair trade. Or any trade at all.*

Millie studied Paula's face for a moment. "This isn't helping, is it?"

"Not really," the younger woman confessed. She cast Millie a fond glance. "But thanks for trying."

"I'm sorry, dear. Is there anything I can do? Can I get you something?"

Paula grinned slyly despite her dour mood. "Nothing the Word of Wisdom would allow," she joked, recalling the satisfying burn of a martini drizzling seductively down her throat after a long day at the office. *That was a lifetime ago. I'd even settle for a little one-on-one with Juan Valdez and his Colombian brew right about now. But hey, the Mormon coffee police would not be amused. Once you become a Saint, it's diet Coke and hot chocolate forever.*

Millie laughed. "Well, I see you haven't completely lost your sense of humor," she said, a note of relief in her voice.

"Maybe not," Paula replied, her gaze returning to the window. "It just comes a little harder these days, I guess." Her hand moved to brush a lock of dark hair away from her eyes. "Where's Rudy, anyway? I haven't seen him all morning." She thought of her gentle, warm-eyed golden retriever, now in his eleventh year and beginning to show his age. He and TJ had literally grown up together; and now that he'd lost his best friend, Rudy seemed to move more slowly and wave his long, feathered tail less frequently. The big dog spent a good deal of time lying outside TJ's room, his golden head resting forlornly on his wide, furry paws. It was heartbreaking for Paula to watch.

"He's in the backyard," Millie reported. "Scotty took him for a run earlier, but he still seemed a little restless, so I thought he might enjoy spending some time outdoors. Shall I go get him?" She moved tentatively toward the sliding glass doors leading to the patio.

"No; he'll let you know when he wants to come in. Besides," Paula said as she pushed her chair back, "I've got some work to do at the office. I'd better get going; I'm already behind schedule." She stood and smoothed the legs of her blue velour sweat suit, then retrieved her handbag and car keys from the breakfast bar.

"Oh." Millie seemed disappointed. "I thought we might go to that Relief Society meeting and luncheon over at the ward house. It starts in a couple of hours. I even put it on the calendar." She glanced pointedly at the refrigerator, where a small magnetized whiteboard calendar hung. There was a notation circled in red under "Saturday."

"Gee, Millie, I'm sorry," Paula said. "It slipped my mind . . . and besides, you know I'm not really into that sort of thing—cookies and crafts and such. Maybe next month, okay? I'm way behind on a couple of major projects at work."

"Well, all right," Millie sighed. "But there are some really nice ladies—and you wouldn't have to sew or glue things together or anything. Just sit and visit, if you like."

"I know, I know," Paula laughed. "You just go and have fun, and I'll try to make it next time. From what I know of the Mormons, there will *always* be another meeting."

"No doubt about that," Millie smiled. "Will you be late?"

"I don't think so; maybe five or sixish," Paula said, moving toward the garage. Halfway to the door, she stopped and turned to face Millie. "But you know where I am . . . in case there's a call or something."

"Yes, dear," the older woman clucked. "I have your office number, your cell phone number, your fax number, your beeper number . . . and I believe there's a carrier pigeon out back, just in case modern technology fails us. Or I could always call 911 . . ."

Paula raised a hand. "Okay, I asked for that," she chuckled. "See you later . . . and watch out for that Super Glue. Remember the time TJ stuck a couple of popsicle sticks to his fingers when he was trying to build a Power Rangers tower?"

"I sure do," Millie said, wincing at the memory. "As I recall, he swore off Super Glue after that—said something about only having eight fingerprints for the rest of his life."

A sudden flutter of sadness rippled through Paula's mind and flickered briefly in her eyes, but she shrugged it off and smiled gamely. "He was lucky to have you," she said. "You were always there for him."

"And so were you," Millie said firmly. "No boy ever had a mother who cared more. You know that, don't you?"

"Some days," she admitted. "Other times, I just wish I'd been . . ." She swallowed a surge of regret and tossed her head. "Hey, I'll be working all night if I don't get out of here. Say hi to the Relief Society ladies for me, will you?" She flashed Millie a little grin and moved quickly toward the door.

"You bet," Millie called after her. "I'll be sure to do that."

"Good grief, it's worse than I thought," Paula mumbled. "Where have I been for the past six weeks?" She had been sitting at her desk for the better part of two hours, staring blankly at a daunting accumulation of project reports, correspondence, memos, and file folders marked "Urgent." And none of it seemed to make any sense.

She swung her high-backed burgundy leather chair around to face the enormous panoramic window covering the east wall of her high-rise office. From her vantage point on the building's twenty-third floor, Paula could gaze out over downtown Los Angeles and literally watch the city's business district pulse with energy and anticipation. Even on Saturdays the streets were clogged with traffic, and occasionally the raucous sound of a souped-up taxi horn would reach her ears through the thick, triple-paned glass. The sidewalks, teeming with people of every age, race, and description, often seemed to be eddies of hope and vitality. She rarely tired of the view, because she thought of herself as part of it. For nearly a dozen years she had worked relentlessly to build her company, Donroe & Associates, into one of the West Coast's prestigious five-star advertising agencies. Paula had succeeded even beyond her own soaring expectations, along the way slogging through a bad marriage, an ugly divorce, and single motherhood to emerge as a glittering star in the professional world. She had earned the right to preside from her exclusive twenty-third-floor domain.

But today, the view seemed lackluster at best. Paula felt scattered, distracted, more inclined to mope than to make a dent in the jumble of papers on her desk. Closing her eyes, she urged herself to focus on the task at hand. *I'll worry later about Mark . . . and Scotty . . . and my life,* she told herself. *Get with the program, Donroe; you've got work to do. Face it—if you'd been working for your company, you would've fired yourself weeks ago.* She smiled at the thought, but it wasn't enough to make her turn her chair around and get back to business. *Just resting my eyes,* she reasoned. *A few more minutes, and I'll be good to go.* She let out a long, slow breath and sank back into the chair's soft leather.

Within seconds her breathing had become deep and regular, and she could feel herself drifting off. For a moment she resisted, but as the steady rhythm of her pulse slowed to a relaxed cadence, she gradually gave in to a luxuriant sensation that felt something like freefloating on a warm day off the coast at Malibu. She could do this, after all—take a little time to pull herself together. She was the boss. Whatever didn't get done today would just have to wait until—

"Paula?" The deep sound of a man's voice, followed by three sharp raps on her open office door, yanked Paula back to the moment. Her eyes flew open, and her heart thumped at this abrupt shattering of her peaceful interlude. She spun her chair around to face the intruder.

Ted Barstow's boyish face and lean, tightly muscled physique came into view. He was dressed in casual slacks and a bright blue polo shirt. "Oh, it's you," she grumbled.

"I'll take that as a 'Gee, this is a pleasant surprise,'" he grinned. Plopping himself down in a chair across from Paula's desk, he rested his right ankle on his left knee. "So how's it going, chief?"

"How does it *look* like it's going?" She gestured toward the stacks of papers and folders in front of her. "One of these days, I might actually find a desk underneath all of this."

"Well, don't look too hard," Ted advised. "Personally, I like a little clutter in my life . . . we creative types tend to enjoy the challenge of trying to remember where we put stuff. Happens every day; you've seen my office." He shook his head good-naturedly and ran the fingers of one hand through his short blonde hair.

"That I have," Paula said with a tiny smile. She couldn't help being just a little glad to see him, despite the interruption. Ted was not only her chief copywriter and the creative backbone of Donroe & Associates, but he'd been a good friend for several years. Not to mention being, as he described himself, a "long-distance" member of the Church. "And speaking of your office," she continued, "what are you doing here, anyway? I thought the golf course was your weekend habitat these days."

"Ah, yes," he admitted. "Golf—a real gentleman's sport. "Truth is"—he wiggled his eyebrows drolly—"I'm no gentleman, and I only play golf when my trick knee warns me that hitting the ski slopes or the mountain trails would be a bad idea. Besides, I have better things to do today." He leaned back and locked his fingers behind his head. Paula noticed that his long, sinewy arms were deeply tanned—a sharp contrast to her own smooth, milky-white skin.

She folded her arms across her chest. "Oh?" she said with a touch of gentle sarcasm. "There's something better than flexing the body beautiful? Something more fun than lifting weights, hanging off a cliff, or sweating Gatorade?"

"Occasionally, yes," he said. A vaguely smug expression on his face told her he had something in mind.

She took the bait. "And what exactly would that 'something' be?"

Ted grinned like a schoolboy on his first day of vacation. "I thought you'd never ask," he said, planting both feet on the floor and sliding to the edge of his chair. He paused expectantly for several seconds, his intense blue eyes boring into hers.

"Well, I asked, didn't I?" Paula finally said with a thin smile.

"So you did," he said lightly, "and I won't keep you in suspense. Here's the deal." He quickly shifted his weight onto one hip and reached behind him to pull something out of his back pocket. It was a small postcard featuring an ocean scene, and he laid it in front of her on the desk. "Wanna get away for a little while? I thought we could go for a stroll on the beach or something." He pointed to the card. "It's Marina Del Rey—we can be there inside of an hour if the traffic cooperates. I know this beautiful, secluded little stretch of sand where we can relax and watch the sea lions all afternoon. What do you say, chief?" Ted was practically bouncing on his chair.

Paula stared at him blankly for a long moment, then her dark eyes narrowed. "You're kidding, right?"

Ted's grin broadened. "I'll take that as a 'Why, yes, I'd love to. What a wonderful idea.' You might want to bring along a sweater or something; the breeze can whip you around a little this time of year. Everything else is taken care of . . . I've got some great food, a blanket, even a pair of high-powered binoculars. We could leave right now and—"

"Whoa, boy," Paula interjected. "Where on earth is this coming from, Ted?"

For the first time he noticed that she wasn't smiling, and his enthusiasm faltered. "What? Oh, well, I, uh—I just thought you might enjoy a little break, that's all. I called your place earlier and Millie said you'd just left for the office, so I knew where to find you. It seemed like a good idea at the time, so I got together a few things and . . ." His voice trailed off as he waited for her response.

She regarded him coolly for a few seconds as her mind raced. *He's just trying to be nice; don't take your frustrations out on him. You've hardly spoken to anyone at the office since TJ's death. Maybe it's time to start smoothing things out a little. At least let him down easy.* She willed herself to relax and gave him a tepid smile. "I'm sorry," she said weakly. "This is all very nice, but I just . . . I just can't. There's too much to do." Her gaze drifted over the clutter on her desk. "I need to spend a big chunk of time here today." *Never mind that I haven't accomplished a thing all morning.*

Ted's eyes darkened. "Are you sure?"

She sighed. "I'm sure. It's just not possible." *Besides, I've got too much on my mind to be chasing sea lions all over the beach. What if Mark calls, and Millie can't reach me?*

"Oh." The single word seemed to be filtered through layers of disappointment. Ted's shoulders slumped, and his gaze dropped to the floor. The two sat in silence for several long, awkward moments.

As a tight ball of guilt formed in her chest, Paula considered her options. Finally, she settled on something of a compromise. "On the other hand . . . ," she began in a pensive tone.

Ted's blonde head shot up like an exclamation point. "On the other hand?" he repeated.

"On the other hand," she continued, "I suppose I could use a short break . . . at least for lunch. I think I could manage that." She looked at him with a half-smile. *A quick trip to the deli, some idle chit-chat. Nothing too deep . . . nothing too revealing.*

"Lunch . . . lunch . . . lunch," Ted pondered. Then his face erupted into a mischievous grin. "Yes, that's it—lunch!"

Paula laughed in spite of herself. "Good grief, Ted, you act like you invented the concept. Come on, let's run down to Meservy's deli for a bite. Then I can get back to—"

"Are you kidding?" Ted cut in. "I've already got everything we need, and I know the perfect place. No muss, no fuss, no bugs, no smog, no travel time. You just wait right here and sharpen your taste-buds, and I'll be back in a New York instant." He leapt to his feet and bounded from the office before she could voice an objection. Oddly, she felt amused and heartened by his sudden burst of eagerness.

Paula had barely returned from a quick trip to the rest room when Ted appeared with an enormous canvas backpack grasped tightly in one hand and a king-sized blanket securely wedged beneath his other arm. An L.A. Dodgers baseball cap was balanced jauntily on his head. "Ready to go?" he asked brightly.

"Go *where?*" she countered, glancing at his gear. "This looks more like a safari than a light lunch."

"Not to worry," he insisted. "Follow me, and I'll make a believer out of you."

"Yeah, right," she muttered, trudging behind him down the hall to the elevator.

"Catch the button, will you?" he said. "I'd do it, but my hands are occupied."

Her mouth pursed as she reached for the DOWN button. "I thought you said we weren't going anywhere," she said.

"Hold on," he laughed. "Let's make that the UP button, shall we?"

A slightly puzzled expression flashed across Paula's face. "But the parking garage is—"

"I know, I know. But we're going UP. Just humor me, okay?" She shrugged and complied.

Inside the elevator, Ted leaned against the wall and said, "Now, press thirty-six."

"Uh-huh." Paula followed his instructions, then waited quietly as the lights flashed in sequence from twenty-three to thirty-six. It was the final number on the panel—the top floor of the building.

As the heavy steel door rumbled open and they walked into a tiled foyer, Paula suddenly recognized this place. She hadn't been here for . . . well, for years. It was like a lost memory coming to life, and she couldn't help smiling.

"Gotcha," Ted whispered behind her.

They were standing at the entrance to the DeJeune Atrium. Named for the original owner and designer of the building, this floor had been preserved as a small oasis at the top of his glass-and-steel monument to commerce and technology. Thirty years earlier, Arthur DeJeune, a prominent architect, conservationist, and patron of the arts, had finished off his newly designed building with an entire floor of luxuriant plant life, artfully arranged to represent dozens of geographical areas of the world. In one casual stroll through "the gardens," as they had come to be known by employees working in the building, one could experience everything from the vivid cactus blooms of the desert Southwest to the profuse, aromatic foliage of more tropical climates. If one had a favorite plant, shrub, or flower, there was no question that it could be found in this temperature-controlled, meticulously groomed sanctuary of life and color. It was like Eden at a glance, only with plant labels and waste containers.

"We have it all to ourselves," Ted observed as they moved through the entrance and toward a small waterfall at the center of the atrium. "It's pretty crowded during the week, but I almost never see anyone here on a Saturday."

Paula nodded, breathing in the slightly humid air. "You come here often on Saturdays?" she questioned as he set the backpack down and spread the blanket on a grassy mound near the waterfall and beneath a tall, glistening ficus plant.

"I wouldn't say often," he replied. "Maybe once every couple of months. I find it . . . peaceful." He flopped onto the blanket and smiled up at her. "And there are no critters—at least none that prefer human flesh to leaves and things." He patted a spot next to him. "Come on down . . . it's a reserved seat, you know."

Paula lowered herself gracefully and sat cross-legged on the plush woolen blanket, noticing how its deep blue shade matched her sweat suit almost perfectly. "And a color-coordinated seat at that," she joked.

"We aim to please," Ted drawled. They sat in companionable silence for a few moments, enjoying the lush greenery of their surroundings. Off to one side, two small canaries perched on a blue-green bush were chirping contentedly.

"This is something," Paula murmured. "I'd forgotten how lovely it is here. When Rich and I were first . . ." She paused, remembering the early years of her marriage to Richard Donroe, when life had seemed perfect. They had set up their small advertising agency in an ugly, one-room, windowless office several blocks from this building, and had come here a few times a week to stroll arm-in-arm through the gardens, dreaming of more prosperous times to come. Then Richard had pulled out of the marriage and the business, leaving Paula with no money and even fewer dreams. But she'd held on, worked hard, and made the agency flourish. Finally, the day had come when she'd been able to move her company to this prestigious building and an elegant suite of offices on the twenty-third floor. But she'd never had the heart to visit the gardens again, even after nearly a decade. *I should have come,* she thought now. *Has it always been this lovely?*

A rustling sound pulled her back to the moment, and she glanced over at Ted, who was rummaging in the oversized backpack. "Welcome back," he said, winking at her. "Pleasant memories, I hope."

Paula chuckled grimly. "More or less." She eyed the backpack. "What have you got in there, anyway?"

"Lunch," Ted replied as he began to pull out various items and arrange them on the blanket. "Let's see . . . we've got delectably ooey-gooey barbecued ribs, two kinds of salad—yep, including your favorite, three-bean—an assortment of veggies and dips, fresh fruit, some of those sesame butter rolls you go wild over, and—of course—strawberry shortcake for dessert." He rubbed his temple. "Now, did I forget anything?"

"Nothing except the army to eat all of this," Paula laughed. She was beginning to relax, and the food looked and smelled wonderful. Snatching two olives from one of the small plastic vegetable trays, she popped them into her mouth. "You really know how to do a meal, Ted."

"Me and Joe Albertson," he said. "Let's hear it for deli magic."

"Hear, hear," Paula agreed, reaching for a rib. "Or is that, 'here, here'? I never could figure out what that toast meant, you know—'here it is,' or 'hear what I'm about to say'? Either way, it doesn't make a whole lot of sense."

"Well, I guess if you've had enough to drink, it really doesn't matter," Ted observed. "Which reminds me . . ." He pushed his arm deep into the backpack and pulled out two shallow, long-stemmed plastic glasses. Then, reaching in again, he slowly drew out a long, gracefully shaped dark-green bottle, its narrow neck tipped with gold foil. "We can't have a proper meal without a little liquid refreshment, now can we?" Smiling widely, he began to peel away the foil.

Paula's mouth suddenly went dry as her face paled. *Champagne? It was always my favorite . . . but why would Ted do this to me now?* She gulped hard and stared at the ground, trying to think of something to say while the seconds ticked by awkwardly. She prayed for a kind and artful reproach, but no words came. By the time she lifted her eyes, he had poured the pale, effervescent liquid into both glasses and was holding one out to her. "Cheers," he said warmly, his blue eyes sparkling as if he was bestowing a great gift.

The time had come; she knew she had to stand her ground. "Ted," she rasped in a paper-dry voice, "how *could* you?" She gestured toward the champagne glass, its contents still so inviting despite her resolve. "You know I don't . . . I don't *do* this anymore. And I can't believe you would actually—" She covered her mouth with her hand and shook her head, unable to continue.

Ted's expression froze for an instant before he gently set both glasses down and reached for Paula's free hand. "Do you mean to tell me," he said in low, solicitous tones, "that you have stopped drinking entirely?"

Paula lowered her hand from her mouth and stared at him incredulously. "Why, yes. Of course," she replied. "Isn't that what the Word of Wisdom is all about?" Her tone became defensive as she pulled her hand away from his. "But then, maybe I shouldn't expect you to understand—"

"I understand," he interrupted, "that you'll die if you don't drink."

She laughed sarcastically. "Water, maybe. Orange juice, maybe. But I hardly think champagne is necessary to sustain life."

Ted leaned forward until his face was inches away from hers. "And who," he breathed, "said anything about champagne?"

Paula snorted softly. "Well, I certainly know a glass of the bubbly when I—"

But Ted had already turned away from her and was retrieving something from the backpack. His eyes were expressionless, his mouth set in a perfectly straight line as he shoved the green bottle firmly into her hands. "Here's your champagne," he said evenly.

Paula felt a sudden rush of warmth to her face as she turned the bottle and examined its label. "Sparkling grape juice," she murmured. "Non-alcoholic."

Ted leaned back on his elbows and regarded her coolly, saying nothing. Finally she broke the silence. "Oboy . . . why do I all of a sudden feel like an idiot?"

"I guess that would be," he said tersely, "because you *are* one." His voice held no trace of humor.

Startled by his response, she tried to lighten the mood. "Hey, my mistake; sorry about that. I just thought—"

"You just thought I had so little respect for your beliefs that I'd pour you a glass of *champagne.*" His cold blue eyes bored into hers accusingly.

"Well, not exactly," Paula said feebly. "It was a joke, right?" She smiled uncertainly.

"Actually, no," he said, sitting up and folding his arms across his chest. "It didn't even occur to me that you'd automatically jump to the conclusion that I was tempting you away from the Word of Wisdom—away from all the promises you'd made." His eyes flashed. "I was there a few weeks ago, you know; I saw you come up out of that baptismal font with a look of pure joy on your face, and I was rooting for you one hundred percent. Why would I *ever* do something to compromise that commitment?" Suddenly the anger drained from his eyes, and his face crumpled into a forlorn expression. "What kind of a friend do you think I am, anyway?"

Paula sighed deeply. "A wonderful friend with an idiot for a boss," she said. "I'm really sorry, Ted; I was way out of line." She rested her hand lightly on his arm. "What can I do to make it up to you?"

He seemed to relax at her touch, and the beginnings of a smile tugged at the corners of his mouth. "Just trust me, okay? I may not be an active Mormon at the moment—although I have been doing some thinking about it lately. But I promise you . . . whatever happens in my own life, I'll never try to sabotage your faith. You've got to believe that."

"Okay, I do. I do believe that," Paula said earnestly. "So now what?"

"Now," Ted declared, a gleam of good humor returning to his eyes, "we get back to the business at hand. For starters, let's take up where we left off when I so rudely called up your previous lush-like behavior." She giggled as he picked up both champagne glasses and handed her one. "To quote an old Mormon toast," he said with a flourish, "'Vino is red, champagne is yellow, I'll take my chances with lucky green Jell-O.'" They both laughed as their glasses touched.

"Mmm, not bad," Paula said after a few swallows of the grape juice. "I could learn to like this."

"Well, save a little to wash some of this food down," Ted cautioned. "There's no way I can eat it all by myself."

"Anything for a friend," Paula said lightly.

They had eaten their fill and settled into an easy, amiable conversation when the shrill sound of a beeper split the peaceful air.

CHAPTER 2

Paula reached into her pocket and pulled out a small, gray, very noisy plastic box. She pushed a button and the beeping stopped, but she continued to focus intently on the tiny silver screen nestled in her palm.

"What's up?" Ted asked after a long moment. "You're staring holes into that thing."

Paula chewed on her lip nervously. "It's Millie," she finally said. "She wouldn't call unless it was really important, and she's probably been trying to call my cell phone. I left it in my office." She stood abruptly, scattering a few olives and salad greens across the blanket. "I think I know what this is about, and it's something I've been waiting for. Do you mind if I . . . ?" She nodded toward the elevator.

Ted shrugged. "Sure, you go ahead; I'll wrap things up here." He looked up at her. "But I hafta ask . . . this wouldn't by any chance have something to do with a recently returned missionary from the great state of Idaho, would it?" Paula had told him about Mark; and once he had picked his jaw up off the ground, he'd quickly gotten used to the idea of Paula's having a twenty-two-year-old son. In fact, he had rather enjoyed teasing her by pointing out that if Mark hurried and found himself a wife, Paula could easily be a grand-mother before her forty-second birthday. She had generously offered to wash his mouth out with laundry detergent.

Now her eyes shone when Ted brought up the possibility. "I don't know," she admitted, "but I certainly intend to find out." She began to walk briskly toward the elevator, then stopped in mid-stride and turned back toward him. Her face broke into a warm smile as she gestured toward the remains of their picnic. "Thanks, Ted . . . for all of this. It means a lot to me; it really does."

He looked at her a little sheepishly. "Then I'm forgiven for my earlier, uh, indiscretion?" He shot a glance at the empty champagne glasses, now perched on a nearby stone bench like a pair of miniature birdbaths.

"Absolutely," she said cheerfully. "And the next bottle is on me."

"I'll look forward to it," he said. "Now get out of here and go make your call." Pulling himself to his knees, he started gathering up the food and blanket. By the time he turned again toward the elevator, Paula had disappeared.

Please let it be him, she pleaded as she waited for a dial tone and punched in the number. It rang once, twice, then a small click told her someone had answered. Millie's cheerful "Hello?" echoed in her ear. She had probably been sitting with one hand on the phone for half an hour.

Paula dispensed with formalities. "What's up?" she questioned eagerly.

"I thought you'd never ask," Millie teased. She spoke deliberately, but there was an unmistakable note of anticipation in her voice.

"Come on, I'm dying here, Millie. Tell me—was it him?" Paula's fingers drummed fiercely against the edge of her glass-topped desk. "He called, didn't he?"

"Oh, all right," Millie said, feigning impatience. "If you must know . . . yes, he called. Elder Richland, in the flesh. From Idaho. Less than an hour ago."

"I *knew* it!" Paula exclaimed, making a thumbs-up sign with one hand. "How is he? Did he ask for me? Why didn't he call sooner? Is he all right? Did you get his number? Has he started school? No; he would have been calling from Utah. Does he want me to call him back? I could do it right now if you'll give me—"

"My goodness, girl, slow down!" Millie laughed. "I said he called; I didn't say he'd given me his life history since leaving California."

"Okay, okay," Paula said, taking a deep breath as she leaned back in her chair. "So tell me what he said. Every word."

"You don't ask for much, do you?" the older woman chuckled. "Really, there isn't much to tell."

"What's that supposed to mean?" Paula asked, feeling an anxious knot taking shape in her midsection.

"Oh, nothing, I suppose. He asked how you are, of course, but he didn't say much about himself. I got the feeling he really wanted to talk with you, not me. It's understandable. After all, you're . . . family." Millie said the words with no hint of envy or reproach.

"Family . . . that's nice," Paula reflected. She couldn't help thinking of Scott, who had lately withdrawn himself from virtually any contact with her or Millie, despite their efforts to include him in their conversations and activities. Where had her family gone over the last six weeks, anyway? She shook off the thought and pressed for more information. "So did Mark leave a number? Ask me to call? Confess to a sudden urge to drop everything and come out to sunny California for the weekend? *What?*"

"None of the above," Millie explained. "He was just on his way somewhere—with his brother Alex, I think. Said he'd be gone until late."

"I could have waited up," Paula sighed. *I would have waited up until Tuesday of next year.*

"I told him that, but he just laughed and said it figured. 'Tell her I'll try again tomorrow,' he said. 'We have a lot to catch up on.'"

"He's right about that," Paula said, suddenly relieved that at least he cared enough to *want* to catch up. "Did he say what time he'd call?"

"Not really, but I think he said something about having church in the morning. Maybe he'll call later on in the afternoon."

"Okay." *I'll be there; can't . . . won't miss his call. Not after I've waited this long.* Paula made a mental note of how many church meetings she would miss if she stayed home and waited for the phone to ring. *I can always go to church—can't always talk to my son. Surely the Lord would understand; He's big on families, after all. And even if Mark isn't technically family anymore . . .* She shook her head to clear the thought away. *Don't go there, Donroe. You can't remake the past, even if you wanted to. Just be grateful he's a good boy, clean and healthy. And a Mormon.*

"Where were you, anyway?" Millie's question cut through Paula's musings.

"Excuse me?" Paula said, her thoughts still far away.

"I said, where were you? I was starting to worry when I called your office, then your cell phone, and couldn't get an answer. 911 was next if the beeper hadn't worked." Millie spoke lightly, her voice edged with curiosity.

"Oh, Ted dropped by and we . . . went for a bite." *And had a fight, then made it right.* Paula smiled at the memory.

"That's nice, dear," Millie said. "He's such a lovely young man, don't you think?"

"I suppose," Paula replied vacantly, her thoughts already hurtling back to Idaho and the tall, brown-eyed young missionary. *Returned* missionary.

"And talented, too . . . all those writing awards." Millie was gushing.

"Uh-huh," Paula agreed idly. *What does a returned missionary do in his spare time—practice speaking civilian? Hang out with the Future Farmers and Former Missionaries of America? Join a support group for other elders who had found their birth mothers in the mission field?*

"He seems to care about you, you know."

"What?" Paula ripped herself back from her intriguing train of thought.

"Ted. He cares about you."

"Yes, of course . . . and I care about him, too. He's a good friend." She pictured Ted offering the Mormon toast and grinned in spite of herself. *Lucky green Jell-O.*

"Let's see now," Millie continued, "didn't you tell me he's divorced?"

"Twice," Paula acknowledged.

"So that would make him . . . single."

"I believe that's the correct term, yes." Paula's lips were beginning to feel tight. What did this have to do with anything?

"Well, well," Millie said coyly. "He's awfully good-looking, too. And a member of the Church."

"In a manner of speaking," Paula said. "I wouldn't exactly call him a mainstream Mormon."

"But he has a history," Millie responded. "That's something. Maybe you could talk to him and—"

"Maybe," Paula cut in, "but right now I have a lot of work to do, and I'm way behind. I'll see you later, okay?"

"Of course, dear. I know you're busy," Millie said hastily. "And I'm late to that Relief Society meeting, too . . . I wanted to be sure you got the message."

Remorse flickered across Paula's mind. "Gee, I'm sorry, Millie. I didn't realize you were waiting around for me to call."

"No matter. I'll just be on my way. We'll see you later, then? Supper will be ready around six."

"Sounds good. But don't knock yourself out; a sandwich would be fine, you know. Ted and I had a pretty big lunch." *Although I could have tolerated a few more of those gooey ribs.*

"I'll keep that in mind," Millie clucked. "Good-bye now." A soft click sounded, followed by silence.

Paula returned the phone to its cradle, then leaned forward until her chin was almost touching the desk. "Well, what do you know," she mused aloud, closing her eyes to savor the news. "He called. He actually called." She felt a satisfied grin idling at the corners of her mouth.

"I *knew* it!"

Paula's eyes flew open just as Ted leaned against the open door of her office. She pressed a hand to her chest. "What are you trying to do, give me a coronary? Sneaking up on me like that . . ." She took a deep breath and fanned her face dramatically.

"So sue me," he said with a little smirk. "I just happened to be in the neighborhood and thought I'd drop by. Want some leftovers?" He held out a few plastic grocery bags.

She started to shake her head, but paused. "Got any more of those ribs?" She thought of the tender white meat dripping with sweet, tangy sauce and her mouth went soft.

"Well, I believe we just might be able to rustle up some of them critters," Ted drawled. He checked three of the bags before he found what he was looking for. "Here you go; might as well take the salad and what's left of the dessert." He stepped forward and plunked a large bag on her desk between two piles of folders.

Paula glanced briefly into the sack, then up at Ted. "What, no champagne?" she asked snidely.

"Heck no," he said, playing along. "I poured the rest of it into one of those round stone basins by the waterfall. By the time I left, our two little canary friends had found it. I bet they're pretty happy campers by now." He grinned and winked at her.

"Yeah, yeah," she said, dipping her finger into a tub of barbecue sauce. "Nothing like a little grape juice to really send you into orbit." She plunged her dripping finger into her mouth and closed her eyes as the sauce oozed over her tongue. It was just as good as she'd remembered. Maybe better.

"So . . . he called, did he?"

Paula nodded, her eyes still closed as she slowly, delicately licked the last bit of sauce from her finger. Finally she looked at Ted, who was staring at her intently. "You know," he said gruffly, "you do that very, uh . . . seductively."

She gazed at him blankly for a moment, then broke into a hearty laugh. "Oh, come on, Ted," she chided. "It's just the champagne talking."

"That must be it," he agreed with a hoarse chuckle. He sat on the broad arm of a chair across from her desk. "So, about that call . . ."

"Well, he did and he didn't," Paula said as she carefully twisted the grocery bag's plastic handles into a knot.

"Excuse me?" Ted looked at her with a puzzled expression. "I thought you said Mark—"

"Oh, he called, all right," she explained. "It's just that he was on his way somewhere . . . told Millie he'd call me tomorrow."

"I see. Did she say how he was? Why he hasn't been in touch sooner?"

"I asked that too—along with a thousand other questions. Millie said he was kind of evasive; just said he'd explain everything when he calls."

"Hmm. After waiting this long, you'd think he'd at least let you know what's going on."

"He will, Ted. I'm sure of it." Paula spoke in sympathetic tones, although she was inclined to agree with his observation. But she was willing to give Mark the benefit of the doubt. "We'll get all caught up tomorrow. In the meantime," she gestured toward the clutter on her desk, "I really have to dig into this mess. We've got meetings with two major clients on Monday, and I need to do some serious strategy planning before then. Even if I don't feel like it."

"If there's anything I can do to help . . ." Ted left the offer hanging.

"Thanks, but I need to do the groundwork first—figure out the budgets and some reasonable time lines for both ad campaigns. If I can get my act together, I should be able to get it done this afternoon; after that, I'll definitely need your creative input. Can we meet first thing Monday?"

"You bet, chief." Ted saluted smartly.

"Seven A.M.?"

He winced, then smiled weakly. "Uh, sure . . . seven A.M."

"I knew you'd love it," Paula grinned. "Now, go chase a golf ball around or something. I have work to do." She was beginning to feel a welcome surge of energy, and she wanted to take advantage of it.

"Okay, okay; I can take a hint." Ted stood, picked up his remaining grocery bags, and sauntered toward the door. Halfway there, he swung around to face her. "But call if you need me, will you?"

"Hmm?" Paula was already absorbed in her work, but looked up to give him a parting smile. "Yes, of course . . . and thanks, Ted. I mean it." She reached over to flip her computer on, and was soon engrossed in tapping out a string of keyboard commands.

"No problem. See you Monday, then." Ted shuffled into the hall, and a few moments later the front office doors opened and closed.

It was nearly nine o'clock by the time Paula cleared the last file folder from her now-immaculate desk, closed up her office, and made her way to the parking garage on one of the building's lower floors. She had ridden an intense wave of creative energy for the past several hours, accomplishing more in less time than she would have thought possible. Now she was exhausted but in high spirits.

Later, at home, she carefully pushed open Scotty's door and made sure he was safely asleep. Then she knelt beside her bed and expressed thanks for the gift of renewed vigor and burgeoning optimism. "Tomorrow will be a wonderful day," she whispered. "An extraordinary day. Tomorrow, Mark will call. My son will call." She drifted off to sleep with a prayer of peaceful anticipation on her lips.

CHAPTER 3

A deep, discordant bellow rumbled through Paula's open bedroom window, pulling her rudely away from a pleasant early-morning dream involving barbecued ribs and a matched pair of tipsy canaries. She groaned, opened one eye a sliver of an inch, and wondered if some poor animal might be lying wounded in the street. A few seconds later the pitiful sound repeated itself, and this time she recognized it at once. *Scotty's friends are here to pick him up in that dinosaur of a Chevy.* She glanced at her bedside clock: seven-thirty. *Right on time.* She had heard the tuneless bleating of the old car's horn nearly every Saturday and Sunday morning for over six weeks now, and it still set her teeth on edge. *Someone should put it out of its misery.* She smiled grimly at the mental picture of a T-shirt-clad firing squad poised to do its duty. *They shoot Volvos, don't they?*

Before the obnoxious horn blared a third time, the front door slammed and Paula heard footsteps hurrying toward the street. Then a rusty metal door screeched open and closed, followed by a string of popping and groaning sounds as the old vehicle shuddered into gear and lurched away from the curb. Paula thought she detected the faint but pungent odor of burning oil as the Chevy lumbered out of earshot. Sandwiching her head between two pillows, she tried to relax back into her tantalizing dream, but it was no use. She was hopelessly awake. *I wish Scotty would stay home just one Sunday,* she mused. *Maybe I could talk him into going to church.*

Stretching languidly, Paula mentally discussed with herself the options for her day. *First priority: be here when Mark calls.* A pleasant chill swept down her arms as she anticipated hearing his voice. *In the meantime, you could catch up on some office work, do a little ironing, watch one of those overdue videos you rented from Blockbuster a month ago, get online and check your investments—*

"Whoa, girl! Hold on just a minute," Paula said aloud. She sat up abruptly and glared at herself in the mirror hanging over her dresser. "All right . . . what have you done with Paula Donroe, the Mormon convert who used to live at this address? You know the one . . . that smart, pretty little thing who swore—oops, not a good word; make that *promised*—to do everything right once she joined the Church. That's right . . . the Sabbath-*keeping* Donroe, not this loathsome *imposter* you see before you. What did you do, spike the barbecue sauce? Shame on you!" Paula made a troll-like face and stuck her tongue out at the image in the mirror. Then she collapsed back against her pillows, giggling until her sides ached. It felt good.

Half an hour later, she had showered and dressed in a pair of casual khaki slacks and a light-blue oxford shirt. Her plan for the day hadn't fully materialized, but as she knelt for a brief morning prayer it occurred to her that despite her compelling desire to be at home when Mark Richland called, she could never justify missing church this afternoon to baby-sit the phone. Surely Mark would understand; he was Mr. Straight Arrow, after all. If she wasn't home, he'd try again later. The thought gave her comfort.

As Paula ran a wide comb through her damp hair, she heard a light but insistent scratching at her bedroom door. Suddenly, her morning began to take shape. *It's been a long time since Rudy and I took a little stroll around the neighborhood,* she mused. Her heart felt light at the prospect. *I've barely paid him any attention since TJ . . .* Moving quickly to the door, she opened it to find the big dog leaning back on his haunches, staring up at her with a somber, worshipful gaze. His dark, luminous eyes were so grave and pensive that she immediately knelt beside him, encircling his shaggy neck with her arms and pressing her lips to the crown of his wide golden head. A surge of emotion rose in her throat as she stroked his back and whispered, "Hey, big guy, how ya doing?" He nuzzled her neck with his cool, damp nose. "Wanna go for a walk?" A tiny gurgle of joy erupted from deep in his chest, and he lifted a paw to gently tap her knee. "Okay, it's a deal. Just let me get my shoes on and grab a sweater." She was back beside him in less than a minute, and the two of them sauntered companionably out into the cool morning.

They took the long way around the neighborhood, stopping often to explore an intriguing stand of shrubs or to listen to a family of squirrels chittering in the trees. Two streets over, there was a small park, if you could call it that—about forty square feet of grass and a couple of squatty stone benches. Paula sat on one of them while Rudy ranged around the perimeters of the lawn, then returned to settle near her feet with a contented sigh. Reaching down to scratch his head, she felt relaxed and optimistic. She knew her frame of mind was directly related to the long-awaited call from Idaho that would soon come, probably today. Closing her eyes, she could almost hear the phone ringing. It would be *so good* to hear her son's voice again. After twenty-two years of not knowing who or where he was, she would never tire of hearing that voice.

Returning to the house more than an hour later, they found Millie, her ample figure bundled in a comfortable-looking chenille robe, sitting in the breakfast nook, spooning sugar onto a bowl of shredded wheat. "Morning," she said as Paula sat down across from her, and Rudy disappeared beneath the table. "I heard you leave earlier; didn't fix anything special for breakfast, since I wasn't sure when you'd be back. I could stir up some muffins, or—"

"Don't you dare, Millie Hampton," Paula interjected cheerfully. "This is supposed to be your day off, after all. Just because you stick around for church doesn't mean you have to feed us, too. Scotty's already gone, and I can manage just fine." To prove her point, Paula poured herself a bowl of cereal and picked up a pitcher of milk with a dramatic flourish.

"It's no bother," Millie protested. "I like taking care of you."

"I know; but really, fending for myself one day a week won't kill me, will it?" Paula reached across the table to pluck two fresh strawberries from a blue ceramic bowl. She popped one into her mouth and bit down slowly, enjoying the sudden nip of the fruit's tangy juice as it flowed over her tongue.

"I suppose not," Millie agreed, "but it hasn't been an easy time these past few weeks. I've worried about you."

"Well, don't," Paula said firmly, lifting the second strawberry to her mouth. "Things will be just fine; you'll see. Now, don't you have a meeting or something this morning?"

Millie nodded. "The Relief Society ladies asked if I'd help with the planning for a little luncheon next month—for the seniors in the ward, I believe. I told them I'd be happy to, so we're meeting to get things organized."

"An inspired invitation," Paula laughed. "Just don't get them hooked on your chicken with plum sauce, or they'll make you the patron saint of lip-smackers before the old folks know what hit them."

"Oh, pooh," Millie said with a shy grin. "I just want to help a little, that's all."

"Uh-huh . . . like Martina Hinges just wants to hit a ball or two over the net every day," Paula joked. She said it lightly, but she couldn't help reflecting that in the short time since they had joined the Church, Millie had already made her way into the very heart of the ward with her sunny disposition and her cheerful willingness to serve. Paula, on the other hand, who was by nature more cautious and solitary, had remained somewhat on the outskirts of this minia-ture city of Saints. It would take her a little more time to get used to the idea of belonging to a four-hundred-member family.

"Let the youngsters play tennis," Millie said, smiling benignly. "I'll take a good old-fashioned dinner party any day." She stood slowly, her gnarled hands gripping the edge of the table, and grimaced slightly as her weight shifted from one foot to the other.

"Your hip giving you grief again?" Paula asked.

"No more than usual," Millie replied. "It limbers up some if I keep moving." She edged carefully toward the entryway. "I'll just run to my room and change, then I'll be on my way. We'll see you at church, then?"

"Wouldn't miss it," Paula smiled, recalling her conversation with a certain bedroom mirror earlier that morning. "You have a nice meeting."

"Thank you, dear," Millie said as she disappeared into the hall. A few seconds later, her bedroom door opened and closed.

Paula lingered at the breakfast table for nearly an hour after Millie's big Buick pulled out of the driveway. She ate two bowls of cereal, polished off the rest of the strawberries, and read the Sunday paper. Recalling Saturday afternoon's welcome burst of energy, she reflected that it felt good to be lazy for a change, instead of depressed. There was a big difference; one could *choose* to be lazy, but when it came to being depressed there was no choice involved—you just plummeted into a deep, black hole and waited at the bottom until it was over. At the moment, she was thoroughly enjoying the consequences of her morning's choice—doing nothing and feeling perfectly cheerful about it. *I'm expressing my gratitude for a fresh outlook on life,* she mused with a contented sigh. *Surely that's an appropriate Sabbath activity.* She leaned back in her chair, closed her eyes, and smiled serenely as the sun's rays filtered meekly through the kitchen window and warmed her face. *I'm preparing myself to feel the Spirit when I go to church.* Her mind and body grew heavy with peace and relaxation, and every problem of her life seemed to slowly recede into a warm cocoon of tranquility. A few bars of "Gently Raise the Sacred Strain" fluttered pleasantly around the edges of her memory.

A piercing electronic bark close to Paula's ear jarred her into alertness, and her mind winced with exasperation at this sudden intrusion on her cozy reverie. *If this is one of those annoying telemarketers . . .* She reached above and behind her for the wall phone. "Yes?" she said curtly into the receiver.

There was a long silence on the other end. *"Hello?"* she finally pressed.

"Paula?" A deep, faraway voice sounded hesitant and uncertain. "Is this 555-2856?"

A sudden rush of color flooded Paula's cheeks as she recognized the caller, and she clamped her lips together to stem a wave of regret. *Nice one, Donroe,* she lamented silently. Swallowing her emotion, she said too sweetly, "Mark? Mark Richland, is that you?" *As if he doesn't know you know. Face it; he has an idiot for a birth mother.*

The voice relaxed, and she could picture him smiling into the phone. "The same," he said. "Uh, sorry if I caught you at a bad time; sounds like you weren't all that excited to get a call."

Paula laughed self-consciously. "No, it's not that at all," she protested. "I was just about a million miles away when the phone rang, and it startled me. Sorry about that . . . sometimes I get a little cranky when . . . well, when I get sidetracked. I hope you'll forgive me."

"No problem," Mark said amiably. He paused, then after a few seconds asked, "So how are you, anyway?"

"Oh, I can't complain," she replied. "I never stop thinking about TJ, of course. Millie and I are still figuring out how to be Mormons, and I manage to stay busy at the office. Other than that, things are pretty much the same."

"And how's Scott?"

Paula's laugh had a sorrowful edge. "Well, he's said about seven words since Thanksgiving, and 'When can I be baptized?' weren't among them. I'd like to say we've pulled together as a family since we lost TJ, but that would be stretching it. I worry about him, Mark. A lot."

"Just keep trying, Paula," Mark said earnestly. "That's all the Lord asks of you."

"I know," she agreed. "But over the past few weeks, it seems like Scotty's withdrawn into his own bitter, angry little world. And I don't know how to bring him out of it."

"I'm sure you'll have some help," Mark said. "The Lord will eventually get to him."

"Well, then, I hope the Lord doesn't mind spending some time in gangland, because that's where Scotty hangs out these days. I can't seem to get him away from the Crawlers."

"If it helps to know, I pray for him every day," Mark said quietly.

"It does, and thank you," Paula replied. "Although I have to wonder . . ." Her voice trailed off before she finished the sentence, and silence followed.

"You have to wonder?" Mark prompted.

Paula briefly considered saying what was really on her mind, dismissed it, then decided to go ahead. *I need to know,* she thought. *He owes me that.*

She took a breath and continued. "Although I have to wonder why you would feel obligated to pray for my son, when you haven't exactly felt the need to stay in touch with his mother." She felt regret flooding over her even as she said the cutting words. *Ouch. Definitely not one of your shining moments, Donroe. You could have—should have been nicer. Kinder.*

An awkward cough was followed by an even more awkward silence on the line. Then, "I—I guess I had that one coming. I'm sorry." Mark's subdued tone seemed bathed in regret, and it was several long moments before he spoke again. "Really . . . I'm so sorry."

He sounded so utterly penitent that Paula's heart churned with remorse. "Hey," she said carefully, "I should be the one apologizing. You know me—more foot per square inch of mouth than anyone else on the planet. Even becoming a Mormon hasn't cured me of that— yet, anyway." She paused for a moment, then decided to explain herself. "It's just that I was so sure I'd hear from you sooner—over the holidays or something. When I didn't, I started to wonder if you'd changed your mind about staying in touch, or if something had happened to—"

"Yes, something has happened." Mark's deep, suddenly intense voice sent a foreboding chill careening down her spine. What exactly was he trying to say—that he'd changed his mind since their tender parting at the airport in early December? That he'd thought it over, and she would never have a place in his life? That it would be best if they just went their separate ways, without dredging up any inconvenient family ties?

I can't believe he's doing this, she thought helplessly. *I should hang up before he says it.* She stood and moved toward the phone receptacle on the wall, but the receiver was frozen to her ear. She squeezed her eyes shut, steeling herself for the words she knew were coming.

"Paula? Are you still there?" His inquiry seemed to reach her through a long, dark tunnel, and she willed herself to respond politely.

"Yes . . . yes, of course. You were saying?" Paula raked a hand through her hair and chewed on her bottom lip as she imagined the worst. *Here it comes.*

"Okay." Mark let out a long, slow breath. "I haven't called because . . . well, it's . . . uh, I don't quite know how to . . . you see, it's . . ." He retreated into silence, and Paula could almost feel his heart pounding in her ear. The boy needed help.

"You can just say it, Mark," she said kindly. *This is almost as hard for him as it is for me.* She felt as if her heart might break twice—once for each of them.

"Thanks," he said gratefully after another deep sigh. "It's just that this is all so . . . hard."

"I understand," Paula lied.

"No, I'm not sure you do," he countered, his voice a little stronger now.

"Well, could you explain it to me?" she asked mildly.

"Yeah . . . I'm getting there." He gave a short laugh with no trace of humor in it, then paused for a few interminable moments.

"Mark?" She was having second thoughts about this whole conversation. "If you'd rather not—"

"It's my mom." His voice sounded hollow and distracted.

"Your mom?" Paula's brows knit in puzzlement. *Mom? Which mom? The one in Idaho, or . . . don't be a pinhead, Donroe. He only has one mom; you gave up your right to that title twenty-two years ago.* "I guess you're right," she added. "I don't understand."

"She . . . she's dying." His voice cracked, then silence.

His words stunned her like a blow to the stomach, and she slumped onto a kitchen chair. "Excuse me?" she rasped, barely recognizing her own voice.

"My mother is dying of cancer," Mark clarified, speaking slowly and deliberately. When Paula made no sound, he went on. "I knew she was sick the second I saw her at the airport, but no one would tell me anything until we got home and had a family council that evening. Then it all came out."

"Dear Lord," Paula breathed, her eyes brimming. Unable to speak, she waited for him to continue.

"It's ovarian cancer—the most aggressive kind. Often not detectable until it's too late. It's not like she didn't have checkups or anything . . ." A tight sob cut off the rest, then he began again. "Anyway, she's been having chemotherapy, and she feels like she's got it beat—at least for the time being. But it's just buying her a little time, that's all." Paula heard a sharp intake of breath, felt the pain in his voice. "Maybe a year or two."

"Oh, Mark," she said, barely above a desolate whisper, "I don't know what to say. I . . . I'm so sorry . . . so *very sorry.*"

A ragged sigh crackled across the line. "Thanks, Paula. That means a lot. And I hope it helps explains things . . . why I haven't been in touch. It's been so crazy, and we're all still getting used to the idea of maybe being . . . without her, you know?" He groaned softly.

"I honestly didn't mean to ignore you, but this has been so hard on the family—"

"Don't, Mark," Paula interrupted, wiping fiercely at her eyes. "Don't you think a thing about it. I understand." This time she wasn't lying. "And if there's anything I can do . . . anything at all . . ."

"Well, there is one thing," he said hesitantly.

"Name it," she said, ready in an instant to muster all the medical, financial, and spiritual resources at her disposal. She could enlist the finest doctors, pay all the bills, fast to within an inch of her life, offer a prayer that would put the prophet Enos to shame. And if that wasn't enough, maybe arrangements could be made for—

"She wants to see you, Paula."

The words pierced her brain like a jolt of electricity, stunning her into numb disbelief. When she could finally speak, her voice sounded like sand trickling over a bed of gravel. "Your mother wants to . . . *see* me? To see *me?*"

For a moment Mark seemed almost cheerful, energetic, optimistic. "Yeah. I told her all about you, and she . . . well, first she started to cry. Then she declared it a miracle, and said she'd never forgive herself if, as she put it, 'my time drained away and I never met the special person who gave my wonderful son the gift of life.'" The soft note of pride in his voice made Paula smile a little.

"Well, gee, I . . . I don't know what to say," she stammered. "Are you sure?"

"As sure as I've ever been about anything," he insisted. "She's mentioned it at least once a day—sometimes two or three—for weeks now. "I think," his voice tightened, "the prospect of meeting you is keeping her going somehow."

"Whew." Paula shook her head. "I never thought something like this would happen—never in a million years."

"Yeah, I know," Mark agreed. "But she says it's a blessing—like tying up all the loose ends before she . . ." He cleared his throat. "So will you think about it? Will you think about coming to visit?"

Paula inhaled deeply. "There's nothing to think about," she said decisively. "I'd consider it an honor to meet your mother."

"And my dad, too." Mark sounded relieved. "He's pretty excited about it—but quieter, if you know what I mean."

"And your dad, too," she repeated.

"And Alex, and Jake, and Andrea, and Ruthie."

"I get the picture," Paula laughed. Then her tone became more serious. "But is your mother up to this?"

"Not right now," he admitted. "The chemo has been very rough on her; most days she doesn't get farther than the chair beside her bed. But it'll be over next month, and she figures she'll be doing a lot better within a few weeks. Maybe by sometime in March."

"I see." She chuckled lightly. "I've never been to Idaho, you know."

"No problem," he replied. "Most everyone speaks English here."

"Well, that's a relief," she joked. "What should I wear?"

"Nothing special. Just make sure it's warm."

"What? Won't it be springtime in the Rockies?"

Mark laughed. "Are you kidding? We're talking the Grand Tetons here, where in the spring a young man's fancy turns to shoveling the walks once instead of twice a day."

"Brrr," Paula responded. "I'll buy mittens."

After a brief pause, Mark spoke quietly. "This means a lot, Paula—to all of us. It'll be terrific to have you here for a few days, and . . . and you'll love Mom. I guarantee it."

"I'm sure I will," she said solemnly. "I just wish the circumstances could be different."

"So do I," Mark replied. "But then, miracles have been known to happen. We've all got to believe that. You'll pray for us, won't you?"

"You know I will," she vowed. "And is there anything else I can do?"

"I don't think so. As Mom says, we'll just take it a day at a time. I can't wait to tell her . . . she's sleeping right now. This'll be the best news she's had in a long time."

Paula sniffed as a solitary tear made its way down her cheek. "It's all so . . . sad," she murmured. "To think that you've just spent two years serving the Lord, giving Him all you had. And now you come home to . . . this. I can't help wondering why."

"That same thought has occurred to me—many times," Mark admitted, his voice wavering slightly.

"And have you come to any conclusions?"

A long silence hung in the air, then he began to speak slowly. "Only that . . . well, no. Actually, I'm still struggling with that one.

There are plenty of convenient answers, but none of them seems to make much sense right now. It'll come in time, I suppose; but at this moment, I just . . . I just want my mom back." He let out a ragged breath.

"I understand," Paula soothed. "But I know you're strong; you'll figure it out. You did when TJ died, remember? If you hadn't been there, I might never have gotten through it." A tender surge of pain shot through her as she thought of her young son.

"I suppose," he sighed. "But I just want to hold on to her . . . if you knew her, you'd know why. She's . . . she's . . ." His voice failed.

"She's an extraordinary woman," Paula said, completing his thought. "I've known that from the moment I met you." She chuckled dryly. "Well, at least from the moment I realized you were serious about wearing a suit and tie twenty-four hours a day. I figure any mother who could raise her son to be"—a sudden welling of emotion caught in her throat—"to be such a gentleman would have to be an extraordinary woman."

"Thank you, Paula," he murmured softly. "And you're right about that . . . she is remarkable." He cleared his throat, then his tone changed abruptly. "Uh-oh," he said, "I've got to go. I promised one of our stake missionaries I'd go with him to visit a few families today, and he'll be here in a couple of minutes." She could hear the smile in his voice as he added, "Gotta go jump into my suit and tie."

"Then you go right ahead, you handsome missionary, you," Paula laughed, relieved that their conversation was ending on a lighter note. "But stay in touch, okay?"

"No doubt about it," he promised. "It's awfully good to talk to you, Paula. I'll call again soon."

"Take care, Mark," she said warmly. "And give your family my best."

"Done," he said. Then, after a brief pause, "And thanks, Paula." A soft click followed, and he was gone.

She sat with the mute phone pressed to her ear for several minutes. "Just hang in there, Mark," she whispered as she finally replaced the receiver. "Just hang in there."

Paula found Millie in the chapel minutes before sacrament meeting began. Squeezing in next to her at the end of a full pew, she huffed good-naturedly. "What is this—the entire Millie Hampton luncheon committee and social club on a single bench?" In one graceful motion, she smoothed her gray wool skirt across her knees and reached for a hymnbook.

Millie smiled and gave Paula's arm a squeeze. "We had a real good meeting," she whispered. "They said I could plan the whole menu for the seniors' luncheon, and they'll help me put it all together. Goodness, I feel like . . . like a queen!" Her gray-blue eyes sparkled with anticipation.

"That's wonderful, your majesty," Paula quipped. "You'll knock their socks off." She gazed affectionately at her old friend, glad to see Millie's gifts being put to good use.

At that moment the bishop stood, and Paula turned her attention to the meeting. This, after all, was why she had come—to sing the songs of Zion; to partake of the emblems of a sacrifice more infinite and divine than she could yet comprehend; and perhaps to uncover a few more layers of this new gospel that she found at once so appealing, so satisfying, and yet so foreign to her understanding. There was no doubting the truth of it; like a marrow transplant, it had seeped into her bones and given new life to her wearied spirit. She just needed a little more time, she supposed, to really make it her own.

But today, try as she might to focus on the messages from the pulpit, her mind's eye was riveted instead on a little family huddled together against an ice-encrusted Idaho winter—a grim season made even crueler now by profound illness, maybe even death. *They're tough*, Paula told herself. *They'll handle it.* But she couldn't shake the thought: *Mark's mother has cancer. And she wants to see me.*

The flicker of a smile pulled at Paula's mouth as she contemplated this woman of mystery—Mark's mother. At the moment, she was a woman without a name, without a face, without an identity. She had a husband and five children and lived on a potato farm. Period. *Not much of a resumé*, Paula mused. She spent long minutes imagining what such a woman might look like. *Tall? Thin? Short? Stumpy? Shaped like—what else—a potato? Plain-faced, with her graying hair in a bun. Worn-looking. Friendly . . . yes, definitely friendly, in a down-home sort of way. Perhaps not highly educated, but a good woman who's raised a good Mormon family and taught them manners. Her name? Bea or June or Laverne or Nancy . . . a nice name. Probably married to Harold or Ben, who has an endearing little spare tire. An honorable man who cares about his wife and kids, but a hard life on the farm has stripped him of any spirit. No, that's not it . . . he still has plenty of spirit, but he's just too tired to let it show. And now with his wife so sick . . . well, maybe the spirit is gone after all. I hope not—for the family's sake. All those children . . . what will he do when they're left without a mother?*

A few tears slid down Paula's cheek, and she wiped them away with a quick brush of her fingers. *This is all so sad . . . so terribly sad.* Two and a half months earlier she had buried her twelve-year-old son, and now she felt her whole body aching for the loss that could come to Mark and his family. *Where's the justice in all of this? Where's the comfort? Where is God, just when they need Him most—just when we all need Him?* Paula bowed her head and covered her eyes with one hand. *Answers . . . there are never any easy answers. But I will pray for you, Mark. I will pray for you.*

CHAPTER 4

"Cancer. I can't believe it. That poor boy." Millie sat at the kitchen table, shaking her head. "No wonder he hasn't called." She slid the slim gold band of a blue topaz ring up and down, up and down the third finger of her right hand. "What can we do?"

Paula sighed and poured herself a glass of lemonade. "I've asked myself that a thousand times since this morning. I guess we just wait and pray. I'll know more after I've been there."

"Been where?" Scott's voice boomed from the entryway, startling both women.

Millie looked up and gave the boy a kind smile. "Hello, dear. We were just sitting down for a bowl of soup. Will you join us? It's your favorite—homemade chicken noodle."

"Yeah, sure. Why not?" He slouched toward the table, his baggy jeans balancing low on his slender hips. A thin line of tanned, muscular flesh was visible beneath the ragged hem of his pale green T-shirt as he settled into a chair and slid down a few inches.

He's grown at least an inch in the last month, Paula thought, observing his lanky frame. *Where have I been?* "Hey, big guy," she said affectionately. "Haven't seen you for a while. What's going on?"

"Nuthin'," he muttered, reaching for a breadstick. "You goin' somewhere?"

"Oh, well, I, uh . . . ," Paula stammered. She exchanged a quick glance with Millie, who nodded slightly. "I guess I'll be going to Idaho for a few days. Not right away; maybe in a month or so."

A slow smirk twisted Scott's mouth into a sardonic grin. "What, missionary boy can't live without seein' his new mama?"

"Scotty!" Paula exclaimed, more surprised than irritated.

"Well, it's true, isn't it?" the boy shot back. "Why else would you be goin' off to some podunk place like Idaho? I bet nuthin' grows there . . . nuthin' but mama's boys." He glared at her belligerently.

Now Paula was angry, and she plumbed her brain for a withering reply. Then she felt the firm pressure of Millie's hand on her arm. Before she could speak, the older woman said evenly, "Scotty, it's not what you think. Mark—Elder Richland and his family are in trouble up there. Your mother's just trying to figure out how to help, that's all."

Scott appeared vaguely interested. "What kinda trouble?"

Millie looked at Paula, who by this time had taken several deep breaths and was more or less in control. "Go ahead, dear. Tell him."

Paula cleared her throat and spoke in measured tones. "Well, okay. It seems that Mrs. Richland—Mark's mother—is very ill. She has cancer."

Scott slumped a few inches farther down in his chair. "Whoa," he breathed, staring straight ahead.

"It's pretty bad," Paula continued. "She's having chemotherapy now, but Mark feels like it may not do much good. Although we're all hoping and praying she'll get better."

"So she might . . . croak," the boy said flatly.

Paula felt a tiny smile rise to her lips in spite of everything. "Yes," she admitted, "she might . . . do that."

"Bummer," Scott said. "Can I have some soup?"

That's my boy, Paula thought, relieved that at least for the moment, the argument had been defused. Now, if she could only figure out how to keep the peace, it would be worth all the chicken soup in the world. And then some.

Millie placed three deep bowls of thick, steaming soup on the table, and Scott quickly reached for his spoon. Plunging it into the hot, golden liquid, he was soon hefting an enormous load of broad noodles and large chunks of white meat toward his open mouth.

"Uh, Scotty?" Paula began. His spoon stopped for a second. "Honey, could we say a blessing first?" she continued sweetly.

Her son scowled and rolled his eyes, but lowered the spoon to his bowl. "Yeah, right," he grumbled. "The Mormon blessing thing." He put one elbow on the table and rested his chin in his hand. "Can we just get it over with? I'm starvin'."

"Okay." Paula bowed her head and offered a brief prayer, then raised her eyes to find Scott staring at her curiously. "What?" she asked.

"You're really into this religion thing, aren't ya?" he responded, his voice laced with sarcasm. "Geez, you practically live at the church on Sundays, you can't leave the house or go to bed without sayin' a stupid prayer, and Millie's always brothering and sistering everyone. What's so cool about it, anyway?"

Paula couldn't help smiling to herself. *With his attitude, this is not exactly a golden missionary moment. But it's worth a try. At least he's talking.* She took a deep breath and smiled gamely. "Well, sweetie, I know it's a pretty big change from the way we did things before, but—"

"You can say that again," Scott broke in, changing his voice to a lilting falsetto. *"No more coffee, no more tea, no more olives in your mar-tee-nee."* He snickered and lifted his soup bowl to his lips, taking several loud gulps of broth.

This is disgusting, Paula thought. She bit her lip and watched him shovel an overloaded spoonful of noodles and vegetables into his mouth. *So, maybe this isn't exactly the moment for an impromptu testimony meeting.* With his free hand, Scott grabbed the baggy sleeve of his T-shirt and wiped it across his dripping chin. Paula's eyes darkened with anger, and she opened her mouth to scold him.

Millie came to the rescue. "What your mother and I would like to help you understand," she explained serenely, "is that being a Latter-day Saint makes you look at life a little differently. When you've made promises to Heavenly Father that you'll live a certain way, then the most important thing is to keep those promises. Since we were baptized, we've been trying awfully hard to do what's right."

"Uh-huh," Scott mumbled, picking a sliver of celery from between his front teeth. "And who gets to decide what's right? Everybody makes their own rules."

"Not quite," Millie smiled. "God makes the rules, and His prophet lets us know what we should be doing. It's as simple as that."

Scott nodded and reached for a bread stick. When he didn't speak, Paula watched him closely, her heart swelling with hope. *Is he coming around? Will we finally be able to share the gospel with him?* Her mind flashed to an image of him three years hence, tall and handsome in his missionary haircut and a crisp new suit, his scriptures grasped securely in one hand as he marched eagerly off into the sunset to preach to the pure in heart. She thought she might burst with pride.

"'Cept if there isn't a God. And if there isn't a prophet. That stuff's for suckers." His words brought Paula crashing back to the present, and she sighed deeply. *Guess I'll hold off on buying the suit.*

"Now, now," Millie chided gently, "just because you don't know it yet doesn't mean it's not true. But when you get a testimony, you'll see—"

"See what?" the boy scoffed. "All I see is you runnin' around makin' casseroles for sick people, an' Mom moonin' over her holier-than-thou missionary boy in Idaho. I'd rather spend my time hangin' with the Crawlers."

Paula cringed at the mention of Scott's gang, but she willed herself to respond calmly. "I can understand that," she conceded. "It's just that Millie and I have found a new way of looking at things since we joined the Church—a happier way, I think." She glanced at Millie, who nodded her agreement. "Of course, we're still pretty new to this Mormonism business, still learning and trying to figure out how it all fits together." Her voice lowered in pitch and increased in intensity. "But I can tell you this, Scotty: in spite of any mistakes we might be making along the way, joining the Church has been a good thing. A very good thing."

He snorted loudly. "So what are you now, the Mormon Martha Stewart?" He crushed a bread stick between his palms and dumped the crumbs into his almost-empty soup bowl. Then he took another bread stick and stirred the broth-and-crumb mixture into a thin gruel.

Paula quelled an impulse to roll her eyes, mentally counted to ten, and reached over to pat her son's arm. "You know, big guy," she said with as much warmth as she could muster, "we all need as much help as we can get to make it in this world. That's what the gospel does—it gives us help and direction."

Scott looked at her and raised one eyebrow. "Help and direction, huh?"

"That's right," she replied, a note of expectancy hovering in her voice.

The expression in his hazel eyes hardened. "Well, now," he said, "your church didn't *help* TJ any, did it? And the only *direction* he went was six feet straight down. Same for what's-his-face's mother in Idaho, okay? So far you're batting a thousand, Mom." He wadded up his paper napkin and tossed it into his soup bowl.

Paula felt her back stiffen at his impertinent remarks, and her temper flared. "Just *stop it,* young man. I don't need this," she murmured through clenched teeth.

"Well, neither do I," he snarled back at her. "I'm outa here. Don't wait up." He pushed his chair back savagely and loped from the room. Two seconds later he jerked open the front door, then slammed it with such force that the windows vibrated with the shock.

The two women sat in stunned silence for a full minute. Finally, Paula looked at Millie and smiled drolly. "I thought that went well, didn't you?"

The older woman chuckled as she stood to clear the dishes. "Well," she said lightly, "I wouldn't go filling the font for him just yet."

Paula leaned back in her chair and folded her arms across her chest. "Seriously, though, I don't get it," she said, her brows knitting into a puzzled expression. "I mean, I know he's a teenager and all, complete with raging hormones and a zero tolerance for anything that remotely resembles authority. But lately he's seemed . . . worse. Much worse. Like he's living in his own weird time zone, daring everyone else to cross his boundaries and get their heads ripped off. You can't reason with him . . . and sometimes it scares me. A lot." She shook her head.

"I know, dear," Millie said, easing into a chair at one end of the table. "But maybe he just needs a little time."

"Time? Time for what—to plan our untimely ends?" Paula gave a short, humorless laugh. "Sometimes I feel like I'm sharing living space with an axe murderer-in-waiting."

"Oh, my!" Millie chortled. "I wouldn't go quite that far . . . but I do think the boy's hurting."

"Well, he's not the only one," Paula mumbled, picking at a loose thread on one of the blue and white checkered place mats.

"Yes, but I'd be willing to bet that he *thinks* he's the only one," Millie observed.

Paula lifted her eyes to meet Millie's kind, steady gaze. "What do you mean?"

"Of course, I'm only saying what I think," Millie began, "but it seems to me that Scotty might feel like he's the one on the outside looking in. Here we are, you and I; we've got the Church, we've got our new ward friends, we've got each other. And if that's not enough, you've got a new son in your life. Then there's Scotty . . . what's he got? A big hole in his heart where his little brother used to be, and a new half-brother that he likely sees as competition."

"Competition?" Paula questioned.

"Or maybe it's jealousy; I don't know. But you never hear him say a civil word about Mark, and it's my guess that he resents that young man and all he stands for—including the Church."

"But I've never given him any reason to think—"

"Think?" Millie laughed. "Who said anything about thinking? He's a teenager, remember?" Her expression sobered. "I just get the feeling sometimes that he's hurting so much, he doesn't know where to turn."

"He seems to be doing okay with the Crawlers," Paula observed.

"I think he's just passing time," Millie stated. "Trying to find out where he belongs."

"Well, I hope he finds out and loses that gang before somebody else in this family gets shot," Paula said. "I don't want to bury another son anytime soon." The thought made her shudder involuntarily, and she looked at her friend through emotion-filled eyes. "What can we do, Millie?"

"I'm not quite sure," she replied. "A little prayer wouldn't hurt; that's a place to start. And he needs to know we care."

"All right," Paula vowed firmly. "I'll try to do better. Try to be more understanding. Try to keep my temper under control." She flashed Millie a tiny smile. "If I bury the hatchet, maybe he'll bury the axe."

"That's a good girl," Millie chirped, reaching over to squeeze her hand. "And who knows? If things go well, we might even have a missionary in the family in a few years."

"Let's just get past puberty, shall we?" Paula laughed. She was beginning to feel a little better.

Later that evening, Paula was in her room when the phone rang. She answered it absently as she sat cross-legged on her bed, thumbing through a Sunday newspaper. "Hello?" a warm, energetic feminine voice said on the other end. "Could I please speak to Paula Donroe?"

"This is she," Paula replied, intrigued by the voice's rich inflection. She glanced at the unfamiliar name on her caller ID.

"Oh, good," the woman said quickly. "You don't know me, but"—she laughed lightly—"I have every reason to believe that we'll be sitting together on a stranger's couch within the next couple of weeks."

"Excuse me?" Paula said. She was a bit confused, but the caller's open, friendly tone piqued her curiosity. "If I don't know you, then why in the world would we share a couch in *anybody's* house? Maybe you have a wrong number, or—"

"Not a chance, *Sister* Donroe," the voice interjected.

"O-o-kay," Paula said slowly, smiling in spite of herself. "You're from the ward, right?"

"What was your first clue?" the congenial voice teased.

"Well, there's not a convent around here that I know of," Paula joked in return. "Uh, have we met?"

"No, but it's time we did," the woman said. "I'm Meg. Meg O'Brien. From the ward, as you so cleverly surmised." There was a breezy, lilting quality to her voice that put Paula at ease.

"Then it's nice to meet you, Sister O'Brien. I—"

"Hey, let's lose the 'sister' stuff, okay? It sounds so . . . so *fuddy-duddy*. Personally, I never use it unless I'm talking to a woman twice my age or three times my size." She laughed amiably. "And since you don't fit either description, it's just Meg. Okay?"

"Okay . . . Meg," Paula agreed. She had no idea where this conversation was going, but she was beginning to enjoy the trip.

"Good," Meg said. "Now, you're probably wondering who in the world I am, and why I'm calling you on an otherwise peaceful Sunday evening."

"You could say that," Paula admitted. "But then I'm pretty new to the Church, and I'm thinking it could be some kind of crazy Mormon ritual." She thought of her conversation with Ted only the day before. "Similar to the Saints' fascination with green Jell-O."

Meg roared at Paula's droll observation. "Good one," she sputtered when she could catch her breath. "This is gonna be fun."

"And 'this' would be—?" Paula questioned.

"Oh, right," Meg said. "This would be our monthly rendezvous with destiny—or at least with three living-room couches and a couple of adorably hyperactive poodles. You, my dear, are about to be initiated into the ranks of the Relief Society visiting teachers. And I am your faithful partner."

Paula was momentarily speechless while her thoughts raced. *Me, a visiting teacher? I've heard the term, but what does a visiting teacher do? She visits, obviously—probably teaches, too. But what do I know about either one? I'm still wet behind the ears in the Church . . . how can they expect me to do this?*

"Hallo, is anyone still home?" Meg's energetic voice broke into Paula's jumble of thoughts. "Are we still connected? I could have sworn I heard a little gasp a minute ago . . . does anyone over there need CPR?"

"Oh, uh, sorry," Paula mumbled, trying to keep her voice light. "It's just that . . . well, if you don't mind my asking, what exactly does this involve? I mean, I hear someone mention visiting teaching almost every Sunday in Relief Society, but I'm afraid I don't have a clue about what it really is. Besides, I'm so new to the Church that I don't think I could possibly—"

"Hey, not to worry," Meg interjected. "Think of it as your 'initiation into the compassionate sisterhood.' And if that still sounds a little too scary, just picture yourself as a cheerleader with a plate of cookies and a message instead of pom-poms."

"Excuse me?" Paula was feeling more confused by the moment.

"On second thought, make that brownies," Meg laughed. "They work every time."

"Come again?" Paula said, her voice tightening a little.

"Uh-oh," Meg replied quickly, "I didn't mean to give you the runaround. I'm pretty much of a blabbermouth, you know, and my tongue gets ahead of my brain on a regular basis. I hope you'll forgive me."

Her tone was so genuine that Paula's tension evaporated. "No problem," she said warmly.

"Whew," Meg breathed appreciatively. "And thanks. Now, back to visiting teaching. How about if we start things out right—say, over dinner? Just the two of us . . . new partners. I can explain everything, and we can figure out a schedule that works for us. How does Marie Callender's sound? My treat."

Paula mentally pictured the comfortable ambience and satisfying food offered by this popular restaurant. "Well," she laughed, "I may not know much about visiting teaching, but I certainly know a good piece of pie when I taste one. How could I possibly refuse?"

"Terrific!" Meg exulted. "My taste buds are standing at attention already. How's Tuesday night for you? Kevin—that's my husband—says he'll be happy to spend some 'quality time' with the kids." She chuckled. "His idea of 'quality time' is ordering in pizza and letting the little darlings choose their toppings. Then they all sit around and play video games until he gets tired of them winning and sends them to bed."

"How many do you have?" Paula asked.

"Oh, I don't know. It's so easy to lose count. Ten or twelve, easy." Meg sighed.

Paula gulped. "You have ten children? Or *twelve?*"

There was a long pause, followed by a brief fit of uncontrolled laughter. "Are you kidding?" Meg finally wheezed. "Do I sound that tired? I was referring to the video games, thank you very much. If I had that many kids, I wouldn't be visiting Marie's, I'd be *hiding out* there. But, since you asked, I have three—Cody, Sean, and Danielle. And, Kevin, of course, makes four."

"I see," Paula grinned. "Well, then, you definitely deserve a night out. Tuesday sounds perfect."

"It's a deal, partner," Meg agreed. "I'll pick you up at six-thirty. Let's see, now . . . 10410 Valley View Drive, right?"

"That's it. I'll be ready and watching for—uh, what exactly should I be watching for?"

"A white Taurus wagon. More or less white, that is . . . depending on whether it's before or after I pick up the kids from a soccer match. I swear, those playing fields aren't regulation unless they're buried under at least two inches of mud."

"Okay, a Taurus wagon," Paula repeated eagerly. "I'll look forward to it."

When they hung up, Paula leaned back against her pillows and contemplated the intriguing new direction her life seemed to be taking. *I'm going to be a visiting teacher,* she mused. *I'm going to visit, and I'm going to teach, and I'm going to be somebody's partner.* She recalled Meg's warm, inviting manner. *Maybe I'm even going to be somebody's friend.* Closing her eyes, she smiled at the thought.

CHAPTER 5

Ted shook his head and sat down slowly when he heard the news. "Wow, that's awful," he said. "Mark always seemed like such a nice kid, so willing to serve a mission, so convinced he was doing the right thing. And now this—his mother dying. Go figure, huh? I'm sorry, Paula; this has got to be a bitter pill for everyone to swallow." She had come to his office to share the news, and he stared intently at her across the desk. "What happens now?"

"Life goes on, I guess," she said solemnly. "I'll go to visit, of course, when she's well enough; it's the least I can do. And besides, it's not all that hopeless. She could get better. Prayers are answered; miracles do happen. Mark said that himself."

Ted smiled grimly. "Where there's life there's hope, right?"

"Something like that," Paula replied.

He traced a small circle on the desk with his finger. "Well, I suppose if there's a *miracle* to be wrought, the Mormons ought to be able to pull it off." His voice was laced with barely concealed sarcasm.

Paula looked at him warily. "You don't sound all that convinced," she said.

He shrugged and leaned back into his deep leather chair. "Well, let's just say that getting answers to prayers hasn't exactly been my strong suit over the past twenty-five years or so."

"And what does that have to do with the Mormons?" she asked pointedly.

Ted's eyes hardened as he returned her steady gaze. "Nothing. Unless one Mormon's adultery counts as a high point in the life of a ten-year-old kid."

Paula's mind instantly flashed back to a conversation they'd had several weeks earlier, when Ted, heartbroken at the news of TJ's death, had come to her home early the next day. Overwhelmed by grief, they had huddled close together on the living-room sofa, holding hands, and Ted had eventually spilled out his story. Born into an active Latter-day Saint family in West Jordan, Utah, in his eleventh year he had watched his family sour and disintegrate when his father strayed into the arms of a woman in their ward. The divorce left Ted's mother to raise four young children alone, and Alma Barstow's bitterness opened a yawning chasm between her family and the Church.

Ted's fragile faith had quickly shriveled into smoldering resentment, and when he left home at eighteen he was determined to put as much distance as possible between himself and the Mormons. A high-flying career as an investigative journalist took him to all parts of the world over the next dozen years, and he never looked back. When a volatile political climate threatened to compromise his integrity and personal safety, he left the international circuit and settled in to write award-winning advertising copy for Paula's agency. Only by accident had she discovered his tenuous connection to the Church; and since her baptism the matter had rarely come up for discussion. He had been genuinely supportive of her decision to become a Latter-day Saint, but he seemed to be giving the Church a wide berth when it came to making any commitments of his own.

Still, she did not really expect Ted's acrimonious response to her news about Mark Richland's mother. Regarding him curiously, she had to ask. "You still blame the Church for what happened to your family, don't you?"

He stared at her for a long moment, then sighed deeply. "I'm not sure 'blame' is really the right word," he said. "But whatever it is, I can't get past it. Not yet, anyway. It's going to take some time."

Paula bit her tongue to quell a stinging remark, but she couldn't help thinking it. *It's going to take some time? Some time? Good grief, it's been a quarter of a century. Isn't it about time you faced up to the past and got on with your life?* Aloud she said, as casually as she could, "And how much longer do you think it's going to take?"

He flashed her a breezy smile, but she could see the muscle in his jaw working. "What is this, the Mormon inquisition? Or is it just the overzealous attitude of a newly dunked member? You're not trying to re-convert me here, are you, Ms. Donroe?" His tone was light, but there was a *don't go there* expression flickering in his intense blue eyes.

Paula bristled at his insinuation, though she knew it held an element of truth. *Can't he understand?* she asked herself. *Can't he catch the vision of the gospel—see it, feel it, taste it? I may be a new member, but already it has touched and healed me in so many ways. He's right, I suppose; I should let him find his own way. In the end, that's what we all have to do—find our own way.* She smiled warmly and held up one hand in a peacemaking gesture. "Hey, Ted, I'm sorry—didn't mean to get all preachy on you. It's just that . . . well, the gospel has made a big difference in my life in only a few weeks, you know?"

Now it was his turn to be contrite. "I know," he said softly. "And it's really great that you've found the Church; I'm happy for you. As for myself, I . . . I can't say one way or another right now. There's a lot to consider, and I'm still working on it. Let's just leave it at that, shall we?"

"No problem," Paula agreed amiably.

"And I'm awfully sorry about Mark's mother," he added. "I really am."

"Thanks, Ted," she replied. "That means a lot. I'll tell him you send your best."

"I'd like that." Ted's face seemed to relax, and he quickly ran the fingers of one hand through his hair. "Now, can we go over a couple of things on the Northridge account?"

"Absolutely," Paula said. Their conversation moved easily into business matters, and a few hours later they had put together the framework of a glitzy advertising campaign featuring Northridge BodyWorks, one of the West Coast's most prestigious fashion retailers. Working head to head across a desk piled with artful photos of alluring women, they traded ideas and images like two youngsters kicking a ball back and forth on a school playground. It was exhausting and exhilarating work, generating a surge of creative energy that seemed to carry them effortlessly through the afternoon.

When they were finished, Paula stretched her slim arms elegantly and sank back against the soft leather couch facing Ted's desk. "As usual, my friend," she said, "you've put your finger on the pulse of the industry. Those Northridge people will fall all over themselves thanking you when their sales go off the charts in everything from lingerie to lip gloss. I'm sure of it." She gazed at him with shameless admiration.

"Well," he grinned, raising an eyebrow lecherously, "it's not all that hard to come up with a good idea or two when you picture a few of these"—he glanced down at the glamour shots strewn across his desk—"in lingerie and lip gloss."

"Still," she protested, "it takes a certain finesse with words to capture the feeling." Picking up a sheet of copy he'd written hurriedly, she took a few seconds to read through it. "This is pure magic, Ted."

"Oh, I don't know about that," he said. "Besides, it was a joint effort." His eyes held hers for a long moment. "Seems like we make a pretty good team."

"No argument there," she laughed, smoothing a lock of dark hair back from her forehead. "It was fun, wasn't it?"

"More fun than a barrel of . . . bagels," he joked. "Now, *there's* an image I'd like to pursue." He leaned back in his chair and closed his eyes.

A soft giggle, followed by a dull thud and a sharp pressure low on his forehead, brought him to instant attention. His eyes flew open just as a small pillow from the couch bounced off his face and landed amid the piles of photos on his desk. Looking up just long enough to see an impish grin crinkle Paula's mouth, he quickly pressed his fingers tightly over one side of his face and let out a long, pain-riddled moan. "My eye," he murmured, hunching over and lowering his head to within inches of the desk. "Edge of the pillow . . . could've cut me . . . oh, my eye."

Paula froze in horror for an instant, then vaulted from the couch and rushed to his side. "Oh, Ted," she wailed, "I'm *so sorry*. What have I—are you all right? I didn't mean to . . . are you bleeding? We should call 911." She was leaning over him, her hands grasping his shoulders, her face a fraction of an inch from his. Her heart pounded wildly with fear and humiliation. *You're such an idiot, Donroe.*

Still applying pressure to his eye, Ted whimpered and rested his forehead on the desk. Paula held him tighter, caressed his cheek, frantically massaged his shoulders. He said nothing, but his free hand reached out to grasp hers tightly. *He's in pain,* she thought. *I've got to get help.* Leaning far forward, she put her lips close to his ear. "Talk to me, Ted," she insisted. "I know you're hurt, but I need to know exactly what to tell the people at 911. What's going on?"

The moaning stopped. He slumped back against her for several seconds, then slowly began to speak. "What's going on," he whispered, turning his head so their faces were less than an inch apart, "is . . . *pure magic.*" She could smell his spicy cologne, feel his breath against her cheek. Then he grinned.

"Wait a minute." Pulling back a little, Paula focused intently on his blue eyes, which by now had darkened to a smoldering cobalt, and studied them for any sign of injury. Finding none, she stood up straight, folded her arms across her chest, and tried to concentrate on being annoyed. "So really, Ted . . . what *is* going on here?"

"Nothing," he replied quickly, still grinning as he reached down to pick up the offending pillow. "Just a pleasant diversion at the end of a long day." He tossed the pillow back on the couch.

"I see," Paula said deliberately. "Then there's nothing wrong with you. Physically, that is."

Avoiding eye contact with her, Ted cleared his throat and began to shuffle through the papers on his desk. "Nothing 911 could do anything about," he murmured.

"Uh-huh." She sank down on the couch and stared at him for a full minute, then sighed dramatically. "I know exactly what you mean."

His head shot up, and he met her gaze with sizzling anticipation. "You do?" he croaked.

"You bet," she replied earnestly, her eyes sparkling. "And I think I've got just the ticket."

"You *do?*" Ted sat riveted to his seat as she stood and moved slowly around to his side of the desk. Her arm encircled his shoulders as she bent forward and inclined her head toward his face. "Let me tell you what I have in mind," she whispered gruffly.

"Okay," he wheezed, closing his eyes and pursing his lips slightly. He held his breath and listened to the pounding of his temples.

"Do you know what would *really* make this a perfect day?" she murmured, teasing a stray lock of blonde hair away from his brow.

"Well, I, uh . . . what?" he rasped, slipping down slightly in his chair.

She smiled and eased even closer as she breathed the word intimately into his ear. *"Shopping."*

Ted's eyes flew open as the intensity of the moment evaporated. "Shopping?" he repeated.

She chuckled softly as she pulled away from him. "Why, of course. After a few hours of highly creative activity, I just need to go *buy* something. It's a woman's answer to instant stress relief. Not to mention," she added, mimicking his earlier explanation, "being a pleasant diversion at the end of a long day."

"Shopping?" Ted stared at her dumbly, his expression hovering between amazement and disbelief. "You want to go *shopping?*"

Paula gazed down at him innocently. "Gee, I can't think of anything I'd rather do."

Ted's shoulders sagged. "I could," he muttered.

She put one hand on her hip, the other lightly on his arm. "Oh? And what might that be?" she asked, the hint of a smile playing across her lips.

"Nothing," he grunted. "Maybe an hour at the gym." He patted her hand absently. "Go shopping. Have a great time."

"Thank you. I think I'll just do that." She moved her hand to the back of his neck and felt his muscles tense. "You know, Ted," she added, "you're quite a guy. I always knew you were a gifted writer, an amazing athlete, an intellectual whiz-kid. But now I see that . . . well, I've obviously underestimated your talents."

He looked up at her curiously. "How do you figure?"

Paula tugged gently on the lobe of his ear. "Now I see that you can act, too." She clapped a hand over one eye and wailed, "Ooh, my eye. The pillow . . . might have cut it. Ooh!" She laughed out loud. "You really had me going there for a minute."

Ted's face broke into a boyish grin. "Yeah, well, you aren't so bad yourself, you know. I'd say you just about evened the score. Shopping!" He grimaced slightly.

"Indeed," Paula smiled. "Even as we speak, there's got to be a purse or a blouse or a pair of shoes with my name on it at the mall." She glanced at her watch and nodded toward the door. "It's after seven; let's call it a day, shall we?"

"I'm right behind you," he said, stretching out his arms to collect the photos strewn across his desk. "Just give me a minute to deal with this chaos, and I'll lock everything up tight. You go ahead." He began to sort various items into separate folders.

"All right, then," she said, flashing him a smile as she hurried out of the office, "I'm on my way. See you tomorrow. And thanks for a truly . . . *memorable* afternoon."

In a few seconds Paula had disappeared down the hall, and Ted heard the smooth, rolling sound of the elevator doors. Resting his head on the desk, he moaned softly. "Shopping," he sighed.

Paula lowered her fork to her plate and smiled contentedly as the last morsel of a miniature crab-and-cheese quiche dissolved in her mouth. *If it's Tuesday, this must be Marie's,* she told herself. *And it's even nicer than I remembered.* She glanced around her at the small grouping of tables in a quiet corner of the restaurant, away from the noisier booths and main traffic areas. The room, bathed in subdued overhead lighting, was decorated in muted tones of green and burgundy. Most of the diners were in pairs, or groups of four; the smooth murmur of their quiet conversations seemed to lend a comfortable intimacy to the very act of nourishing oneself. And now, in some benevolent way, this time and place seemed to welcome the beginning of a new friendship. At least it seemed so to Paula.

She looked across the table and studied Meg O'Brien in the mellow light. *A perfect match,* she thought, recalling their recent phone conversation. *She looks just like she sounds—warm, bright, open, energetic. Nice. Very nice. Almost like I've met her before . . . just can't remember where or when.* Meg, who was tall and exquisitely proportioned, wore a tailored navy pantsuit with a crisp white blouse set off by a glistening silver chain at her throat. But fashion aside, it was her smooth, chin-length, wheat-colored hair and vivid cornflower-blue eyes that made her truly striking. When she smiled, the light from those extraordinary eyes seemed to ignite the rich gold of her hair. *It's got to be natural,* Paula mused. *Blonde like that could never come from a bottle.*

Meg interrupted this train of thought by smacking her full lips with a certain elegance. "Scrumptious appetizers," she declared, lightly touching a napkin to her mouth. "I tried making a quiche once, but my kids bolted for the nearest Pizza Hut. Kevin liked it, though; he still remembers what it was like in college, when we could hardly make ends meet. Sometimes we spent the last week of the month eating peanut butter and jelly sandwiches—without the jelly." She smiled. "Those were some of the best times."

They chatted easily through a dinner of garden salad and roasted chicken breast with spring vegetables and new potatoes. By the time they had drained their water glasses twice, Paula had cheerfully embraced the idea of visiting teaching and was eager to get on with it. "It's not always easy to connect with our ladies—or even with each other—every month," Meg explained, "but I can guarantee it'll never be boring." She smiled, then launched into energetic descriptions of the three women assigned to them.

Caroline Wintersweet, a wealthy widow in her mid-seventies, lived in a nine-bedroom mansion on the privileged side of town with two toy poodles and her full-time gardener, Rollie. "Some people say she had an affair with him years ago, before her husband died and she joined the Church," Meg said. "But personally, I can't see it. He always seems to have a leaf or something caught between his teeth, and his wardrobe isn't exactly what you'd call fastidious. I think they just like to carp at each other. Caroline's a sweetie, once you get to know her—a little snooty at first blush, but she'll warm up right away if you say nice things about her poodles." Meg chuckled. "I found that out the hard way—ignored them on my first visit, and almost didn't get invited back. So just remember to drool a little over the babies, Jacques and Heidi, and you'll be a shoo-in."

"Not a problem," Paula smiled, thinking of her own golden-maned Rudy.

Meg described the second woman, Sylvie Randoph, as "a needy soul—in almost every way you can think of." She had been raised in the Church, attended a year of college, then married a handsome returned missionary and worked to put him partway through medical school. "That's where the fairy tale ended," Meg said. "It was the stress or something; you never know about these things. He turned abusive—nearly killed her a couple of times. He went to jail for a year or so, dropped out of the Church, never went back to school. They've been divorced for about three years now, and Sylvie's alone with two little girls, trying to keep their family together, barely scraping by as a temp office clerk. The ward helps with food and necessities, but it's awfully sad. If you catch her on a good day, her testimony can light up a room; but most of the time she struggles with depression. She just needs good friends—someone to listen."

"And that's where we come in, right?" Paula asked a little hesitantly.

"My, my . . . spoken like a true visiting teacher," Meg beamed. "You're going to be good at this—I can tell."

"I hope so," Paula said, chewing on her bottom lip while her thoughts raced. *Oboy . . . what have I gotten myself into?*

"Which brings us," Meg continued, "to the last—but certainly not the least—of our illustrious teachees. And believe me, this one is a killer."

Paula's eyes grew wide as the word snapped her mind back into focus. "A killer?"

"Well, not in the strictest sense of the word," Meg clarified. "I mean, she hasn't put poison in anyone's Postum or anything. But I wouldn't be surprised if she's cracked a few bones along the way to her three divorces. The woman's a female Schwarzenegger, I tell you—a black belt in karate. She runs a first-rate martial arts studio downtown, and *everybody* shows up at her classes on time. Or else."

"And she's the quilting leader in the ward, right?" Paula joked.

"Well, that'd be one way to get people out to our Relief Society enrichment meetings," Meg laughed. "The thing is, Bonnie's totally, unconditionally, blissfully inactive. I think she joined up with the Mormons about ten years ago when her first husband made a bet with some of his drinking buddies that he could talk a couple of young elders into having a brew with him. He failed, of course, then somehow ended up converting during one of his rare moments of sobriety. She went along with it, I guess—stayed a member even after he fell off the wagon and out of her life. I don't think she's been inside a church for at least ten years and three husbands; but her name stays on the records, so she still gets visiting teachers. And the amazing thing is, she loves to have us come! Calls us her 'home ladies,' and gives us a bone-crunching hug every month. Has a great sense of humor, too—and the kindest heart of anyone I know. You'll love her, even if she takes some getting used to. Our job, as I see it, is just to show up and have a good time, no churchy message, no strings attached. Who knows? One day, we might actually see Bonnie Solomon in church. And you can bet she'll be on time."

"Whoa," Paula breathed. "Sounds like a challenge."

"We're all God's children, my dear," Meg said warmly, "and every one of us has—or is—a challenge. That's what living the gospel is all about—helping each other through life. And speaking of challenges—are you up for one of Marie's famous desserts?"

Paula considered the question for a nanosecond. "Only if it's chocolate or something equally comfort-intensive," she replied.

"Then join me for the nth degree of gratification with a slice of chocolate-cherry-pecan cheesecake," Meg grinned. "I've been there before, and trust me, it's poetry on a fork. An entire epic, in fact."

"I'll take your word for it," Paula said, her mouth already watering.

The two women savored their desserts in companionable silence for several minutes. Finally, Meg lowered her fork and spoke in measured tones. "Paula," she said, "I'm afraid I have something to confess to you."

Her statement caught Paula's attention. "I'm listening," she said. *What is this—some deep, dark secret from her past? I don't think so; we've only just met, after all. She looks pretty normal to me—not prone to spilling her life's story to a stranger.*

"The thing is," Meg went on, "all of this—our being partners, I mean—wasn't just an accident. It was planned."

Paula laughed lightly. "Meg," she said, "I've only been a Mormon for a couple of months, but I've been around long enough to know that *most* things in the Church are planned, at least to some degree."

"I guess you're right about that," Meg agreed. "But this . . . this was just a tiny bit different." She hesitated.

"Go on," Paula urged.

"Well, you and I haven't actually met before now, but I've been very much aware of you since last November, when you . . . when you lost your son."

"I see," Paula said.

"TJ, wasn't it?"

"Yes, that's right. TJ." Paula's throat constricted in a knot of grief at the unexpected mention of his name, and tears welled suddenly in her eyes. She tried to give Meg a reassuring smile, but her lower lip quivered without mercy.

Meg reached quickly across the table to squeeze Paula's hand. "I'm so sorry," she said. "I didn't mean to upset you." Her own eyes glistened.

"Not to worry," Paula replied, dabbing at a stray tear on her cheek. "It's just that . . . the memories are still so fresh. And more than a little painful, when I let myself stop to think about them. Which is about a hundred times a day." She sniffled, then managed a halfhearted grin. "You were saying?"

"Oh, yes." Meg cleared her throat and continued. "My middle boy, Sean, was—is—just about TJ's age. He turned twelve a few months ago. Apparently they were in the same Sunday School class in those few weeks while TJ was getting acquainted with the Church. They played on the ward basketball team together, too. Sean thought he was the greatest, and they got to be rather good friends in just the short time before TJ—" She stopped and swallowed hard. "Anyway, he was all Sean could talk about—TJ loved old movies. TJ loved Western novels. TJ was *so good* at jump shots and free throws. TJ this and TJ that."

"He was quite a kid," Paula added softly.

"I know," Meg said. "So you can imagine how his death affected my Sean. He'd never lost anyone close to him—and honestly, I wasn't sure if he'd survive it. We spent a lot of late nights talking about things, praying for understanding, crying together. It hurt me so much to see him in pain." Meg's voice quavered, and she was quiet for a few seconds.

"I—I'm sorry, I don't really remember your son," Paula interjected. "There were so many people at the funeral, and I hardly knew anyone . . ." Her voice trailed off.

"That's understandable," Meg replied. "Sean was the tall, skinny, red-haired kid who served as one of the pallbearers." Paula nodded as if she faintly remembered the boy. "He insisted on doing it, and was the first to volunteer. Kevin and I had planned a combination business/vacation trip that week with all the kids. The others went along with us, but Sean wouldn't be budged. He said he had to do this one last thing . . . for his buddy. My mother, bless her, came and stayed with him so he wouldn't be alone. It meant the world to him, and I'm sure she handled it better than I could have."

Both women sat quietly for a time, lost in thought. Finally, Meg went on. "Later, when I heard you'd joined the Church, a whole flood of memories made me realize that we just might have something in common."

Paula stared at Meg, her eyes questioning. She liked this woman, but couldn't imagine their lives intersecting in any meaningful way—at least not until they had shared the experience of having their spinal columns rearranged by a hug from Bonnie Solomon. She smiled a little at the thought, then asked, "Something in common—besides a love for Marie Callender's chocolate-cherry-pecan cheesecake?"

"Oh, I know that'd be a hard act to follow," Meg laughed, swirling another bite of dessert on her fork, "but at least let me give it a shot."

"You're on," Paula agreed, still curious.

"Okay. The only thing you need to know, really, is that I'm a convert, too—about twelve years ago now. Kevin and I were in our mid-twenties; he was just finishing up his accounting degree, and I had my hands full with two-year-old Cody, not to mention being barely pregnant with Sean and sicker than any dog I've ever laid eyes on. Then one day these two hopelessly cheerful young men knocked at my door. They even smiled when I lost my lunch in front of them, then tended Cody while I got myself cleaned up. To be honest with you, I wasn't all that interested in hearing their message; but I was so embarrassed that, just to be nice, I let them come back the next day. The rest, as they say, is history. Kevin and I held out for a couple of months, but when we went to a ward dinner and found out about the green Jell-O thing, which at that time happened to be a staple of our student diet, it was all over." She leaned back in her chair and flashed Paula a wide, ingenuous smile. "So you see, as fellow dunkees, we *do* have something in common."

"Uh-huh," Paula nodded. "This is all beginning to make sense. Is there more?"

"Of course," Meg said. "And this is where the confession part comes in."

Paula smiled slyly at her new friend. "Don't tell me—you switched to orange Jell-O and were excommunicated."

"Heck no," Meg laughed. "Our little branch in Michigan was desperate for a Primary pianist, and I was the only one who could plunk out a note, so they had to keep me. Kevin stayed on for the ride. More than a dozen years later, we're still a-plunkin' and a-ridin'," she finished with an exaggerated Western drawl.

Paula brought her back to the subject at hand. "And you were saying . . . uh, confessing?"

"Oh, that," she said. "The thing is, I know what it's like to be a new member—so full of questions, uncertainties, even doubts sometimes. 'Did I do the right thing?' 'How can I ever be a perfect Latter-day Saint?' 'Does Somebody up there really know and care about me?' 'How does my one little life fit into the vast plan of salvation?' And most important, 'In the premortal world, did I have this many bad hair days?'"

"Amen," Paula giggled.

"But seriously," Meg continued, "it can be a challenge to get the hang of being a Mormon in a non-Mormon world—even if you *know* it's true, and even if you're in a fabulous ward like ours. When Sean first told me you'd been baptized, I didn't think too much about it. 'She'll be fine,' I said to myself, and life went on. But then, as I watched Sean struggle with TJ's death over the next few weeks, I realized that you were going through an even deeper loss—and at the same time you were trying to figure out what you'd really gotten yourself into when you stepped into that baptismal font."

"I've had my moments," Paula admitted.

"We've all had them, trust me. In the meantime, something kept nudging thoughts of you into my mind. Not that I ever did anything about them—I'm pretty much of a slug when it comes to things like that, and I had my own busy life and family to take care of. But then a couple of weeks ago my visiting teaching companion moved out of the ward, and there I was without a partner in crime. So—better late than never, right?—I asked the Relief Society president if I could have you. And Eloise Martin, fairy godmother that she is, thought it was a perfect idea."

Paula smiled as she remembered Sister Martin's familiar, loving arms around her on the day of TJ's funeral, and her many kindnesses since. If anyone understood her need, it was Eloise. *I should have known,* she thought.

"So, that's basically the story—uh, the confession," Meg summarized. "And now here we are—Donroe and O'Brien. Sounds like some kind of high-powered law firm or something, doesn't it?" She looked intently at Paula. "High-powered, maybe," she said. "But let's just be friends first, okay? If you think you can tolerate my bad jokes and slightly irreverent approach to life, that is."

"Hey, anyone who springs for both dinner and dessert can't be all bad," Paula grinned. "Besides, at the risk of sounding like Paul Harvey, I'm dying to tell you . . . the rest of the story."

"The rest of the story?" Meg looked slightly baffled for a moment, then her eyes lit up. "I'm game, if you're up for another sliver of cheesecake."

"Done," Paula agreed, pushing her dessert plate to one side as Meg motioned for the waiter. "Want to hear *my* conversion story? It's a heart-stopper."

"See these?" Meg asked, tugging on both earlobes simultaneously. "They're all yours." She rested an elbow on the table, cupped her chin in one palm, and looked at Paula expectantly. Her vivid blue eyes danced in the mellow light of a small candle flickering in the table's centerpiece.

Half an hour later, Paula had told her everything—about the long-ago separation from her newborn son; TJ's friendship with the Mormon elders; the devastating argument between mother and son when she refused to allow his baptism; his death before she had a chance to apologize; the bottomless grief that somehow opened her heart to the elders and their message; and finally, after her baptism, the stunning discovery that one of these eager young missionaries was the very son she had given away so many years before. Then, almost as an afterthought, she added the wrenching news about Mark Richland's mother. When she finished, she leaned back in her chair and studied Meg's reaction. "I told you it was a heart-stopper," she said.

"Yeah, but you didn't warn me it was going to be a six-hanky affair," Meg hiccuped, wiping steadily at the tears streaming down her cheeks. "This one definitely deserves a spot on *Touched by an Angel*. It'd be an all-time winner." She inhaled deeply for a few seconds to calm the overflow of emotion, then gave Paula a watery smile. "You know," she said, "that's just about the most beautiful story I've ever heard. In my whole life. I'll never forget it if I live to be three hundred."

"Me neither," Paula said. "Of course, by that time I hope to be safely tucked away in some pleasant little corner of the universe, catching up on some quality time with my sons." Her eyes clouded with a faraway look. "Especially TJ. I could spend an eternity apologizing to him, and it still wouldn't be long enough."

"Well, I'm sure he doesn't see it that way," Meg said, a note of gentle reprimand in her voice. "After all, if it hadn't happened, you might never have found the gospel—or your missionary son, for that matter." She began to sniffle again. "Sorry to be such a bawl baby . . . but this is just so unbelievable. So utterly wonderful."

"I know," Paula said softly. "Unbelievable. Thanks for letting me share it."

"No, thank *you*. Can I tell Kevin?"

"Of course."

"And Sean? Sean would love it. He'd write it in his journal."

"I'd be honored," Paula said, remembering the journal TJ's Sunday School teacher had given him only a week or two before . . . She shook her head as tears threatened again.

The sound of someone clearing his throat nearby startled the women. Looking up, Meg saw their college-age waiter standing to one side of the table, watching them curiously. Now he spoke hesitantly, his gaze moving from one to the other. "Uh, excuse me . . . your check, ma'am." He shoved a small slip of paper awkwardly toward Meg.

"Thanks." She took the paper and smiled up at him. As he quickly disappeared around a corner, she turned to Paula. "Shall we call it a night? If I'm not home to supervise, Kevin will turn bedtime into a Stephen King story fest, and my nine-year-old will be sleeping with a baseball bat under her pillow—just in case. I'm thinking of signing her up for one of Bonnie's karate classes so she can keep the monsters at bay."

"Not a bad idea," Paula observed, standing up and slinging her purse strap over her shoulder. "If my Scotty gets any more out of control, I might need one of those classes myself."

Meg looked at her, waiting for an explanation.

"Don't get me wrong—he's a good kid," Paula said quickly, "but he's going through some pretty tough times at the moment. Which is a story for another piece of cheesecake. Meanwhile, I brought some work home tonight, and I need to get to it."

"Okay," Meg conceded as they walked out into the mild January evening. "Scotty's story: to be continued. In the meantime, how's your schedule for visiting teaching, say, week after next? I'll be happy to set up the appointments. We can usually see everyone in one evening—sometimes two, depending on our CQ."

"CQ?" Paula questioned. *I haven't heard that one before . . . must be some kind of insider Mormon terminology. I still have so much to learn.*

"Chat quotient," Meg said with a little smirk. "As visiting teachers, we live and die by it. You know the part of that Tennyson poem that says, 'More things are wrought by prayer than this world dreams of'? Well, in the Church it's also true that 'more things are wrought by *chatting* than this world dreams of.'"

"I see," Paula said, shaking her head a little. *I can visit . . . I can teach . . . but can I chat?*

"Not to worry, you'll get the hang of it," Meg insisted, patting her arm. "After all, you'll have a master teacher. Chatting was my major in college."

"Well, that's a relief," Paula laughed as they buckled themselves into the Taurus. "Week after next should be fine, as far as I know. I'll check my schedule and give you a call tomorrow if there's any problem."

Meg slipped a cassette into the stereo, and Sinatra's golden voice filled the car's interior. Neither woman spoke, but both could feel the tentative bonds of a new friendship beginning to take hold. *I could enjoy this,* Paula thought privately as the car pulled into her driveway.

But Meg laid everything out in the open. "I can feel it," she said, turning toward Paula with a wide, dimpled grin stretching across her face. "We're going to have more fun than any two visiting teachers have a right to."

As she snuggled into bed past midnight, Paula hoped it would be true.

CHAPTER 6

Paula bounded downstairs earlier than usual the next morning, humming an old Sinatra tune and feeling remarkably energetic despite only a few hours' sleep. *It must be the cheesecake,* she thought idly—*a triple whammy, ten-hour sugar rush. Or it could be my intriguing new insight into a very important gospel principle: the notion of chatting one's way into the celestial kingdom.* Either way, she felt ready to take on this day and make it her own.

"Morning, Millie," she said brightly, plopping herself down at the breakfast bar. "Is that bacon I smell—and cinnamon buns?" She inhaled deeply and felt her stomach flutter with anticipation.

The older woman was standing in front of the open refrigerator, reaching for a carton of orange juice. When she turned toward Paula, her face was solemn and pinched-looking. She managed a weak smile, but the heavy circles beneath her eyes seemed to cast long shadows that canceled it out.

"Good grief, Millie, you look terrible," Paula blurted out. "What in the world is the matter? Is it your arthritis again? If you need to go back to bed and rest for a while, or—"

"No, dear, I'm fine," Millie said, setting the juice on the bar. "It's just that . . ." She seemed hesitant to continue. ". . . this has never happened before. I thought he would surely call, or—" She began to wring her gnarled hands, and her expression seemed even more pained than before.

"Millie, what's going on? Tell me . . . now," Paula said firmly.

Following a long pause, Millie looked at her glumly. "The thing is . . . Scotty didn't come home last night."

"He *what?* Are you sure?" Paula's tone was incredulous. *The one night I was too tired to check on him, and now this.*

Millie nodded. "He was out with his friends, and—"

"That gang, I'll bet." Paula drummed her fingers against the bar.

"I suppose. Anyway, he hadn't come in when I went to bed a little after nine, but that's not unusual. Then I went to wake him early this morning; he'd asked me to get him up about six so he could study for a test or something. I knocked on his door, but there was no answer . . . not even his usual growl . . . so I went in. No Scotty. His bed hadn't even been slept in. I looked all over the house—sometimes he falls asleep watching TV downstairs, you know. Nothing. It's plain to see; he hasn't been here since late yesterday afternoon." She stuffed her hands into the pockets of her apron and stared at the floor.

Paula shook her head and groaned, then her eyes flashed with anger. "That kid is going to have some tall answering to do. He knows the rules, and they most certainly do *not* include overnighters in the middle of the week. There's got to be a serious punishment to fit this crime. Why, anything could've hap—"

She broke off as a series of images ripped through her mind: grim-faced police officers, the sterile white lights of a hospital emergency room, a youthful figure lying unnaturally still on a sheeted bed. *Good Lord,* she cried silently, *is this going to be an instant replay of what happened that terrible night in November? Please, no. I can't do that again. I can't lose another son.* Her complexion faded to a pasty gray color, and she began to tremble.

Millie shuffled around the bar and squeezed Paula's shoulders. "I know what you're thinking—all the memories of TJ," she said. "But I'm sure it's not the same. After what happened, I don't think Scotty would ever go downtown that way again. He was in the car when TJ got shot, for goodness' sake. He was *driving.* You don't forget something like that; you think twice about going back."

"Or you don't think at all," Paula reflected, feeling a sudden chill snake up her spine. "Or maybe you're drawn back to the scene of the tragedy over and over again, just to see how far you can tempt fate. And maybe one last time, fate finally catches up with you." She closed her eyes and moaned helplessly. *Wasn't I happy just a few minutes ago, humming one of Sinatra's best? Where's "It Was a Very Good*

Year" when I really need it? "What should we do, Millie? Should we call someone, or—"

"I was thinking," Millie interjected, "that a prayer would be nice. Then we'll figure out what else to do."

"Yes, of course. A prayer," Paula agreed as tiny waves of optimism rippled through her chest. "Heavenly Father knows where Scotty is, doesn't He? He'll know what to do." *And please, Father . . . please don't decide You need my son more than I do at the moment. Fair is fair; TJ was enough. Just let me keep Scotty, and I'll be a model Mormon, okay? You can count on it.* "Would you do the honors?" She looked at Millie expectantly, and was relieved when she nodded eagerly.

They knelt next to the kitchen table, and Millie offered a brief, heartfelt petition for direction and comfort. After a whispered "amen," Paula lifted her head and gazed at her friend through tear-filled eyes. "When . . . how did you learn to pray so beautifully?" she asked.

"It just comes from my heart," Millie replied softly. "I picture a kind, fatherly gentleman who's anxious to hear what I have to say—someone who knows me from the inside out and loves me without any ifs, ands, or buts. Then I tell Him what's on my mind, and I believe He listens." She smiled shyly.

Paula returned her smile and reached out to touch one of her age-creased cheeks. "I'm sure He does, Millie. I'm sure he does. So, what do you think we should do now?" she questioned as she helped the older woman to her feet. Glancing at her watch, she realized it was still early.

"Let's talk about it over breakfast," Millie suggested. She nodded toward the table, where she had laid the morning paper earlier. "Sit down, dear, and I'll fix us each a plate. No use worrying on an empty stomach."

"I suppose you're right," Paula admitted. "We can't really start calling the neighbors at this hour, anyway." Sitting down, she picked up the paper and glanced idly at the front page. Before long, she felt Rudy's warm muzzle resting gently on her foot. "Good morning, pal," she said, reaching under the table to scratch the top of his head. His feathered tail thumped the floor in easy greeting, and Paula found comfort in this familiar display of affection.

A few minutes later, she had only picked at her scrambled eggs, which now lay clumped coldly together at one side of her plate like a small yellow-and-white moat surrounding a crumbling castle of toast and bacon bits. Every so often she thumbed absently through a page or two of the paper.

"Any interesting news?" Millie asked in the middle of a long silence.

Paula sighed. "Oh, I suppose it's the usual mix of politics, violence, and misery. About the only thing that changes from day to day is who does what to whom." She folded the paper over and reached for her glass of orange juice. "Maybe I'll call the office and leave a message that I won't be in until later. There's no way I'm going anywhere before we find out what's going on."

"I'm glad," Millie said firmly. "It's good not to be alone at a time like this."

Was she referring to the fact that Paula had been out of reach, sitting alone in a darkened movie theater, at the very moment when TJ had been gunned down? Paula shuddered at the thought, but kept it to herself. *A guilt trip will get you exactly nowhere, Donroe. Just try to relax and stay focused on a positive outcome to this mess.* She lifted the juice glass to her lips for a long, slow drink.

Before she had taken three swallows, Paula felt Rudy's head jerk abruptly away from her foot and heard a low rumble in his throat. Half a second later he shot out from under the table and trotted purposefully into the entryway, where he sat back stiffly on his haunches, staring intently at the glass-paneled front door. At the same moment, Paula heard a soft click as the antique brass knob turned slowly, carefully, almost silently. Almost. To the two women, it was an ear-splittingly joyful sound. "He's home!" Millie exclaimed. "Lord be praised, he's home!"

Paula froze in her chair, but Millie hurried to the entryway. She and Rudy both pounced on Scott's tall, angular frame as it tentatively slipped through a narrow opening when the door swung inward. Paula could almost hear the boy's bones creak as Millie wrapped her sturdy arms around him and squeezed. "Oh, sweetie, we were so worried," she cried.

Hearing Millie's unrestrained welcome, Paula felt her heart pounding with excitement at the prospect of seeing her son again.

He's alive, whole, and walking on his own steam, she thought. *Millie was right . . . the Lord be praised!*

"Where's Mom?" Scott asked in little more than a whisper. Paula smiled broadly. *He's asking for me! He knows how glad I am he's all right, how good it feels to have him home. No matter what, he's my boy; we'll straighten all this out, then we'll sit down and have a wonderful breakfast together. It's going to be a good day, after all . . . Donroe, why are you always so paranoid?*

"She's in the kitchen," Millie answered as Paula pushed her chair back and prepared to make a grand, benevolent entrance into the foyer of their happy home.

She had taken exactly one step when her son's bitter snort, followed by a string of profanities, stopped her cold. His next words made her blood boil. "She waitin' to see if I come crawlin' back like some spineless little Mormon?"

"*Scotty!*" the older woman gasped. "I'm sure you didn't mean that. Your mother's been plenty worried, and we were just minutes from calling the police. We couldn't imagine why in the world you—"

"Why you didn't bother to come home last night," Paula snapped as she strode into the entryway. She leaned against the door and folded her arms across her chest. *So much for warm-fuzzy homecomings.* "Do you want to tell me about it now, or would you rather spend the day in your room, thinking about it?"

"I got school," he said sullenly.

"And I got work," Paula barked. "But they can both wait until I find out exactly what's going on."

The boy stuffed his hands into his jeans pockets and glared at the floor, saying nothing. Paula saw the muscles in his jaw twitching, and her anger deepened. "Millie, will you excuse us?" she said in a voice of deadly calm, her eyes never leaving Scott's face.

"Sure, . . . I'll just go and . . . load the dishwasher," Millie said meekly. She turned and hurried from the entryway.

"Well?" Paula moved closer to her son as she eyed him up and down. His clothes were rumpled and dirty, his green T-shirt stained with some kind of brownish liquid, his thick, dark hair matted and sticking out from his scalp at odd angles. A sickening odor hovered around him, and when he raised his eyes for an instant she could see that they were bloodshot and puffy.

"Well, what?" he said through clenched teeth. She stepped toward him again, and he backed away. "Give a guy a little room, will ya?" Instead, she closed in on him until his back thudded against the wall. He finally raised his head defiantly, his face no more than six inches from hers, and her fury intensified when she was assaulted by the unmistakable smell of alcohol on his stale breath. "So, Mommie dearest," he sneered, "who do you think you are, anyway, my Mormon Nazi jailer or—"

Her open hand made fierce contact with his stubbled cheek before either of them realized what was happening. The slap echoed across the entryway, and Paula heard Millie's sudden intake of breath from the kitchen even before she felt the sudden sting on her palm. Her slim frame began to tremble when she saw Scott's red-streaked eyes widen in pain and disbelief. "Whoa," he breathed, sliding down the wall into a rumpled heap of astonishment.

Paula quickly opened her mouth to apologize, but changed her mind at the last moment. *He disobeyed all the rules,* she reminded herself. *He stayed out all night—and he's been drinking, for heaven's sake. This is no time to go soft, Donroe.* When she spoke, her voice was calm but edged with profound intensity. "Go get yourself cleaned up, and Millie will fix you some breakfast. Then I expect you to go to school and be home no later than three-thirty, and you'll go right to your room. You're grounded, Scott—no Driver's Ed classes, no telephone, no Crawlers, no TV or computer games. Just homework and bed."

His surly expression, which had been momentarily replaced by a few seconds of complete bewilderment, now returned. "How long?" he asked gruffly.

"Probably for the rest of your life," Paula responded icily. "Now go. We'll talk later." She pointed toward the stairs, and he shuffled unsteadily toward his room. Rudy, who had kept his distance during their argument, moved to follow Scott. "Stay here, Rudy," Paula ordered curtly. The big dog stopped in his tracks, then turned obediently and headed for the kitchen and his quiet place under the table.

Paula began to tremble more violently; she felt chilled to the bone, and her knees threatened to buckle as she leaned heavily against the door. From where she was standing, she could see into the living room and across to the far wall, where a graceful charcoal drawing of TJ smiled out at her from an elegant gold frame. The sensitive portrait, painstakingly fashioned by Scott in the weeks following his brother's death, had been his Christmas gift to Paula. Since then she had spent countless hours studying it, memorizing its intricate, life-like detail, admiring Scott's obvious artistic gifts. But at this moment TJ's boyish grin seemed to fade a little, taking on a more pensive expression. Was it her imagination, or could he be trying to communicate with her from another dimension—and if so, what was he trying to say? Paula closed her eyes and felt hot tears on her cheeks. *What's happening to us?* she thought. *Why can't I keep this family together? I've got to do something before it's too late . . . but what? Or maybe it's already too late. Dear Lord, please . . .* A sharp sob caught in her throat, and she pressed her hand to her mouth.

Millie's kind voice sounded close to her ear. "It's all right, dear. It's all right." Paula fell into her friend's ready embrace. "There, now," Millie soothed, stroking her dark hair. "We'll get through this. You'll see."

"I don't know how," Paula sobbed as they walked slowly toward the kitchen. "Do you know what I did, Millie? I *hit* Scotty . . . I *struck my son.* How can any good come of that? I've never thought of myself as an abusive parent before, but now I . . . I . . ." She sank onto a chair and buried her face in her hands.

"Shh," Millie whispered, rubbing Paula's shoulders. "We've all been under a lot of stress and strain these past few months—and Scotty hasn't exactly been easy to live with, that's for sure. Maybe this will bring things into the open for both of you. You'll talk tonight; things will work out."

"Maybe," Paula sniffed, wiping at her eyes. "In the meantime, I guess I'd better go upstairs and redo my face. If I show up at work looking like this, everyone'll think it's Halloween." She stood and gave Millie a quick hug. "Thanks for feeding our little truant . . . and for all the rest of it, too."

"I'm glad I could be here. And I'll make sure he gets right to his room after school."

"You're the best, Millie. I mean that." Paula smiled tentatively. "You know, if you'd been his mother from the get-go, he'd probably be a straight-A student and an Eagle Scout by now. Instead, he'll be lucky to get his GED and a couple of low-level merit badges for miscellaneous Scout-like activities."

"Oh, pooh." Millie shook her head good-naturedly. "We all follow our own paths," she said. "In Scotty's case, the path just happens to be taking some unfortunate detours at the moment."

"Like through the cellar, into the gutter, and out to play with the Crawlers," Paula added. "Anyway, I'll talk to him tonight. Have a *lovely* day, Millie . . . the way I figure, things can only get better—I hope."

"There's always hope, dear," Millie said firmly. "I believe that." She gave Paula's arm a squeeze, then turned to the task of preparing breakfast for one slightly hung-over teenager who was in big, big trouble.

It was past eight P.M. by the time Paula coaxed her shiny red Jaguar into the garage and wearily reached to shut off the ignition. *I'll just sit here for a few minutes,* she told herself. *Get myself ready to face the music with Scotty.* Thinking back on her day, with its frantic pace from beginning to end, she couldn't help feeling grateful that there had been literally no spare moments—not so much as a tiny sliver of time to reflect on the morning's events, or even to think ahead to this unavoidable encounter with her son. *I do much better in my executive mode,* she reasoned. *If Scott was my employee, I'd know exactly what to do, and I'd do it—tell him to shape up or find another job. But this mothering thing . . . I can't just say, "Well, my boy, your performance as a son is just not cutting it. So you can either get your act together or find another family."* An unexpected surge of emotion rose in her throat as an unsettling thought needled its way into her brain. *But that's just what some parents do, isn't it? They actually* fire *their kids—kick them out, tell them they can't come home again, leave them to fend for themselves. I should know; that's what my own parents did when I was foolish enough to fall in love.*

Paula shivered, even though the air in the garage was warm. She gripped the steering wheel and squeezed her eyes tightly shut. *There's got to be a better way, Father. Please help me find it.*

Almost half an hour later, she made her way slowly upstairs and stood for a few moments outside Scott's room before she knocked softly on his door. No answer. She knocked again. Still no answer. "Scotty?" she called, her face nearly touching the oak door frame. "Scotty, are you awake?"

"It's open," a deep voice responded.

Pushing the door inward, Paula stood quietly and waited until her eyes adjusted to the room's dim light. Then she kicked off her suede pumps, located a rust-colored banana chair near the bed, and lowered herself into it. "Nice furniture," she joked.

Scott was lying face-up on his bed, his hands tucked behind his head. A pair of stereo earphones circled his neck and rested against his light-yellow T-shirt.

"Been listening to some good music?" Paula asked. *As if the aboriginal pounding of heavy metal could be classified as music.*

"Tchaikovsky," he said tonelessly, his eyes riveted on the ceiling.

Paula's jaw dropped. "Tchaikovsky," she repeated incredulously. "I didn't realize you were into the classics."

Only Scott's mouth moved. "Yeah, well, I guess there are a few things you didn't realize."

"I suppose," she conceded.

The two sat for a few minutes in deep silence while Paula gathered her thoughts. Finally, she spoke. "Scotty, about this morning . . . I . . . I . . ." She gulped audibly. *Come on, Donroe; you closed a two-million-dollar advertising deal this afternoon. You can do this one little thing for your own son.* "The thing is, I just wanted to say . . . well, I'm sorry." *Okay. That's more like it.* She took a deep breath. "I was so angry, really frustrated and disappointed. But I never should have hit you. I hope you can forgive me, and I—"

"No." He said the word in a level tone, but it pierced her heart like a scud missile. She had obviously done irreparable damage to their relationship—whatever was left of it.

Paula scooted forward and balanced on the edge of the banana chair. "Please don't shut me out here," she pleaded, her eyes glistening. "I know it was awful this morning, but don't you think we can—"

"I said *no,*" Scott interjected again, and her heart sank. He sat up, swung his long, muscular legs off the bed, and planted his feet solidly on the floor. Then he looked her squarely in the face and said firmly, "I won't accept your apology."

"But Scotty," she urged, "if you could only try to understand . . ." Her throat constricted, and she couldn't finish.

He made a fist with one large hand, and for a moment Paula thought he was about to return the morning's favor. Instead, he rested the fist on his knee and looked at her gravely. "Could you just *listen* for a minute here?"

Paula nodded as despair washed over her. *He's going to tell me where to go, and then some. I know it.*

Scott's eyes were darkly intense as he spoke. "I won't accept your apology because *I* was wrong. You did what you had to do, Mom; I deserved that smack on the chops. And I should be the one apologizing."

She stared at him blankly for five, ten, twenty seconds, her senses numbed to the reality of what he was saying. "Excuse me?" she finally rasped, holding tightly to the edges of the banana chair.

Scott's mouth curved into a tiny smile as he studied his mother's bewildered expression. "I said it was my fault. I've had all day to think about it, and I know what I did was way out of line. Not to mention stupid. Whatever punishment you decide on is okay by me." He tugged nervously at the dark, shaggy curls along his hairline and stared at the floor.

Paula was speechless. She closed her eyes and leaned far back into the banana chair, causing it to tip precariously to one side. *Can this be happening—an intelligent, civil conversation with my rude, belligerent son? If this is a dream, I hope nobody wakes me for at least a month.* She opened her eyes and saw him looking at her, his gaze forthright and almost penitent. Although she knew she was taking a chance, she had to take it further. "And just . . . what did you do?" she asked. "Last night, I mean."

"It was no big deal," he began. "Me 'n the guys just went down to the clubhouse to hang out, play some video games, stuff like that. I would've been home by nine, but, uh . . . somethin' came up." He started pulling at a small string hanging from his shirt sleeve.

"Something that kept you out all night?" Paula questioned. *Keep it casual,* she warned herself. *Now that he's talking, you can't afford to shut him down.* She quickly pasted a benign expression on her face and nodded her encouragement.

"Well, not exactly," he continued, "at least to begin with. Benny's dad owns a couple of grocery stores, ya know? So last night around eight, he came over to the clubhouse and said he'd hire us to move a bunch of stuff from one store to another—a lot of boxes and cans, things like that. Said he'd pay us each ten bucks an hour. It was a sweet deal, so all six of us went over to the store. The plan was to finish up in a couple of hours, but . . ." He chewed his lip anxiously. "But it didn't exactly turn out that way."

"I'm listening," Paula said after a long silence.

"That's what I was afraid of," he joked grimly. "This is where the 'stupid' part comes in."

She nodded and touched his knee lightly, still partially stunned by his apparent willingness to communicate. *He could be pulling my leg,* she thought, *just moving his lips and taking me for a ride. But why? He knows it wouldn't do any good; the truth would come out sooner or later.* "Go on," she said.

"Well, things were going great, and it was actually fun movin' all those boxes and stuff around. And to be getting paid for it, too . . . that was cool. Then Ben's dad had to go somewhere, so he told us to just finish what we were doing and lock up before we left. We kept workin' for a while, then we just started goofin' off a little, ya know? Next thing I knew, Benny was taking a bunch of beer cans out of some coolers in the back, handing 'em to us. So we started drinkin', and it was . . . it was . . ." He paused and shook his head.

Paula couldn't help smiling to herself as she recalled her own first—and last—experience with beer. *Now comes the part where he tells me how foul-smelling, bitter, and repulsive the stuff is. How it made him sick and miserable; how he'll never let another drop cross his tongue. Poor kid; I'll help him put it into words.* "It was awful, wasn't it?" she prompted.

"Actually, it was pretty fun," Scott replied. "The first few swallows took some getting used to, but after that it went down re-e-e-al smooth." He made a horizontal motion with one hand. "And after three or four cans, I felt like I was having an out-of-body experience or something. If you wanna know, it was cool. Totally cool."

"Uh-huh," Paula muttered. *No, I really didn't wanna know. An out-of-body experience? Stay calm, Donroe; he hasn't even gotten to the "stupid" part yet . . . something to look forward to.* "So then what happened?"

He rubbed the back of his neck. "Geez, things get a little hazy from here on."

Surprise, surprise. What did he expect after three or four cans? "I'll bet they do," she said sweetly.

"Anyway," he went on, "about midnight we all piled in Benny's car and somehow made it back to the clubhouse. I don't even know who was driving, but I'm pretty sure he was just as smashed as I was. We didn't get pulled over or anything, but it was a miracle we didn't get dragged down to the 34th Precinct. I guess all the cops were somewhere else, probably trying to stop a bunch of gang fights. We were lucky dudes, all right."

A sudden rush of anger colored Paula's cheeks, though she tried to maintain control as she spoke. "You think you were lucky because you didn't get *caught?*"

"Fer sure," he replied, flashing her a self-assured smile. "It could've been real bad news, 'specially since we're all under age. We coulda rotted for a couple nights in the tank, got fined big-time, an' spent the next hundred years doing community service. Bummer." He lay back and let out a long, slow breath.

Paula pushed herself out of the banana chair and sat beside him on the bed. "Scott," she said, and there was no mistaking the intensity in her voice, "you were *drunk*. There could have been a terrible accident. You could have *killed* someone. *You* could have been killed." She shuddered at a fleeting mental image of twisted metal and broken bodies strewn across the highway.

"Yeah, that too," Scott said matter-of-factly. "But it turned out okay."

"Okay? I don't think so," Paula corrected. "You're right about one thing, though: that was a really, really stupid thing to do."

Scott's laugh was a low rumble in his throat. "Sheesh, Mom, I haven't even told you about the *really* stupid thing yet."

"Oh?" Paula's alarm threshold was at its saturation point. "And what might that be?"

"You shoulda seen it," her son began, his eyes squinting with revulsion. "I wouldn'ta believed it if I hadn't been there myself. It was awful." He covered part of his face with his arm.

She was instantly sympathetic as she rested her hand on his outstretched leg. "It's all right, Scotty; you can tell me. We'll get through this together."

"Well, okay," he mumbled. "When we got to the clubhouse, we thought we'd just go inside and lay around for a while—you know, until the beer wore off. The thing is, almost the second we got inside the door, we all got sick. Rotgut sick—hurling all over the place, making a mess like you wouldn't believe. And the smell—-whew!" He fanned the air in front of his face. "Benny and Joe passed out on the front-room floor in the middle of it. Ricky made it to the bathroom, and the rest of us sacked out in the bedroom. When we left this morning, the place needed fumigating. We talked about just torching it, but nobody had a match. That was the totally stupid thing— messin' up our place like that. It'll never be the same without new carpet and a paint job. That's what we get for being idiots, I guess." He sighed mournfully.

"I see," Paula said, struggling to keep a straight face. "And just what do you think you've learned from this little adventure?"

"That's a no-brainer," he smirked. "Absolutely don't drink."

"Good," she smiled. "Very good."

"Unless you can hold your liquor. Or find a good place to puke."

Paula made a tiny choking sound. "Well, that's not exactly what I had in mind," she said, "but at least it's a start." *And at least we're talking, not slapping each other around.*

She decided to pursue the matter a bit further. "Scotty, I know it's not unusual for kids your age to try a little alcohol once in a while. But, honey . . . I just don't think it's a good idea." She felt his leg stiffen slightly beneath her hand.

"It was just a couple beers, Mom." His tone was mildly defensive.

"I know that. But what I'm trying to say is, even a little bit of alcohol can make you lose control—and it can lead to a lot of other things that aren't very pretty, either. Trust me . . . you don't want to go there."

Scott raised himself slowly until he was sitting side by side with his mother on the bed. His voice sounded much deeper, more mature than a sixteen-year-old's when he spoke. "And this from a woman who's had a monster martini—or two or three—every night of her life for as long as I've known her. And has still managed to make a very big name for herself in business. I'd say drinking hasn't seemed to hurt you any."

His words hung like an indictment in the still, dark air, and Paula felt a stinging rush of—what was it? shame? guilt? embarrassment?—rise to her cheeks. Suddenly grateful for the room's dusky light, she was sure her face had taken on a deep scarlet hue. *Oboy,* she thought. *He's got me cold on this one.* Then she paused to reconsider as an idea came to her. *Or maybe not.*

She cleared her throat and forced herself to lift her head and gaze steadily into his eyes. "You're right about that. It doesn't seem to have done me any harm," she admitted. "But I was one of the lucky ones. I could tell you about at least a dozen of my college friends—bright, promising kids with no limits when it came to potential—who started out with weekend beer busts, moved on to hard liquor and drugs, then ended up dropping out of school and life. Three of them died before their twenty-fifth birthdays, and at least four have done hard prison time for drug trafficking. It hasn't been a pretty thing to watch; and if I were you, I'd want to stay as far away from that corner of the universe as I could."

Scott eyed her carefully. "But you were an exception. I could be, too."

Paula shook her head fiercely. "Don't even *think* about it, Scott. It's not worth the risk, because the numbers are against you, and you'd probably lose. Besides," she rested her hand firmly on his shoulder, "it's *wrong.* I didn't know that twenty years ago, five years ago, or even three months ago, but I'm sure of it now. And you haven't seen me snarfing green olives with anything but turkey sandwiches since mid-November, right?"

"Yeah, right," he murmured. "The Mormon thing."

"Exactly—the Mormon thing," she smiled. "Some day I hope you'll know it for yourself." Scott rolled his eyes and groaned softly. "But in the meantime, for you as a member of this family, the rule is *no drinking.* Understood?"

He looked away, but she grasped his chin in her hand and turned his head back toward her. "*Understood?*" she repeated firmly.

"Yeah, yeah. Understood," he grumbled, pulling away. She was relieved when his customary volley of profanities didn't materialize.

"That's my boy," she chirped, leaning over to press a light kiss against his cheek. "Now, about your penance . . ."

"Aw, geez," he whined, "haven't I been through enough already?"

"Almost," Paula said. "But you really need to pay the piper for all the rules you broke. I think four weeks should be sufficient."

Scott's eyes grew wide in horror and disbelief. "Four weeks? You're grounding me for *four weeks?* My life is over." He slumped back against the wall.

"Who said anything about grounding?" Paula asked cheerfully.

He looked at her quizzically. "But you just said—"

"I said four weeks. Let me clarify that: you'll be attending church with Millie and me for four weeks. Starting this Sunday."

"Terrific," he groused. "All of a sudden, being grounded doesn't sound all that bad."

"Oh, don't be such an old curmudgeon," Paula said playfully. "It'll be fun—we'll be just like a real . . . *family.* What a unique concept! And who knows? Some of the 'Mormon thing' might just rub off on that handsome hide of yours. Then there's the good news: we'll try not to make it too hard on you—sacrament meeting only, for about an hour. You're gonna love it!" She grinned as Scott slid down on the bed and buried his head under two pillows. "Good night, sweetie . . . pleasant dreams." She heard a low moan as she tiptoed from the room.

Later, as Paula drifted into a relaxed sleep, she breathed a prayer of thanks for the small gifts of rational conversation she had shared with her son. Theirs was an uneasy peace at best; but for the moment, it would have to do.

CHAPTER 7

A light rain had begun to fall by the time Meg O'Brien's Taurus pulled into the Donroes' driveway sometime after ten P.M. Meg shut off the motor and turned toward her new friend with a satisfied grin. "See? I told you it'd be fun. There's nothing quite like an evening of visiting teaching to put everything into perspective."

"You're right about that," Paula said. "You couldn't find three more different ladies if you'd picked them at random from the telephone book." As she said it, her thoughts meandered back over the three hours she had just spent getting acquainted with as unlikely a trio of Latter-day Saints as she could ever have conjured up in her own vivid imagination.

Caroline Wintersweet—rich, elegant, fine-boned, inordinately proper—had ushered them into her prim Victorian drawing room with a decorous sweep of her wispy, silk-clad arm. The room was steeped in the dense fragrance of several dozen roses, fresh-cut from her garden and meticulously arranged in a tall crystal vase here, a shallow porcelain bowl there, an antique brass cuspidor by the enormous floor-to-ceiling window. The space was bright and airy, perfectly accented by a longish blue-and-white-striped chintz sofa and two burgundy wing-backed chairs facing each other across a narrow, cream-colored Oriental rug. When Caroline lowered herself gracefully into one of the chairs, she seemed to become part of the furnishings.

Their conversation was cordial, restrained, tasteful—and punctuated occasionally by a keen but mannerly bark from one or the other of two small white poodles who had miraculously appeared on Caroline's lap at the very moment her cultured derrière made contact with the chair's rich leather upholstery. Recalling Meg's earlier comments regarding the familial status of Jacques and Heidi, Paula clucked and cooed over them until Heidi, intrigued by this attentive stranger, hopped down from Caroline's lap and trotted over to have a closer look. A few curious sniffs later, encouraged by Paula's friendly scratch behind her ears, the little dog had satisfied herself that the dark-haired visitor's attentions were genuine. Like a spring lamb frolicking in the pasture, she took a couple of quick turns around the circular coffee table, then bounded onto the sofa and confidently snuggled the length of her furry body against Paula, who smiled and gently stroked the tiny white back.

Jacques, who had been observing this bonding moment from his safe place at Caroline's side, soon joined them. Paula inhaled their pampered, freshly bathed and perfumed smell as if relishing the scent of a fragrant candle. The two dogs sprawled contentedly beside her for the remainder of the visit, then delicately flicked their smooth pink tongues against her hand as a parting gesture of affection.

"You were a hit. An absolute, unqualified hit," Meg smiled as they walked to her car at one edge of the long driveway. "Caroline loved you."

"Yeah, right," Paula laughed. "She barely said a dozen words to me, and those included 'How do you do?' and 'Lovely to have met you.' Not exactly a declaration of undying friendship. And I didn't even chat very well."

"But I could tell," Meg insisted. "With Caroline, it's all in the eyes; hers are the most extraordinary gray-blue color, and they change dramatically with her moods and feelings. You probably didn't notice, but when those little dogs made friends with you, Caroline's eyes positively glowed with satisfaction. I've been visiting her for two years now, and I've never seen anything quite like it."

"I'm glad," Paula said. "She reminds me a little of my mother—cool and reserved on the outside, but a real softie where it counts." She tapped her chest. "And it only took me forty years to figure it out. Someday I'll tell you the story."

"Deal," Meg agreed.

Their visit with Sylvie Randolph was less elegant, but Paula was captivated by this young mother and her bubbly three- and four-year-old daughters, Missy and Emmeline. Their tiny two-bedroom apartment was cramped and run-down; the carpet was worn so thin in places that the rough planking beneath it showed through; and the sparse, mismatched furnishings in the living room were barely serviceable. Sitting on a drab green vinyl couch that wobbled on uneven legs, Paula looked around her and noticed that for all its dreariness, the room was impeccably tidy. And so were the golden-haired children, who smiled shyly at her from their seats—two polished wooden stools placed next to a small table where they had been coloring. A few pictures of Mormon temples decorated the walls, and a painting of Jesus ministering to a cluster of children hung next to a weathered "Families Are Forever" placard.

Sylvie was a short, slightly rounded woman in her late twenties with straight blonde hair and large brown eyes. She smiled often, but those lovely eyes held some deep, inscrutable sadness that Paula couldn't quite define. As they visited, Paula vaguely remembered Meg's description of Sylvie's circumstances—a violent, abusive marriage; a painful divorce; a young mother struggling to keep her family together on a shoestring. *This woman has seen a lot of heartache in her short life*, she mused. *How can I possibly help?* At the moment, all she could do was listen politely as Sylvie rehearsed the events of her month and Meg gently plied her with questions, trying to determine if her needs were being met. At one point, Sylvie's eyes misted over as she related a difficult encounter with the girls' father, and Meg reached out to squeeze her hand for a long moment.

When it was almost time to leave, the children scampered into the kitchen and gleefully emerged a few seconds later, each with a small plate of Rice Krispies treats. "These are for you," Emmeline said proudly. "Mommy helped us make 'em." She helped her younger sister hand one to each of the women.

Missy grinned and smacked her lips. "They're go-o-o-d!" she exclaimed.

"My favorite!" Meg replied, dropping to her knees to give each of the girls a hug. Paula followed her lead, and the youngsters came to her eagerly. Something about the feel of them in her arms brought a lump to her throat.

Paula didn't speak for several minutes as they drove to their next appointment. Finally she said what was on her mind. "How in the world does she manage? I can't imagine living like that."

Meg sighed. "It's pretty much day to day, hand to mouth. When Sylvie first married, she had every expectation that her life would be one of those 'happily ever after' scenarios. Didn't happen. But now, in spite of everything, she's trying awfully hard to make the best of it, and she desperately wants to raise those little girls in the Church. I pick them up sometimes on Sundays when she has to work. Or sometimes when she's feeling too low to take care of them." There was a rich note of compassion in Meg's voice when she added, "That's what it's all about, I guess—caring for one another. You never know when your turn will come to be on the receiving end." Paula nodded, but without real understanding. *This is all too new,* she reflected. *I'm not sure if I'm up to it.*

"Not to worry," Meg said softly, as if reading her thoughts. "You'll figure it out as you go along."

At that moment they pulled up in front of a yard that had all the charm of a perpetual garage sale. A pair of disabled trucks straddled the driveway, and miscellaneous tools, toys, and household appliances littered the half-mowed lawn. "This is the place," Meg announced. "Solomon's sideshow." She gestured toward the motley collection. "Bonnie's not like this at all. If I were her, I'd dump husband number three before he could say, 'Whoa, that's my dirt bike in your living room.' But she seems to like the guy, so I guess that's something in his favor. Just watch your step in the kitchen; that's where he cleans his hunting rifles."

Bonnie greeted them with a wide, toothy grin and a handshake that left Paula discreetly massaging her fingers for ten minutes. The wiry, auburn-haired woman had just arrived home from teaching an evening martial arts class, and for the first few minutes of their visit she moved constantly about the room like a cat on the prowl. When she finally settled down, it was to sit cross-legged on the floor next to a dilapidated exercise bicycle and rest her elbow on one of its over-sized pedals. "So, what's cookin', ladies?" she inquired brightly.

Their conversation reminded Paula of the time she'd gone rollerblading with TJ in a lovely little park near their home—so many nice trees and flowers, but they were all a blur. Her mind raced to keep up as Bonnie recounted her adventures of the previous month— something about a midnight brawl with one of her former husbands; vandals tossing a cement statue of Mickey Mouse through her studio window; a motorcycle wreck featuring her sixteen-year-old son's fractured tibia; and—last but certainly not least—an invitation from the bishop to serve in the nursery every Sunday morning. "I told him he'd better be talking about plants," she laughed, "'cause I was never much good at growin' kids." She had graciously declined the offer, citing her preference for early-morning television infomercials over "all that churchy stuff." Meg laughed out loud at Bonnie's decidedly un-Mormon mannerisms, and Paula joined in. She had little or no idea of what she was laughing at, but it seemed a good idea at the time.

"Not much of a chatter, is she?" Bonnie whispered to Meg as they rose to leave and Paula hurried out the door. "She didn't even wait around to get her Solomon hug."

"Give her time," Meg said cheerfully. "She's just new to the Church, you know, and—"

"Oh, well, that explains it," Bonnie cut in. "I've scared her off, haven't I? She's thinking, 'If this is a Mormon lady, I might as well throw in the towel right now.' Her face drooped slightly. "Tell her I'm sorry, will you? I didn't mean to go on and on, but—"

"I know; that's just you," Meg smiled, opening her arms for the expected hug. "I'll let her know. And we'll see you next month."

"Wouldn't miss it." Bonnie waved breezily at Paula, who by this time was securely belted into the Taurus. She half-lifted her arm in a clumsy gesture of farewell.

"It's okay," Meg said as she slipped into the driver's seat and Paula tried to apologize. "She takes some getting used to."

Paula chuckled self-consciously. "I—I guess I just expected everyone in the Church to be 'true to the faith,' and all that sort of thing. But Bonnie is . . . well, she's . . ."

"Downright irreverent," Meg supplied. "But you've got to remember that she's not really 'in' the Church, so to speak—not yet, anyway. Honestly, I'm not sure she even knows what it's all about. The way I see it, our job is just to take whatever she has to give, lumps and all—or is that *karate chops* and all?—and let her know we care about her no matter what. You'll see—she's easy to love when you don't take her too seriously."

"Uh-huh," Paula responded. "More like an acquired taste than, say, the natural appeal of chocolate-cherry-pecan cheesecake."

"You got it," Meg beamed. "Bonnie's one of a kind—even better, in fact. She's rocky road in a sea of vanilla. We really should run down to her studio and watch her in action sometime." She patted Paula's shoulder. "In the meantime, I'll bet you've had just about all the visiting you can take for one night."

"You could say that," Paula said with a wan smile. "It was fun, but my evenings are usually more . . . solitary."

"Honey, for me, this *is* solitary!" Meg rejoined. "But let's get you home, and I'll get back to my brood. There's probably still some chance for a moment or two of privacy at the end of a long day." She turned the key and the station wagon's motor came to life.

Now, as they lingered briefly in Paula's driveway before saying good night, Meg turned the conversation in another direction. "By the way," she said, "that's a mighty good-looking young man you've had with you in church the past two weeks. Is he any relation, or just some studly dude you picked up off the street in a fit of missionary zeal?"

Paula laughed in spite of her weariness. "That's Scott, my oldest—well, my oldest if you don't count Mark Richland." Her eyes shone with a faraway look for just an instant. "My only child left at home." Her throat knotted with familiar grief as she thought of TJ. Would the pain ever go away—or at least be bearable? She didn't think so.

"Oh, that's right . . . I remember your telling me about Scott." Meg looked a bit puzzled. "But from what you said, I didn't think he was likely to show up at church any time before the Millennium."

"That makes two of us," Paula replied. "But when he got into some trouble a couple of weeks ago, I decided he should do a little 'community service' to make things right. Hence his assignment to attend four weeks of sacrament meeting with Millie and me."

"What a great idea!" Meg enthused. "And who knows? Maybe he'll even—"

"Don't hold your breath," Paula interjected. "So far, he hasn't cursed out loud or spit on the carpet during a meeting. I'm taking that as a good sign. As for anything more significant, I'm afraid the jury is still way, way out on this one. Like in Czechoslovakia."

"Well, you never know," Meg said warmly.

"Well, yes I do," Paula stated resolutely.

But later, as she lay in bed waiting for sleep to wash over her, she remembered the song. *How gentle God's commands, how kind his precepts are. . . .* Scott had sat silently during the first verse of the closing hymn, then had picked up the melody and sung the next two stanzas in a pure, solemn baritone voice that had sent warmth rippling through Paula's body. She had wiped quickly at her tears during the prayer, and when she put her arm around Scott after the "amen," he didn't flinch or pull away. It had been one of those halcyon moments that would linger in her heart, along with a tiny bit of hope and a grain of faith. *Come cast your burden at his feet, and bear a song away.*

❤ ❤ ❤

It was just after noon, and Paula stood at her office window, looking twenty-three stories down at the street below. There had been some kind of an accident, and emergency vehicles were lined up at the curb. She watched with mild interest as a pair of police officers began to redirect traffic. *They all look like toys from up here,* she thought. *Is that how we look to God from 'up there'?* She smiled as an image flitted across her mind—the white-robed Creator, down on His knees, blithely tinkering with a miniature train set. *I suppose He could have whatever cars He wanted,* she mused. *Even the Cannonball Express. Just a snap of His omnipotent fingers, and voilà! One of the angels on duty appears with the best set heavenly money can buy. Maybe they use leftover gold from paving the streets to do their business on high.*

Paula was startled by a brisk knock at her open office door. She whirled around to see her assistant, Carmine, walking toward the desk. "Sorry to bother you," the chunky redhead apologized.

"No problem," Paula said. "I was just having an intriguing, uh, train of thought." She smiled mysteriously.

When she said nothing further, Carmine went on. The woman was in her late twenties, but still spoke with a slightly adolescent drawl when she wasn't entertaining clients or presiding over an office staff meeting. "Okay. I thought you'd want to know about this *majorly* interesting phone call I got a few minutes ago."

"Oh?" Paula said absently, leaning over to shuffle through a small pile of paperwork on her desk. "Who was it from?"

Carmine cleared her throat importantly. "Green Pointe."

Paula's head shot up, her eyes riveted on Carmine. "You mean . . . *the* Green Pointe?"

"The same." Carmine's face had erupted into a satisfied grin. "It was Cal Brady, their new head honcho, who called. He's on his way back to Chicago late this afternoon, but wanted to stop by and see you before he leaves."

The news was enough to propel Paula backward into her burgundy leather chair. Her mind whirled as she considered the possible implications of such a visit. Green Pointe Spirits was the largest manufacturer and distributor of upscale alcoholic beverages in the Midwest, and its products were unrivaled when it came to quality and customer appeal. Until three months ago, in fact, Paula's own liquor cabinet had been well stocked with Green Pointe labels. Gin, bourbon, vodka, and her personal favorite, Bristol creme, had smoothed the gritty edges of her days more often than she could remember. Even now, at the memory, her mouth suddenly felt parched with dryness and deprivation. "I wonder why Brady wants to see me," she said.

"He mentioned something about a coast-to-coast ad campaign." Carmine said it casually, but there was a ripple of excitement in her voice. "I set up an appointment for two-thirty."

Paula glanced at her watch, then back at Carmine. "Do we have any information on Green Pointe in the files?" she asked.

"You mean something like . . . this?" Carmine grinned, holding out a slim manila folder balanced on the tips of her long, thick fingers. "Dick still had a company profile and some financials left over from when he courted the old CEO a couple of years ago. I got the rest off the Internet."

Paula gave her an appreciative smile. "This is terrific, Carmine. Now I know why we pay you the big bucks."

The young woman laughed amiably. "Yeah, well, just remember how grateful you are when bonus time rolls around. I'll have fresh coffee ready for you and . . . oh." Her sunny expression clouded for a moment. "I mean . . . with all due respect to your new religiosity, do you want some cocoa or something?" The question was punctuated with studied politeness, but Paula could almost hear the words forming themselves in her assistant's mind: *Crazy Mormons.*

"No thanks, Carmine. Coffee for Mr. Brady, and a glass of mineral water will be fine for me."

"Sure thing. I'll just leave you to your boning up, then." Carmine pivoted on one three-inch heel and moved briskly out of the office, closing the door behind her.

By the time Cal Brady appeared and settled easily onto the small, cream-colored leather sofa across from her desk, Paula had made herself familiar enough with the Green Pointe operation to know that this man represented more power, wealth, and influence in the business community than most of her other clients combined. As he laid out his vision of their cooperative advertising effort, she studied his meticulously groomed hair, slightly graying at the temples; his heavy gold diamond-encrusted Rolex watch; his three-piece Armani suit, with creases in the trousers that looked sharp enough to slice bread; his hand-tooled leather wingtips. The man looked prosperous. *No, not just prosperous,* she thought. *Rich . . . filthy rich. If people's auras were visible, Cal Brady's would be green.*

"So, what do you think?" Brady's thick, silver-toned voice brought their conversation sharply back into focus. "If you'd like to take us on, it could mean tremendous benefits for everyone concerned. Your usual fee for services rendered, plus a healthy percentage of the profits from the campaign, would make a sizable difference in your annual revenues."

"I can see that," Paula said, glancing at a spreadsheet of projections he had placed on the desk in front of her. *This is unbelievable,* she thought as the figures burned themselves into her brain. *With the Green Pointe account, Donroe & Associates could easily double—maybe even triple—its income in less than a year. This gives new meaning to the term "big business."* She looked up at Brady and smiled demurely. "I do have one question, though."

"Shoot," he said eagerly. His deep-green eyes shone with an almost boyish enthusiasm that Paula found appealing.

"What brought you to Donroe?" she asked. "Any of the big New York agencies would have jumped through hoops to work with you." *And to get a slice of your profit pie.*

"It must have been fate," he answered warmly. "Lauren Banks did some consulting work with us a few months ago, and when she heard we were looking for a new agency she put in a good word for you. Well, several thousand good words, actually." Paula nodded in recognition as she heard the name of her old graduate-school friend. *I should have known. Lauren has been singing the praises of Green Pointe creme de menthe ever since she literally took a bath in it on a dare the night before her master's oral exam. Said it softened her skin and helped her sleep like a baby.*

"Besides," Brady continued, "your reputation wasn't exactly lost on us in the first place. Even if Lauren hadn't brought it up, I'm sure we would've been knocking on your door sooner or later. I think her recommendation just made it sooner."

"That's very nice," Paula said. She was always a little awestruck to realize that her company was actually known and admired in the advertising world; and the fact that an internationally recognized enterprise like Green Pointe would seek her out was a definite coup. *Something of a step up from eight years ago, when we were eating cheap microwaved burritos for lunch so we'd have enough money to have our advertising flyers printed up.*

Brady pushed back his sleeve to glance at his watch. *The man is surprisingly agile with that chunk of metal and diamonds on his wrist,* Paula thought. *If I were wearing something like that, my arm would be in a sling.* "I need to be on my way," he said, rising from the sofa. "We'd like to set up this campaign over the next month or so; can we count on your help?"

Paula also rose and walked around her desk to escort him to the door. "It certainly sounds like a promising collaboration, Cal," she said. "Let me run it by my executive committee, will you? We need to be moving in the same direction with a project of this magnitude." *Okay, so I don't exactly have an "executive committee." I'm sure I can find someone to talk it over with. Rudy, perhaps?* "I'll get back to you by the end of the week, if that's all right."

"Perfect," Brady said with a smile, revealing two perfectly matched rows of gleaming white teeth. They shook hands, and Paula was momentarily taken aback by the incredible smoothness of his palm against hers. *Maybe Lauren Banks isn't the only one who uses*

Green Pointe products creatively, she reflected. After she had closed the door behind him, she couldn't help giggling a little at the mental image of Cal Brady meticulously sponging a pale green ring of creme de menthe from around the perimeter of his elegant marble bathtub.

The next morning, Paula laid the Green Pointe spreadsheet on Ted's desk and pointed to the projected income figures. He whistled softly. "It's a big chunk of change," he said. "What do you think?"

She leaned against the credenza at one side of his desk and tucked one hand into her skirt pocket. "I think we could put together a fabulous campaign. It's a natural for the consumer market. But I—"

"My feelings exactly," he broke in, barely able to contain his excitement. "In fact, I've already got a terrific hook in mind, and I'm sure we can—"

"Just hold on a minute, Mr. Whiz Kid," Paula interrupted, holding up her hand. "Before we get into all of that, I need your input on a more . . . *personal* level."

He looked at her quizzically. "A more personal level?"

"That's right." Paula lowered herself onto the couch across from his desk. Then she gave him a small, enigmatic smile and started to explain. "The truth is, Rudy and I talked about this until very late last night, but he was uncharacteristically reserved about offering his opinion, so nothing was resolved. I thought you might be able to offer some perspective on the situation."

Ted rolled his eyes dramatically. "So, now I'm playing second fiddle to a dog, am I? Well, I guess it's about time I learned my place." He put his elbow on the desk and rested his chin on his hand. "I'm all ears—although Rudy's are admittedly bigger. See? I'm outclassed before I even start." The corners of his mouth turned down as he scowled at her, but she could see his blue eyes sparkling beneath his scrunched-up brows.

"All right, all right," she laughed. Then her expression sobered a bit as she said, "I've really got a little problem here, you know."

"No, I don't know," Ted replied. "But I have a feeling you're going to tell me."

Paula nodded and leaned back against the couch, closing her eyes briefly. "It's this thing about being a Mormon," she said a few seconds later.

Ted stared at her in genuine bewilderment. "What about it?" he asked. "Uh-oh . . . don't tell me you've changed your mind, and you don't want to be one of the 'elect' after all. Of course, I can understand how—"

"And the Green Pointe account." She leveled her gaze directly at him.

Still puzzled, Ted repeated her last words. "Being a Mormon and the Green Pointe . . . oh. *Oh.*" A flicker of comprehension darted across his face. "Now I get it. You're wondering about the ethics of running a liquor campaign when you're on the wagon yourself."

"Something like that," Paula admitted.

He shrugged. "Hey, if you want to know what I think, it doesn't bother me."

He had her attention. "How do you figure?" she asked.

"Pretty simple, really. It all boils down to a matter of choice." He leaned back in his chair. "Red or blue, up or down, left or right, bourbon or ginger ale—like they say at our friendly neighborhood Chuck-A-Rama, 'The choice is yours.' It's exactly the same when we introduce a product to the public: ultimately, the customers choose what *they* want. If they just happen to choose Green Pointe, then we've done our job; but we're not *making* them choose Green Pointe, or any other liquid refreshment, for that matter. Good advertising is just good business—and I don't see any reason to feel guilty about running a brilliant, highly successful ad campaign." His face crinkled into an engaging smile. "Especially when there are *so many* numbers in front of the decimal point on the line that says 'Projected Profits.'"

"Maybe," Paula said dubiously. She glanced at the sheet of figures on his desk. "It is a lot of money."

"You bet it is," Ted grinned. "And that's only the beginning. If we do this one right, Donroe & Associates has a future without limits."

"A future without limits. I like the sound of that," Paula smiled. It was what she had spent a decade dreaming about and working for, and now it seemed within her reach. "I'll have to think about it a little more, but I do like the sound of that."

Back in her office, she spent hours staring out her window into the gray, smog-filled sky, contemplating the decision that was hers alone to make. The Green Pointe account could make Donroe &

Associates an international advertising force to be reckoned with; she was sure of it, and the challenge set her mind spinning with possibilities. As for the moral dilemma, Ted had a point; millions of people bought hard liquor every day, and, as he had suggested, it wasn't up to her to make them all into teetotalers, but merely to give them choices. They were, after all, mature adults and could make up their own minds. Besides, the profit potential was staggering; if she worked it right, this would be her ticket to unqualified financial independence.

At one point she wondered if, given her newfound direction in life, she should be thinking in such worldly terms. *Don't be silly, Donroe,* she finally told herself, dismissing any further internal argument on the subject. *The more money you make, the more tithing you pay, right? Everybody wins.* She smiled at the thought. *I'd sure like to see the look on Bishop Peters' face when he opens* that *little gray envelope!*

Late in the afternoon, she buzzed Carmine on the intercom. "Get me Cal Brady in Chicago," she said. "We have an ad campaign to put together."

CHAPTER 8

On a tranquil Sunday morning in early March, Paula sat at the kitchen table, patiently coaxing one last drop of Millie's homemade strawberry preserves out of a small glass bottle and onto the thick slice of hot, buttered toast on her plate. "Come on," she urged, holding the jar upside down and foraging inside with the tip of a knife. "Just one . . . more . . . delectable . . . little . . . morsel." She smiled as a tiny chunk of strawberry, carried on a mini-tide of succulent red juices, slid elegantly over the lip of the bottle and plunged headlong into a dollop of butter. "There we go," she cooed, using her knife to swirl the tasty mixture delicately over the toast. She lifted it to her lips just as Millie bustled into the kitchen. "Too late," Paula said, glancing apologetically toward the empty jar. "I snarfed it all."

Millie's carefree little chuckle seemed to brighten up the room. "That's what I made it for, dear," she beamed. "I just thought I'd fix myself some cereal. Can I get you anything?"

"No, thanks," Paula replied. "I've had so much of this scrumptious stuff that I may not eat again until the Millennium—or until dinnertime, whichever comes first. Right now, I think I'll head upstairs and meditate for a couple of hours on what I'm going to wear to church." She took a final bite of toast and pushed back her chair.

"It was nice when Scotty went with us," Millie said quietly.

"I know," Paula concurred. "He actually behaved pretty well during those four sacrament meetings, too. I can't say I really expected him to keep coming to church after his 'sentence' had been served, and he certainly proved me right. But at least he's been pleasant enough since then, and I haven't heard quite so much foul language lately. Then again, that may only be wishful thinking—and it might have something to do with the fact that we hardly ever see him."

"We have to think the best," Millie said. "He does seem a little more cheerful."

"I believe you're right—on both counts," Paula smiled. "Now, if you'll excuse me, I'll just go up and get myself together—maybe even read the Sunday School lesson for a change."

She turned and walked into the entryway just as the phone rang, then stopped halfway up the stairs when she heard Millie say, "Well, my goodness! Of course she's here; just hold on a minute." She heard quick footsteps across the tile, then Millie's urgent voice. "Paula!" she sang out. "Paula, it's for you. It's *Mark Richland!*"

The words penetrated Paula's mind like a firebrand. *My son is calling!* It had been almost two months to the day since she'd spoken with him and heard the terrible news about his mother's fight for life—and about her desire to meet Paula. Was it time now? She had waited, hoped, longed to hear Mark's voice again with each passing day, but in the end had decided to keep a respectful distance and allow him to make the next contact. *I can't be barging in on their grief at a time like this,* she had thought. *He'll call again when he's ready.* And now, apparently, he was ready. Her heart beat wildly in her chest as she gripped the bannister. *What will the news be?*

"Paula?" Millie's insistent voice cut through the haze. "Paula, he's waiting. It's long-distance from Idaho, you know."

She couldn't help smiling at her friend's pragmatic observation. "I know, Millie," she responded. "I'll get it upstairs." Less than twenty seconds later, sitting cross-legged on her floral chintz comforter, she put the phone to her ear. "Mark," she said warmly. "It's wonderful to hear from you. How are . . . things?" She held her breath, anticipating the worst, hardly able to bear the thought of what she might hear.

"Hey, Paula!" Mark boomed, his voice pulsing with energy. "Fine . . . I'm fine . . . we're all fine. Except, of course, for the fact that it's twenty below outside. There are three cows in the barn, and they're *udderly* freezing." He laughed at his own joke, and Paula willingly joined him. *Like mother like son,* she thought. *He has my weird sense of humor, even if he doesn't know it. But what about his* other *mother—the one with cancer and a slim-to-none chance of survival?* She waited to hear what he'd say next.

"I guess you're wondering what's been going on up here," he finally said in a more subdued tone. "With my mother and all."

"You know I have," Paula confirmed. "You've been in my prayers every day."

"Well, they must have worked," he said. She could literally feel the warmth of his response through the phone. "Mom's better. A *lot* better."

A wave of relief swept over her. "Oh, Mark, that's wonderful—really fabulous! What do the doctors say?"

"They're calling it a miracle. She was in such bad shape before the chemo, and that made her even sicker. Then it just sort of turned around, and at her appointment last week they told her she was in remission. Can you believe it?" He sounded like a wide-eyed five-year-old on Christmas morning.

"Yes, Mark, I can believe it," Paula said earnestly. "You're a good man, a man of faith, and I would expect the Lord to honor your prayers. Obviously, your mother still has a lot of living to do."

There was a brief pause on the line, then Mark began to speak slowly and intensely, his words balancing on a plateau of raw emotion. "It's like getting another chance, you know? Like turning back the clock for a little while, seeing her like a brand-new person, watching her do little everyday things like it was the first time. Realizing all over again how much I love her. Am I making any sense here?"

Paula smiled and wiped at the tears on her cheeks. The recent memory of his tall frame leaning toward her in a dimly lit airport lobby flashed into her mind, and she felt his arms around her again. *Another chance . . . turning back the clock . . . a brand-new person . . . so much love.* "Yes, Mark," she said softly, "you're making sense. Perfect sense."

"I thought you'd understand," he said. "So, when are you coming up to the frozen northland?"

His question caught her off guard. "Me? You mean . . . to visit?"

He chuckled. "Well, at this time of year it wouldn't be to take in the scenery." After a few moments during which Paula said nothing, he went on. "Seriously, we'd love to have you come—the sooner the better."

"Gosh, I—I don't know," she stammered. "I thought now that your mom is better . . . of course I'd love to see you, but maybe your family just needs some time to get back to normal, and I don't want to—"

"Paula," his voice cut in firmly, "don't you see? *You* are a part of what will make us normal again. Ever since I told my folks about you, they've hardly talked about anything else—especially Mom, who's been wondering about you for twenty-two of her fifty-three years. And even though her improving health has cut back on the urgency of the situation, she's still as anxious to meet you as ever. She made me promise to tell you that if you don't mind meeting a bald, tired old lady with needle tracks on her arms, she'll do her best to show you a good time."

Paula laughed. "With an invitation like that, how can I refuse? Of course I'll come."

"Terrific!" Mark exclaimed. "How about next week—say, for a long weekend? That'll give you a few days to book a flight on one of our Skywest puddle-jumpers, pack up your mittens and galoshes, and put your office on auto pilot. What do you say?"

His excitement was contagious, and more than anything Paula wanted to look deep into those chocolate-brown eyes again, to bask in the wide, dimpled smile that so reminded her of his father. Why postpone the inevitable? "I'll be there," she promised. "But only if you're sure it won't be too much trouble."

"Trouble!" Mark hooted. "Trouble is when the tractor blows a tire. Trouble is when my little sister misses curfew. Trouble is when Dad tries to help in the kitchen. Trouble is *not* when Paula Donroe comes to visit. You can be sure of that."

"Well, okay," she said, her heart flooding with sudden warmth. "It's twenty below, you say?"

"Naw, I was just kidding," he said cheerfully.

"Whew," she sighed, her relief obvious.

"Actually, it's thirty below. And holding."

Paula gulped, then groaned. "No chance of an early thaw, huh?"

"Are you kidding?" Mark said exuberantly. "We're in the *middle* of an early thaw. You should have been here *last* week. With the wind chill, it hit minus fifty."

"Oh, then I'll just pack my bikini," she quipped. "To celebrate the balmy weather." She made a mental note to buy thermal underwear.

A few minutes later they hung up, and Paula leaned back against the cluster of pillows on her bed, holding the now-silent phone to her chest. Her mind could barely grasp the idea of seeing her son again—much less the reality of meeting the couple who had shared their lives, their faith, and their love with him for the past twenty-two years. Yet it was true; they actually *wanted* to know her. The thought was terrifying and exhilarating beyond anything she could imagine.

When Paula went downstairs and broke the news to Millie an hour later, the older woman was ecstatic. "You just leave everything to me," she declared, her eyes gleaming. "I'll call the airlines tomorrow, then I'll go shopping. We'll have you ticketed, packed, winterized, and ready to go before you can shake a leg."

"Or get cold feet," Paula added wryly.

"That too," Millie said. She smiled down at Paula, who had curled herself up in the huge overstuffed chair in her den, and was looking rather small and fragile. "You're not having second thoughts, are you, dear?" she asked.

"Oh, no," Paula replied quickly. "Well, maybe one or two. It's just such an *unusual* situation, you know? I'm not quite sure how it'll all turn out."

"Don't you think another thing about it," Millie said, reaching out to squeeze Paula's hand. "They'll love you."

"How can you be so sure?" Paula asked, her eyes wide with apprehension.

"Because *I* love you," Millie said warmly. "And I have great taste."

At that moment, Paula felt a familiar pressure and glanced down to see Rudy's shaggy head coming to rest sanguinely against her knee. He squeezed his eyes shut and moaned contentedly when she rubbed the soft, furry space between his brows.

"See?" Millie observed. "Here's someone else who loves you, and he's an impeccable judge of character. Rudy sees right through to the heart, don't you, boy?" She reached over and patted the broad golden back, and his long tail made a slow, feathery arc in the still air. "No doubt about it," Millie concluded. "Those folks in Idaho have got themselves a real treat coming."

Rudy woofed in agreement, and Paula rewarded him with a leisurely stroll around the neighborhood before church. "Someday," she said to him as they sat for a moment under a spreading willow tree in the park, "I must introduce you to Jacques and Heidi. They're small, but they've got heart, and I think you'd like them." She grinned. "They're Mormons, you know."

❤ ❤ ❤

Thursday morning, Paula slumped down in her orange plastic chair and glanced nervously at the airport clock. *Same day of the week,* she thought. *Same time. Same gate. Same stylish furniture. Same destination: Salt Lake City, then Idaho Falls, Idaho. Last time I was saying good-bye to my son. This time I'm getting ready to say hello to his mother.* She swallowed the knot of anxiety in her throat and focused on the *Ensign* magazine Millie had given her as she pulled her big Buick up in front of the airport doors. "Have a wonderful time, dear," she'd said, leaning across the seat to give Paula a motherly hug. Then she was gone, and Paula had her thoughts to herself.

She had barely read the *Ensign*'s table of contents six times when her flight was called. The big Delta jet was crowded, and a rather round, gregarious gentleman occupied the seat next to her, so the ninety-minute shuttle passed quickly in idle conversation. He courteously inquired as to her destination and the purpose of her trip. *What should I tell him?* she wondered. *That I'm going to Idaho to meet my son's mother?* She smiled at a mental image of the little man scratching his bald head, asking her to repeat what she'd just said, then decided to play it safe. "Visiting friends in Idaho for a long weekend," she explained. *No use saying anything more. He might be a reporter—or worse, the friend of a friend who knows someone who loves a good story. I could turn up as a colorful character in someone's trashy novel.*

Their landing in Salt Lake City was obscured by a heavy snowfall. Paula spent her hour-long layover standing transfixed at one of the airport's wide, panoramic windows. The large, graceful flakes seemed to tumble in slow motion from the gray sky, clinging here and there to the glass or joining their fellows in a carefree meander to the asphalt below. *Magnificent,* she thought. She had seen snow like this as a young girl on her parents' country estate in Connecticut, had twirled and danced winsome circles in it, leaning far forward to capture as many of the cool, bright bursts on her tongue as she could. Years later, after her divorce, she and the boys had taken a few weekend snow trips into the mountains east of Los Angeles, where she would sit on the deck of a rustic ski lodge, sipping enormous cups of steaming gourmet coffee to stay warm, and watch them careen downhill on skis or toboggans. *Those were good times*, she remembered, staring up into the whirling snow. *We were younger then, more in tune with ourselves, just trying to make each other happy.* She smiled at the sad, sweet memories.

"Skywest flight 2165, with service to Idaho Falls, is now boarding." The brisk announcement startled Paula from her reverie, and she hurried to the gate. She was ushered down a long, frigid corridor and out into the storm, where she and eighteen or so other passengers made a dash for the small turbo-prop plane perched about fifty yards downwind. By the time she had stomped the snow off her suede loafers, climbed a steep flight of boxy stairs into the body of the plane, and deposited herself in a narrow window seat, she was chilled through and thoroughly annoyed. *Just relax,* she told herself. *In an hour and fifteen minutes, you'll be safely on the ground in Idaho Falls. More or less.*

Just then Paula felt an icy trickle on her forehead. Reaching up to wipe away the dampness, she groaned as she realized that the cabin's warmer temperature was beginning to melt the thin coating of snow on her hair, brows, and lashes. When the trickling increased, she rummaged in her purse to find a tissue, then blotted her hair and wiped frantically at her forehead and temples to preserve her makeup. *Terrific*, she mused as her mascara made dark trails down her cheeks. *I'm going to meet Mark's family looking like a water-logged street urchin.* She glanced out the small, cube-like window to her right, seeing nothing but huge snowflakes pelting the glass. *That is, if I ever make it to Idaho Falls.* She breathed a small, silent prayer for a safe journey, closing with *And please . . . please don't let it be anyone on this plane's time to go. I'd really prefer not to be part of a group exit.*

A few minutes later, Paula took in a sharp breath as the tiny plane seemed to hop rather than lift off the runway. She glanced anxiously out the window; there was still nothing to see but swirling flakes, so she lowered the shade, closed her eyes, and eased back against the seat. Before long, the steady drone from the engines began to have a hypnotic effect, and she drifted into an uneasy, dreamless sleep.

The flight attendant's voice jolted her back to consciousness. "Ladies and gentlemen, we'll be starting our descent into Idaho Falls in a few minutes. Please fasten your seat belts." Paula's eyes opened a crack. *So far so good*, she reasoned, lifting a hand to smooth her hair. It was still damp and hung limply against her cheeks. She tossed her head irritably, then caught herself. *Oh, don't be such a ninny. You may look like a drowned muskrat, but a good blow-dry will take care of that. Mark's mother doesn't even* have *any hair, for goodness' sake.*

She flicked up the window shade and peered down at Idaho. "Oh, my!" she gasped aloud as her eyes widened in astonishment. She pressed one hand tightly against her chest.

"Is everything all right, miss?" a deep voice called from across the aisle. "You look upset or something."

Paula turned to see a thin, middle-aged man dressed in a dark business suit staring at her. *He must be tall,* she surmised at first glance. *He's folded like a paper clip into that little seat.* She quickly collected herself and smiled disarmingly in his direction. "I'm fine," she said cheerfully. "It just that I . . . well, I'm coming from California, and everything here is so . . . so *white.*"

"Not to mention *cold,*" the man grinned. "You get used to it. Glad you're okay." He turned back to reading his in-flight magazine.

Moving close to the window again, Paula stared in amazement at the landscape below. It was true; by and large, everything she saw was intensely, uncompromisingly white—vast, snow-covered fields stretching for miles in every direction, their flatness interrupted only by an occasional white-roofed farmhouse or barn. But the extraordinary thing, she decided, was not the snow itself; rather, it was the visual fire ignited by the early-afternoon sun as its beams shot through the naked blue sky and exploded against row upon row of pristine drifts.

The effect was so breathtaking that Paula felt moisture spring to her eyes. *Even "spectacular" would be too tame a description for this scenery,* she mused, her gaze riveted to the shimmering countryside whizzing beneath her. *If I had to describe my idea of heaven right here and now, this would be it.* She smiled playfully. *Well, I'd add a few space heaters. And maybe a hot tub.*

As the plane began its descent and the perimeter of Idaho Falls came into view, Paula tore her gaze from the window and began to contemplate the next hour of her life. She was rushing headlong into the massive, uncharted territory of a place she'd never seen, people she didn't know, emotions she couldn't anticipate. After this weekend, nothing would ever be quite the same again; she could feel it up and down the length of her slim, forty-year-old bones. But what did it mean? *You'll find out soon enough,* she reminded herself. *Until then, go slow, be polite, compliment the cook*—she felt the wheels beneath her bump down crazily on the runway—*and book a flight home on one of the big planes.*

As the unwieldy vehicle lurched to a stop, Paula collected her things from under the seat in front of her. She sat quietly nursing the knot of apprehension in her stomach while the other passengers filed by, then stepped reluctantly into the aisle and moved to the front of the plane. When a sudden blast of sub-zero wind whipped through the open door, she tucked her chin into the collar of her brown suede jacket and hurried down the narrow steps. By the time she had sprinted the few dozen yards to a narrow airport entrance door, her lips were numb and she could barely feel her ungloved fingers clutching the straps of her bulky overnight bag. *So much for my idea of Idaho heaven,* she thought wryly as she pushed through the door. *Woodland Hills may not be paradise, but it's definitely more hospitable than*—

The words evaporated in Paula's brain as she raised her head and saw Mark Richland's lanky profile hovering near the edge of the crowd. She stopped in her tracks, and at that same moment his deep, chocolate-brown eyes fixed on hers. He spread his arms wide and she rushed into them, oblivious to anything but the feel of him crushing her to his chest, lifting her off the floor, whispering words of welcome and delight into her ear.

"Whew!" she laughed when he set her down and she finally found her voice. "I could use a hug like that at least once a day."

"You've got it," he vowed, smiling down at her. "As long as you're a guest in the Richland home, hugs are mandatory."

She reached up to pat her straggly hair. "Even when I look like this? I got snowed on in Salt Lake, and—"

"You're beautiful," he interjected, then his face erupted into that dimpled grin she remembered so well. "Even if you're old enough to be . . . my mother." His eyes danced as he said the word.

"Well," she replied, "I may be over the hill, but I still know a good-looking dude when I see one." Almost shyly, she touched her fingers to his cheek. His dark hair was a bit longer than she remembered; a few relaxed curls brushed the collar of his down jacket. He looked older, more settled somehow. More at ease in his own skin.

Still grinning, Mark reached down to retrieve her carry-on bag. "Shall we?" He nodded toward the baggage claim area, and they walked arm in arm toward one of the shiny circular conveyor belts where miscellaneous pieces of luggage were beginning to appear.

It was a forty-minute drive on snow-packed roads to the far corner of Roberts and the Richland farm. Paula settled back into the soft, electronically heated leather passenger seat of their forest-green Suburban and gazed out a side window at the glittering frozen landscape. "I was totally dazzled when I saw all of this white stuff from the plane," she admitted.

"Yeah," Mark agreed, "there's something about sunlight on snowdrifts that takes your breath away. I missed that while I was in California. What I *didn't* miss was getting up at four A.M. to feed a bunch of cranky chickens. Even my most obnoxious missionary companion was no match for those little pecking fools."

Paula laughed, enjoying their easy conversation. After a while, they lapsed into a comfortable silence. "You know," she said several minutes later, "I'm really looking forward to meeting your family. But on the other hand, I'm . . . well, I guess I'm a little nervous."

"Not to worry," he said, reaching over to pat her knee in a fatherly way. "I can tell you right now that you're not the only one. Our whole household has been a little crazed since Sunday, when I told everyone you were coming."

Paula glanced over at his strong profile. "Really?" she asked incredulously.

"Really." His mouth curved into an engaging smirk. "Personally, I think they're jealous. After all, it's not every day a member of the family brings his past home to meet his present and share a part of his future. The kids think it's *so cool.*" Their eyes met briefly as he turned his head toward her. "And so do I," he said.

Paula had to ask. "And what about your parents?"

"Oh, you'll see," he answered mysteriously, shifting into four-wheel drive as they turned off the main road. "You'll see."

The narrow ribbon of ice-encrusted road they were traveling seemed to sideslip under them as they approached the crest of a small hill. Mark didn't seem concerned, but Paula's rigid grip on the door handle told another story. *You've come this far, courtesy of Skywest's White-knuckle Express,* she reminded herself. *This is no time for a panic attack.* She took in a long, deep breath and willed herself to relax.

Then, suddenly, they were at the top. Mark pressed his foot to the brake and turned toward her. "Welcome to the Richland spread, Sister Donroe," he said with a flourish.

Paula gasped audibly at the sight before her. "This . . . this is where you live?" she questioned.

"Last time I checked the mailbox," Mark answered lightly. "Now, come on . . . it's time you met the family."

As the Suburban started its gradual descent down the slick road, Paula stared wide-eyed at a cluster of buildings in the distance. The imposing main house, facing the road and standing apart from three smaller structures, was situated on a gentle rise in front of a long, freshly plowed circular driveway. It vaulted at least three stories into the blue-gray winter sky, and a gleaming white wood exterior gave it the appearance of a dignified country estate. *But friendlier,* Paula thought, her gaze taking in the deep-green shutters framing several windows on each floor. *Like an upscale bed-and-breakfast.* She smiled, recalling the pleasant week she'd spent in Connecticut at the Westbury Inn the previous October as a guest speaker at Yale University.

Off to one side of the house's wide, enclosed porch was a stand of several massive evergreens, their regal branches now weighted almost to breaking with piled-up, drifted snow. A sweeping path to the front entrance was lined by what Paula supposed to be dozens of small bushes or shrubs, although they were completely obscured by the shimmering white stuff. *Like little square sentinels,* she thought.

Guarding the way home. She quickly surveyed the broad expanse of snow-covered fields in every direction. *Not that anything would need guarding in a remote place like this.*

"Wow," Paula breathed as they pulled into the drive. "This is really impressive." Now that they were closer, she could even see the intricate wood carvings on the house's massive double front doors.

"It's been a good life," Mark said matter-of-factly. "The farm has done well most years, and we've been comfortable." He made a sweeping gesture with one arm. "This place has a certain charm during the winter, but it really comes alive in the spring. It's so fresh and green."

"I can imagine," Paula said, though she really couldn't. *Maybe someday I'll get to see it when it's green.*

"You'll have to come to visit when it's that way," he said. "Green, I mean."

"The thought had occurred to me," she smiled.

The Suburban crunched to a stop in front of the house. "Ready?" Mark asked.

Paula gulped. "As I'll ever be," she said, rubbing her hands nervously against the soft, chocolate-brown wool of her slacks.

"Good." He glanced down at her suede loafers. "You'll need to hold on to me; the walk will be a little bit slippery without boots. I'll get the luggage later." She nodded, and he pushed open his door. In a few seconds he was helping her out of the vehicle, and she gripped his arm tightly—not altogether for safety reasons—as they made their way up the path. Her breath hung in the glacial air like a thin stream of quicksilver, and she was chilled through by the time they had climbed the four broad steps to the porch.

Mark paused outside the door to give her shoulders a squeeze, and at the same moment she curled an arm around his lean waist. Without a word, he reached out and turned the knob noiselessly, then pushed. The door's hinges creaked amiably as it swung inward. "Mom? Dad? We're home," he called out. "They'll be in the living room," he whispered as they stepped inside. He grasped Paula's elbow and steered her across the entry and down a short, carpeted hallway to the right.

Almost without warning, the narrow space opened into an expansive, high-ceilinged room that seemed to be flooded with light from every direction. It was an unusual room, and Paula's first inclination was to take it all in with her curious, sweeping gaze. But instead, a movement to her far right wrested her attention, and from the corner of her eye she saw a tall man rise from a sofa in one corner of the room. Behind him, still seated, was a dark-eyed woman wearing a silk turban-like scarf on her head. After a few seconds, the man extended a massive hand toward the woman. Reaching to grasp it tightly, she gracefully pulled herself up to stand beside him.

Paula hesitated, wanting, needing a few more moments to observe this striking pair and approach them on her own terms. But Mark was already pressing his hand to her back, urging her gently across the broad swath of off-white carpet to within a few feet of the solemn-faced couple. Time and breath hung expectantly in the still, warm air, and no one moved or spoke.

Finally, Mark broke into a wide, generous smile. "Well, here we are," he beamed. "Paula, I'm very pleased to introduce you to my mother,—"

"Oh, my goodness," the dark-eyed woman said in a low, melodious voice, as if suddenly plumbing the depths of a discovery beyond mortal comprehension. "You've come. You've really come." Her eyes brimmed and overflowed as she pressed a hand to her trembling lips. In an instant she had closed the distance between them, and was wrapping her slender arms around Paula. Returning the embrace in a warm rush of emotion, Paula felt the thin flesh and sharp bones in her back through the silky fabric of her blouse. *Like a fragile china doll,* she thought, easing back from the hug for fear of hurting her. The woman rested her long, delicate fingers lightly on Paula's arm and smiled from the depths of her luminous brown eyes. "Welcome to our home," she said.

"Ahem." Mark cleared his throat softly, his eyes dancing with anticipation. "Now, as I was saying . . . Paula, I'd like you to meet my mother, Jakarta Richland." The woman's smile broadened. "And Mother, I'd like you to meet my mother, Paula Donroe." He paused, then sang out, "Now I ask you, how can one guy get so lucky?" Both women laughed shyly.

"It must be in the genes," a husky voice said nearby. "Two beautiful women, two beautiful mothers." Paula turned to the large man standing beside them. *This isn't a man,* she thought at first glance. *This is a mountain.*

"And this, of course," Mark said, interrupting her thoughts, "is my dad. Paula, meet Samuel Jacob Richland."

Even as she extended her hand in greeting, Paula found it necessary to lean back and look up—way, way up—to find the face, neck, shoulders, and arms that were connected to the two huge hands enfolding hers. And the eyes . . . penetrating gray-green eyes that shimmered with emotion. There was a poignant feeling and sadness in those eyes, and as he smiled down at her she wondered if life had somehow dealt him a blow from which he had not yet recovered. "It's awfully good to meet you," he said, and she knew he meant it.

"Thank you so much," Paula said, allowing the joy of the moment to wash over her. "It's wonderful to be here. Just wonderful."

CHAPTER 9

"Jakarta," Paula repeated, turning to Mark's mother. "What a lovely name. I've only heard it before in connection with—" She paused, trying to recall a long-forgotten geography lesson.

"Indonesia," the woman smiled. "My grandparents were Indos, born and raised on the Malay Archipelago. Mams—my mother—named me after the city where she was born. I've never seen it; she married an American businessman and moved to the States before I was born. But she often told me long, romantic stories about what an exotic, beautiful place it was."

Paula looked more closely at Jakarta and could see the rich Indonesian heritage in her elegantly defined facial features—deep, long-lashed eyes the color of liquid chocolate, and full, expressive lips. Her skin was a pale vanilla color, almost translucent; Paula thought its delicate appearance might have something to do with her recent illness. She was taller than Paula by two or three inches, but probably weighed less, although her figure was definitely more voluptuous. *If I look like that in my fifties*, Paula thought, *I'll be deliriously happy. Heck, if I looked like that* now *I'd be delirious.*

Samuel moved to his wife's side and gently put his arm around her shoulders. The top of her turbaned head barely came to his shoulder as she nestled comfortably against him. Images of the legendary Paul Bunyan came to mind as Paula observed the man's large, muscular frame and his ruddy, slightly weathered complexion. His thick hair was a deep chestnut color, sun-bleached on top and graying at the temples. Paula noticed again the melancholy cast of his gray-green eyes; but this time she noticed the deep laugh lines, too.

They've had a good life, she thought. *They fit together.*

"Well, why don't you all take a load off?" Mark suggested. "I'll go get the luggage and take it up to Paula's room."

"Thank you, dear," Jakarta said, then turned to Paula. "Please, sit down." She motioned toward a pair of deep-green leather chairs across from a burgundy velvet sofa in one corner of the room. Paula lowered herself into one of the chairs while Mark's parents settled close together on the sofa.

For the first time since their meeting, Paula tore her gaze from this intriguing couple and focused on her surroundings. "This is absolutely beautiful," she murmured, and Jakarta broke into a satisfied smile.

The living room was not large, but its unique design used light and shadow, color and texture to create an area that felt spacious and intimate at the same time. A few pieces of tasteful furniture, including an ebony baby grand piano, were pleasantly arranged here and there on the thick ivory carpet. But it was the room itself that took Paula by surprise. Its shape was a perfect oval, the graceful curve of its walls broken only by the six-foot-wide arch through which she and Mark had entered. A vibrant mauve wallpaper accented by tiny, crisp white flowers circled the lower half of the room. Above it was a series of eight-foot-high beveled vertical window panes spanning the entire east wall, capturing every available particle of sunlight and catapulting it into the room. Across from the windows, behind an antique brass railing, the room opened onto the house's small second-story atrium, alive with exotic blooming foliage of every description. A row of glistening vine-like plants draped their virescent leaves gracefully beneath the railing. "Whoa," Paula breathed, gazing upward. "This is like . . . paradise."

"It was Mom's idea," Mark said, settling into the chair beside Paula. "I think it was her way of bringing a little class to your run-of-the-mill Idaho potato farm." He winked at his mother, who smiled and rested her hand on Samuel's knee.

"Really, Jakarta," Paula said, "I'd say this represents more than just a *little* class. And if I ever get around to building my dream house, I'd certainly like to borrow your architect."

The woman across from her laughed, and the sound reminded Paula of the friendly, mellow tones of her pewter wind chimes at home. "Please, call me Karti. We're just Sam and Karti. And I'll take that as a compliment—although I'm afraid the 'architect' and I come as a package." She glanced at her husband, whose ruddy complexion deepened a shade or two. "We designed our home together."

"In between having babies and planting spuds," Mark added.

"Well, 'just Sam and Karti,' I'd love to see the rest of it," Paula said.

The distant slam of a door prompted Sam to look at his watch. "That'll be the girls," he explained. "Andrea picks Ruthie up after school."

The foursome sat in expectant silence, waiting for the two youngest members of the family to make an appearance. They could hear light chatter coming from the direction of the kitchen, accompanied by the sound of four snow boots thudding to the floor. Paula's fingers drummed nervously against the arm of her chair. Mark leaned toward her. "They're great kids," he whispered. "You'll love them." She smiled at him and chided herself for being anxious.

Within moments, the girls had cleared one side of the arched entrance to the living room. They hesitated for a second or two, then both padded in stockinged feet across the thick carpet to their mother's side. The taller girl, whose long, thick hair was exactly the chestnut color of her father's, bent over and pressed a quick kiss to Karti's cheek, then straightened her long, willowy frame and stood behind the couch, her cool gaze shifting toward Paula. Her younger sister, clearly delighted to see her parents again after their day's separation, wrapped each of them in an eager hug, then squeezed between them on the sofa. Her shoulder-length hair was very dark with subtle auburn highlights, and her enormous round eyes were the blackest Paula had ever seen. They glittered now with curiosity as the youngster stared openly at their visitor.

"My dears," Karti said genially, "I'd like you to meet a very special new friend—the one we told you was coming to visit." Gesturing toward Paula with a graceful sweep of her hand, she continued. "This is Sister Donroe, who lives in California. Your brother Mark taught her the gospel while he was on his mission, and she joined the Church a few months ago."

"I *know* that, Mommy," the smaller girl whispered loudly. "You told us all about it, remember?" She folded her arms and huffed impatiently, but Paula could see the excitement in her dark eyes. The older girl continued to regard Paula coolly, a distant expression shading her deep-green eyes.

Karti continued with the introductions. "Paula, these are the youngest members of the Richland clan." She reached back and squeezed the tall girl's arm. "This is Andrea, who's sixteen. She's a straight-A student and plays the flute and piano gloriously. She's also the newest driver in our family—just got her license last month. We're very proud of her." The girl shifted from one foot to the other and stared at the floor.

"It's so nice to meet you, Andrea," Paula said, flashing her a warm smile. "I have a son, Scott, who's sixteen, too. He's taking driver's training in school, and he's due to get his license quite soon. That's a big accomplishment."

"Yeah," Andrea mumbled, twining a strand of thick hair around her index finger.

Must be a teenage thing—speaking in words of one syllable or less, Paula thought. *She and Scotty would make a terrific team.*

And this," Karti said, affectionately rubbing her hand up and down the younger girl's arm, "is our baby, Ruthie."

"Mom!" the youngster protested. "I'm not a baby, and I'm grown-up enough to use my *real* name." She pursed her lips and tossed her head indignantly, all the while keeping her gaze riveted on Paula.

"Oh, dear, I'm *so sorry,"* Karti said quickly, her eyes twinkling with amusement. "Excuse me, Paula . . . may I introduce Miss Ruth Ann Richland, age ten, dancer and gymnast extraordinaire." The child's eyes glowed at her mother's words of praise, and the earlier slight was forgotten.

"A pleasure to meet you," Paula said rather formally, then her face broke into a wide grin. "I used to dance all the time when I was your age. There was a huge lawn in back of my father's house, and I'd sneak outside early in the morning and make up my own dances."

"Really? Cool." The girl moved daintily from the couch and stood close to Paula's chair. Crossing one foot over the other and stuffing her small hands into the pockets of her corduroy trousers, she spent a full minute studying Paula's features from every conceivable angle. Finally, she smiled shyly. "You're very pretty," she said.

Paula felt a slight blush creep into her cheeks. "Why, thank you, Ruth Ann," she said. *I could learn to like this kid,* she told herself. *I could like her a lot.* "You're very pretty, too."

"Then I guess we have a lot in common," Ruth Ann said matter-of-factly. "So you can call me Ruthie."

"Deal—Ruthie," Paula replied. She was beginning to relax, and found herself wondering when she would meet the other two children. They were boys, if she remembered correctly.

She felt the light touch of a small hand on her knee, and she met Ruthie's forthright, innocent gaze. "My mommy told me your little boy got shot, and he's living with Heavenly Father now," she said.

Paula heard Karti's sharp intake of breath. "Please, Ruthie," she insisted, "this is not the time or place to—"

"It's all right . . . really it is," Paula interjected, surprised at the steady sound of her own voice. This child's simple observation seemed so natural, so uncomplicated by the baggage of grief or regret, that it was easy to respond to. "Yes, Ruthie," she said quietly. "His name was TJ, and he was twelve years old." Saying the words, she felt a flutter of longing rise in her chest.

"Are you sad?" Ruthie asked.

Paula inhaled deeply and let out a long breath. "I miss him very much, and yes, I'm sad," she answered honestly.

"Well, don't be," Ruthie declared with a firm pat to her new friend's shoulder. "Heavenly Father is taking good care of him."

Paula couldn't help smiling at this open-hearted wisp of a girl who dispensed such good advice. "I'm sure He is, Ruthie," she agreed. And she believed it.

"Okay, my little chickadees," Sam broke in with a mildly authoritative tone, "we have the next few days to get acquainted with Sister Donroe, and—"

"Please, just Paula," she said, circling Ruthie's waist with one arm. The girl beamed.

"Yes . . . Paula," he repeated. "But right now, you girls have chores and homework to do before supper. So let's get going, shall we?"

Andrea took her cue and left the room immediately. But Ruthie tossed her head, plunked her hands on her hips, and rolled her eyes. Then, leaning close to Paula's ear, she whispered, "He's always like this when we have company—all hotsy-totsy 'hurry and get your work done' mister man, so they think he's the boss. But y'know what? He's really just a big ol' *marshmallow.*"

"Uh-huh," Paula chuckled. "Then who's the real boss?"

Ruthie straightened up to her full height and threw her shoulders back importantly. "My mom and I trade off," she declared.

While Paula struggled to keep a straight face, Sam jumped up from the couch and scooped Ruthie into his long arms. "Okay, okay," he growled, brushing his stubbly chin against her soft neck until she giggled uncontrollably. "Enough of this conspiring against your old daddy. There are a couple of hungry dawgs out back that need feedin', or they might just mistake a Ruthie arm or leg for their dinner. An' don't you have a multiplication table or two to memorize before Friday? Last time I checked, that was tomorrow."

Ruthie gave him a quick peck on the cheek. "Okay, Daddy-O, you win." She jumped lithely from his arms to the floor, then crooked her neck to look up at him with a determined expression. "But I get to sit by Sister Paula at supper."

"I think that could be arranged," he replied, bending down to give her a gentle swat on the seat of the pants. "Now off to your chores, young lady." She aimed a saucy smile in Paula's direction, then scampered from the room.

"I'll help," Mark said protectively. "She may need some help getting through that deep snow out back." In two or three long strides, he had disappeared through the arch.

Sam reclaimed his place next to Karti. He leaned back on the sofa and smiled wryly. "That little one sure has a mind of her own."

"So I see," Paula agreed. *That was me thirty years ago,* she thought privately. "She's adorable."

Karti nodded and smiled—a bit wistfully, Paula thought. "Ruthie was our unexpected blessing," she explained. "I was forty-three when she was born, six years after we had Andrea. We weren't really planning on a fifth child. But then"—she laughed in her light, melodious way—"we weren't really planning on our second, third, or fourth, either." Her glistening, doe-like eyes focused intently on Paula. "Our family has been a miracle . . . and it all started with you."

For a moment Paula felt slightly confused, and her mind didn't compute a meaning in Karti's words. Then, as understanding dawned, she blushed slightly. "Oh . . . you mean Mark."

"No," Karti said firmly, "I mean *you*. If you hadn't made that incredibly unselfish decision twenty-two years ago, our lives might have taken a very different direction. As it turned out, having Mark in our home made it just that—a real home. Before then, we'd been happy; no question about that." She leaned comfortably against Sam's shoulder, and Paula was reminded of two pieces of a jigsaw puzzle fitting perfectly together. "But a child . . . this child added a dimension to our lives that was beyond expression. After ten years of wishing, hoping, praying for a family, there were simply no words to describe the joy . . ." Her voice broke, and she wiped at her moist cheeks.

"I'll never forget the first moment we saw him—so tiny, so perfect," Sam said, picking up where his wife had left off. "When we learned he'd been born, we caught the next flight to Connecticut. He was less than two days old when the social worker brought him to us in a small room off the maternity wing in the Branham County Hospital."

Now it was Paula's turn to dab at her eyes as the memories surfaced. "That would have been about five minutes after I kissed him good-bye," she said softly. Closing her eyes, she could feel again the softness of his newborn skin against her cheek.

"Oh, my," Karti murmured, pressing a slender hand to her lips. "We never knew you were . . . still there." Paula nodded, unable to speak. This new revelation seemed to bind them to one another in ways that could not be defined . . . at least for the present.

After a brief, contemplative silence, Paula cleared her throat and smiled brightly through her tears. "Well," she said, "you've done a great job with him. Even before I knew we were, uh, *connected*, I envied the parents of such a remarkable young man. If TJ had lived, they would have loved each other like . . . well, like the brothers they were. But then . . ." Her voice trailed off, and a faraway look veiled her eyes as a familiar pain pressed against her heart.

"You were saying?" Sam urged gently after a few seconds.

"Sorry. I was just thinking . . . if TJ had lived, I might never have discovered who Mark really was. I was too pig-headed to listen to the gospel when I first heard it, and it took losing my son to help me see what really mattered in life. Then Mark was able to teach me . . . and the rest, as they say, is—"

"History," Sam and Karti said in unison. "Meant to be," Karti stated simply.

"Yes," Paula echoed, realizing it was true. "Meant to be."

"And speaking of history," Karti smiled, "we've got pictures, home movies, scrapbooks, old baby blankets—everything you've always wanted to know about your son's life. What's more, we've got the whole weekend to sort it all out." She glanced at her watch. "But right now, you'd probably like to get settled and freshen up a bit, and I need to get supper started. Let me show you your room." She rose carefully from the sofa and shook her head when Sam reached for her elbow. "I'm fine," she whispered, brushing the side of his face lightly with her hand. As the two women moved toward the archway, Paula glanced back to see Sam hunched forward on the sofa, gazing at his wife with an expression that could only be described as an exquisite balance between passion and pain. *I have never seen such love in a man's eyes,* she thought. *Or such longing for . . . for what?* She couldn't tell; but she knew it was a look worth spending one's life for. No doubt about it.

As they made their way slowly up a long, spiraling staircase to the second floor, Karti leaned heavily against the oak railing. She seemed out of breath when they reached the landing, which opened into the plant-filled atrium overlooking the living room. "Are you all right?" Paula asked, hesitantly touching her arm. She could feel skin against bone through the silky fabric of Karti's long, caftan-like blouse.

Karti's reply was preceded by an utterly charming smile that seemed to bubble up from her generous lips into those extraordinary brown eyes. "Oh, yes," she said cheerfully. "I'm just a little tired, that's all. I suppose I haven't quite bounced back from the chemotherapy yet. They say it takes a while." She pointed toward a short, carpeted hallway to one side of the circular landing. "The guest room is this way." Her tone dismissed any further discussion, and Paula followed her docilely toward a golden oak door at the end of the hall.

"This is lovely," Paula said as they entered a cozy room with peach-colored wallpaper and a small attached bath. On a wall above the bed hung a rich oil painting of a young girl sniffing an armful of multi-hued flowers; facing it was a large window framing a breath-taking chain of snow-covered mountains. "I could look at this view all day," Paula murmured.

"Not a chance," Karti laughed. "We've only got you for the weekend, and we intend to see just as much of you as we possibly can." Her eyes danced with anticipation. "For purely selfish reasons, I'd like to get to know the amazing woman who has made such a difference in our lives—even if from a distance." She gave Paula another buoyant smile. "Now, take your time getting settled; have a little rest if you'd like. Then I'd love some company in the kitchen, if you're feeling domestic."

"I'm afraid I'm a whole lot better at making deals than I am at making meals," Paula admitted. "Although I do have great respect and endless appreciation for the culinary arts. My housekeeper, Millie, is an expert in that area; she's taught me well, at least in the appreciation part. Frankly, she won't let me near the kitchen—last time she did, I made biscuits that could double for hockey pucks. But she can put on a food fest that leaves you smiling for days."

"Ah, yes . . . Millie," Karti nodded. "I seem to recall Mark's blow-by-blow, palate-tingling description of the 'totally awesome' spread she laid out last Thanksgiving . . . not long after you were baptized, wasn't it?"

"Uh-huh," Paula said. "It was my first holiday on the wagon, so to speak. I spent the morning cleaning out my liquor cabinet. My dog, Rudy, complained loudly; he's a champagne lover, you know. But once I explained to him the finer points of the Word of Wisdom, he was okay with it. He's actually turned out to be a pretty good Mormon—for a golden retriever."

"Hmm . . . you ought to have Rudy talk to our two Bernese mountain dogs," Karti suggested. "Bruno and Alfie have never quite caught the vision of home teaching." They couldn't help giggling like schoolgirls.

"This is nice," Karti said when she could catch her breath. "I was hoping we could be . . . friends."

"Me too," Paula agreed. "Friends." Later, after Karti left to get the meal underway, she deposited herself in a large overstuffed chair by the bed and stared out the window, quietly contemplating the glacial majesty of the Grand Tetons. *Friends,* she thought. *I like the sound of that.*

"Mom makes a killer meat loaf," Mark whispered to Paula as they sat at the dining-room table. "It's—how can I say this?—gourmet, without being . . . trendy," he added with a little chuckle. And he was right. Served up on a lustrous pewter tray, it was nestled among tiny new potatoes and pearl onions, sprigs of crisp parsley, and small clusters of deep-red cherry tomatoes. The loaf itself was topped with sliced mushrooms and a rich, dark gravy. Paula's mouth watered at the sight and aroma of it, and her taste buds were not disappointed when the tender meat gently broke into a thousand delicate bursts of flavor on her tongue.

"Mmm, this is fabulous," she said between bites. Karti smiled contentedly.

Suddenly, Paula was aware of a poking sensation in her side. Turning to her right, she saw a ten-year-old elbow nudging her in the ribs. She set her fork down and focused her attention on Ruthie, who was staring up at her expectantly. "Yes?" she said, intrigued by the girl's impish grin.

"My mom's an awesome cook, right?" Ruthie asked. When Paula nodded eagerly, she continued. "Well, if you think this is good, just wait till *tomorrow* night." Seeing a question form in Paula's eyes, she hurried to explain. "That's *my* night to cook." She leaned back in her chair and folded her arms triumphantly, seemingly oblivious to the good-natured groans rippling around the table. "We're having my favorite."

"Which is . . . ?" Paula glanced up just in time to see Andrea's eyes roll unbelievably far back into her head.

"No fair asking," Ruthie said resolutely. "It's a secret—but you're gonna love it."

"I see," Paula replied. "Well, in that case, I can hardly wait."

"Me either. And if I were you, I wouldn't each lunch," the child advised. "That way, you'll have room for everything."

Paula nodded obediently. "Sounds like a plan," she said. Ruthie seemed satisfied and returned to her meal.

Lifting her water glass to her lips, Paula took a moment to glance around the table as members of the family resumed a casual conversation based on the day's events. Sam sat at one end of the long oval table, Karti at the other. Paula thought she looked exhausted; she smiled often and laughed easily, but the dusky circles beneath her eyes told another story. Sam was cheerful enough and bantered lightly with the family, but his gaze rarely left his wife's face. Mark's younger brothers, Alex and Jake, both tall and sandy-haired, had rushed in just as the meal began; their drive home from classes at Ricks College had been slowed by treacherous road conditions. Then there was Andrea, who only picked at her food and occasionally cast a piercing stare in Paula's direction. The expression in her deep-green eyes remained cool and cautious.

At the meal's end, Sam asked Andrea and Ruthie to clear away the dishes. "Your mother's tired," he said. "She needs a good night's rest." Everyone nodded, and the girls had already started collecting plates when Sam's deep voice stopped them. "Let's have prayer, then I'll get this beautiful lady tucked in while you finish up." He winked at Karti, who smiled gratefully.

"C'mon," Ruthie said, tugging on Paula's sleeve. They followed the rest of the family to the living room, where they knelt in a small circle. At Sam's request, Alex offered a simple prayer of thanks for blessings enjoyed, among them Paula's presence in their midst. This was followed by a heartfelt supplication for Karti's continuing improvement, as well as a plea for peace and protection through the night. In her heart, Paula felt certain that this humble prayer, so pure and direct, would be heard and answered.

The "amen" was said, and as the family rose, Karti moved to Paula's side. "I'm so sorry to leave you like this," she said. "It's just that this has been a very busy day, and I do still get so tired . . ."

Paula held up a hand, then laid it on Karti's arm. "Not a problem," she insisted. "The important thing is that you take care of yourself. I'll be just fine; the family and I will spend some time getting acquainted this evening, then tomorrow will be all ours. I'm actually feeling a little ragged around the edges myself, and turning in early sounds appealing. I hope you'll rest well . . . and thanks for a wonderful dinner. Your meat loaf will be a hard act to follow." She glanced sideways and winked at Ruthie.

"Just wait," the little girl said smugly. "You'll see."

"Until tomorrow, then," Karti said, giving Paula a weary smile and a parting embrace. "I'm always much better in the morning." She pressed tender kisses to the cheeks of each of her children; then Sam put his arm around her shoulders, and the pair disappeared through the archway.

"He'll stay with her," Mark observed quietly. "Since she's been sick, he's gotten in the habit of sitting with her, watching her until she falls asleep. I think she enjoys it."

Paula looked at him and hesitated for a moment, then decided to address the obvious. "She looks quite . . . frail. When you told me she was much better, I guess I thought"—she shook her head—"well, maybe I really didn't know *what* I thought. I—I don't mean to be an alarmist, but . . . is she doing okay?"

Mark's face relaxed into an easy smile. "No question. I mean, if you'd seen her two months ago, you'd be amazed at how good she looks now. It's just a matter of getting her strength back, putting on a little more of the weight she's lost—"

"And growin' some *hair!*" Ruthie chimed in. "Her hair was so-o-o pretty . . . long and dark and mooshy." She closed her eyes and hugged herself, as if lost in memory.

"Mooshy?" Paula questioned, smiling at the image the word brought to mind.

"Yeah, mooshy—like so soft and thick and squishy I could use it for a pillow. I did, too; when she was sick at first, I'd lay on the bed and snuggle against her hair and smell how fresh and clean it was, like an angel breathed on it." The child's eyes glowed, then dimmed a little. "I loved her hair. It all fell out, but she gave me some to keep, and she promised it would grow back just as mooshy as ever. I hope it hurries . . . that little bit of fuzzy stuff she has now just tickles my nose." She giggled softly.

While Paula was digesting this information, Mark quickly crossed the room and retrieved two silver-framed photos from the glass sofa table, then retraced his steps and stood close to her. "These pictures were taken about a year ago," he explained. "Before they found the cancer."

Paula stared intently at the photos. One was an 8"x10" professional portrait of Sam and Karti, the other an enlargement of a casual family snapshot. In both pictures, Karti's extraordinary beauty was framed and highlighted by an exuberant mane of the deepest, richest walnut-colored hair Paula had ever seen. Its gentle curls fell thickly, sensuously above her dark eyes, against her cheeks and neck, across her shoulders, begging to be touched, smoothed, caressed. In fact, Paula couldn't help touching the photos, one at a time, as if she might actually be able to reach through the glass and feel the incredible texture of those gleaming locks for herself. How could she ever describe their effect?

"See? I told you," a ten-year-old voice said close to her. "Mooshy."

Paula looked down into Ruthie's wide, raven eyes. "I think you're exactly right," she smiled. "Mooshy."

The evening passed quickly in pleasant, animated conversation. Everyone relocated to the downstairs family room, where a blazing fire warmed them as they relaxed on large, comfortable couches and recliners. Paula learned that Mark, who had been working at a local lumber and building supply store since returning from his mission, planned to resume his studies at BYU in June, now that Karti seemed to be on the mend. "I'm thinking of going into medicine," he said, and Paula heard a depth of feeling in his declaration.

Alex would finish another year at Ricks, then work toward an engineering degree at Idaho State. And Jake, almost nineteen, would serve a mission before completing his degree in agricultural economics. "That's a fancy term for 'stayin' down on the farm and out of the red,'" he grinned. "Dad has worked awfully hard to make this farm a success; after my mission and college, I'd like to stay right here and help keep it in the family."

When it was her turn, Paula eagerly answered a flurry of questions about her life, her business, and her family. A glimmer of interest rose in Andrea's eyes when Paula described Scott, but it quickly faded back to a bored, insolent expression. Ruthie, on the other hand, seemed captivated by Paula's story, and sat close beside her on the couch closest to the wide stone fireplace. At eight-thirty, when Mark reminded her of bedtime, she pouted dramatically and looked to Paula for deliverance. "I don't have to go, do I?" she pleaded, her huge, soulful eyes fixed on Paula's face. Her small hand coyly patted her new friend's knee.

"Hey," Paula said, willing herself to keep from smiling at this child's charming impudence, "tomorrow's a school day. You don't want to fall asleep during math, now do you?"

"Oh, gag," Ruthie scoffed. "Reading is okay, but I *hate* fractions." She crossed her eyes and gripped her throat dramatically.

"I know exactly how you feel," Paula laughed. "But I think you'd better listen to your big brother. I'm not the boss, you know."

"She's right," Mark pointed out. "You'll have plenty of time to get to know each other this weekend. But for right now, you need your beauty sleep, kiddo."

Paula's heart thudded in her chest when the word caught her by surprise, bringing a lump to her throat. *Kiddo. That's what I called TJ.* She pushed the thought aside and smiled as she felt Ruthie's lips brush her cheek. "Good night, Sister Paula," she said in a faintly petulant tone. "I'll come right home from school tomorrow, and we can play before I fix dinner."

"Deal," Paula agreed. "Sleep tight." She reached out to give Ruthie a little squeeze. *This is nice,* she mused. Before her mind could pursue the thought further, the little girl had slipped away and scurried up the stairs. Her older sister followed silently a few seconds later. "You, too, Andrea—sleep well," Paula called out. There was no response. She shrugged. *Can't win 'em all, I guess.*

By nine-thirty, the fire had died down and the conversation was following suit. Mark stood up and stretched his long, sinewy arms toward the ceiling as Alex and Jake said good night and headed up the stairs. "We turn in fairly early around here," he said. "Morning chores never take a vacation." He gave Paula a crooked grin. "Could I interest you in a five A.M. tour of the barn, chicken coop, and other scenic attractions?"

"Oh, gee, thanks," Paula responded with a dramatic sigh. "You know I'd really love to; but to be honest, I'd be more inclined to hibernate until noon. Isn't that what most people do here—at least until it warms up to twenty below?" She shivered at the thought.

"Only transplanted Californians," he laughed. He sat beside her on the couch, and his expression grew serious. "It's really terrific to have you here, Paula," he said. "I hope you know that."

Paula stared into the smoldering firelight and shook her head. "It's incredible, you know? Being here like this, with you . . . meeting everyone. I never thought it could happen—not in my wildest dreams."

"Well, dreams are meant to come true—especially the wild ones," he chuckled. "As for me, I think I've never been happier. Now that Mom's health is improving, and you've come back into my life . . . well, it just doesn't get any better than this." He leaned back and sighed with contentment.

"Oh, I don't know about that," Paula said, reaching out to barely touch an unruly lock of his dark hair. "Just wait."

He gave her a puzzled glance. "Just wait?"

She nodded. "Until you fall in love."

Mark closed his eyes and nodded slowly, a tiny smile crinkling his mouth. "Ah, yes . . . love. Mom brings the subject up every so often. Quite often, actually."

"Well, great minds . . . ," Paula said with a little smirk.

"Uh-huh," he murmured. "'When you find the right girl,' she says, 'you'll wonder how you ever lived without her.'"

"Listen to your mother, Mark," she said playfully. "Both of them."

He sat up suddenly and leaned forward, his eyes boring into hers. "Is that how it was with you and my father, Paula? Did you love him?"

His questions caught her off guard, and she felt a wave of emotion wash over her, leaving her heart pulsing with tender memories, her eyes bright with unshed tears. But there was no hesitation in her voice as she answered. "Yes, Mark, that's how it was. And oh, yes, I did. I did love him." She paused, and an almost imperceptible sob caught in her throat. "I loved him *so much.*" She looked at her son for a long moment. "You have his eyes, you know. And his smile. That incredible smile."

"But he died," Mark said.

She nodded. "Before we even knew I was pregnant. We were very young, and my parents had basically disowned me when Greg and I eloped, so I was utterly alone when he was killed in that horrible motorcycle accident. I knew I couldn't go home, and I wanted something better for my child—for you—than I could provide, so I made the toughest decision of my life." She patted his arm. "I've always told myself that I didn't give you up . . . I gave you more. I guess it turned out all right in the end."

Mark smiled his agreement. "After all of that happened . . . you went back to school. Then you married someone else."

She nodded again. "Richard Donroe." Saying the name left a disagreeable taste in her mouth, and she winced.

"Not exactly a marriage made in heaven, eh?" Mark asked.

"Or anywhere near it," she said with a bitter laugh. "It was more like a business merger—basically a marriage of convenience. Except that after a couple of years I realized it wasn't really a marriage, and it certainly wasn't convenient. The only thing good about it was that I had two great kids. Nothing can ever change that." She smiled pensively.

"But even after such a terrible experience, you still believe in love?" His eyes were probing hers, questioning.

"Never doubt it," Paula said earnestly. "I've always loved my children—even the one I gave away." She rested her hand on his knee. "And now that I've found him . . . you . . . I understand even better what the word 'always' means. Then there's the gospel—a pure definition of love if there ever was one. Husbands and wives, parents and children, brothers and sisters, friends caring for one another under the watchful eye of Heavenly Father . . . I'm learning that it's all part of the plan. Unfortunately, sometimes the real thing gets mixed up with fear and anger and a bunch of other emotions; goodness knows I'm better than average at doing that. But when it comes right down to it, love is the glue that holds everything together. It created you; it brought Sam and Karti together; it was what prompted you to spend two years of your life sharing the gospel with strangers. And one day, it will make you wonder how you ever survived until you met the woman you love. I know it." She leaned back against the couch and gazed at him affectionately.

Mark regarded her solemnly for a long moment. "Do you think you'll ever get married again?" he finally asked.

Paula chewed her lip and considered the question for a full minute before answering. "Maybe," she said. "But only if the process has absolutely nothing to do with classified ads or singles' dances."

"I hear ya," Mark laughed. "Tell you what: let's keep an eye out for each other, okay? You check out the foxy California babes in your ward for me, and I'll . . . gee, I'm sure I'll be able to think of *something* for you." He made a gargoyle-like face, and she smacked him with a green-and-white striped sofa pillow.

"Some matchmaker you are," she growled.

"We aim to please," he grinned. "Meanwhile, I've got an early day at work tomorrow, so I guess I'll say good night." They both stood, and he drew Paula to him in a warm embrace.

"You know," she said, reaching up to pat his cheek, "I think I've had more hugs today than I've had in the entire rest of my life. Not that I'm complaining."

"We like to think of it as a family tradition," Mark explained. "It's kind of like a mission statement: More hugs per square inch in the Richland household than anywhere else in the state. Maybe the world."

"Well, I could get used to a tradition like that," Paula observed. "It makes me feel right at home."

"Then it's working," he said. "You're welcome in our home anytime."

"Thank you, Mark," she murmured. "You can't know how much that means to me."

"No problem," he said quickly, his voice gruff with emotion. "We'll see you tomorrow, then." He gave her arm a final squeeze, then turned and disappeared up the stairs.

"Sweet dreams, my boy," she whispered after him. "I love you."

CHAPTER 10

A low, moaning sound somewhere in the far distance cut through Paula's favorite early-morning dream—a peaceful scene in which she was reclining in a fragrant, sunlit meadow next to a gently whistling brook, eating Twinkies and elegantly sipping chocolate milk through a straw. Whenever she awoke after this dream, usually with a smile on her face, she knew she had slept well. And this morning in particular, as she stirred and stretched languidly beneath the thick down comforter on her bed, she anticipated the day with a sense of refreshment and well-being.

The mournful sound came again, and for a moment she couldn't place it. Then she remembered. *In California, this would be about the time our milkman makes his rounds of the neighborhood. But here on the farm, we're getting the real thing—before it's been pasteurized, homogenized, or bottle-ized. Complete with a morning serenade by the Holstein Sisters themselves. Let's hear it for the barnyard symphony!* She snuggled into her pillow and listened for a few more minutes before throwing off the covers and heading to the shower.

By the time Paula had dressed and made her way downstairs, the kitchen was alive with morning sun and tempting aromas. Karti was standing next to the tiled counter, keeping a watchful eye on the large square waffle iron in front of her. She looked up and smiled brightly when Paula entered the room. Clearly, the night's rest had done her good; she was still a bit pale, but the deep shadows under her eyes were almost gone, and her face seemed animated with warmth and energy. Even her slim body, now clothed in casual Levi's and a green flannel shirt, appeared relaxed and invigorated. "Good morning!" she beamed. "Did you sleep well?"

"Perfectly," Paula said, returning her smile. She glanced around the empty kitchen and over to the breakfast nook, where a long, rectangular oak table waited with eight flowered place mats in readiness for the morning meal. "Guess we beat everyone else up, huh?" she said a little smugly.

Karti cleared her throat and bit down on her lip, all the while staring at a blinking red light on the waffle iron. "Have a seat, Paula," she said, gesturing toward the table. "Looks like this waffle will be ready any second. We can split it." She opened a cupboard and took down two stoneware plates.

"It sounds wonderful," Paula said, "but I'm not in any hurry if you'd like to wait for the others. I suppose Mark will be—"

"Gone to work," Karti reported, moving to the stove to stir a small pan of fresh maple syrup.

Paula rubbed her forehead. "Oh, that's right; he said he had to leave early. But the girls will want to—"

"Gone to school." Karti retrieved a bottle of orange juice from the fridge and carried it to the table.

Paula squinted at a porcelain clock above the stove. Seven-thirty. "Alex and Jake?"

"Gone to Ricks. Basketball practice." Karti raised the lid of the waffle iron, lifted out four perfectly browned squares with a fork, and deposited two on each plate.

"And Sam?"

"Gone to town." Karti looked at Paula then, and her eyes twinkled with amusement.

"So," Paula said, her cheeks coloring slightly as she caught the implication, "you're telling me I'm the Lone Ranger in a household of early risers?"

"Something like that," Karti said with a musical laugh. "It gives us a good start on the day. Except for Andrea. She gets up at six, wakes up around nine. I'm not sure she's even conscious during her first couple of classes."

Paula nodded. "Sounds like a certain sixteen-year-old I know," she said, thinking of her son's curious sleeping habits. "Scotty stays up all night with his friends, but I swear he's in a coma whenever I try to have a conversation with him."

Karti picked up the two waffle-laden plates. "Tell me about your family, Paula," she said. Her invitation was so warm and genuine that Paula followed her willingly to the table, where they nibbled their breakfast, sipped hot cocoa, and talked long into the morning.

Paula related her story, and Karti drank in every detail—especially the ones related to Mark and Greg, Mark's birth father—with such eager interest that Paula felt, at least for the moment, as though she had somehow been placed squarely at the center of the universe. Karti's respect and admiration for her appeared boundless, and her life, on this golden morning, seemed to matter immensely. When she rehearsed the events surrounding Greg's death, and later described her incomprehensible loss when TJ died, Karti clasped Paula's hand in both of hers. Great tears of empathy and compassion brimmed in her limpid brown eyes, then made glistening trails down her soft cheeks. "So much heartache," she murmured, and in some marvelous way Paula knew she understood.

Around ten o'clock, the back door opened and an explosion of arctic air into the kitchen announced Sam's arrival. Karti watched her husband pull off his hat, boots, and gloves and hang his heavy wool jacket on one of several large brass hooks by the door. Without moving or speaking, Karti waited until their eyes met. In that instant, something like an electrical current passed between them, and her gaze seemed to draw him to her side like a powerful magnet. Paula had never seen anything like it.

Sam stood behind Karti's chair and rested his huge hands on her shoulders, then bent to press his lips against the deep-green silk scarf that swathed her head. His mouth moved to her ear, where he whispered a few words that brought a demure smile to her full lips. When he straightened up, he nodded a cheerful greeting to Paula. "Have you two solved the problems of the world this morning?" he inquired.

"Almost—but we'll need another couple of hours to finish the job," Karti said. "Will you join us for lunch?" She reached up to run two of her fingers along the length of his hand.

"I may have to pass on that," he said. "I saw Tom Bailey in town earlier; he's having some trouble with his milking machines, and I told him I'd be over as soon as I could to try to figure out what the problem is. You know how grumpy those cows get when they've got all that milk and nowhere to put it. Sorry, babe." He gently massaged her shoulders. "But I wouldn't miss supper for a million bucks." They both laughed, and Sam grinned at Paula. "You haven't lived until you've had one of Ruthie's Friday Night Specials."

"Something to look forward to," Paula smiled. *Hey, she said I was pretty. I'd eat worms if she cooked them.*

"Well, I'll let you ladies get back to your visiting. I'm off to the Baileys'." Sam bent over his wife again, this time pressing a lingering kiss to the side of her neck. Then he donned his hat, boots, gloves, and jacket again and disappeared through the back door. Paula shivered at the blast of freezing air he let in.

"Brrr," Karti said, echoing Paula's thoughts. She glanced toward a window, where an indoor/outdoor thermometer perched on the sill. "Twenty-two below," she reported. "I could use some more hot cocoa; how about you?"

"I wouldn't turn it down," Paula said. Five minutes later, they were sipping the steaming chocolaty liquid from oversized ceramic mugs and getting back to the business at hand.

Now it was Paula's turn to listen as Karti, speaking in low, melodic tones, unfolded the captivating scenario of a life both commonplace and extraordinary. Born in the Florida Keys to a large, prosperous family, Jakarta Lillian deClerq was the fifth of seven children, raised in a gospel-centered home where spirituality, education, and hard work were revered. Early in life, the dark-eyed beauty found creative expression in art and modern dance, and during her senior year in high school she blended the two by producing a one-woman dance recital using her own vivid paintings and abstract sculpture as backdrops. The project won her offers of full-ride scholarships to several prestigious universities, including the Sorbonne in Paris, where she studied for a year.

"Wow," Paula breathed. "That must have really been something."

"Oh, yes," Karti smiled. "One of the best times of my life. I lived a few blocks from campus with an elderly couple, the Brousseaus. They were such sweet, faithful members of the Church, and they came to every one of my gallery shows and dance recitals. We were very close, and I hated to leave them when my year was up. Of course, I could have stayed longer, but . . ." Her voice trailed off, and her gazed drifted toward the window.

"But . . . ," Paula prompted.

"But," Karti finally went on, "it wasn't to be. I'd fallen hopelessly in love, and I had to follow my heart."

Paula's eyebrows stood at attention. "Oooh, this sounds interesting." She propped an elbow on the table and rested her chin in the palm of one hand. "Tell me *every detail.*"

The light shining from Karti's eyes had a mischievous glint to it as she took a leisurely sip of cocoa, set her mug down on one of the floral placemats, and began slowly circling the edge of the mug with her graceful index finger. The protracted ritual was elegant and methodical, even sensuous when combined with the delicate pout of her generous lips. Finally, her gaze met Paula's. "You'll recognize the name," she said. "Elder Richland."

Paula's jaw dropped. "You're kidding." Karti shook her head. "You're not kidding. You mean . . . *Sam?*"

Karti nodded. "The very one." Almost instinctively, she pressed a hand over her heart. "He was serving a mission, and one day at church the Brousseaus invited the elders over for dinner. I was standing next to Sister B., and I . . . well, I . . ." She smiled a little and looked deeply into her cocoa as a crimson blush spread across her pale cheeks.

"You fell for him, didn't you? You fell in love with a Mormon missionary!" Paula finished her sentence with a dramatic flourish. When Karti shrugged, she pressed for more information. "But how could you . . . when did you . . . what did you—"

"It was easy." A radiant smile spread across Karti's face. "I loved him. He loved me. We both knew it the instant we met."

"Ah, yes . . . love at first sight," Paula sighed theatrically. "The pretty young coed, far from home; the handsome young missionary, seeing his future in those gorgeous brown eyes; the . . . the . . . uh, help me out here, Karti. What happened next?"

Karti chuckled softly. "Unfortunately, in the mission field there were rules about that sort of thing. Well, just one rule, really: *Don't.* So we had to make it up as we went along." She smiled mysteriously.

Paula's attention was riveted on this story. "And?" she urged.

Karti leaned back in her chair. "And," she said, "that's exactly what we did. The very first time we met—after a sacrament meeting on a cold, wet day in February—it was as though we were suddenly linked together by an invisible lifeline that stretched both backward and forward through the eternities. Neither of us said anything, but we both *knew;* and the feeling only deepened every time we looked into each other's eyes. For the next four months, until he left to go home, we carried on a chaste little courtship right in front of the Brousseaus, the mission president, and the whole branch—and nobody knew! It was our little secret." Her eyes glistened at the memory. "We never broke any mission rules, never spent a moment alone together, never got closer than a handshake, never said anything even vaguely romantic to each other. Unless, of course, you counted the times we played our little game. He'd say something like, 'Don't you just LOVE France in the MARRY month of May, Sister deClerq?" And I'd reply, 'Why, yes, Elder Richland, I believe I DO.' Then we'd both giggle a little—but not enough to arouse suspicion. That was about as torrid as it ever got." She paused and raised the cocoa mug to her lips for several long, slow swallows.

"Soul mates," Paula said, and Karti nodded. "How did you finally work it all out?"

"I thought you'd never ask," she said, relishing this opportunity to relive a bit of the past. "One fine June morning, I packed my bags and followed him to BYU. I knew he was attending summer school, so I decided to give him something to do besides homework. When he came home from class one day, I was sitting on the front steps of his apartment building. I'll never, ever forget the look on his face—or the kiss he gave me right before he said, 'Will you marry me?' And I've never looked back."

"Unbelievable," Paula said, her voice choked with emotion. "That has to be the most romantic story I've ever heard." She reached into her pocket for a tissue and dabbed at her eyes. "And clearly, you've been happy."

"Oh, yes," Karti declared without hesitation. "Although I can't say there haven't been some tense moments—especially while we waited more than ten years to have a family." She smiled and blushed a little as she added, "Not for lack of trying, you understand. It just didn't happen. By the time Mark came along, we had almost given up hope. I wouldn't say our marriage was in serious trouble, but we'd grown apart. Sam was terribly busy with the farm and his small accounting business, and I had opened a dance studio in town, as well as doing freelance artwork for several children's magazines. We were active in the Church, but it was hard to watch all our friends having babies and growing their families." She paused. "That all changed, of course, when Mark came to us. He was the beginning of the miracle."

"I'm glad," Paula said quietly. "You've done a marvelous job with him—better than I ever could."

"I'm not so sure about that," Karti smiled, "but I do know it's been a privilege to have him in our home. And now, to be able to meet you . . . I can hardly believe it."

"Me neither," Paula said. "It's just nice to have some kind of a connection after all these years, you know?"

"I do know," Karti agreed, "and I feel the connection in a very special way." She noticed Paula's curious look. "I'll explain later," she said, pushing aside her mug. "But right now, could I interest you in a guided tour of our home?"

"I'd love it." Paula scooted her chair back and stretched her legs. "I need to move around a little."

"Good. Let's take it from the top—literally," Karti said. She led the way up one flight of carpeted stairs to the atrium, then up another flight to a rather small, foyer-like space. They paused for a moment before moving down the hall toward a set of enormous white-oak sliding doors. Nodding in the direction of the doors, Karti spoke in an almost reverential tone. "This is my favorite place," she said. "My studio." Paula said nothing, but an intriguing flutter of anticipation rose in her chest as Karti barely touched the doors and they parted silently. Then she stood aside and motioned for Paula to enter.

She had not taken more than three steps forward when she turned back to Karti and whispered, "This is *incredible.*"

The broad, expansive room was alive with light and shadows. On one wall, an enormous window reached toward the high, arched ceiling in a series of cathedral-shaped etchings along its borders. The window looked out on the same breathtaking mountain landscape Paula had seen from her own guest quarters, but its effect was dramatically intensified by the fact that across the room, the wall facing this window was covered by a floor-to-ceiling mirror that perfectly reflected the stunning natural panorama. Standing on the polished hardwood floor between the window and the mirror, Paula felt as though she was completely surrounded by the vast out-of-doors. "Whoa," she breathed, captivated by the sensation.

Karti moved silently in front of Paula and perched herself on the arm of a low, tapestry-covered sofa near the window. "I never get tired of the view," she said. "Depending on the season, the weather, and the time of day, it can change completely in a matter of seconds."

"I can see how it would," Paula responded. She remained standing in the center of the room as her gaze took in the details of this ethereal space. Near the window and to one side of where Karti was sitting, a large artist's easel and work table were situated close together. The easel was empty, but half a dozen unfinished pen-and-ink drawings, mostly of children and landscapes, lay on the table. A few feet away, centered on a rich teal-and-cream oriental carpet, sat a large wooden quilting frame. Vibrant glints of blue and gold caught and held Paula's eye as she viewed the current work in progress, anchored securely to the frame's smooth railings.

"It's a gift for Sam's parents," Karti explained. "Their sixtieth anniversary. I took up quilting a few years ago, and it's become my passion." She chuckled. "There's nothing like a piece of fine art to keep you warm on a cold winter's night." After a pause she added, "It's been a blessing, too, during these past few months when I've been so . . . tired. It doesn't take much to push a needle, and it gives me great satisfaction."

Moving closer to the frame, Paula could see that this quilt was indeed a work of art. Its delicately entwined fabrics and designs, painstakingly outlined by hundreds of tiny, perfect stitches, reminded her of the Amish quilt collection she had once seen on display at the Smithsonian. Except that this quilt, with its wide, graceful flourishes and lush strips of luminous color, was much prettier and more inviting than the more austere, primitive Amish pieces. She brushed her hand lightly across one corner of the quilt, and was amazed to feel several different textures and thicknesses of fabric. "This is gorgeous," she said. "I'd love to learn how to do it." *As if I'd ever have the time—or the patience. Or the fabric swatches,* she thought. "But I don't know anyone who could teach me."

Karti reached into a drawer beneath the work table and pulled out a book of intricate quilt patterns. "After I learned the basics from an elderly sister in the ward, I graduated to these. Now I make my own." She pointed to an arrangement of small, elegantly crafted quilts hanging on a green-papered wall across the room. "Those are a few of my favorites." She turned to Paula with an almost shy expression in her eyes. "Perhaps some day I could teach you . . . if you'd like."

Paula felt a sudden, inexplicable rush of emotion. "Yes," she replied. "Yes, I'd like that." She sat beside Karti on the sofa. They lounged in tranquil silence for several minutes, watching the slow, opulent drift of a cluster of cumulus clouds across the mountains. Occasionally the clouds' fullness obscured the sun for a few seconds, and the studio was bathed in a luminous silver glow; then, when the clouds passed, the sun's rays on the rich wood flooring seemed to warm the room by several degrees, all in a matter of moments. There was no sound, but Paula could almost feel the air pulse with contentment. She was mesmerized.

"Well, I suppose we could sit here all day, soaking up this cozy ambience," Karti said finally, stretching her long, slender body like a satisfied feline. "Goodness knows I've done it so often that I'm beginning to feel like a General Foods International Coffees commercial. But let me show you around the rest of the place, then we'll have some lunch. After that, it's only a matter of time before Ruthie's home, and the fun begins. Especially when she cooks." Her expression grew whimsical. "All of my children are special, you know. But Ruthie . . . she's something more. Something extraordinary. Maybe it's because she's the baby of the family, or because she came along several years after we thought we'd finished having children. We've been inseparable since she was born, and even more so since I've gone through all of this cancer business. I'm just grateful it's over now." She rose gingerly from the sofa. "Shall we?"

Paula nodded and followed her through the double doors. As they stepped into the hall and the doors tapped softly together behind them, Paula felt a tiny flicker of regret tug at her mind. "I've never had a daughter," she said quietly as they made their way down the stairs to the second floor.

"There's nothing quite like it," Karti responded. "I was thrilled with my three sons, of course. But when Andrea and Ruthie came

along, they made me feel . . . whole, somehow. It's hard to explain."
She looked over at Paula. "You're still young yet. Maybe someday
you'll have a little girl of your own."

Paula's laughter sounded in the stairwell. "Me? I don't think so.
Forty-plus is a little old to be starting another family—even if there
were a potential husband lurking somewhere out there. At this point,
I think the most I can hope for is a sweet little granddaughter or two
from Scott in a few years—and of course from Mark's side of the
family as well." She considered the prospect for a moment, then her
eyes lit up. "Hey, can you imagine the fun they'd have calling us *both*
Grandma?"

Karti's expression clouded for a fraction of a second before she
mirrored Paula's smile. "That would be lovely," she agreed. "I couldn't
think of anything more lovely."

They passed the plant-filled atrium on the second-floor landing
and walked down a wide hall in the opposite direction from Paula's
guest quarters. A brief tour of the bedrooms followed. "Mark and
Alex share a room; so do Andrea and Ruthie," Karti explained. A tiny
grin lifted the corners of her mouth. "So do Sam and I. Jake has his
own space; no one wanted to share a bed with his extensive model
airplane collection." All of the rooms were of modest size, each one
decorated to reflect its occupants' tastes. Paula raised an eyebrow
when she saw the broad red ribbon strung lengthwise between
Andrea's and Ruthie's beds. "Andrea's idea," Karti noted. "She toler-
ates Ruthie, but *no one* is allowed on her side of the room."

"I see," Paula said. *Scotty would probably do the same thing if he
had to share a room. Except he'd use barbed wire.*

When Karti ushered her into the spacious master suite, Paula was
not surprised to see a broad expanse of windows on the east wall and
a collection of vibrantly healthy green plants displayed on filigreed
wrought iron stands in one corner. Photo collages of the children and
several delicate watercolor landscapes adorned another wall, and a
large impressionistic painting of the Salt Lake Temple hung majesti-
cally above the king-sized bed. Paula's gaze was drawn to an exquisite
ecru-and-salmon-colored quilt folded neatly at the foot of the bed,
and a glance in Karti's direction assured her that its creation had been
personalized for this very room.

"This is a wonderful place," Paula said, her voice almost a whisper. "It's so warm and inviting, so comfortable, so—" She stopped abruptly in mid-sentence, her eyes suddenly riveted to an object sitting alone on a mirrored pedestal at one end of a polished mahogany dresser. Moving quickly across the deep carpet to the other side of the room, she stopped next to the object and leaned forward to examine it closely. "I can't believe it," she murmured. "It's you . . . and Sam."

She was staring at a small bronzed sculpture, a bust only ten or eleven inches tall, but the faces were unmistakable as they shared a deep, expectant kiss. No, it was more than just a kiss; it seemed to be a moment of intimate communion, captured forever by the gifted hands and intuitive fingers of a consummate artist. The likenesses of a younger Sam and Karti were so distinct—her fine, high cheekbones and thick, lustrous hair; his deeply cleft chin and a broad forehead set above slightly bushy brows—that Paula wondered who could have fashioned this amazing piece. It was, in fact, beyond amazing—even beyond artistic genius. It was a source of power; a microcosm of passion. She turned questioning eyes toward Karti. "Who did this?"

"It's titled 'First Kiss,'" Karti said in a slightly uneven voice, her dark eyes glistening. "Do you like it?"

"Like it? I'd pay a fortune to know who created it, and then I'd go right out and pay him another fortune to do a piece for me. It's exquisite." Paula touched Karti's arm. "You must absolutely treasure it; I've never seen love expressed so completely in a work of art, or with such tenderness. And he's captured your faces almost perfectly. Is he a friend of yours—maybe someone you met at the Sorbonne?"

"You could say that," Karti answered, reaching out to caress the bust with the tips of her fingers. "Only . . ." She hesitated, then began again. "Only he is a . . . she."

"Yes, of course . . . I should have known," Paula said, staring even more intently at the statue. "A woman's touch. Did she have you sit for a preliminary sketch, or what?"

"Not exactly," Karti replied. "She did it kind of in . . . freestyle."

"Wow," Paula breathed. "That's even more impressive. Who is she, anyway? Have I seen her work in any of the major museums?"

"I'm not sure," Karti said. "Let's see . . . I think her name is some-where on the base." She picked up the bust and lifted it up to the light, then pointed to a small area near the bottom of the piece. "Ah, yes . . . right here."

She held the statue out to Paula, who cradled it in her hands and turned it carefully to reveal the artist's signature. "There it is," she said after a few seconds. "It's small, but I think I can read it." She repositioned the piece so the window's full light fell on it. "Let's see; looks like a J . . . J . . . J. Rich . . . J. Richland." She shot a razor-edged glance at Karti, who shrugged and stared back at her with a wide-eyed, innocent expression. "*J. Richland.* That wouldn't by any chance stand for *Jakarta* Richland, would it?"

"Turn it over," Karti said evenly.

The words Paula saw engraved on the smooth underside of the bust removed any doubt: *To Samuel, love of my heart . . . forever. Karti.*

Suddenly Paula's legs felt less than steady, and she sank into a velvet-covered chair next to the bed. "I can't believe it," she whispered, hugging the statue to her chest. She looked up at Karti. "I had no idea you were such a gifted artist."

Karti kicked her terry slippers off and sat cross-legged on the bed. "Sculpting was always my first love," she began in the low, euphonic voice that Paula had grown so fond of. "Even more than dance or painting. I think I was pretty good at it, too; I sold dozens of pieces to private collectors during the first years we were married. But this"—she nodded toward the statue Paula held—"this was different. This was my best . . . I think because it had such special meaning for both of us."

"Tell me," Paula said reverently.

Karti chewed gently on her bottom lip. "Funny," she said after a while, "it seems more like last week than over thirty years ago. May I?" She reached out toward Paula, who reluctantly placed the statue in her hands. "I did this in celebration of our first anniversary; it represents the very first time we kissed as husband and wife on our wedding night. There was so much love, so much anticipation, so much passion in that kiss; I wanted it to last forever." Her eyes shone with the memory as she continued. "I worked on it for six months, and Sam never even knew. He cried when he saw it." She tenderly stroked the male figure's cheek with a slender finger. "Even now, sometimes I see him just staring at it."

"I can understand why," Paula said. "It's inspired. I've never seen anything like it. Except maybe . . ." She paused.

Karti looked at her curiously, and Paula could see that before the chemotherapy, her perfectly arched brows would have formed elegant question marks above those extraordinary brown eyes. Now there was just a hint that her fine, dark brows were beginning to come back. "You were saying?" Karti said, and Paula started a little.

"Oh, yes. Except maybe in real life—this morning, when I saw the two of you looking at each other across the kitchen. I could have sworn you were newlyweds."

"I know," Karti sighed. "It's amazing, isn't it? After three decades and five children, you'd think things would cool down a little." She glanced sideways at the bed and skimmed her hand almost shyly across its thick, cream-colored blanket. "But we're closer now than ever. Being with him is incredible."

Paula cleared her throat awkwardly and picked at a bit of fuzz on her pant leg. "Uh, that's nice. Really nice. That's great," she murmured. *As if I needed to know all the family secrets.*

Karti giggled. "I've embarrassed you," she said. "How refreshing."

"No you didn't, not really. It's just that I—" Paula stopped in mid-sentence. "What was that you said? Refreshing?"

"Exactly," Karti said. "I just think it's terribly heartening to know that in today's world of bathroom humor, mindless promiscuity, and non-existent morals, a woman of your obvious accomplishment and sophistication is actually taken aback by such things. I'm impressed."

Paula decided to return the favor. "Well, I do know a good set of pecs when I see one," she observed, batting her eyelashes and pasting a demure smile on her lips.

Karti began to laugh, and both women were soon hooting at this turn of the conversation. "You've got style, Paula Donroe," Karti finally hiccupped. "Can you come over to play again next weekend?"

Paula wiped at her eyes and shook her head. "Hey, don't tempt me. I haven't enjoyed myself this much since my college days, when my roommates and I made it our personal mission to elevate joke-telling to an art form. Of course, everything was a little funnier when accompanied by a vodka tonic and three or four creme de menthes. What wasn't funny was the hangover the next morning." She grimaced. "When I tried to eat a little breakfast, I could actually hear my teeth screaming for mercy."

"Sounds like the morning after chemotherapy," Karti said, reaching up to touch the silk scarf covering her head. "And the next morning. And the next. Finally, when you feel good enough to get up and comb your hair, there isn't any." She made a ghoulish face, and Paula couldn't help laughing. "The kids tell me that my favorite daytime soap ought to be *The Bald and the Beautiful.*"

"In college, ours was *The Young and the Retchless,*" Paula grinned. "We kind of saw its main characters as role models for holding one's liquor."

They laughed again until Karti fell back on the bed, exhausted. "Are you okay?" Paula asked lightly.

"Oh, yes," she replied "Just a little out of breath—but for a good cause." Paula could see her slim midsection still jiggling with mirth beneath her flannel shirt. "It's a fabulous feeling—so easy and light." She sat up, the bronze statue clasped firmly in one hand, and looked fondly at her new friend. "Thank you, Paula."

"For what?" Paula asked, a genuinely puzzled expression settling in her eyes.

"For making me laugh, for laughing with me, for . . . for looking past the tired, sick old lady to the real Jakarta Richland. To the pre-cancer Jakarta Richland." She regarded Paula with unreserved admiration.

"What's that?" Paula made an elaborate show of squinting and casting her gaze slowly, carefully about the room. "Excuse me, but I don't see any tired, sick old lady around here. Only a young, gorgeous babe with a slightly outrageous headdress and a smile that could melt a glacier in ten seconds flat." Paula's eyes sparkled as Karti breathed in her words as though they were giving her new life.

"On second thought, make that *two* gorgeous babes," Paula added. "But I'm still working on the smile. Maybe you could help me out a little." She twisted her mouth into several comical shapes before pressing her lips together and shaking her head dolefully. "Oh, well . . . I guess it takes a man to put a smile like that on someone's face."

"Only if his name is Samuel," Karti said.

Paula gestured toward the bronze statue cradled in Karti's hands. "And only if he's a world-class kisser."

"Here, here," Karti agreed, and they laughed again.

After a moment, Karti set the bust on a nightstand next to the bed and rested her hands elegantly on her knees. "I meant what I said, you know. About your seeing the real Jakarta Richland."

"I know," Paula said, her voice matching Karti's suddenly reserved tones. She paused, not knowing exactly where the conversation was headed.

"It's the cancer," Karti went on. "Over the past year, it's been an unwelcome guest—a member of the family, really. But believe me, this is one relation nobody wants to claim. Most days, it's a dark cloud hanging over everything. Oh, I've tried my best to joke about it, to laugh off the side effects of the chemo, to 'be of good cheer,' as the scriptures say. Sam and the children have tried, too—but when I look into their eyes and see twelve black holes of fear and helplessness, I know it's unreasonable to expect them—us—to be the same carefree, teasing, lighthearted family we were before this happened. And even now, when we've had such good news from the doctors, I worry that they still don't quite believe it."

"And do *you* believe it?" Paula asked gently.

"I believe," Karti said slowly, thoughtfully, "that my life is in the Lord's hands."

An icy shiver raced up Paula's spine. *In the Lord's hands . . . that's exactly what the elders said about TJ's life after they gave him a blessing. Then he died. But it isn't always like that, is it? Sometimes the Lord has a life in His hands, and then He gives it back. Changes His mind or something. Karti still has a family to raise, for goodness' sake. Surely He knows that.*

"Of course, all of our lives are in His hands," Karti continued. "Who knows? Sam could have a massive heart attack tomorrow and be gone; one of the kids could have an accident at school and never come home. Your plane could fall out of the sky on Sunday, and—"

"Thank you *so much* for sharing that," Paula said with a nervous laugh. She made a mental note to see about updating her will.

"Sorry," Karti chuckled. "The point is, we're all living on borrowed time anyway. But I'd like to think I still have a good, long ways to go." Her expression brightened. "So I guess the answer to your question is yes, I do believe the doctors when they say I'm in remission. I do believe I've been given a miraculous gift of more time. And I do believe I'll be here for all the important moments in my children's lives. But even if I'm not, I'll still believe. Life will still go on." Her eyes glistened with faith and conviction as she met Paula's gaze. "Besides, now that I have a marvelous new friend, I'm not about to abandon ship without a fight."

"I should hope not," Paula said. "That would be awfully inconsiderate of you."

Karti nodded. "I know. That's what my husband keeps telling me." She stood and moved across the room to the dresser, where she carefully replaced the bust on its mirrored pedestal. "Now, what do you say we go downstairs and lose ourselves in scrapbooks and memories for a while?"

Paula's face lit up. "Can't think of anything I'd rather do," she said, bounding from her chair to follow Karti into the hall.

They were halfway down the stairs when the kitchen door opened and slammed. Within seconds an excited, high-pitched voice split the air like a firecracker. "Hi, Mom . . . Hi, Sister Paula!" it echoed through the large, still house. "I'm home . . . and it's time! It's time!"

CHAPTER 11

Karti winked at Paula. "The Friday Night Special," she whispered.

"Ah, yes," Paula smiled. "Ruthie's night to cook."

At that moment the little girl skipped up the stairs and into her mother's arms, nearly knocking her off balance. "How's it goin', Momsie?" she giggled, planting a loud kiss on Karti's cheek. Then she turned and wrapped her willowy arms around Paula's waist. Paula returned the hug, burying her nose briefly in the child's fragrant brown hair.

An instant later, Ruthie grabbed her mother's hand and began pumping it as the threesome walked down the stairs. "I can get everything ready right now," she said eagerly, her wide eyes dancing with anticipation. "It'll only take a few minutes, and we can—"

"Hey, hold on a minute, young lady," Karti interrupted, stopping on the bottom stair to pat her daughter's shoulder affectionately. She glanced at her watch. "It's not even three-thirty yet, and suppertime isn't until after six."

"I know, but I thought I could start making dessert, and—"

Karti laughed. "Well, unless you're planning to make the ice cream yourself, I think we've already got that covered. And you made cookies two days ago, remember?"

"Oh . . . right," Ruthie admitted. Her mouth formed a small pout, but it disappeared as she glanced up at Paula. "Do you like peanut butter chocolate chip cookies?"

Paula closed her eyes, and an expression of pure delight flashed across her face. "Mmm . . .my favorite," she said.

"I *knew* it!" Ruthie exclaimed. "Do you want one now? I baked extra."

A low rumble in Paula's stomach reminded her that in their absorbtion with other things, she and Karti hadn't eaten lunch. Still, she was hesitant. "Gee, I don't know . . ."

"Well, *I* do," Karti broke in. "And I won't have any guest of mine wasting away for lack of nourishment." She turned to Paula. "Sorry about lunch—or the lack thereof," she whispered. "My appetite is a little slow coming back, and sometimes I forget that other people actually enjoy eating." She tugged at a stray lock of Ruthie's hair. "Sweetie, Paula and I are going downstairs to look at some pictures and things. Why don't you fix us a nice tray of cookies and milk? And don't forget some for yourself."

"Cool!" the girl blurted out. She was halfway to the kitchen when she skidded to a stop and turned back. "Oops, I almost forgot. Andrea dropped me off, then went over to the Siddoways' for a while. She and Barbi are working on a history project or something. Said she'd be home by suppertime. Okay?"

"Okay," Karti replied.

Downstairs, Karti led Paula to a large, built-in cabinet on one wall, and they pulled out several thick photo albums. "These should last us until supper," Karti smiled. "They take us up through Mark's first birthday."

"Good grief!" Paula cried with mock astonishment. "I don't think I've taken this many pictures of all my kids put together." She squinted, cocked her head to one side, and mustered up a little scowl. "Is this one of those Mormon things—you know, a requirement to get to heaven? 'Be ye therefore a perfect picture-taker'?"

Karti's rich laugh echoed across the family room. "If it were, I'd be sitting pretty about now." She lowered herself onto one of the long couches, and Paula sat beside her. "It's just that after ten years, I'd pretty much worn out my camera on Sam. Sam on his tractor; Sam with his fishing gear; Sam at his desk; Sam milking the cows; Sam with Mickey Mouse at Disneyland; Sam holding the first potato of the new harvest; Sam re-roofing the house. When I caught myself clicking the shutter at Sam putting in his new contact lenses, I knew it was time to find another hobby." She paused. "But then, when we finally got Mark, I just went crazy. I'm surprised he didn't develop permanent red-eye from the flashes. It's just that he was so . . . so *wonderful*. But then, you'll see that for yourself."

Karti opened the first album, and Paula gasped. Staring up at her was the hospital photo of her day-old son—the picture she'd given to a social worker for delivery to his new parents more than two decades earlier. Carefully mounted beside it was the agonized letter she had written to him, explaining the circumstances of his birth and begging his forgiveness. She had, of course, kept copies of these bittersweet mementos; but at this moment, seeing the originals for the first time in twenty-two years, she felt tears stinging her eyes. *It still hurts . . . even now, when I know he's been well and happy. So happy.* She pressed her fingers tightly against her trembling lips and shook her head to clear out the piercing memories.

"It's all right," Karti said gently. "I knew when I read your letter that we'd been given an extraordinary gift from an exceptional woman. It would seem that I was right—on both counts." She reached out to squeeze Paula's free hand, and they sat for a few moments in reflective silence.

"Ta-*dah!* Afternoon snack, at your dispo-o-o-sal!" Ruthie's spirited announcement startled them, and Paula quickly wiped a hand across her cheek. Unaware of the emotionally charged moment, Ruthie blithely knelt beside the glass-topped table in front of the couch, careful not to jiggle the plate of cookies and three tall glasses of milk balanced on the tray she carried. Depositing the tray on the table, she grinned triumphantly. "Dig in!" she ordered. "I'll go first." She scooped up two cookies with one hand and grabbed a glass of milk with the other, then plopped herself down next to Paula and began to nibble on the edge of a cookie. "Mmm," she said between bites, her face a study in contentment. "Just as good as I remembered."

"She makes a batch at least once a week," Karti whispered.

Paula picked up one of the cookies and sniffed it appreciatively, then sank her teeth into its soft, moist surface. The flavor was a unique blend of chocolate and peanut butter that seemed to tempt and satisfy at the same time, and Paula was on her third cookie before she noticed Ruthie's enormous grin. "What?" she said, reaching for a glass of milk. "I was hungry, okay?" She shrugged and filled her mouth with the ice-cold liquid, letting it drizzle slowly down her throat. Then she grinned back at Ruthie. "Besides, these are absolutely the best cookies I've ever tasted. I mean it." To prove her point, she reached for a fourth.

Ruthie's delight exploded into an attack of wiggles, her small body bouncing back and forth, side to side on the couch. She finally settled down, but her eyes shone with satisfaction. When she got up to take the empty tray back to the kitchen, she glanced at her mother, pointed a stern finger at Paula, and spoke in a remarkable imitation of Karti's voice. "Just don't you let this spoil your supper," she warned in a gruff but motherly tone. Then she giggled and hurried up the stairs.

After a few moments of contented silence, Karti turned to Paula. "You know," she said gently, "I hardly know anything about your boys. Would you tell me about them?"

"I can do better than that," Paula smiled. "You just wait right here, and I'll be back in a New York instant." She patted Karti's knee, bolted off the couch, and strode up the stairs. Less than five minutes later, she returned with a small brown wallet-sized folder in her hand. "I've got pictures," she grinned. "They go everywhere with me; Scotty hates it when I pull them out in front of him. He has this darling little dimple at the corner of his mouth that only shows up when he's embarrassed." She sat down beside Karti and began turning the plastic-covered pages. "I took most of these last summer. Every couple of years or so, I go crazy with a camera." She paused. "I'm just glad I got the urge when I did, because three months later TJ . . ." She swallowed and coughed a little. "Anyway, here's Scotty with a couple of his school friends on the day he got his learner's permit. He's the tall, dark-haired, buff-looking kid on the left—a natural athlete with a crazy sense of humor and real artistic talent. He just needs a sense of direction."

"A very handsome young man," Karti observed. "He and Mark look enough alike to be—brothers." She smiled endearingly. "I hope they'll get to know each other."

"That would be terrific," Paula said. "They played basketball a couple of times on Mark's P-Days, and I think they got along pretty well. Unfortunately, I think he might resent Mark a little at the moment—kind of a delayed sibling rivalry or something. I'd love it if they could get to be friends, but I just don't know if it'll ever happen."

"Not to worry," Karti said with conviction. "These things have a way of working out."

"I hope so." Paula turned another page. "Here's Scotty at the beach, and this one was taken on the ski slopes at Lake Tahoe a couple of winters ago. He really loves the outdoors."

"I can see that," Karti agreed. "Did TJ share his interests?"

"Not exactly. He was quieter, less social, more apt to have his nose in a book. Except, of course, when he was tossing hoops, which was his first love." She pointed to the next picture. "Here he is on the basketball court—his favorite place in the whole world. Here's one with his best friend, Rudy. And this," Paula's throat constricted as she held the photo briefly to her heart before turning it toward Karti, "is the picture Millie took of TJ and his new friends, Elders Richland and Stucki." She removed the photo from its protective sleeve and tucked it into Karti's hand. "You can keep this one. I have a copy."

"Thank you." Karti studied TJ's thick, unruly sand-colored hair, his mischievous brown eyes, freckled nose, and wide, infectious grin. "He's adorable," she said. "Obviously one of a kind."

"You've got that right," Paula said quietly. "Now, do you have some more memories of Mark you'd like to share?"

"Well, just a few," Karti beamed.

The next two hours passed in what seemed to Paula a free-fall of emotion as she and Karti pored over the albums and scrapbooks documenting Mark's life. While she smiled and cooed and laughed and joked over the hundreds of photos and memorabilia, the deepest chambers of Paula's heart were silently filling with the tears and regrets of a woman who had never quite forgiven herself. But forgiven herself for what? For falling in love with a man who would tragically die too soon to have really lived? For wanting a better life for herself and for her baby? For still caring so much, even after twenty-two years, that she couldn't let it rest? Finally, a snapshot of Mark, bursting with pride as a brand-new Eagle Scout, set her senses reeling, and she slumped back against the couch. Suddenly her head was pounding, and she closed her eyes tightly.

Karti was quick to assess the situation. Closing the scrapbook, she took one of Paula's hands in both of hers. Paula could feel the smooth, delicate texture of Karti's skin as she gently rubbed her thumb in tiny circles on the back of her hand. "I know," Karti said. "This must be difficult for you. I was just so anxious for you to know him, to see what a fine boy he was, what a fine man he's become. But maybe it wasn't such a good idea—all of it at once, I mean. I'm so sorry if I—"

"Please, don't. I *needed* to do this." Paula opened her eyes and forced herself to smile. "I don't suppose it'll ever really be easy; I gave up on that possibility many years ago." She patted the cover of the scrapbook. "But this—this is the only way I know to finally make peace with it. Until a few weeks ago, I thought I'd never have that chance; but I can see that being here with you is a wonderful opportunity to . . ." Taking a deep breath, she nodded resolutely. "To come to terms with the past, to accept the present, and to get on with the future." She paused. "I can do this, you know," she declared. "But in the meantime, as we say to our clients who want something done yesterday, 'Your patience will be appreciated.'" She flashed Karti a small, hopeful smile.

"I'd say your clients are among the most fortunate people on the planet," Karti said. "You're bright, beautiful, funny, and I'm sure you're a consummate professional. How did you get into advertising, anyway?"

"Long story," Paula replied. "Maybe next time I come to visit, I'll . . ." A light suddenly rose in her eyes. "Or, better still, *you* could come visit *me*. I'd show you all the sights, take you to the beach, introduce you at the office, let Millie feed you until you resemble a stuffed pork chop. Then I'd take you to church and watch everyone lining up to shake Elder Richland's mother's hand. He's admired and loved by a lot of people out there, you know. We could have a *spectacular* time. Mark could come, too—maybe he and Scotty could spend some time together. And Sam is welcome, too, if he can get away. What do you think?" She studied Karti's face expectantly.

For just an instant, Karti's dark eyes widened like those of a startled doe caught in the glare of a spotlight. Then she quickly smiled and reached up to touch the scarf on her head. "Why, that would be lovely," she said. "Just as soon as I'm a little more back to . . . normal."

"Fair enough," Paula agreed. "You just let me know when you're ready, and we'll roll out the red carpet. Or at least the red Jaguar."

"Ah, yes," Karti nodded. "Mark told me about your snazzy new convertible. I can hardly wait to feel the wind whipping through my . . . follicles." Both women giggled.

Paula was launching into an animated description of traffic on the California freeways when Ruthie's high, insistent voice tumbled from above and caught them by surprise. "Supper!" it announced importantly. "Come and get it! Everybody's here!"

Karti winked at Paula and cupped her hands around her mouth. "Coming, *mon cherie,*" she called back. "Shall we?" she asked, gesturing toward the stairs.

"But of course," Paula said grandly, and they hurried up to the dining room. In the wake of her recent cookie feast, Paula was more curious than hungry; she couldn't help wondering what delicacies would be featured on a ten-year-old's menu. As they took their seats at the table, an unexpected twinge of memory nipped at her heart. *My mother would never have allowed this,* she mused. *"That's what servants are for," she always said when I asked. Seemed to me like the servants had all the fun. They never made my favorite, either.*

The table had been set with obvious care, from the cheerful yellow linen tablecloth to the sparkling water goblets. Clearly, Ruthie was in charge of this meal, and the family members regarded her with a mixture of amusement and indulgence. Only Andrea appeared bored and fretful, her arms folded churlishly across her chest. She rolled her eyes and puffed out her cheeks when Karti gave her a warning glance.

Ruthie was oblivious to the dynamics of the moment. For this evening, she and her father had traded places, and she sat beaming at the head of the table while Sam sat contentedly beside his wife. "Mom," she said efficiently, "would you please ask the blessing?" Karti cheerfully complied, and at the very instant the "amen" passed her lips, Ruthie vaulted from her chair and bustled into the kitchen. Paula noticed that some food had already been placed on the table. Next to the centerpiece—a cluster of blue silk flowers in a small plastic vase—sat a napkin-lined basket of steaming dinner rolls. On each plate, a few dark leaves of lettuce cradled half a pear topped with a dollop of mayonnaise and sprinkled with grated cheese. Paula's appetite was making a mild comeback.

Within seconds, Ruthie reappeared with the vegetable course—a large, oblong serving dish piled high with fresh-frozen garden peas, steamed to an emerald-green color and capped with several plump squares of rapidly melting butter. She carefully lowered the bowl to the table near her own plate, then squared her shoulders and grinned at Paula. "Main course, coming up!" she announced. Without further comment, she spun around and disappeared into the kitchen.

"Yippee skippy," Andrea said, her voice dripping with sarcasm. "As if this is gonna be a HUGE surprise." She slouched back against her chair and focused her attention on the ceiling while she fingered a long, silver chain around her neck.

"Watch your manners, *sweetie,*" Karti whispered curtly. "Your sister is trying."

Andrea smirked. "Trying what—to gag us to death?" She giggled sourly.

Now it was Karti's turn to roll her eyes, which she did with such dramatic flair, accompanied by a deep sigh and a hand to her forehead, that Paula couldn't help laughing. By the time Ruthie was ready to serve up the main course, the entire family had joined in—with the exception of Andrea, who was shaking her head in disbelief.

"What?" Ruthie asked, approaching the table with a large, covered ceramic bowl nestled securely in her arms.

"Nothing, dear," Karti said, then quickly changed the subject. "What has our favorite little chef prepared for us this evening?"

"Gimme a break," Andrea moaned. She clamped her lips together when Karti shot her a severe look.

The younger girl's cheerfulness seemed to cancel out her sister's peevish attitude. Ruthie stepped confidently to Paula's side and deposited the oversize bowl on the table in front of her. *She's got her mother's sense of theatrical timing,* Paula thought as this exuberant child reached to uncover the bowl. "It's my favorite," Ruthie declared with a satisfied grin. "The whole family loves it, too."

"Well," Paula responded warmly, "then I'm sure I—"

Her lips froze in mid-sentence as the bowl's contents came into full view. Before her, shimmering and glinting gold like a newly discovered treasure, sat the largest mound of macaroni and cheese she had ever seen.

Paula's jaw dropped like a nutcracker, and she stared up at Ruthie through half-open eyes. "I don't believe it," she muttered, shaking her head.

The girl's face drooped, and the joy drained from her countenance. Her lower lip trembled ever so slightly as she spoke. "You mean you don't . . . you don't like . . ." She couldn't find the words, couldn't mask her disappointment. For a long, excruciating moment, the family held its collective breath.

Seeing her young friend's crestfallen look, Paula quickly explained herself. "Oh, no . . . it's not that at all. Not at *all.*" A glimmer of hope settled in Ruthie's eyes as she continued. "You see, I just couldn't believe it when I saw all that *scrumptious* macaroni and cheese." She closed her eyes and licked her lips to make the point, then put a hand to her heart. "I *love* that stuff!"

Ruthie's enormous dark eyes widened even further. "You *do?*" she asked, then shot a triumphant glance toward Andrea, whose own eyes had by this time taken up permanent residence at the back of her skull.

"Hey, if it's Kraft macaroni and cheese, fresh from the box, this must be heaven," Paula grinned. As she said it, she could sense a wave of relief and good humor bathing the room in light and energy. She decided to capitalize on the moment. "You know, I grew up in kind of a hoity-toity family; we always had proper sit-down dinners, and I got pretty tired of *steak tartare,* broccoli florets, and fruit compotes almost every night of the week." She made a ghoulish face, and everyone laughed. "Sometimes I'd just pick at my food and go to bed early, then in the middle of the night I'd sneak down to the kitchen and have a ball mixing up my favorite—mac and cheese. I'd eat the whole thing, right then and there, then clean up and go back to bed with a smile on my face. Nobody knew—not even the maid, who would've hyperventilated if she'd figured it out. I'd actually save up my allowance money, then stop at the store on my way home from school and buy a bunch of boxes. I hid 'em in my room—kind of like my own personal year's supply. And I wasn't even a Mormon at the time." She winked at Ruthie. "But you know what? Now that I'm grown up, *and* a Mormon, when I get around to doing the food storage thing, good ol' Kraft macaroni and cheese will be at the top of my list. You can come visit me, and we'll have an all-night mac-and-cheese party. And green peas, too."

"All *right!*" Ruthie exclaimed, her cheeks flushed with sheer joy.

Paula looked at Karti impishly. "See?" she whispered loudly. "I might not do quilts, but I can certainly do Krafts."

By the time the meal was over, Karti's face was drawn and pale with exhaustion. "It's been an intense day for you," Paula said. "Why don't you turn in early? Ruthie and I will clean up." Without hesitation she wrapped her arms around Karti's thin frame and hugged her gently, thinking how close she had grown to this woman in little more than twenty-four hours.

Karti sighed. "Thanks; I think I'll do that. It's amazing how tired I get these days. I can hardly wait until this is all behind me."

"And it will be, soon enough," Paula said reassuringly. "Meanwhile, just take care of yourself, okay? We'll see you in the morning." She watched as Sam carefully linked Karti's arm through his and guided her toward the stairs. *Like a gentle giant,* she thought with a rush of admiration. *How would it be to have someone care that much?* She was suddenly aware of a dark, empty place at the center of her heart. *How would it be to have someone care at all?*

The question gnawed at her through the evening as she observed the Richland family talking, laughing, playing silly games, challenging each other to a friendly arm-wrestling match. Even Andrea, who generally seemed aloof and distracted, eventually warmed to the good-natured bantering of her older brothers. If this was a slice of Mormon family life, Paula reasoned, then she wanted the whole pie. But how and where did one begin? *Probably with a good man,* she thought ruefully. *As if there are any good ones left roaming the streets of Los Angeles, a temple recommend in one hand and a sharp eye out for a middle-aged convert who only last month, when someone in the ward asked her if she knew where the stake house was, responded that she preferred the Red Lobster.* She couldn't help chuckling at the memory.

"Paula? Hey, Paula . . . you're a million miles away." Mark's deep voice startled her back to the present as he settled next to her on the family-room couch. She smiled into his deep-brown eyes, thinking how much he looked like the rest of the family. At the thought, she steeled herself for a stab of pain, but it never came. Instead, she ran her finger along the firm line of his jaw and noticed how contented he looked. For the moment, anyway, that seemed to be enough.

"Just thinking," she said. "Still amazed that you and I are finally together. And in Idaho, of all places!" She laughed a little, then her expression sobered. "It's a miracle, isn't it?"

"A miracle, plain and simple," he agreed. "I hope we'll always stay in touch." A tide of affection rose in his eyes as he added, "A guy can always use another good mother."

Later that night, as she knelt by her bed and gave thanks for an extraordinary day, Paula added her own benediction to Mark's statement. *And a mother can always use another good son.*

On Saturday, the family had planned a snowmobile excursion to introduce Paula first-hand to the frozen beauty of an Idaho winter. A morning sky full of dark, lowering clouds gave them second thoughts, however, and by nine o'clock a fierce blizzard had virtually obliterated the landscape and confined them to the house for the storm's duration. "The plows won't be out until the weather lets up," Sam explained. "Could be later today—or next week." He smirked a little as Paula's eyes widened in alarm. "Not to worry," he said calmly. "We'll get you out of here by early summer." Then he laughed—a deep, cheerful, reassuring cadence that echoed through the house. Paula loved the sound of it.

Karti, whose energy level had improved dramatically overnight, punched her husband playfully in the ribs. "Thank you, my love, for that encouraging weather report." She turned to Paula, grabbed her hand, and smiled enticingly. "Come on," she said, leading her toward the stairs. "I want to show you something."

By the time they reached the third-floor landing, Paula had a pretty good idea of where they were headed, and it hardly surprised her when Karti pushed open the doors to her studio. "Go ahead," she whispered, nudging Paula forward into the room. "It's better than Disneyland."

Paula did as she was told, taking a few steps into the studio. Then suddenly, at the center of the room, she caught her breath as the space seemed to take on a life if its own, dipping and twirling in a mighty rush of motion around her. Outside the huge window, an undulating wall of silver-dollar-sized snowflakes had wiped out the view and was twisting in the fierce wind like a white sheet hung out to dry. Every few seconds the sheet would break apart in an explosion of crystalline energy, hammering the window with millions of super-charged flakes. Replicated exactly in the mirror across the room, the scene was dizzying in its intensity, and Paula was mesmerized by the sensation.

She felt as though she was at the very center of the storm, and expected at any moment to feel a rush of arctic missiles pounding her face. Closing her eyes and parting her lips slightly, she could almost feel the flakes pelting her lips, dissolving against her tongue. She shivered and hugged herself as she imagined their icy residue trickling down her throat.

"Pretty amazing, isn't it?" Karti was standing beside her on the polished wood floor. "I love watching the big storms from here; you feel like you're right in the middle of things, and no two are ever the same. Every time it happens, it's a brand-new demonstration of God's power."

Paula opened her eyes, and for several minutes the two women stood together, gazing reverently at the natural phenomenon surrounding them. Finally, Paula broke the silence. "You mentioned God's power." Her mind raced over some of the concepts she had learned since becoming a member of the Church. "It's all done by the priesthood . . . I mean, that's the essence of His power, isn't it?"

"Yes, it is," Karti said quietly. She gestured toward the window. "And if He can manage and control these tremendous forces of nature, just think what He's capable of doing in the lives of His children."

"You're right," Paula agreed. "I suppose He can do just about anything He wants to. All the same, it makes you wonder . . ." Her voice trailed off as she stared pensively into the storm.

"Wonder what?" Karti asked.

Paula took a deep breath and continued. "Wonder why even all His power isn't enough sometimes. Seems like it wasn't enough to keep the *Titanic* from sinking, or to stop the riots in L.A. a few years ago, or to protect innocent children from horrible abuse, or to prevent what happened to all of those poor people in Kosovo." A lump rose in her throat. "Or to keep TJ alive."

She felt her friend's arm around her shoulders, and they moved to a sofa near the window. "Oh, He has the power, all right," Karti said. "But His plan is to give us our agency and let us find our own way—to test and try us, and all of that good stuff." She smiled solemnly and shook her head. "Seems like there ought to be an easier way than sin and death and destruction." Paula nodded in agreement.

"But all of that can build and refine our faith by requiring us to face and endure things we don't understand. I think that's why the Lord allows it to happen—so we can learn how to trust Him more completely."

Paula's eyes bored into Karti's. "Do you trust Him?" she asked.

"I do," Karti answered without wavering. "I've been through too much in my life to doubt either His presence or His love for me. For all of us."

"And do you trust Him with your life at this moment, when even a single stray cancer cell could make all the difference?"

Karti leaned back against the couch, and her sigh seemed to echo from the deepest chambers of her soul. "I've made my peace with it," she said slowly. "I honestly don't know what will happen to this poor old body of mine; after all that chemo, it feels like it's been to Auschwitz and back. Still, we've had good news from the doctor, and right now I feel like I'll probably be around to annoy everybody for many years to come—or at least a lot longer than we were first led to believe. All that, of course, is in the Lord's hands; and whatever comes, I think I can deal with it. But I do worry . . ." She paused and shook her head.

"About what?" Paula asked.

"I worry about Sam," she said.

"You mean if you . . ." Paula couldn't finish the sentence.

"That's right . . . if I cash in my chips first," Karti grinned, shaking off the seriousness of the moment. "He's a *man,* after all; what do they know about cleaning the toilet, or kitchen survival skills? I've tried to teach him, but so far he's only memorized the Pizza Hut number."

"Well," Paula laughed, "then I guess you'd better stick around to take care of him."

Karti's expression sobered ever so slightly. "That, my friend," she said without hesitation, "is exactly what I intend to do."

They sat together in silence, enjoying the storm's spectacle, for another half hour, then rejoined the family downstairs. The morning passed quickly as they played board games and watched videos— except for Andrea, who sat on the far side of the room, her nose buried in a book. Paula glanced over at her a time or two, only to find the teenager studying her with a cold, almost hostile glare. She found it a little disquieting, but chalked it up to normal adolescent behavior.

After lunch, when the storm eased up a little, Sam and the boys went out to check on the animals and plow the main walks. Paula and Karti were seated comfortably in the living room, chatting quietly, when Ruthie burst in and made a beeline for Paula. "Hey," she said, dancing from one foot to the other, "wanna make cookies? Our favorite . . . peanut butter chocolate chip." She licked her lips and grinned irresistibly. "I'll teach ya *exactly* how to make 'em." She glanced over at Karti. "Can we, Mom, huh? Can we?"

Karti shrugged. "Whatever our guest would like to do."

"Oh, goodie!" the child exclaimed, grabbing Paula's hand in both of hers and tugging her to a standing position. "C'mon—I've got everything set up in the kitchen. Let's go!"

"That's my Ruthie," Karti chuckled, watching Paula being dragged, wide-eyed, behind the ten-year-old cook. "Have fun," she called out as this unlikely pair disappeared into the hall.

On their way to the kitchen, they encountered Andrea. "Hi, Anders," Ruthie sang out. "Wanna help us make cookies? It'll be loads of fun, an' I'll let ya eat some of the batter like always."

Andrea stopped abruptly, and her icy gaze traveled quickly from Paula's feet up to her eyes. "I don't think so. I've got better things to do." Without further comment, she turned and headed up the stairs. Paula shivered involuntarily at a sudden chill in the air.

Ruthie's enthusiasm was undampened. "Never mind," she said brightly. "She's a real snot sometimes." Paula had to laugh when her young friend huffed dramatically. "We can do it ourselves," Ruthie declared. "She'll change her mind when she smells 'em baking."

A few hours later, the whole family—including Andrea, who was still grumpy but willing to be fed—gathered around the big-screen TV downstairs for a light supper of potato-cheese soup served in the biggest mugs Paula had ever seen, and accompanied by crusty wheat rolls, homemade apple cider, and Ruthie's fresh-baked cookies for dessert. A roaring blaze in the fireplace seemed the perfect backdrop for an evening of home videos. "Kind of like a combination 'This Is Your Life, Mark Richland' and 'This Is Your Son, Paula Donroe,'" Karti explained. Mark groaned good-naturedly and Paula smiled meekly, not entirely sure what to expect. But by the end of the evening, having viewed Mark in everything from his birthday suit to his Little League uniform to his brand-new missionary togs, she felt a connection to this young man—and to his family—that moved and warmed her in ways she had never experienced. "Thank you," she said simply when the last image had flickered across the screen.

Karti pressed the "eject" button and gathered the video, together with several others they had watched, into her hands. She moved wearily, but her eyes sparkled as she shuffled over to Paula and held the tapes out to her. "For you," she said. "We had them all copied."

A lump the size of Connecticut rose instantly in Paula's throat. She couldn't speak, but the gratitude in her brimming eyes said it all as she clutched the tapes to her chest.

Behind her, a sudden snort cut through the peaceful air. She turned a little to her left just in time to see Andrea, her face a mask of irritation, move quickly up the stairs and out of sight. Paula shot a questioning glance toward Karti, who shrugged. "A little teenage cabin fever, I guess," she said. "I'll talk to her in the morning."

Paula nodded, then the shadow of an idea rose in her eyes. "Would you mind if I . . . looked in on her?" she asked.

"Not at all," Karti replied. "She's really a very nice young lady when the mood suits her. When is your flight in the morning?"

"Eleven," Paula said. "I really need to get a few things done before Monday—get my life organized, you know."

"Of course," Karti smiled. "At least that will give us time for a leisurely breakfast, then Mark can run you to the airport. I'll say good night, then." Almost instantly, Sam appeared at her side. He curled an arm securely around her shoulders as they made their way upstairs.

Paula stretched her arms above her head and looked fondly at Mark, Alex, Jake, and Ruthie, who were finishing up the last of the cookies. "This has been a scrumptious day," she said. "I hope you guys weren't too bored by all the videos and stuff; you'd probably rather have been outdoors on your snowmobiles."

"Naw," Mark said. "It's not often we get to spend time with . . ." He grinned, and the dimples on either side of his mouth deepened. "Long-lost relatives."

"Especially drop-dead gorgeous ones," Alex added, and Jake

nodded his agreement. They seemed to enjoy watching Paula's cheeks light up like red Christmas bulbs.

"And the bestest was making these," Ruthie said, waving the sole surviving cookie in the air with a flourish before popping it into her mouth. "When you come again, we'll make a bunch more."

"It's a deal," Paula laughed. "Now, if you'll excuse me, I think I'll call it a night. She hugged each of them warmly, then headed upstairs.

Three doors down from the guest room, she paused in front of a large, hand-painted sign that read "Andrea's Place—Stay Out!" She couldn't help smiling at the warning. *Hmm. Shades of Scotty—always wants his own space,* she thought, and suddenly felt a gentle, unexpected tug at her heart. *I really do miss him . . . hope he's there when I get home.* Then her focus returned to the mumpish teenager on the other side of this door, and she wondered if she dared intrude. Finally, she took a deep breath and knocked. No answer. She knocked again.

"Aw, Mom," a whiny voice called through the door, "Can't it wait till tomorrow? I'm busy, ya know?"

Paula put a smile in her voice as she replied, "Actually, Andrea, it's not your mom. It's me . . . Paula."

Dead silence.

"Andrea? Can we talk? I'm leaving in the morning, and I didn't want to go without . . ." Her voice faded as she listened for a response. There was none.

"I know you're in there, Andrea. Please, I just wanted to ask you something. Please?" Her own voice seemed to mock her in the soundless hall, and Andrea wasn't about to make things any easier. Finally, after a minute or two of profound silence, Paula sighed and turned away. It wasn't worth the effort; after all, she hardly knew anything about this girl—and she didn't much like what she *did* know.

A soft click behind her was followed by a petulant "Yeah?" She spun around to see Andrea eyeing her through a narrow opening. As Paula approached, the door opened a little farther.

"Hey," Paula said, putting on her cheeriest countenance, "are you up for a little company?"

Without speaking, Andrea shrugged and swung the door wide, motioning for her to enter. "Thanks," Paula said, a muscle in her cheek twitching nervously. "I didn't know if you'd already gone to bed, or—"

"You wanted to ask me something?" Andrea broke in tersely. She sat cross-legged on her queen-size bed and stared passively at Paula, who remained standing.

"Well, yes, I did—sort of. I guess I just don't know quite how to—"

"I'm listening." Andrea folded her arms across her chest, lifted her chin a little, and stared directly into Paula's eyes.

"Okay." Paula inhaled deeply, let out a long breath, and moved a bit closer to the bed. "I've noticed how you've looked at me and spoken to me these past couple of days, and it's obvious that you don't like me very much." Andrea's gaze dropped to the coral bedspread. "Could I ask why?"

"You could ask, but I'd think it'd be obvious," Andrea said, her voice edged with disdain.

Paula responded in measured tones. "Well, I'm afraid it's not all that obvious to me. Have I said or done something to offend you, or—"

"Oh, you did that a *long time ago*," Andrea shot back, her dark eyes glinting with anger.

"Excuse me?" Paula said, her brows knitting together in puzzlement. "We've known each other for what, two days? Could you help me out a little here?" Paula was curious, bordering on frustrated. *Stay calm,* she told herself. *Maybe for a teenager, two days is a long time.*

Andrea leaned back on her elbows and stretched her legs out in front of her. When she spoke, the words fell from her tongue like tiny, lethal drops of cyanide. "Well, let me spell it out for you." She paused just long enough to make Paula squirm a little. "First of all, I've got this flick, like, running around in my head, ya know? The star is this wimpy teenager, maybe a year older than me, who has a baby boy and then gives him away. *Gives him away.* I don't see how *anyone* could give a baby away . . . not in a million years." She shook her head in disgust. "Do *you* know of anyone who might do a rotten thing like that?"

Paula was beginning to get the picture. A painful knot of emotion formed in her throat, but she said nothing.

"And second of all, the story picks up when she meets her son again after more than twenty years—after he's all grown up and happy and stuff. So then she figures she can just take a little trip to see his family—his *real* family—and try to get him back again." She glared at Paula. "Isn't that what she wants to do—get him back again?" Her gaze hardened still further. "To make up for the one who died?"

The color drained from Paula's face as she listened to Andrea's accusing words. *So that's it . . . she blames me. For everything.* She held her breath in the electric silence that followed, clenching and unclenching her fists at her sides. She wanted to be enraged at the audacity of this child's biting insinuations, to scream at her that she couldn't *possibly* know what she was talking about, to slap her or shake her or strangle her into taking it all back. But a sudden rush of tears blinded her, and the searing gnarl of pain in her throat cut off any sound. At the same moment the muscles in her legs turned to rubber, and she sank into a chair near the bed, burying her face in her hands.

Long moments later, she felt a tentative touch on her shoulder. "Uh, Paula, are you . . . okay?" Andrea's voice sounded more human—no, make that more *humane*—than at any time during their brief, imperfect relationship. Was it a trick? Paula didn't care; she'd take whatever crumbs of compassion this unusual teenager was willing to offer.

"I—I'm sorry," Paula mumbled, using her hands to wipe at her eyes. "I didn't expect anything like this. It's just that what you said . . ." Fresh tears erupted and cascaded down her flushed cheeks.

"Here. You could probably use some of these." Paula looked up to find Andrea kneeling in front of her, a box of tissues in one hand. "Your makeup is, like, a mess." Her voice was softer now, almost apologetic.

"Thanks," Paula sniffed, and made good use of the tissues. When she was somewhat composed, she looked at Andrea with pain-filled eyes. "Please," she breathed, "don't think I've come to steal Mark away. I never, *ever* wanted to do that. I love him, of course, and to find him after all these years—well, it's been phenomenal. But he's *your* family, Andrea, not mine. I know it's hard to understand, but I gave him up because I wanted a better life for him than what I could manage. And I couldn't have found a better place for him if I'd picked it myself. He's your brother . . . forever."

"I love him," Andrea said, her voice quavering.

"We both do," Paula said, wiping at a stray tear. "That's the wonderful thing about love—there's always enough to go around. Especially in families like yours. I've learned a lot about love since I've been here." She paused. "I'm just sorry you've been so . . . upset. Maybe someday you'll understand . . . well, why I did what I did." A ragged sigh escaped her throat.

"I think I do understand a little better now," Andrea said. Their eyes met, but this time without rancor. "You really did care about that little baby, didn't you?" Paula nodded earnestly. "I believe you. I can see it in your eyes. And you're not really trying to break up our family, are you?" Paula shook her head so hard her vision blurred. "I believe that, too." Andrea bit her lip and bowed her head, then looked up with brimming eyes. "I'm sorry, Paula; I was a dweeb. It's just that . . . with my mom being so sick and all, wondering if I might lose her, I couldn't stand to think of losing Mark, too." Tears rolled down her cheeks. "He means everything to me, you know?"

Paula reached out and pulled her into a warm embrace. "I know," she whispered, stroking Andrea's smooth chestnut hair. "I know."

By Sunday morning, the storm was over and the sun shone brilliantly on the pristine drifts that had piled up overnight. Following a cozy breakfast of French toast, scrambled eggs, and creamy hot chocolate, Paula stood at the front door, ready to take her leave of the Richlands. No doubt about it: this weekend had been an unforgettable island of time during which she had soaked up enough love, laughter, and peanut butter chocolate chip cookies to bolster her spirits for a long time to come. And as she hugged each member of the family, she told them so.

Finally, she and Karti stood face to face in the entryway. There were no words deep or eloquent enough to express their feelings, so they dispensed with the formalities and simply wrapped their arms around each other for a long, silent leave-taking. "Come again—soon," Karti said close to her new friend's ear.

"I will," Paula replied, her emotions barely in check as they pulled apart. "Soon. Take care of yourself, will you?"

"As if my life depended on it," Karti smiled, and the affection in her eyes sealed the promise.

A few minutes later, Paula leaned back in her seat as Mark guided the Suburban's studded snow tires resolutely along the freshly plowed road leading to the interstate and the airport. "This is beautiful country, even in the dead of winter," she said.

"Keep reminding me of that," Mark laughed. "After four months of white-knuckle driving, I'm more than ready to break out the old John Deere and enjoy the sweet smell of new-mown grass." He paused. "But yes, it is beautiful, any time of the year. I've had a great life." He looked over at Paula and grinned broadly. "They're a pretty terrific family, aren't they?"

"The best," she agreed. "Really fabulous. I had a wonderful time."

"I knew you would. We're all looking forward to your next visit."

"Me, too." She twisted in her seat to look behind them as the Richland property disappeared behind the large stand of trees separating it from the highway.

They rode in silence for several miles while Paula chewed her lower lip nervously. There was something important she had to ask, but she couldn't quite find the words. At length, she tossed aside any sense of decorum and reached across to put her hand on Mark's shoulder. "Can I ask you something?" she said. "Something kind of personal?"

"You bet," he answered cheerfully. "You're family now, after all. Shoot." He laughed. "Just a figure of speech."

"Right," she said, chuckling at his good humor. "Thanks." She waited for a long moment, then continued with carefully chosen words. "It's about Karti. She's an extraordinary woman, isn't she?"

"No argument there," Mark conceded. His voice took on a somber note as he added, "But that's not what you wanted to ask about, is it?"

"No." Paula forced her lips to form the question. "Is she all right, Mark? Is she really going to beat this cancer?" There; she'd said it. Now all she could do was hold her breath and wait for the inevitable. Wait for the awkward clearing of his throat, then listen to his tense declaration of faith and hope, complete with a brave smile that couldn't quite mask the despair in his eyes. Wait for the reality to come crashing down around her heart. It was the last thing in the world she wanted to know; but Karti was a part of her life now, and she had no choice but to deal with the truth and whatever sad, painful consequences it might bring. She straightened her back and steeled herself for the news.

"Actually, yes. I believe she's going to beat it. No one can say for sure; but if anybody can come through this thing with her health intact, not to mention her hair, it's Mom."

Paula stared at him incredulously. He seemed calm and at ease with his declaration—utterly sure of himself, in fact. Not at all nervous or waffling. "You're quite certain?" she asked. "I mean, when I talked with you in January, you felt like the chemo was only buying her a little time." *Please tell me you've prayed about it,* she pled silently, *and the Lord told you everything would be all right.*

"Well," he said, "I've prayed about it. And that, together with the doctor's very positive report last week, leads me to believe that everything will be all right."

She chuckled softly, then a little louder. "What's so funny?" he asked.

"Nothing," she smiled. "I'm just relieved, that's all. Your mother and I have become fast friends, you know, and I'd like to plan on keeping our relationship going for a good, long time."

"Like—for eternity?" Mark suggested as he turned into the airport drive.

"Quite possibly," she replied. "Or at least until I've heard all of her stories from your childhood."

"That would be roughly the same thing—eternity," Mark grinned. "You'll come again, won't you?"

"You couldn't keep me away," she said. "I know a good source of peanut butter chocolate chip cookies when I see one."

"Jake's missionary farewell will be sometime this summer. Maybe you could join us for that." Mark looked at her expectantly.

"I'd love to; sounds like a wonderful plan."

"And you could bring Scott, too. Let him see what it's like to be going on a mission. You never know; someday he might—"

"Whoa!" Paula sputtered. "Right now, I'll be ecstatic if I can just talk him out of getting his belly button pierced. But you're right; it would definitely be a good experience for him to see an honest-to-goodness Mormon family in action. If he hasn't burned the house down or run away from home by then, I'll bring him along."

Passengers were already boarding by the time they arrived at the gate. Paula smiled as she reached out to grasp Mark's hand. "You're a son any mother would be proud of, you know that?" she said. "And if there's ever any doubt in your mind, just go ask your mother. Then go ask the other one."

"Double jeopardy, eh?" He reached down to gather her into his arms for a warm embrace. "Thanks for coming, Paula," he said. "It's done us all a lot of good." He stepped back and put his hands lightly on her shoulders. "Don't be a stranger."

"Not a chance," she vowed, her eyes shining. "I'll call as soon as I get home." She kissed the tips of her fingers and laid them gently against his cheek for a moment, then turned and made her way quickly through the gate's open door.

As the plane sliced through a thin cloud cover and leveled off, Paula closed her eyes and replayed, in minute detail, every moment of the weekend. Now that she had met and bonded with this extraordinary family—even with Andrea, who overnight had blossomed into something of a Donroe groupie—she couldn't help wondering how their lives would intertwine in the months and years ahead. It was all so unusual, this singular connection between two mothers and a son that had brought them together. How would it really play out in the long run? Her life, it seemed, was taking on some new and intriguing dimensions. And she could hardly wait to discover the possibilities.

CHAPTER 12

As days slipped into weeks, Paula's life seemed to take on a new rhythm and buoyancy, as though her long weekend in Idaho had somehow smoothed her rough edges a little, redefined her fledgling faith, even bolstered her confidence in the future. Frequent conversations with Karti and other members of the Richland family added a sweetness to her days that came close to compensating for Scott's distant behavior; and a weekly package of peanut butter chocolate chip cookies, lovingly wrapped in several layers of aluminum foil and addressed to "Sister Paula," sent pulses of contentment fluttering up her spine.

Even her "chat quotient" improved as she and Meg O'Brien put their own unique spin on the concept of visiting teaching. "Okay," Meg said one Friday evening as they collected several baskets of Sylvie Randolph's laundry in the wake of a major appliance failure, "so we modify the terms a little. This week, we're her visiting *bleachers.*"

Paula rolled her eyes, but the warmth in her heart was genuine. What she hadn't expected was the lump that rose in her throat as they sorted the laundry before washing it. "This is unbelievable," she murmured, fingering the children's threadbare clothing and worn underwear. "You can almost see right through their little socks and panties."

"Sylvie's things aren't any better," Meg reported, holding up a few items. "Her temple garments have seen way better days, and these jeans . . . well, the holes might be a fashion statement for the rich and famous, but I suspect she'd rather do without them."

Paula put a small undershirt back into the basket. "You know," she said slowly, "I'm thinking what a doggone *shame* it would be if some of this ratty stuff somehow got lost or misplaced—maybe gobbled up by a hungry washer or something—and ended up being, shall we say, 'recycled' into a new generation of wearing apparel." She looked squarely at Meg. "What do you think?"

"I think," her partner beamed, "you're really starting to get the hang of this visiting teaching gig. I know a cozy little factory outlet mall a few miles from here; they have great kids' stuff, and not a bad selection of grownups' things—all at bargain prices. They're open late, too."

Paula grinned. "Then what, my fair accomplice in crime, are we waiting for? Let's take the Taurus; it'll hold more."

Three hours later, they had replaced every piece of bedraggled underwear, every mateless sock, every lifeless hair ribbon with the most cheerful and appealing new items they could find, including three sets of matching mom-and-kid Levi's, tennis shoes, and T-shirts. Finally, they purchased a small stuffed animal for each of the girls and an inexpensive but stylish dress for Sylvie to replace the faded, shabby skirt and blouse at the bottom of her laundry basket. Paula insisted on footing the bill, ignoring Meg's protests.

"Well, okay," Meg relented at last, "but I get to put the frosting on the cake. And you have to promise you'll let me."

Paula gave her a puzzled look. "But I thought we'd already gotten everything we could think—"

"Almost everything." Meg's striking blue eyes were alive with anticipation. "She desperately needs new garments; and we could pick them up at the distribution center in the morning, and still be at Sylvie's before noon. Let me do this, Paula—just a few pairs will give her a whole new lease on life. There's absolutely nothing like the feel of that precious new fabric against your skin. Someday, you'll know what I mean. I'd like to do this part. Please."

Her earnestness moved Paula almost to tears. "Of course," she said, smiling at her friend. "That would be lovely."

They delivered Sylvie's laundry the next morning, having placed some of the old clothes on top of each basket to conceal the new items. When four-year-old Emmeline scampered into the living room and discovered the baskets on the floor, she hurried to the one nearest her. "Oh, goodie," she said, "I need my pretty red ribbons." She began rummaging through the basket, but she soon stopped and gave her mother a puzzled frown. "These aren't our things, Mommy," she said. "They're . . . brand-new!"

Sylvie cast a sideways glance at her visiting teachers, who shrugged innocently. Then she knelt beside the baskets, and for a few minutes there was silence in the room as she examined their contents. When she finally raised her head and turned toward Meg and Paula, bright tears streaked her face. She held a small pink package of garments close to her chest. "How did you . . . why . . . when . . . ?" Her questions were lost in the excited chatter of two little girls exclaiming over their new treasures.

"Terrible mixup at the laundromat," Paula explained with a straight face. "We may never get it figured out. In the meantime—"

Sylvie cut her off with a crushing hug, then did the same to Meg. "My angels," she whispered. "My visiting angels."

Later, in the car, Meg glanced over at Paula. "It's a good thing I'm driving," she observed.

"I know," Paula sniffed. "I was doing pretty well until she called us angels. I've never been called an angel before." She dabbed at her eyes with a tissue.

"Well, get used to it," Meg declared. "I see a great future for you in the fairy godmother department. Doing that for Sylvie and her little ones— that was a brilliant idea. Pure inspiration."

Paula's heart swelled with joy. *Thank You, Father,* she offered in silent gratitude.

In addition to her growing affinity for service, she had never been more focused or productive at the office. She was deluged with ideas for the new Green Pointe account, and she couldn't remember when she'd ever had such fun working on a project. Cloistered together for hours at a time in the conference room, she and Ted bounced around ideas, came up with outrageous slogans, brainstormed through a string of late-night pizza dinners, laughed at old jokes, even made up little songs and sang them to each other when they needed a catchy lyric or two. Once they put on a CD of old Elvis Presley tunes and danced around the conference table— "to get our creative juices flowing," Ted explained. It worked—although Ted seemed to feel the need to hold Paula in his arms for quite a long time before the inspiration flowed. "Just making sure the ideas are pure gold," he said, dipping her almost to the floor during the final stanza of "Fools Rush In." When they finally got back to the table, he fixed his vivid blue eyes on her and smiled. "Yep, pure gold."

Inside of three weeks, after adding art and multimedia support, they had put together enough of their campaign to make a preview presentation to the Green Pointe management team. It went so well that Cal Brady, who clearly relished his role as CEO and top decision-maker, actually doubled his original offer for their services. As Paula and Ted stared at him wide-eyed, his green eyes sparkled and he broke into a boyish grin. "You can just hitch those jaws back up now and start smiling like the rest of us," he kidded. "If this campaign is anywhere near as good as I think it's going to be, it'll be well worth the investment." He stood and shook their hands warmly. "Let's meet again in, say, a month, and we'll finalize everything in writing. Deal?"

"Deal," Paula croaked, still staring. Then she caught Ted's eye across the table, and his expression said it all. *We have ARRIVED, boss. We're at the TOP.* He gave her a subtle thumbs-up signal as she escorted the Green Pointe executives from the room.

Minutes later, having taken leave of Brady and his colleagues, Paula hurried back to the conference room. Ted was standing close to the window, his back to the door, his shoulders hunched slightly as he contemplated the hazy early-evening sky. Her eyes rested for a moment on the cut of his tailored suit and the unique way it hung from his broad, rangy shoulders. She smirked a little as a thought occurred to her. *This guy's so happy, even his shoulder blades are smiling. I know exactly how he feels.*

She moved wordlessly across the room until she was standing directly behind him, close enough to catch the musky scent of his cologne. Then she spoke in her deepest, most alluring tone. "Well, now, Mr. Barstow . . . are we great, or what?"

Ted's back straightened almost imperceptibly as he turned slowly, deliberately, to face her. His vivid blue eyes were glowing with animation as he struggled to maintain a serious expression. "Why, yes, Ms. Donroe, I believe we are. Great, that is." A second later his entire face erupted into a buoyant grin as he added, "No 'whats' about it." He spread his arms, and she came into them without hesitation. His lips brushed the top of her head, and he whispered something she didn't quite hear. But no matter; this moment of celebration was already perfect.

Her arms curled around his waist, and she gave him a warm squeeze before pulling back a little to look up into his face. "I can't believe it," she said in a half-whisper. "I mean, we've worked and hoped for something like this for years, but I never thought . . . well, it's a dream come—"

The words evaporated as she felt his mouth on hers—a light, feathery brush of the lips that lasted only an instant and was over before she could even think about responding. She giggled self-consciously and pressed her hands against his chest in mock annoyance. "Anything for a cheap thrill, huh?"

Ted stepped back quickly and raised both hands into the air. "Hey, give a guy a little success, a pretty girl, and . . . well, you never know."

Paula laughed, and the tension between them drained away. Nothing could spoil the joy, the absolute euphoria of this moment.

Ted checked his watch. "Hey, it's past closing time. What say we head out for a little celebratory dinner? I know this hole-in-the-wall Italian place over on Figueroa Street where the cannelloni is so good that it's been known to bring people to tears. And for a price," he winked at her, "they'll even turn wine into water."

"Oooh, you're bad!" she said, punching him playfully on the arm. "It sounds wonderful."

They ate and laughed and talked far into the evening, riding a wave of elation and optimism that could barely be contained. The prosperous future of Donroe & Associates now seemed to be assured, and Paula was ecstatic. Over dessert, she reached across the small table and squeezed Ted's hand. "It wouldn't have been possible without you, my friend." Her eyes shone with admiration. "How can I ever thank you?"

Instead of answering, he lifted her hand to his lips, turned it gently, and pressed a lingering kiss to her palm. Then he raised his eyes to meet hers, which had misted over a little. "That look on your face is thanks enough," he smiled. Releasing her hand, he leaned back in his chair. "Well," he added, "almost enough."

She regarded him quizzically. "Almost?"

Ted closed his eyes and nodded, then cleared his throat and took a long, deep breath, as though gearing up for something important. When he opened his eyes, their sudden dark intensity caught Paula's attention. "Yes, well, I guess I've just got something to say." He swallowed hard.

"I'm listening." Paula leaned forward, and the cheap, half-burned candle, stuck carelessly into a dark green wine bottle between them, seemed to flame in her dark eyes.

A small, sheepish grin played across his lips. "Gee, I really didn't mean to say anything yet, especially tonight, after all the great stuff that's happened. Wouldn't want to take away from the moment, for you or anybody. But I . . . I . . ." His voice trailed off, and he reached up to loosen his tie. "Uh, maybe it can wait."

"Not a chance, buddy," she said good-naturedly, folding her slender arms in front of her on the table and fixing her eyes firmly on his face. "You know how crazy I get when my curiosity is piqued. It absolutely can't wait." She paused, eyeing him expectantly.

He sighed deeply. "Okay. It's just that I've been thinking about things lately—well, actually for a long time now—and my feelings are getting harder and harder to ignore." He stared into the air above her head for long moments, then focused for a few seconds on his slightly sweaty hands, then adjusted his gaze to meet hers. When the silence became excruciating, he finally found his voice again. "What I'm trying to say, Paula, is that I can't do this anymore. We've been through a lot together— we've plowed in and done some incredibly hard work, and we've had some really great times. Like tonight." He smiled warmly and glanced around at their cozy surroundings. "And we've built a terrific friendship."

"A dynamite friendship," she interjected with obvious feeling.

"I know. But somehow, it just isn't enough." He took another deep breath as his eyes burned into hers. "I want more, Paula. A lot more."

Time seemed to stop along with Ted's breathing, and their gaze remained locked for an infinity of moments. Finally, Paula lowered her eyes and began to trace one perfectly manicured finger around the rim of her half-empty water glass. When she spoke, it was in a soft, agreeable tone. "I understand completely." A winsome smile rose from her lips to her eyes. "And I think it's high time we did something about it."

"You do? Really?" Ted gulped audibly, then reached up to wipe a few beads of perspiration from his forehead.

"Absolutely. In fact, I'm sure I would have brought it up myself if you hadn't. Maybe not tonight, but very soon." Her smile was even wider, brighter now.

He thought his heart would burst from his chest, but he managed to appear outwardly calm. "Wow. I mean, I never thought it would be this easy."

Paula laughed endearingly. "And why not? This should have happened a long time ago. But things just weren't . . . in place, so to speak."

She lifted her glass for a long, slow drink, and Ted watched the rhythmic movements of her throat as she swallowed. "So, uh . . . where do we go from here?" he asked with no breath to spare.

Lowering the glass, she looked at him with perfect sincerity. "I'll see to it first thing in the morning."

He stared at her for a moment. "What do you mean, first thing in the morning?"

"Well, silly," she chuckled, "we can't very well do anything about it tonight, can we?" He was still staring at her without comprehension, so she continued. "I mean, Carmine will have to get the ball rolling." She picked up a bread stick left over from dinner and began to nibble on it.

"What in the world," he murmured, "does Carmine have to do with this?"

"Ted," she replied, a tiny hint of condescension edging her voice, "I'm sure you understand that in an arrangement like this, there are certain . . . formalities. I just need to check with Carmine on the procedure. She runs the office, after all. In the meantime, we can talk specifics." Laying aside the bread stick, she began rummaging in her purse while he watched her incredulously. "Oh, here's something we can use," she said, pulling out a small leather appointment book with a silver pen fitted snugly inside. She opened the book to a blank page and wrote something on it, then tore it out and handed it across the table to him. "How does that look?"

His gaze took in a string of six figures, but his numb brain didn't compute its meaning, so he had to ask. "What is this?"

"Your new salary, of course," Paula beamed. "As I said, it should have happened a long time ago. I'm just glad you asked. It's about time you got more . . . a lot more."

Ted's hand began shaking, and the paper fluttered in his grasp. "Is this what you thought? I don't believe it," he moaned, raking the fingers of his free hand through his short blonde hair.

A look of mild disappointment washed over Paula's countenance. "Gee, Ted, I thought it was a pretty decent raise—almost twice what you've been making. But if you want more, I think we could—"

"No, no; it's not that," he broke in. "This is more than enough— certainly more than I ever expected. It's just that I . . . I thought . . ." He waited for a moment as a hollow flicker of understanding and resignation seemed to settle in his eyes. "Nothing. This is great, Paula. Really wonderful. And so generous. Thank you." His shoulders hunched slightly as he forced his lips into a grateful smile and reached across the table to squeeze her arm. "Thank you so much."

She rested her hand lightly on his. "No problem. You've helped to make it all happen, you know. Donroe & Associates would be exactly nowhere without your creative gifts. And personally, I can't imagine what I would have done without you." She raised her glass. "To friendship—and success."

Ted followed her cue, and the not-quite-crystal clink of the goblets toasted their future. "To friendship—and success," he repeated. But when the glass touched his lips, he couldn't quite bring himself to swallow.

Paula returned the appointment book to her purse and checked her watch. "Good grief! It's one A.M., and I have a seven-thirty meeting with the top brass at Northridge. What say we wrap up this celebration and call it a night?" She pushed back her chair and motioned to a nearby waiter. "Check, please."

Ted pulled himself out of his glum reverie long enough to object. "Hey, boss, let me get it, okay? I'm newly enhanced financially, after all." He flashed her a genuine smile, and his blue eyes sparkled in the dim candlelight.

"Well, okay," she agreed. "But I'll get the tip."

"Fair enough."

While he settled, Paula waited at the front door of the tiny restaurant. He drove her back to the office garage, where he parked beside her glitzy red Jaguar convertible and watched her slip elegantly into its deep leather driver's seat. "All set?" he asked as he heard the soft click of her seat belt.

"All set." She looked over at him, her eyes filled with contentment and affection. "Thanks, Ted . . . for everything."

"You bet. Drive safely. I'll follow you out." He quickly shifted the Cherokee into drive, then glanced at her one more time. "It was great. See you tomorrow."

She waved as they went opposite directions at the garage exit. Ted lifted his arm to return the gesture, but it seemed too heavy at the moment, and he felt it fall back to the steering wheel.

When Paula pulled into the broad cement driveway of her home less than half an hour later, the sweet, alluring scent of blooming lilacs prompted her to stop the car just short of the garage. "When was the last time I took a minute to enjoy something like this?" she wondered aloud, her voice barely a whisper. She leaned back against the cushioned headrest and filled her lungs with the fragrance, then closed her eyes and exhaled ever so slowly into the mild night air. After several inhalations she smiled, feeling deep relaxation and tranquility spreading through her body. "Life is good," she breathed. "So very, very good." Later, in the cool stillness of her room, she knelt for a silent moment of thanksgiving. Nothing, she felt, could be better than this moment in time.

The next week passed rapidly. Paula was riding high on the Green Pointe success, and she cheerfully arranged for Ted's substantial salary increase. He politely thanked her by e-mail, but his days were spent behind a closed office door. Paula kept her distance, allowing him whatever time he needed to catch up on his other projects. *It's the least I can do,* she thought. *We'll get back to Green Pointe when he's ready. I just hope it won't be too long; Cal Brady is anxious to see the final product.* She couldn't help smiling, then gently chastised herself. *Hey, you're the boss here, Donroe; you decide when we get back to it. Okay, then . . . next week. For sure.* She made a note on her calendar.

She needn't have worried. First thing Monday morning, she glanced up from her paperwork to see Ted leaning casually against the oak frame of her open office door. He looked fit and rested, and his easy smile told her he was in a decent mood. "Well," she said affably, "it's nice to see you again. I was beginning to wonder if you'd given up the ghost behind that office door of yours."

His blue eyes deepened as his lips pressed together for a fraction of a second, but the engaging smile returned almost as quickly as it had faded. He shrugged. "Sorry. I had some things to . . . sort out. And a whole lot of work to do."

"I know," Paula said, "but I'm sure you're on top of it by now. Anything I should know about?"

"Not really," he replied slowly, his eyes moving to the panoramic window behind her. The late spring sun was making a rare appearance between patches of dense smog. "Nice day. Clearer than most."

"And it was a good weekend," Paula added. "Yesterday after church, Millie and I spent most of the afternoon out on the patio, just relaxing. It was lovely. Scotty even joined us later."

Ted shifted from one foot to the other. "How's he doing?"

"Good. He seems less hostile these days, and we actually had a rather pleasant conversation. I'm hoping maybe those few Sundays he went to sacrament meeting had a tiny bit of influence, after all. He asked a couple of questions about the Church."

"That's great. Terrific." Ted cleared his throat, then shifted gears. "Hey, shouldn't we be getting busy on the Green Pointe campaign again pretty soon? The way I figure it, we'll need to have a final presentation within the next couple of weeks. What do you think?" His voice sounded hesitant but hopeful.

Paula's eyes lit up. "Wal, I thought y'all would nevah ask!" she said with an exaggerated drawl. "But I've gotta hand it to you, Ted—your timing's perfect. I'm even more excited about this project than ever; I've just been waiting for you to say the word. How's your schedule this week?"

"Clear as a day at the beach," he grinned, her enthusiasm re-igniting his eagerness to get back to work. He could put aside any personal baggage long enough to enjoy the professional challenge. After that—who knew? "What say we get started this afternoon?"

"Perfect. The conference room, one-thirty." She flashed him a broad smile.

"Deal. Ready to go, boss." He winked and saluted smartly, then turned and marched down the hall to his office, where he settled himself behind his desk. The flick of a switch brought his computer to life. "Let the games begin," he murmured.

For the next day and a half, their energy never flagged as they created, polished, reworked, clarified, and perfected the ad campaign until it seemed virtually flawless. It was intense, exacting work, and by early Tuesday evening they felt exhaustion beginning to take its toll on their mental sharpness. But they were *so close* . . .

"We're killing ourselves, you know?" Paula said, pressing her fingers to her throbbing temples. Ted nodded as he watched her stand and stretch near the window, her trim profile silhouetted against the red-orange sky. "I think we've got the project pretty well tied down, don't you?"

"Just a few final touches, and it should be ready for the Brady bunch," he agreed. "I'm not totally sure about that last ad concept, though."

She leaned against the narrow window sill. "I know what you mean. But it's pretty much hopeless to squeeze any more blood out of these two turnips"—she pointed to their heads—"tonight. We're ahead of schedule;

let's let it rest for couple of days, shall we? Then we can come back to it fresh and finish it in another day or so. Maybe plan to tie it up the first of next week."

"Amen," Ted agreed, running his fingers along the smooth edge of the table. "This has been great, but I'm tuckered. Next week is fine." He rubbed the back of his neck.

"Here, let me help. It's the least I can do, after all your incredible work." She moved quickly behind his chair and began a deep, rhythmic massage of the tops of his shoulders. Her fingers deftly kneaded his muscles for a few seconds, and he closed his eyes and moaned softly. "Better?"

"Much," he murmured. "But I . . ." He glanced at his watch, and his eyes registered alarm. "Uh-oh, I *really* need to get going." He quickly shrugged her hands from his shoulders and stood, looking down into her dark, puzzled eyes.

"Well, okay," she smiled. "But I've never known you to pass up one of my free massages."

"And I certainly never thought I'd . . ." A tight little chuckle escaped his throat. "The thing is, I promised to meet some kids at the church by eight. The ward basketball coach is laid up with the flu, and he asked if I'd fill in for him at practice tonight. Big game next week." He hurriedly gathered up a sheaf of papers scattered across the table.

She stared at him, wide-eyed. "You're hanging out with Church kids now?"

He grinned disarmingly. "Hey, it's only basketball. Nothing too doctrinal—although I could probably learn a thing or two from those guys. They're great young men . . . they remind me a little of your Elder Richland, only a few years younger. I'll see you tomorrow, chief. Go home and get some rest."

"On my way. Have a good practice," Paula said, still in a state of mild disbelief as she watched him disappear into the hall. She stayed half an hour longer to finish up some correspondence, then took a leisurely route home, bypassing the interstate to drive instead through a dozen quiet neighborhoods. She was satisfied to slow down for the moment—content with letting the Green Pointe project rest for a few days. Tying up all the loose ends next week would be the best part.

❤ ❤ ❤

Thursday morning, Paula was awakened by the slamming of Scott's bedroom door, followed by footsteps down the long hall. She glanced at the small crystal clock on her bedside table—seven-thirty A.M. She was usually at the office by now, but had given herself permission to sleep in this morning after a late-night meeting with her tax attorney. Now she was glad of it. *It's been weeks—maybe months—since I've had breakfast with Scotty*, she mused. *I'll just trundle on down there and share a few friendly Froot Loops with my son. It'll be great.* She sprang from bed and quickly wrapped herself in a long cotton robe, then shuffled into her terry slippers and hurried downstairs.

"Good morning," she said brightly, then bit her lip as she watched Scott lift an oversized cereal bowl to his lips and loudly gulp down several swallows of milk. *Don't be annoyed, Donroe. He's a teenager, remember. Manners come later—after law school or something. Be nice.* "You look great today, Scotty." And she meant it. Aside from his milk mustache, he was downright presentable in a pair of tan Dockers and a green T-shirt that was only three or four sizes too big. *He'll grow into it.* She smiled benevolently in his direction while Millie hurriedly set out a place mat and poured her a glass of orange juice. Sitting down at the table, she felt Rudy's wide body against her leg.

"Hey, Mom." Scott reached for a piece of toast and slathered it with strawberry preserves. "I thought you were already outta here." He unhinged his jaw and bit off half the toast.

"Not quite. I decided to be a lady of leisure today." He shrugged and inhaled the rest of the toast. "So, what's going on? School's out in a week or so; you must be gearing up for finals."

"Next week," Scott replied. "No biggie."

"I hope that means you're expecting to ace every one of them," Paula said.

He smirked. "You worry too much, Mom."

"Of course I do," she replied cheerfully. "That's my job."

"Uh-huh," he grunted.

"And as long as we're having this little chat," she added, keeping her tone light, "have you got any plans for the summer? I mean, you might want to think about retaking that algebra class, or—"

"Sheesh, what are you—a walking ad for cruel and unusual punishment?" He shook his head peevishly. "I've already got it covered."

"Oh? And how is that?"

"I'm gettin' a job." He leaned back in his chair and gave her a self-satisfied grin.

Paula didn't know quite how to react, so she played the middle road. "I see. And what sort of employment did you have in mind?" *Computer programming, perhaps?*

"Twinkie's dad needs some muscle in his sporting goods store, an' since I'm so *buff,*" he raised his arm and flexed an impressive bicep, "he said I could help out. Six hours a day, Monday through Saturday. Cool, huh?"

"Well, I must say I'm impressed," Paula said. *It could be worse . . . he could be wearing a little paper hat and tossing fries.* "You could learn a lot this summer."

"Yeah—not to mention the money. I'm plannin' to have enough by September to get me an awesome set of wheels." His eyes were gleaming.

Oboy. I should've seen it coming. "Well, we'll talk about that when—"

"Aw, geez!" Scott had just glanced at the kitchen clock. "I'm gonna miss the bus again!" His long body exploded out of the chair, and he sprinted for the door. Seconds later, they saw him loping across the front lawn.

"He'll be okay," Millie chuckled. "You'd think by now he'd realize that after he missed the bus a dozen times or so, I set the clock ahead by five minutes—just in case."

"That's my boy," Paula said with a little laugh.

She reached under the table to pat Rudy's head, and her hand bumped against something bulky. Pulling it up to her lap, she recognized it immediately. "Scotty's backpack." She fingered the forest-green canvas bag's worn leather straps. "I just hope he hasn't forgotten anything important—homework or something. It feels pretty heavy; there must be a lot of books in here."

"Maybe you'd better check," Millie suggested. "The bus has surely gone by now, but if there's something he needs, I can run it over to the school in a bit. Goodness knows I've done it before; seems like he's always forgetting one thing or another. More than once, it's been his gym shorts." She smiled at the memory.

"Okay, let's see what we've got here." Paula opened the clasp and began rummaging through the bag's contents. "Nothing really critical so far—a couple of English and history books, some car magazines, half a dozen candy bars, a bunch of crumpled papers, some kind of a psychedelic yo-yo. I think he can get along without—" Her voice froze in mid-sentence as she touched something at the very bottom of the backpack. Curling her fingers around a smooth object that was flat on one side and rounded on the other, she tugged on it. "What in the world could this—" One final tug, and it rose into plain view.

Refusing to breathe, Paula held a medium-sized tinted glass bottle in both hands. Its flat surface was facing upward while her palms cradled the rounded side, obscuring the label. Inside, a brownish liquid sloshed lazily back and forth. She knew without looking what the label would reveal; the bottle's shape, feel, and unique color were all too familiar. But she was in no hurry to confirm the evidence. A few beads of perspiration dotted her upper lip as she stared at the container for endless moments, her hands trembling slightly.

Finally, she felt Millie's hand on her shoulder. "Not exactly apple cider, is it?" the older woman said quietly.

Paula bit down on her lower lip as she slowly, methodically turned the bottle until its label came into full view. Then she let out a long, agonized moan. "I knew it. Bourbon. Green Pointe."

CHAPTER 13

A thin line of grim determination had replaced Paula's mouth by the time she pushed through the glass doors to her office suite. Carmine looked up from the reception desk with a welcoming grin, but quickly stifled her cheerful greeting when Paula strode briskly down the long, carpeted hallway without so much as a glance to either side. "Uh-oh. Trouble," the redhead murmured under her breath as she turned back to her computer. "And it's not even ten o'clock."

Quickly passing her own office, Paula moved resolutely forward until she made an abrupt stop in front of Ted's closed office door. Clenching her teeth until her jaw muscles twitched, she wrapped her hand around the heavy brass knob and pushed firmly. The door swung inward on a sudden rush of air, and she took exactly five steps into the room.

Ted looked up, startled, to see her eyes flashing. He loved it when her eyes flashed; they made her so . . . well, so *alive*. "Hey, boss," he grinned. "This is certainly a pleasant—"

"Cancel the Green Pointe account." She spoke with absolute clarity, and her voice sizzled like battery acid.

Ted's eyebrows shot up. "Excuse me?"

"You heard me the first time. I said cancel the Green Pointe account. Now."

He pushed back his leather chair and rose deliberately, buying a few seconds to collect his thoughts. "Come again? You can't be serious, Paula. What in the—"

"*Now.*"

He squeezed his eyes shut in total disbelief, and thought he heard a door slam somewhere far away. When he opened his eyes, she was gone.

Ted took a few deep gulps of air, then forced himself to saunter leisurely down the hall to her office. He knocked twice, then opened the door. Paula was facing the window; he saw only the tall, burgundy back of her leather swivel chair. She gave no indication that she'd heard him enter. He decided to tread lightly. "Uh, excuse me?" he said carefully. When she made no response, he forced his voice into a casual, upbeat timbre. "You know, I could have sworn that only seconds ago, some devilishly beautiful woman, expertly masquerading as Paula Donroe, came to my office and made a *most* unusual request." Still no response. "You wouldn't by any chance be hiding a lovely but misguided twin in your bathroom or something, would you?" Met with stone silence, he chuckled nervously and ran the fingers of one hand through his hair. "Well, maybe I was mistaken. Maybe I only *imagined* that someone fitting your description actually asked me to—"

"Imagination had nothing to do with it." Paula's voice was chilled to perfection, and her icy gaze sent a shiver up Ted's spine when she swung around to face him. "In case you didn't hear me the first time, I'll repeat myself. Cancel the Green Pointe account. Now."

"That's what I was afraid of," he murmured. His legs seemed to fail him, and he sagged into a chair near the desk. He studied Paula's face for a clue, but her expression was a mask of defiance. He wanted to be angry, but all he could muster was a confused sigh. "What's up, chief? I've never seen you like this."

At his words, her steely facade crumbled, and she bit down hard on her trembling lower lip. "I mean it," she said, her voice low and pouty. "We can't go on with this campaign."

Ted's eyes probed hers, but he couldn't see beyond the mixture of pain and fury brimming in them. "And that would be because . . . ?"

She leaned forward and stared at him intently. "Because, all of a sudden, this whole thing has become very . . . very . . . *personal.*"

Now he felt a flash of indignation, but controlled his impulse to say something about this being *just like a woman.* Couldn't they ever get beyond this *personal* stuff? "What kind of personal?" he asked politely.

Paula rested her hands on the desk and cleared her throat. "This morning, I found a bottle of Green Pointe bourbon in my son's backpack."

"Oh, *that* kind of personal," Ted breathed. He straightened in his chair, determined to appeal to her sense of reason. "But surely you're not going to let one kid's momentary lapse in judgment cheat us out of a multi-million-dollar—"

"Not one kid. *My* kid. And it's too close for comfort."

Ted felt an angry throbbing at his temples, and he heard himself lash out. "Oh, yeah? Well, let me remind you of something. *Every* kid tries it. I did. You did. I'd bet good money that even your straight-arrow Mormon missionary son probably swallowed a teaspoonful after his senior prom. Scott will get over it. But *we* won't get over it . . . we will *never* get over losing the biggest account of our lives if we do something stupid like this."

Paula held up a hand and shook her head. "I don't want to talk about it."

Ted stood and paced furiously. "No, I don't suppose you do. But if you really want to go through with this insanity, *you* call Brady and give him our excuses. Tell him . . . tell him you're a *Mormon* or something—although that didn't seem to make much *personal* difference when we were signing the deal, did it? I won't be your henchman on this one." He turned abruptly and strode from the office, leaving Paula staring after him, her eyes blazing.

"Fine. I'll do it myself," she murmured through clenched teeth. "First thing tomorrow." *After I've grounded my son for the next twenty years.*

Paula spent the morning, afternoon, and early evening closeted in her office, stewing in her own juices. She thought about Ted's insolent manner, and her blood boiled. She focused on Scott's betrayal of her trust, and a flush of rage turned her face crimson. She mentally reviewed the Green Pointe account, and cursed herself for wanting their business in spite of everything—for wanting it so much it set her teeth on edge. What she really hungered for, in the end, was to get even with all of them for making her look like an idiot. Or had she done that all by herself? In any case, Scott would answer for his sins tonight—and it wouldn't be pretty. By the time she left the building after nine P.M. and aimed her snappy sports car toward home, she had conjured up a scathing lecture—not to mention an ingenious punishment to fit the crime. *It's showtime*, she thought as the car slipped silently into the garage. She barely noticed that the automatic garage door had been left open.

Entering the house, she stepped quickly into the darkened hallway leading to the kitchen. *Good grief*, she thought, *Millie could've at least left a lamp on somewhere. It's black as tar in here.* She felt along the wall for a switch, and finally the kitchen came to life in a soft wash of light. "That's better," she said aloud, kicking her shoes into a corner by the table. There was a note from Millie on the breakfast bar. She was sorry about the garage door being stuck open; a repairman would fix it first thing in the morning. She'd gone to spend the night with Sister Bell, a new friend from the ward who was ill and needed some company. Rudy was at the vet's; they'd kept him overnight to monitor an electrolyte problem after removing a couple of bad teeth. Dinner was in the fridge, ready for the microwave. The contents of the note registered only briefly in Paula's brain as she shuffled toward the entryway. Her mind was already upstairs with Scott, making him wish he'd never popped the cap of that liquor bottle.

As she crossed the entryway, Paula thought she heard a faint sound coming from the family room. She stopped and listened carefully. No doubt about it—that was MTV, and her son was down there watching it. A fresh wave of indignation rose in her throat. *I told Millie to send him to his room the second he got home from school. Well, we'll just see about this. I'll catch him in the act.* She paused for a moment to get her bearings in the dim light, then moved stealthily down the few steps to the family room. It was completely dark except for the television's gaudy glow in a far corner. But as she made her way silently toward the couch where the unsuspecting boy would be lounging, a movement in her peripheral vision caused her to turn her head sharply toward the other end of the room.

Paula gasped and froze in place, beads of cold sweat breaking out on her forehead as she realized that the dark shadow coming toward her was not her son. He was too big, too mean, too ugly. She backed away, then willed herself to confront him. "Who are you?" she said in a half-whisper. "Wh—what are you doing in my—"

A large, fleshy hand grabbed her wrist, and another clamped itself across her mouth and half her face. An instant later, she felt her waist being squeezed in the viselike grip of an enormous, muscular arm. Immobilized, her arms pinned to her sides and her breath cut off without a sound, she felt sheer panic constrict her chest as she struggled to break free. *This can't be happening,* she screamed silently. *This is my house. I . . . won't . . . allow . . . it.* The thought seemed to give her a momentary infusion of courage, and she did the only thing she could manage—she pushed back fiercely against the intruder's chest and tried to butt his chin with the top of her head. The unexpected jolt, though not effective against his overall strength, set him slightly off balance, and the suffocating pressure of his hand over her mouth eased for a second or two. She acted quickly, drawing back until she could drop her jaw. Almost simultaneously, she sank her teeth viciously into one beefy side of the monstrous hand and bit down with a vengeance. She tasted blood before he shook her off, snarling obscenities, and hurled his massive fist into one side of her face. A thousand stars exploded behind her eyes, and she fell backward into oblivion. From somewhere far away, she thought she heard a throaty, disembodied scream.

When she came to a few seconds later, he was kneeling beside her, his beefy fingers around her neck, his knee pinning one of her arms to the floor. *Dear Lord, help!* she prayed frantically. *Help me!* She struggled feebly against the suffocating pressure constricting her throat.

No! she cried silently. *I can't let this happen! Lord, help me!* In a last, desperate move to free herself, she focused every ounce of strength on her one free arm. Striking at his head, she raked her fingernails savagely down his hairline and across one side of his face.

"Swine!" the attacker snarled. "You'll pay for that!" He reared back, grabbed her arm, and twisted it viciously until she felt bones and tendons wrenching apart under the strain. The pain was excruciating, and in that moment Paula knew she had lost. It was useless— he would certainly kill her. Any second her arm would snap, she would lose consciousness from the pain, and it would be over. Even as she felt darkness closing in around her, she still struggled. But he was so strong . . .

At precisely the moment when she was ready to let go and fade into pain-free blackness, Paula felt the man's grip on her arm relax.

An instant later his full weight crashed heavily onto her body and he lay still, an enormous hulk pinning her down, pressing her into the carpet like a shoe crushing a bug. But he wasn't moving, wasn't threatening her, wasn't squeezing the breath out of her. He was just *lying* there. Barely conscious, Paula couldn't reason it out. She only knew that for the moment, at least, she was still alive. Her breath came in jagged gasps as she fought to gain control of her senses.

"Mom? Mom? Are you okay?" The voice at first seemed liquid and far away, then very loud and raucous as it screamed in her ear. "MOM! Can you hear me? Are you all right? I knocked him out." Paula felt a strong hand gripping, then shaking her shoulder. "ARE YOU OKAY?"

She nodded feebly, then somehow managed a tremulous smile as she opened her eyes to see Scott kneeling beside her, his face drained of color. She spoke slowly, carefully, squeezing the words out around the oppressive weight on her diaphragm. "But . . . I'd be . . . a lot better . . . if you could . . . please . . . get him . . . off me."

For a moment Scott hesitated, then broke into a self-conscious grin. "Oh, yeah . . . sure. I shoulda thought of that. Hold on just a sec." He lifted the unconscious man's arm to roll him off to one side. "Sheesh," the boy muttered with a pained expression, "this guy smells like rotting fish." He shoved a sneaker underneath the body and pushed it a few feet behind him, then switched on a small table lamp and knelt to help his mother sit up. "So, you sure you're okay?" he asked.

"I—I think so," Paula replied, rubbing her twisted arm. She didn't think it was broken, but her bruised muscles protested as she sat up. "We'd better call the police." She glanced at the still form lying next to the couch. "What happened, anyway? I mean, how in the world did you—"

"No big deal," Scott said. With one long arm, he reached out and grasped an object lying near the television. As he lifted it, Paula recognized one of Millie's vintage cast-iron frying pans, part of a matched set she'd had for twenty years or more, wonderful for frying chicken—and now, in a pinch, obviously heavy enough to do serious damage to the thickest head. Paula's mouth dropped open, and she stared at her son.

"I was in my room, listenin' to stuff on my walkman," he explained. "When I remembered I'd left the TV on, I came down to shut it off, but stopped at the fridge first to get a sandwich or somethin'. Next thing I know, there's this scream downstairs. I didn't know what was goin' on, so I grabbed a pan just in case. It was pretty dark down here, but I could see enough to know you were in trouble." Scott's voice wavered, and he hesitated. "I'm glad I made it in time," he finally continued. "I don't know what I'd do if anything had . . . happened." He stared at her for a long moment, his expression strained, almost haunted.

Paula reached up to stroke his cheek. "You saved my life, son," she murmured. "If you hadn't been here, he would have killed me. I know it."

The muscles in Scott's jaw began to work furiously. "Yeah, well," he finally blurted out, "I couldn't let it happen again." He ran the fingers of one hand nervously through his thick, dark hair.

She looked at him curiously. "Excuse me?"

"Nuthin'," he replied. "After what happened before, I couldn't just . . . well, I had to do somethin'." He shrugged and got to his feet. "I better call 911 before this scumbag wakes up." He extended his hand. "Need somethin' to hold on to?"

"Sure. Thanks." She rose to her knees, still massaging her throbbing arm. "But am I missing something here?" Her brows were knit together in puzzlement as she reached out to grab his hand. "Something we should talk about?"

He chuckled without mirth. "Naw. It's just crazy stuff, anyways. I don't think you'd wanna . . . UNNH!" Without warning, a huge, bloodstreaked hand gripped one side of Scott's waist, while a second set of fleshy fingers curled around his knee and squeezed like a vise until he yelped in pain and crashed sidelong to the floor. The sharp corner of a lamp table caught his temple as he fell, dazing him for a few critical seconds.

"It's him!" Paula cried, lurching backward, horror etched into her face. "Scotty!" Her heart plummeted as the attacker lumbered toward her, his eyes burning with hatred. She raised her arms in a frantic effort to protect herself, but he was on her in an instant, again coiling his massive fingers around her throat in a death grip. He began to squeeze, and she felt her strength evaporating.

"No-o-o-!" Scott bellowed from where he had fallen. Rocketing to his feet, he launched himself into the enemy's body, knocking him off balance if not off his feet. Stunned by the unexpected blow, the man released his hold on Paula and whirled around, aiming a huge, powerful fist at the boy's jaw. But his earlier bout with the frying pan had slowed his reflexes, and Scott was able to fend him off with a well-placed forearm, followed by a lip-splitting blow to the mouth. Enraged, the man spat blood into Scott's face before collapsing to his knees. He swayed dizzily, and Paula thought—hoped—he might pass out again.

Scott didn't hesitate. Glaring down at his assailant, he grabbed the man's filthy black hair with one hand, and with the other leveled a knockout punch to the center of his face. His large body crumpled against Scott's leg; his breathing was labored, and he made no effort to defend himself. But Scott wasn't finished; his eyes turned hard, and he began kicking the man viciously in the back and stomach.

"Scott! Stop it!" she shouted. "Enough already! He's out cold! It's all right!" A tremor of sheer dread washed over her when he turned blazing eyes toward her for a second, then promptly returned to his attack.

Paula watched in breathless disbelief. When she realized he was getting ready to bash the inert form in the head with the hard rubber toes of his sneakers, she knew exactly what the outcome would be if she didn't do something. *Good Lord, he's lost it! Scotty's going to keep going until he kills this guy!* In a flash of blinding clarity, she knew that in a matter of seconds she would be a witness to the total disintegration of her son's life. And she had to stop it.

There was only one thing to do. Millie's frying pan lay near the couch; Paula reached for it, grasping its heavy iron handle with both hands as she came to her feet behind Scott. She swung it clumsily away from her body, then brought it forward with a frenzied momentum. *Please don't let this hurt him too much,* she prayed, closing her eyes as the pan made solid contact with Scott's right shoulder.

He shrugged off the blow and kept kicking. So she hit him again—hard enough to bounce the pan several inches off his body.

It worked. He spun around to face her, his eyes wide and glazed with an unnatural brightness. Then he raised a trembling fist into the air. "Leave me alone," he growled, his voice hollow and menacing. "I just wanna kill the son of a—"

"No!" she screamed. "It isn't right! You can't do this!"

"Just watch me!" he raged, turning back toward the body.

"I said NO!" Paula repeated. With the ferocity of a cornered lioness, she took hold of one sleeve of his T-shirt and literally jerked him around until she had a clear view of his face. He stared at her, but his wasted eyes showed no recognition. *Help me get him back!* she begged silently. Then she extended her fingers, drew her arm back as far as it would go, and slapped him across the face with every particle of strength she could muster. Pain shot up her injured arm as her hand made fierce contact with the hard bone and muscles of his jaw.

Suddenly, everything stopped—time, movement, breathing, emotion—all instantly suspended by a mother's primal instinct to somehow save her child from himself. Would he be saved, or had she simply done more harm? She took a step backward, waiting.

For interminable moments, Scott stood frozen in the dim lamp-light, his eyes squeezed tightly shut, his face a scowl of pain, his hands balled into fists at his sides, every nerve and muscle at the snapping point. Then gradually, almost imperceptibly, his shoulders sagged, his hands relaxed, and the tension seemed to drain from his body as he took a long, shuddering breath. His head fell slowly forward until his chin almost brushed his chest; Paula could see large beads of sweat glistening in his dark hair, then breaking loose and pooling at his temples. She reached out a tentative hand to touch him, but pulled back before she made contact with his damp skin.

Finally his eyes opened—Paula could tell by the movement of his long, thick lashes—but his head was still bowed. Deliberately, as though moving in slow motion, he raised his arms and clasped his hands behind his neck. Then he straightened his back and looked at her with the gaze of a displaced, bewildered child. "Mom?" His voice was as dry and fragile as parchment. He sank to his knees on the blood-spattered carpet and stared up at her. "Mommy?"

The childlike word sent tears coursing down her cheeks as she knelt and gathered him into her arms. "Yes, Scotty, I'm here," she murmured. He pressed his face to her shoulder, and she gently stroked the back of his head, her lips close to his ear. "It's okay," she whispered. "It's over now. Everything's going to be all right."

Half a dozen deep, tortured sobs rose from Scott's chest as he tried to speak. "I—I don't know . . . if anything will . . . ever be all right . . . ever again." He pulled away slightly and raised his eyes, where Paula saw a fathomless well of pain. *Has it been there all the time,* she wondered, *just waiting to explode like this? Where did it come from, and why?* She sensed that this kind of anguish was not going to go away on its own. *But what can I do?*

She had to start somewhere. "Are you hurt, sweetie?" she asked carefully.

"No, just a couple of scratches." He touched his temple where it had caught the table's corner, then looked down at his bruised knuckles, then back at her. "And a sore jaw."

She ran her fingers gingerly across the wide red mark on the side of his face. "I'm so sorry, Scotty. It was the only thing I could think of to—"

"I know," he said quickly. "You did good. I was out of my mind. But I . . ." He shook his head, as if he couldn't quite believe what had just happened. When he looked at his mother again, fear had joined the pain in his expression. "Did I kill him?"

Paula glanced at the hulk sprawled behind them. "I don't think so," she said, "but I don't want to get close enough to find out. We need to call the police."

"Yeah," Scott agreed. "I'll do it." He hurriedly wiped at his eyes and started to get up.

"No, I'll do it." Paula was already on her feet. "You stay here, and make sure nothing happens."

"Okay—but hurry. If he wakes up . . ." Scott's hand involuntarily curled into a tight fist.

"I'm hurrying." She had reached the phone and dialed 911 almost before she said the words.

Past midnight, after the police, ambulance, and detectives had come and gone, Paula lay down beside her son and held him for a long time. Finally, when she felt his taut body relax a little, she ventured a question. "Want to talk about it?"

Five, ten minutes passed in silence, and she thought he'd fallen asleep. Then he cleared his throat softly. "It never should've happened."

"I know," Paula sighed. "He probably walked right in through the open garage door, and of course Millie and Rudy were both gone. I'll bet Millie didn't even think to lock the door into the kitchen, either; we've always just left it open. Come to think of it, when I got home it was—"

"Not that, Mom," Scott interjected. He moved to sit up on the edge of his bed.

She did the same, and they sat shoulder to shoulder. "What, then?" she questioned, not certain where this conversation was headed.

"Like I said, it never should've happened. And I almost did it again." His shoulders slumped, and he stared at the floor.

She patted his knee and looked at him indulgently. "I'm afraid you've lost me, sweetie. Tell you what: it's been a long night, and maybe we should talk about this in the—"

"Don't you get it?" he cut in, his voice suddenly urgent. "I went *crazy* tonight, Mom. I almost killed that guy. When I saw him choking you, I just snapped. Pow!" He slammed his right fist into the palm of his left hand, then repeated the action. "I *knew* I couldn't let it happen like the last time."

"The last time?" Paula was beginning to sense the importance of this moment, but she couldn't quite identify the source of her concern as she waited for Scott's answer.

"That night. The night TJ got shot."

TJ. At the mention of his name, an unexpected spasm of grief sucked the breath out of her lungs. *Will I ever get used to this? Of course not; one never gets used to the death of a child.* She pressed a hand to her chest and waited a few seconds until it passed, then spoke slowly, deliberately. "I don't see what any of this has to do with TJ."

Scott shook his head morosely. "What *doesn't* have to do with TJ these days?" He turned to face her squarely, his eyes boring into hers with disquieting intensity. "I can't live with it anymore, Mom. I just can't. It's eatin' me up." He leaned forward and covered his face with trembling hands.

Paula laid her hand on his shoulder. "What in the world are you talking about, Scotty? I don't know why—"

When he looked up at her, his face was a mask of torment. "I killed him, Mom. I killed my own little brother. *I killed TJ.*"

CHAPTER 14

Paula watched silently as tears filled Scott's eyes and trickled down his cheeks. She had never seen him suffer like this. More than anything, she wanted to say something to ease his pain, but no words would come. Instead, she leaned against him and nestled her head on his shoulder. "Tell me," she said.

He wiped at his face and took in a labored breath, letting it out in short little chunks. "It should've been me, ya know? I talked him into goin' downtown—thought he'd get a kick out of it. He was sittin' between me and Ben Salter in the front seat, then Benny gets this cool idea to let me drive, so I get behind the wheel, he takes the middle, and TJ moves over to the passenger side. That's where he was when this idiot with a gun . . ." His voice failed, and he whispered the rest. "If I would've stayed put, 'stead of playing the big driver-dude, he'd still be . . . he'd still be alive. It was all my fault. I killed him." Scott's mouth clamped shut, and he swallowed hard.

Paula lifted her head and stared wordlessly at her son. With sudden insight, she realized that this was the first and only time since TJ's death that she and Scott had actually *talked* about it. Nearly six months had passed, and virtually all of their conversations—if you could call them that—had ended in heated arguments or volleys of unspoken resentment. And now, having seen and heard for herself the crushing guilt and self-recrimination boiling out of Scott's tortured imaginings, Paula knew why. *Was I so busy wallowing in my own grief that I couldn't see his? So focused on getting back to normal that I didn't have a clue about what "normal" really was? So caught up in wondering about my oldest son that my younger son didn't stand a chance?* The thought sent a deep shudder rumbling through her body. *I've got to fix this. Now.*

She touched his chin and gently turned his head to face her. "Scotty, listen to me." He closed his eyes and tried to twist away, but she cradled his cheeks in her hands and held on. "Please, honey," she begged, "*listen* to me. I want you to understand something. You *have* to understand something." He looked at her cautiously, and she saw a wave of fresh pain well in his eyes. An almost imperceptible nod of his head prompted her to continue.

She took one of his bruised hands in both of hers and pressed it to her lips before she began to speak. "All these months," she said, "I didn't even know you blamed yourself for what happened. I've been so wrapped up in . . . well, there just aren't any excuses. It's been horrible for you, hasn't it?" He didn't respond, but the quivering muscles in his jaw told her what she needed to know.

"It's why you've been drinking—to get rid of some of the pain," she continued. His deep, ragged sigh acknowledged the truth of what she was saying. "And you really believed you were somehow responsible."

His eyes flashed in the dim bedroom light. "I *know* it, Mom. If it hadn't been for me, he never would've—"

"Wrong!" Paula interjected sharply, then paused to give him the tiniest hint of a smile as her dark eyes glowed with intensity. "And by the way, quit stealing my lines."

"Huh?" Scott blinked several times, obviously puzzled.

"My dear, handsome, totally awesome son," she said, gripping his hand even more tightly, "let's get something cleared up right now, shall we?" He shrugged, and she went on. "Here's the thing: I don't care what you say, it's *not your fault* TJ died. Never has been, never will be. And I can prove it."

She had his attention. "How?" he pressed, looking at her dubiously. "You weren't even there."

"No. But I can sure as heck tell you why it happened, and who was responsible."

"No way. None of the other guys had anything to do with it. I was the one who—"

"Wrong again." Paula's gaze was locked into his, her eyes burning with emotion.

"You're talkin' in circles, Mom. Can't you just leave it—"

"*I* was the one, Scotty. *I* did it. *I* killed TJ." Her words ripped through the air like a firebomb, startling both of them.

"'Scuse me?" Scott could barely croak out the words.

"And that," Paula added, "is why I said that thing about stealing my lines. You see, if anyone's to blame here, it's me. If I hadn't ignored TJ's feelings about the Church and told him he couldn't be baptized, he would've spent the afternoon playing basketball instead of trying to make himself feel better by doing what he knew I wouldn't approve of. Just as sure as you were driving that car, I was driving him to go with you. If it hadn't been for *me*, he never would've—" A stab of pain choked off her voice. She let go of Scott and lay back on the bed, her hands covering her face as she struggled to control her rising emotion. *I didn't think it would hurt this much to just say the words. But it's true, isn't it? I couldn't admit it . . . couldn't even think it until now. If it hadn't been for me . . .* A well of profound sorrow seemed to open in her chest, and she thought she might fall into it and drown.

Long moments later, Paula opened her eyes to the sound of her son's soft chuckle. He was looking at her, shaking his head very slowly, the small beginnings of a smile tugging at his lips. She sat up and slid to the edge of the bed, but he said nothing. "What?" she finally asked.

"I guess we're a pair," he replied, the smile fading. "Both of us blaming ourselves, figuring it was our fault. Both of us trying to pretend things are the same as they ever were—life goes on, an' all that." He looked her squarely in the eye. "When all we really want is . . . for it never to have happened." He glanced down at his shoes, then back up at Paula. "For us never to have lost TJ in the first place. Nothing else makes any difference."

"I know," Paula, said, raising her hand to squeeze his shoulder gently. "And I'm sorry . . . for all the pretending. We should have talked about this months ago."

"Yeah," he agreed. "Before somethin' like this happened—I mean, me almost wastin' that dirtbag." A solemn intensity radiated from his hazel eyes. "I swear, when I saw him messing with you, it was like being with TJ all over again. Only this time, I wasn't gonna let some piece of scum hurt anyone I . . ." His tone softened. "Anyone I care about. So I let him have it."

"You certainly did," Paula observed wryly. "And he took it like a real wimp."

Scott grinned. "Geez, that was only because he was so . . . unconscious." He brushed a hand across his forehead. "I tell ya, I was shakin' in my shorts till I knew he was totally out of it, and then my stupid temper took over. I mean, I'm big, but I can't really fight, ya know?" He squared his shoulders. "Guess I'm more of a cool sports guy."

"Well, 'cool sports guy,' you did the job—and you saved my life. No doubt about it." She smiled warmly and pressed her lips to his cheek. "Tell you what: let's play hooky from school and work tomorrow—maybe catch a movie, take a walk on the beach, or just hang out around here. I don't know about you, but I feel like we still have a lot to talk about; tonight was only a start. We need to find a way to get through all of this—TJ's death, the horror of what happened earlier tonight, what's been going on in our family . . ."

". . . why I had a bottle of bourbon in my backpack." Scott glanced at her sheepishly.

"That too," she affirmed. "But I think we can work it out along with the other stuff. What do you say?"

"Deal." His tone was relieved, almost expectant.

"All right, then," she declared. "Now, let's try to get a little sleep." She gave him a quick hug and stood up. "I'll see you in the morning, okay?"

"Okay," he said as she moved away from him. "And Mom?"

She turned back. "Yes, sweetie?"

"Leave your door open, would ya?"

"You bet, kiddo. Yours too?"

"Yeah. See ya." He lay on his side, drew his long legs up to his chest, and watched her as she padded softly from the room. She left the hall light on.

❤ ❤ ❤

Paula glanced at the clock above the stove: ten-thirty A.M. She had already showered and dressed, called and left a message at her office, fixed French toast, and was pouring hot chocolate into large ceramic mugs when Scott shuffled into the kitchen. He sat down at the table, leaned back in his chair, and closed his eyes for a moment before mumbling, "Morning."

She studied his sunken eyes and haggard complexion; they were similar to what she had seen earlier in her own mirror. Placing his mug on the table, she bent to brush her lips across his forehead. "Tough night, huh?"

"Yeah. Didn't sleep much." He touched his fingers to the small bandage covering the cut on his temple and groaned a little. "Everything kinda hurt, ya know? An' I kept thinkin' about . . . stuff."

"I know," Paula said. "Me, too." She eased herself into a chair across from him. "And from what I've heard about people who've been through an attack like that, it'll take a while for the memories to fade. And the trauma might not even go away on its own."

He looked at her. "What do you mean?"

"Well, I'm not sure, but it could take some professional help to get us through this."

"You mean, like a shrink?" His eyes glinted, and she could tell it wasn't his favorite idea.

"I honestly don't know, sweetie," she soothed. "I'm sorry I brought it up; it's really too early to tell, and everybody's different when it comes to dealing with something like this." She smiled as brightly as she could, but the deep bruise covering one side of her face made the effort painful. "Let's just spend some quality down-time today, and we'll see what happens after that, okay?"

"Okay." He seemed to relax as he stirred his hot chocolate.

They picked at their food, neither one particularly hungry, then talked a little about how they might spend their day. "Are those detectives coming back?" Scott asked.

"I'm sure they are; in fact, I believe one of them said something about coming this morning. They need to ask us some more questions and check downstairs for evidence—as if they didn't have enough already." She made a face. "Earlier this morning, I thought I'd try to clean the carpet down there. But then, just in time, I remembered that we're not supposed to touch a thing until they've checked it out one more time. If I'd so much as put the lamp table back in place, they'd probably have put me behind bars." She laughed nervously. "When Millie comes home and sees that mess, she'll have a fit."

"No, Mom." He reached across the table to touch her hand, and the unexpected gentleness in his voice warmed her. "You know as well as I do what'll happen—she'll get all emotional. 'Thank the good Lord,' she'll say, 'that nothing worse happened. We can clean the carpet and replace the furniture any old day.'"

"You're exactly right," Paula smiled. "And we'll agree with her one hundred percent. I just hope her sick friend is—"

The doorbell chimed, and Paula sighed. "Well, so much for a cozy, uninterrupted morning. I suppose it's the police, or maybe the garage-door repairman. Millie said he'd be here first thing—sometime before noon, anyway." She glanced at his plate of French toast, still mostly uneaten. "I'll get it; you try to eat something." She pushed her chair back and stood, every muscle sore and complaining, sharp reminders of the brutal assault she had suffered half a day earlier. Rubbing her twisted arm and trying not to limp, she moved slowly across the entryway and pulled open the door.

A tall man was standing on the porch with his back to the door, gazing out over the front lawn, one hand in his back pocket. He wasn't in uniform, Paula noted, and he seemed too well-dressed to be a repairman. "May I help you?" she said cautiously.

The man spun around, and a wave of relief and delight washed over her. "Ted! What in the world are you doing here?" Her eyes quickly took in his brown Italian leather shoes, tan sport slacks, pale-blue button-down shirt, and navy tie with quirky-looking zebras cavorting from top to bottom. He must have come from the office— maybe stopped somewhere to pick up the small, colorful bouquet of flowers he held in one hand. "I certainly didn't expect—" Their eyes met, and the intensity of his expression stopped her in mid-sentence.

"Didn't expect anyone to wonder what in heaven's name was going on—especially after that enlightening message you left for Carmine? 'We had an intruder last night, and Scott and I are pretty messed up. I won't be in today. See you on Monday.' My dear boss lady, do you have *any idea* how many definitions of 'messed up' have been running through my crazy and highly imaginative little brain? Everything up to and including death and dismemberment, I can tell you that." His gaze traveled from her bruised face to the way she held one arm carefully at her side. "And it appears that some of my mental images weren't too far off."

For some reason, seeing him there on her porch, his blue eyes filled with concern, Paula felt an overwhelming surge of emotion. It caught her off guard, and she felt her knees begin to buckle. "Oh, Ted," she murmured, "I can't tell you how glad I am to . . ." She reached out to steady herself against the door frame.

"Glad can wait," he said brusquely, stepping into the entryway and circling her shoulders with his arm. "Let's take a load off." He guided her firmly to the living room, where they sat together at one end of a long sofa. She lay back and closed her eyes, breathing deeply, while he put the flowers on a small glass table beside the sofa. "Just take your time," he whispered, rubbing her hand and arm. I'm not going anywhere."

"Thanks," she sighed, leaning against his shoulder.

They heard a few heavy clomping sounds in the entryway, then Scott rounded the corner into the living room. "Hey, Mom, is that the cops, or—oh, hi, Mr. Barstow." The boy grinned self-consciously. "Didn't know it was you."

Ted returned the smile. "I was just stopping by to check up on the two of you. Heard you had an unexpected visitor last night."

Scott's eyes narrowed. "Yeah. This filthy, smelly, totally scummed-out lowlife got hold of my mom and tried to . . ." He squared his shoulders. "Well, he woulda really hurt her if I hadn't got there first." He glanced at Paula. "Is she okay? She seemed all right earlier, when we were eating. But now, she's so . . . so pale."

"Not to worry, big guy," Paula said, her eyes still closed. "I'm just a little tired, that's all. I'll be fine."

Ted looked at the teenager, who was himself a little wan. "Give us a few minutes, will you?" he asked in a kind voice.

"Sure thing. I'll be hangin' out in my room. Later." Without another word, Scott shuffled across the entryway and disappeared up the stairs.

Paula's breathing gradually became more even, and after a minute or two she opened her eyes and drew back to look up at Ted. He was gazing at her with a veiled expression that seemed to mingle concern with protectiveness, puzzlement with pure affection. When he saw her expressive eyes regarding him curiously, he cocked his head to one side and smiled disarmingly. "Feeling better?" he inquired, still gently massaging her hand and arm.

"Much, thank you." She brushed several locks of unruly dark hair away from her face. "Strange . . . I thought I was pretty well under control, considering everything that happened last night. But somehow, seeing you at my door, I suddenly realized how utterly *alone* I've been, even with Scotty here. I guess I've been forcing myself to be strong—for him." She sighed and shook her head.

"And exactly what *did* happen last night, Paula?" Ted's hand stopped moving on her arm, and she felt its solid, reassuring pressure against her skin.

For the next hour, she described every detail: the vicious assault, Scott's life-saving intervention, his senseless attack on the unconscious intruder, her quick action to save Scott from his own rage, and finally, their long-overdue conversation about TJ's death. Ted listened intently, never taking his eyes from her face, though he pressed his lips together and blinked rapidly from time to time.

When she was finished, he carefully wiped a stray tear from her bruised cheekbone. "I had no idea," he murmured. "There I was at home, sleeping like a doggone baby all night, while you and Scotty were smack in the middle of an unbelievable nightmare." He paused, as if considering a deeper implication. "It could have turned out much differently, you know." She was still leaning against him, and she felt his body shudder.

"I know," she said. "I could have lost Scotty, or—"

"Or I . . . uh, Scotty could have lost you." His eyes were glistening now, stark blue against his flushed countenance, and his voice flattened into a whisper. "Someone must've been watching out for you."

"I believe that," Paula agreed. "And He still is. He sent you when I needed you, didn't He? How could you have known that I—" Words failed her, so she reached up and pressed her fingers to his cheek.

Ted quickly covered her hand with his and held it firmly against his face. After a long moment he cleared his throat, then gave her a tiny grin as he released her hand. "Yeah, well, I guess it has something to do with what that guy said about—how did he put it?—bearing one another's burdens, comforting folks that stand in need of comfort. Stuff like that."

Paula felt her chin drop slightly as she placed her hand over her heart and stared at him. "Why, Ted Barstow, I do believe you've been reading the book."

"The book?" His eyes widened innocently, but there was an impish sparkle to them.

"Of Mormon. You know—the little blue beauty I gave you just after I took the plunge."

"Oh, *that* book." His eyes moved to Scott's portrait of TJ, hanging on a wall across the room, then back to Paula. "Well, maybe a little here and there, on a boring Sunday afternoon or something. No big deal." He shrugged and began picking at a piece of lint clinging to his trousers. "Some of it makes sense."

"Uh-huh," Paula smiled.

"The important thing is, everyone's all right." He glanced at her discolored face, then at her body reclining gingerly against the sofa. "More or less."

"As you said, it could have been much worse. We'll be okay, but it may take some time." She closed her eyes and sighed wearily.

"Don't worry about the office," Ted soothed. "It'll still be there when you're ready to come back. In the meantime, I'll do what I can to keep things going. We all will."

"I know you will, Ted. I, um, appreciate it," she murmured through swollen lips. Her eyelids suddenly felt weighted, and all she wanted to do was give in to bone-weariness. Hardly able to speak or move, she felt herself being carried out to sea on a wave of exhaustion. At this moment, a long day of uninterrupted sleep seemed the greatest gift that any being, human or divine, could bestow.

"There is one little thing . . ." Ted's voice came to her as if from the end of a long, cotton-filled tube.

"Mmm?" She tried to open her eyes, but all she could manage to raise was one eyebrow.

"The Green Pointe account. We left it a little . . . up in the air."

Green Pointe. Sounds familiar . . . oh, yes. Green Pointe. I could use a little chug of that creme de menthe right about now. But later . . . after I wake up. Oops—not exactly a Mormon-like fantasy. Just let me sleep; I'll get over it. She nodded slightly, hoping Ted would leave it alone. She was just too tired right now.

"I haven't called them yet, but if we're going to make a change, we probably should do it pretty soon. If you've given it any more thought . . ."

Paula managed to turn her head a little from side to side. "Just let me think about it," she whispered. "Can't decide anything now. In a few days. Need to think." Then she slipped into oblivion.

"Okay, chief. We'll handle it later. You get some rest." He sat with her for a few minutes longer, counting her even breaths, studying the relentless pulse of a vein at her temple. Finally he stood and slowly, gently swung her legs and feet up to the sofa, positioning her body the way he felt would be most comfortable, nestling her head on a soft cushion retrieved from a nearby chair. Then he moved quietly down a hall until he came to what looked like a closet. Opening it, he found an assortment of blankets, afghans, and comforters. He chose a soft, forest-green throw, returned to the living room, and tenderly covered Paula. Kneeling beside her, he carefully adjusted the throw beneath her chin, then feathered a light kiss across her forehead. "Rest well," he murmured against her cheek. "See you soon." A few moments later, the front door opened and closed softly.

"Well, so much for a day of fun and games," Paula observed. She glanced across the kitchen table at Scott, who was lazily blowing into a cup of hot chocolate. The clock above the stove said five-thirty P.M. "Where did it go, anyway?"

"Beats me," he said, stirring his cocoa with half a slice of buttered toast. "But I'm feeling a little better—not so sore, anyhow. I guess we needed the down-time."

"I suppose," she agreed, raising her own cup of smooth, chocolaty liquid to her lips. They had both slept the afternoon away—Scott upstairs in his room, Paula on the sofa. Sometime after four, two police detectives had arrived with rubber gloves, evidence collection bags, and a fresh barrage of questions. They were followed shortly by the garage-door repairman, who fixed the opener mechanism in less than ten minutes and charged Paula a hundred dollars for his trouble. Millie had left a message on the answering machine; she'd be spending another day with her ailing friend. Now, in the calm silence of early evening, mother and son sat across from each other, saying nothing, feeling everything. Neither could put a finger on it, but both knew that in the wake of their shared near-catastrophe, things had somehow changed between them.

"You know, this is all so bizarre," Paula observed, lowering her cup to the place mat. "We've lived in this house forever; you and TJ haven't known any other home. But now, it suddenly seems like it's not really *ours* anymore—like it's beyond protection, and some stranger could just come in and take it all away. Like we'll never be safe or secure or have any real privacy, ever again." She shivered involuntarily and glanced nervously toward the garage door, then out the window, where dusk was beginning to fade into a blue-black sky. Her thoughts flew back to early afternoon. *I wish Ted had stayed for another couple of hours—or months.* "Am I making any sense?"

"Unfortunately, you are," Scott said with a grimace. "I've been thinking that same thing myself. Maybe we need to get a security system installed, or something like that. 'Course, Rudy's usually here, but he's getting pretty old. And he was never very good at playing attack dog. He's too *nice.*" They both smiled at the incongruous image of their affable golden retriever defending the home front with anything more threatening than a deep-throated *woof!* "But he's a good ol' boy; I wouldn't trade him for a pit bull with a black belt in karate any day."

Paula laughed; it felt good to share this warm moment with her son, regardless of the circumstances. They'd get through this; she knew they would. In fact . . .

Without warning, his final words triggered a sharp flash of memory in her brain. *Of course!* It had to be worth a try.

"Hey, Scott," she began in a casual tone, "I'm so sorry we didn't get much talking or playing done today. But if you're feeling up to it now, what do you say to a little drive in the Jag?" She knew she'd hit the right button when his eyes lit up like Christmas bulbs. "Maybe we could stop for ice cream . . . and there's something I'd like to show you, too."

"The Jag . . . cool! Uh," his eyes widened, and he looked at her hopefully, "you don't s'pose I could . . ."

"I don't think so," she responded. *No one* but Paula drove the Jag. When his face fell, she decided to amend the rules a bit. "At least not right now, when you've just been through so much. But later . . . maybe before too long." The light returned to his eyes, and he grinned expectantly.

A few minutes later, the cocky red convertible was hurtling down the interstate, its two passengers laughing as the cool, snappy wind twisted their hair and made conversation nearly impossible. "Where we going?" Scott shouted, dangling his arm outside the vehicle and letting it flap in the breeze.

"You'll never guess," Paula taunted with a light jab to his shoulder. "But I think you're gonna like it." She couldn't help giving him a little smirk.

"Yeah, right," he huffed good-naturedly, then settled back into his deep leather seat to enjoy the ride. After a moment, he turned back toward her. "It's good to be out, ya know? Feels clean or something."

"Yes," she said. "I know." She rubbed her bruised arm. "Clean and free."

The Vincente Street exit caught her attention, and she maneuvered the car into the right-hand lane. *This is where Meg said it was,* she thought, remembering the lively description her visiting teaching partner had given. *I hope I can find it . . . should've checked the phone book for an address.* The car slowed as they left the highway and proceeded down a narrow but clean, well-lit street crowded with storefronts. Paula had no idea how far it was, so she barely nudged the Jag from corner to corner as she scoured first one side of the street and then the other. *I really should have checked the phone book,* she scolded herself as a long line of vehicles behind her chose this moment to test their horns. *It can't be much farther.* Four, six, eight blocks later, she was beginning to think she'd made a big mistake.

"Mom, are you crazy?" Scott was staring at the long queue of irate drivers behind them. "I don't know what you're lookin' for, but one of those gnarly four-by-fours is gonna eat us for supper if you don't get out of the—"

"A*ha!* There it is!" Paula's expression was triumphant as she pulled quickly to the curb. Dozens of vehicles immediately sped past her, many of them still honking.

"There *what* is?" Scott glanced up and down the street. "I don't see no Baskin-Robbins anywhere." She pointed, and his gaze followed hers to a nondescript one-story white building about half a block from where they were parked.

He read the lettering aloud. "'Ninja Academy of Martial Arts. Bonita M. Solomon, Instructor.'"

"That would be my friend, Bonnie." Paula said. "I'm her visiting teacher."

Scott glanced sideways at his mother and raised an eyebrow, then continued reading. "'Karate. Judo. Kick Boxing. Tae Kwon Do. Self-Defense. The Family that Kicks Together, Sticks Together!'" He rolled his eyes and slid down in his seat. "Oh, brother."

Paula smiled broadly and patted him on the shoulder. "See? I said you'd never guess. C'mon, let's go inside. Bonnie's invited me to come see her studio, and I figure this is as good a time as any."

"You've gotta be kidding." Scott peered through the building's large front window into a spacious room where several white-clad figures appeared to be doing stretching exercises. "It's just a bunch of wimpy-looking guys in their pajamas."

"Then there's nothing to be afraid of, is there?" Paula was already unbuckling her seat belt. "We'll only stay for a few minutes. Just indulge your old mom for a little bit here, would you? There's a hot fudge sundae in it if you mind your manners."

"Hey, I'm not a little kid anymore, Mom. If you're trying to bribe me . . ."

"Okay, okay, *two* hot fudge sundaes. With nuts."

Scott sighed. "All right. But only for a couple of minutes—max." Grasping the frame of the convertible with both hands, he propelled himself over the door and into the air. His feet hit the sidewalk just as Paula stepped onto the curb, and he grinned as she approached him. "What took ya so long?" he smirked.

"I'm old. Gimme a break," she replied, grabbing the sleeve of his T-shirt and pulling him toward the studio door.

Inside, they sat on a bench at one end of the long, mirrored room. No one seemed to notice them. A dozen boys and girls, ranging in age from mid to late teens, seemed intent on reaching, stretching, flexing, and extending their young bodies to the limit. Their catlike movements were graceful and controlled, their repetitive motions deliberate and focused as they performed their exercises on thin mats spread across the wood floor. Their crisp martial arts uniforms projected an air of order and civility. Paula was fascinated. "This is so interesting," she whispered to Scott, who appeared slightly less enthralled than a comatose iguana. "What kind of martial arts do you think they're doing?"

"Sissy stuff," Scott mumbled. He scuffed one rubber-soled sneaker against the wood floor until it produced a loud squeak.

"What, you think this is a walk in the flower garden?" a husky voice boomed close to his ear. He started, then looked up to see a wiry, auburn-haired woman standing beside him, her hands on her slim hips. She was dressed in a white uniform identical to those of the students, except for a heavy black cotton belt circling her waist.

"Bonnie!" Paula exclaimed, vaulting to her feet. "I hope you don't mind our just dropping by. We were in the neighborhood, and—"

Her explanation was cut short by a pair of strong, sinewy arms around her, squeezing her lungs dry. When Bonnie finally drew back, her generous mouth opened into a wide smile. "Well, look here! It's one of my home ladies! You're always welcome in my studio, Paula." Her dark eyes moved back to the bench. "And this devilishly handsome young man must be—"

"My son, Scott." Paula noticed a light flush coloring his cheeks as he rose and nodded stoically.

"A pleasure," Bonnie said, extending her hand. Paula managed to keep a straight face as her son winced at the woman's viselike grip. He sat down and let out a deep sigh when it was over.

She turned to Paula. "Have you and Scott ever seen a martial arts demonstration?"

"Not really," Paula admitted. "But some things have happened recently, and—"

"So I see," Bonnie broke in, reaching out to carefully touch Paula's cheek with the tips of her fingers. Her gaze also took in the bandage affixed to Scott's temple. "What went down?"

"We had an intruder," Paula explained, "and he messed us both up pretty bad. So we've been wondering if . . . well, if there might be some kind of self-defense we could learn that doesn't involve weapons of mass destruction."

Scott's head shot up and he glared at his mother, his eyes flashing a surly message. *Have you lost it? We've been wondering? Speak for yourself! Who wants anything to do with a bunch of barefoot kids runnin' around in sissy uniforms, bowin' to each other, just waitin' to get their stupid heads blown off?*

Paula rested her hand on his shoulder. "Scott and I would *love* to see a demonstration," she said sweetly. A large knot of muscles tightened beneath her palm, but she squeezed firmly and looked down at him benevolently. "Wouldn't we, dear?"

"Right," he mumbled.

"Terrific!" Bonnie was clearly delighted. "You've come at the perfect time. One of my intermediate/advanced karate classes is about to start. Sit back and enjoy; they'll definitely give you your money's worth."

"Yeah, just what it's worth . . . nuthin'," Scott growled under his breath.

"I heard that," Bonnie declared. Her tone was severe, but when he looked up at her she was beaming. "And I'll bet you an extra-large, triple-deluxe pizza that one hour from now, you'll be eating those words."

"Or, more likely, my extra-large, triple-deluxe pizza." He leaned back against the bench, folded his arms across his chest, and flashed her a snide grin. "I'm feeling a little hungry already."

"We're on, then," Bonnie said, her green eyes sparkling. "Now, if you'll excuse me, I have a class to attend to." She turned abruptly and marched to the opposite end of the room. The students, seeing her approach, left their exercising and came to perfect attention.

As the warmups and introductory routines began, Paula was fascinated, while Scott maintained a stonelike expression of mild annoyance. But a few minutes later, when the students paired off and starting practicing their carefully choreographed defensive moves and techniques, Scott slid forward to the edge of the bench and watched intently. "Why do they put the little kids with the big ones?" he wondered out loud. "Somebody's gonna get creamed. They oughta match 'em up with kids their own size. Bonnie could get sued for—"

SMACK! One of the students hit the mat, and the sound reverberated through the studio. Scott took in a sharp breath as he realized that the white-clad figure on the floor was by far the biggest, tallest, heaviest person in the room—at least six foot three, well over two hundred pounds, someone you definitely wouldn't relish meeting in a dark alley. But now here he was, flat on his back, out of breath, staring blankly up into the face of his opponent. Scott could almost feel his own back stinging in sympathy.

A few seconds later the young man grinned and scrambled to his feet, ready for another skirmish. As this hulk of a teenager stood next to his partner—the impressive opponent who had prostrated him with a seemingly effortless twist of the arm and a well-placed kick to the backs of his knees—Scott's eyes widened in total disbelief. "It's a *girl!*" he sputtered. He glanced quickly at Paula, whose lower jaw seemed to be resting on her knees. *"Did you see that, Mom?"* She nodded, not quite able to speak. This girl was barely five feet tall, maybe fourteen years old, and probably weighed less than a hundred pounds soaking wet. She patted her partner amiably on the stomach before they went at it again. This time, he charged her and she tossed him over her shoulder.

"Wow!" Scott and Paula exclaimed in unison. Their eyes never left the pair on the mat.

"It's a learned skill," Bonnie's voice said beside them. "Sara started classes when she was twelve, and she's been one of our outstanding students. Brad's a relative newcomer, but he's progressing nicely. In another few months, he'll be able to hold his own against the better part of a football team. It's all timing and leverage. And, of course, concentration." They watched as the couple switched partners, and Brad's new male opponent quickly felt the sting of the mat. Sara easily disabled a tall, thin girl who looked as though she might be more at home on a modeling runway; but during their second bout, Sara made an indecisive move and landed on her back. "We teach people of all ages to use their bodies as tools of self-discipline, self-control, self-esteem, and self-defense," Bonnie explained. "Put all of those qualities together and add a few calculated physical moves and defensive techniques, and I don't care whose army you're fighting, you'll come out on top. It's kind of a nonviolent approach to . . . well, to staying alive."

"I see," Paula said. But frankly, it doesn't look all that nonviolent to me."

Bonnie smiled. "Everything's relative, honey. We figure a sharp, temporarily disabling kick to the solar plexus or a distracting jab to the eye is basically nonviolent when compared to, say, a bullet ripping through one's chest or brain. The objective of using martial arts is not to kill, but to honorably defend oneself. And believe me, it works." She noticed a student trying to catch her attention. "Oh, gotta run. See you later, kids." With a friendly squeeze of Paula's arm, she was off to supervise.

More than an hour later, mother and son still sat mesmerized, having hardly blinked as they observed what seemed the impossible—youngsters using their bodies as ingenious weapons to outmaneuver, outsmart, outbluff, outface, outwill, and outdo their opponents. All without bloodshed or broken bones—and they hardly even seemed out of breath. As the last of the students filed from the room, Scott pressed his shoulder against Paula's and said in a low voice, "I gotta do this, Mom. I mean, I thought I knew what this karate stuff was all about, but this is just too awesome."

"I know what you mean," Paula replied. "I might just do it myself . . . that is, if I'm not too old. When I think of the damage I could have inflicted on that creep last night . . ." She rubbed her sore arm as the memories washed over her.

"I hear ya," Scott nodded. "Where do I—uh, we—sign up?"

Within minutes, Bonnie appeared in her "civvies"—a pair of loose-fitting jeans and a turquoise sweatshirt. "I usually just wear my uniform home," she explained, "but this is a special occasion." She looked pointedly at Scott. "Anyone for pizza?"

He smile sheepishly. "Yeah. I guess you got me."

"Me, too," Paula interjected. "And I'll spring for the pizza. We've got some talking to do. For starters, I have a question: Can you teach this old dog a few new tricks?"

Bonnie's laugh seemed to fill the studio. "Hon, there's nothing old about you. Heck, last month I started teaching a little gal who just turned seventy-four. She's doing fantastic, and so will you. But first things first. I know this pizza dive that'll knock your socks off. Let's get out of here!" She reached for a switch, and suddenly the bright studio was transformed into a cavernous gray ghost of itself, illuminated only by a few dim lights in the ceiling. Scott watched their three dark reflections in the mirror as they moved past the exit sign and out into the cool evening.

Much later, having satisfied their bodies with a transcendent extra-large, triple-deluxe pizza, and their minds with the prospect of a tantalizing new adventure, mother and son stood together in the upper hall of their home. "This is gonna be great, Mom," Scott said, and the light in his eyes told Paula he really meant it. "Classes start next week, and in a couple of months I'll be showin' the Crawlers how to *really* kick butt."

"Yes, I'm sure you will, dear," Paula chuckled. "Just promise me you won't kick mine."

"No way. Bonnie would nuke me. Besides, you'll be learning this stuff, too—and I saw for myself tonight how hard the big guys can fall."

"Good. Just so we understand each other." She wrapped her arms around Scott, hugged him to her, and felt him return the embrace. "Good night, son. Sweet dreams." Earlier in the day she had sensed a turning point, then hoped for a deeper dimension in their relationship because of what they had faced together. Now she knew it was no longer a nebulous hope but a bright new reality, cloaked in mutual trust and a simple white cotton uniform. *Maybe it's true,* she thought as she softly closed her bedroom door and paused to smile at the wide band of moonlight streaming through her window. *The family that kicks together, sticks together.*

CHAPTER 15

Millie shook her head as she sprinkled cinnamon sugar over a small stack of buttered pancakes. "I don't know what's come over that boy," she said, "but he's certainly not the Scotty I knew three weeks ago." She smiled across the table at Paula. "Not that I'm complaining, of course. It's just that he's so . . . *pleasant.* Makes a body wonder if he's been taking some kind of happy pills or something."

Paula nodded and poured herself a glass of fresh-squeezed orange juice. "I know; it's amazing, isn't it? But I can assure you, my friend, that the only thing he's 'high' on at the moment is Bonnie Solomon's karate classes. At least twice a week, right after school, and every Saturday morning, he and couple of his buddies from the Crawlers show up at her studio. I swear, he's going to have that whole gang enrolled by the end of the month. He's good at it, too; Bonnie tells me she's never seen a student learn so fast. 'A natural,' she calls him."

"I can see that," the older woman agreed. "He's always been athletic, and now he's found a way to put it all together and make himself into—how do they say it?—a 'lean, mean fighting machine.'" She laughed merrily, then became more serious. "It's a wonderful skill he's learning, you know—to be able to protect himself and others from vermin like the one who attacked you."

"Exactly," Paula said. "And I think he's learning some pretty important things about himself in the process—discipline, self-confidence, leadership, all those good qualities that'll make him happy and successful in the long run." She paused and looked into Millie's eyes. "I guess it took a near catastrophe to bring us to this point. But if it's helped him find some direction, it was worth it."

"Yes, indeed," Millie said quietly. "The Lord works in mysterious ways." She poured steaming hot chocolate into a cup near her plate. "And how are your classes going?"

"Not too bad," Paula reported. "At least I haven't sprained, dislocated, or broken anything yet, and I've actually learned a few good moves. One night a week is all I can fit in, which is just about the limit of what this old lady's bones and muscles can tolerate. Of course, Scotty's leaving me in the dust, which is perfectly fine with me. We compare notes, and I've never seen him so excited, so anxious to learn. I don't mind telling you, I'm *so proud* of that kid." She smiled, and her eyes shimmered. "You know, I never thought I'd say this, but I really think he's going to make it now. And you're absolutely right, Millie . . . the Lord does work in mysterious ways."

Paula leaned back in her chair and mentally reviewed the events of the past few weeks. Life had been better than good, marred only briefly by her disagreement with Ted over the Green Pointe account. In the end, after a thorough examination and re-examination of her values as a new member of the Church and a concerned parent, she had simply put her foot down and terminated her contract with the liquor company. "We can still offer the people choices," she explained to Ted, "but as far as Donroe & Associates is concerned, from now on we won't even *think* about offering them choices that conflict with gospel standards. Period."

To her surprise, he supported her decision. "It's probably the right thing to do," he conceded. "After all," he added breezily, "what's ten or twenty million dollars in the grand scheme of things?" The next morning, a single red rose appeared on Paula's desk, along with a note in his broad scrawl: "I like the way you think, chief. Go, Mormons!"

Meanwhile, despite her demanding work schedule, those body- and mind-stretching karate classes, and time spent nurturing relationships with her son, as well as with Meg O'Brien and the women they visit taught, Paula's thoughts were never very far from the Richland family. Ruthie's weekly parcel of peanut butter chocolate chip cookies had become a regular staple of the Donroes' diet, and frequent phone calls kept the two families comfortably connected. Karti had sounded weary at the beginning of their last conversation several days earlier, but she declared that all was well, and Paula was relieved to hear the animation return to her friend's voice as she spoke of Mark and his plans to return to BYU for the summer term. "Alex starts classes at Idaho State this summer, too; and of course we'll be sending Jake into the mission field around the same time." She sighed. "The nest is already beginning to feel a little empty. Thank goodness for my angel girls; I don't know what I'd do without them." The pure love in her tone warmed Paula's heart, and she vowed to make a quick visit to Idaho before too long. She smiled to herself as a delicious thought entered her mind. *It's good to have friends. Good to have someone to care about.*

A firm but gentle pressure against Paula's leg brought her back to the present just as Millie cleared her throat. Glancing beneath the table, Paula was not surprised to find Rudy sprawled on the floor, his massive head resting against her lower calf. "I think someone's trying to tell you something," Millie said. The dog then lowered his head to the top of her foot, and she could feel his warm, thick fur against her ankle. He looked up to meet her gaze, and the expression in his mellow brown eyes melted any earlier resolve to spend the day at her office.

"So, you're ready for a little walk in the sunshine, huh, pal?" Three thumps of his tail on the floor answered her question. "Well, buddy, I can't think of anything better to do on a lovely Saturday morning, can you? After all, the beautiful month of May only comes once a year, and I can go to work later this afternoon." Giving Millie a wink, she pushed her chair back and watched Rudy saunter toward the front door, looking back every few seconds to make sure Paula was right behind him. She grabbed a lead from the hall closet and was outside almost before Rudy had cleared the entryway. "See you in an hour or so," she called as the door closed behind them.

The phone was ringing as the pair returned, Paula flushed by her brisk walk in the cool morning air, Rudy winded and utterly content at the prospect of sleeping the day away beneath his favorite shade tree. Leaving the phone for Millie to answer, Paula let Rudy into the backyard, then headed up to her own room for a quick shower.

Millie's voice stopped her halfway up the stairs. "Call for you, dear. From Idaho."

"Great! I'll get it in my room." She took the remaining stairs two at a time, bounded eagerly down the hall, and kicked her bedroom door closed behind her. Plopping cross-legged on her bed, she took a moment to catch her breath, then reached for the phone and lifted the receiver. "Good morning!" she said, feeling an infectious smile burst into her vocal cords. She could hardly wait to catch up on all the news.

"Paula." The deep voice paused. "I'm glad you're home."

"Mark? Mark, is that you?" A vague shiver of apprehension crept up the back of her neck, but she shook it off. "Sounds like you have a terrible cold. I hope your mother's cooking up a big pot of chicken soup and giving you lots of TLC. Whenever my boys were sick, we would—"

"It's not a cold," he broke in, his tone even lower than before. "It's something else."

"What, then? Pneumonia? Bronchitis? You sound awful . . . like you've been eating gravel. Now, *there's* an eating disorder for you." She waited for his easy, contagious laugh, but there was only silence. "Mark, what's going on?"

"It's Mom."

The apprehension returned, accompanied by a massive knot of dread in the pit of her stomach. She could barely force the words out. "Is it the cancer?"

"Yes . . . but it's not what you think."

She didn't know *what* she was thinking, but her mind was screaming for more information. "Last time we spoke, she was doing fine . . . still in remission."

"And she still is," Mark clarified.

"Well, then, that's good news . . . isn't it?"

"It would be, if . . ." He coughed, then started again. "There's no easy way to say this, but they've found a secondary malignancy. Last week they did a routine MRI, and it showed a tumor in her pancreas. A big one. It's a death sentence, Paula; it's already too late." He paused. "I've been trying to work up the courage to call you for the past few days."

"Oh, *no,*" she groaned from the deepest part of her soul. "I was so sure—we were all so sure we'd seen a miracle, and she'd outlive us all."

"I know. Just as things are getting back to normal, this hits us like a blast out of nowhere. It's ripping Dad to pieces."

Paula thought of Sam, so quiet and strong, his kind eyes saying what words could never express as he gazed across the kitchen table at his beloved wife. His Karti. The image flooded her heart with intractable pain. "Oh, Mark," she whispered, "I'm so sorry. So terribly sorry." She wiped at her eyes and felt her lips and chin tremble uncontrollably. "What about treatments—surgery, chemotherapy, anything?"

"No options," he said flatly. "She's too run down for any more chemo, and the same goes for surgery. Besides, the doctor says pancreatic cancer at this stage is always fatal; the most they can do, even with treatments, is prolong the inevitable for a few weeks or months." He spoke the words slowly, evenly, as if he had rehearsed them a hundred times and still wasn't quite sure how to say them.

"Do the girls know?" She pictured Andrea and Ruthie, youthful and vibrant, just beginning to savor life and its possibilities, now facing a future without their mother.

"Dad told them a couple of days ago. I don't think they quite understand yet; Ruthie's convinced that 'just one more priesthood blessing, especially for Mommy,' will do the trick."

Paula had to smile through her tears. "Well, now, she just may have a point. Anything's possible with the good Lord on our side, isn't it? Case in point: He got me to join the Church. With such a miracle behind Him, I would think He'd consider cancer a piece of cake."

She heard a little chuckle. "Of course you're right, Paula," he agreed. "Anything's possible. But," the somber voice returned, "we've all done a lot of praying about it—fasting, too—and it just doesn't seem like she's going to get well this time. Mom and Dad say they've had a spiritual experience telling them so; and while Mom's willing to hold on to hope and fight until her last breath to stay with us, she's also resigned to the Lord's will. Kind of an interesting juxtaposition of tenacity and submission, isn't it? But then, that's the way she's always lived her life . . . more than ready to embrace any opportunity or challenge, but absolutely willing to choose obedience to a higher law over her own comfort or convenience. So now, when the chips are down, she's ready." He took in a ragged breath. "Dad and the rest of us are having a little tougher time with it, seeing as how we'll be . . . without her. For the rest of our lives."

Paula didn't want to ask, but she forced the words out between parched lips. "How long?"

"The doctor said it will go fast. Six weeks. Maybe a couple of months."

"Dear Lord." She covered her mouth to muffle an anguished sob. *Too soon. Too soon.* Taking in a breath, she tried to speak normally. "How is she doing today? Can I talk to her?"

"She's resting right now, but I know she's planning to call you soon. She's actually feeling quite good at the moment—still in a state of shock, I think, but physically she really hasn't started to . . . uh . . . deteriorate yet." He swallowed hard. "That's what makes this whole thing so hard to believe—to think that before the summer's gone, she will be, too. It blows your mind, you know?" Paula could hear his agony behind every word.

"I know," she agreed, her own voice none too steady. "What can I do, Mark? Of course I'll want to come to see her right away, and—"

"I'm not sure," he said. "We're all still getting used to this, and she'll let you know how she wants to handle it. In the meantime, your prayers will help a lot."

"Absolutely; that's the least I can do. Please give her my love, and tell her I'll try to—"

"Hello, Paula?" She recognized Karti's voice instantly. "I picked up the phone a second ago to make a call, and imagine my surprise to hear my son talking to his mother." The warm, melodious voice crackled with delight. "I just *love* saying that."

Paula laughed in spite of herself. "We're three of a kind, that's for sure. I doubt that anyone else in the world could claim such a unique 'love triangle.'"

"Or two more terrific mothers," Mark added.

"Quite true," Karti said lightly. "Now, son, would you kindly excuse us? We'd like to talk about you, and we don't want to run the risk of burning your ears."

"Yeah, yeah," he murmured, sounding almost relieved. Catch you later." The phone clicked, and the two women were alone.

"So," Karti began after a brief pause, "I guess he told you." She said it casually, still clinging to a shred of the bantering tone she had used a moment earlier.

"Yes," Paula confirmed. "I . . . I don't know what to say."

"Don't say anything." Her tone had become even and somber. "Except, of course, that you'll come to say good-bye."

The implication of her friend's words suddenly became all too real, and a riptide of emotion rose in Paula's chest. "Then it's true," she moaned.

"Oh, yes, it's true. I've come to terms with that."

"How?"

"By staying on my knees until I was finally able to reconcile myself to the Lord's will, and then letting it go, placing it in His care."

Paula chuckled without humor. "You make it sound so simple."

"I wish," Karti replied with a deep, unfathomable sigh. "It's been the hardest thing I've ever done—with the possible exception," her voice lightened a bit, "of going through seventeen hours of hard labor before Alex was born." She hesitated for a moment. "At least then I knew I'd be bringing something wonderful into the world. But this business of dying . . . well, it's never exactly a welcome development, and I suppose one always feels like a lot has been left undone. I've just found *you*, for goodness' sake. Sam and I had so looked forward to growing old together. And eventually there will be grandchildren . . ." Another pause. "But I've come this far believing—*knowing*—the gospel is true, the plan of salvation is real, and the immortality of the soul is so much more than just a vague hope conjured up by someone who was afraid to die and needed something to hold on to. Because I know these things, I *must* accept the Lord's timetable for my life. Of course, that doesn't mean I won't stick around as long as I possibly can. It just means that when the time comes, I'll be able to leave with no regrets." She gave a tenuous little laugh. "At least that's the way I hope it'll work. I'm a novice at this death thing, you know."

Paula could hardly speak around the knot of grief and admiration in her throat. "Everything you say makes perfect sense—if there's any sense in a beautiful life ending way too early." She held tighter to the phone as another rush of emotion threatened. "I just wish we had a little more time. I'll come to see you next week, and we can—"

"Forgive me, Paula, but I don't think so," Karti broke in. "We've known and cared for each other for a few months now—though I truly believe I've loved you from the moment I first held Mark in my arms—and we've made some incredible memories. But I think the time has already passed for doing that, and I need to give my husband and children my undivided attention between now and . . . then. Whenever it comes."

Paula bristled a little as she wiped at her tears. "You mean . . . you mean you don't want to see me?"

"Oh, I *do* want to see you. More than anything." Karti's words vibrated with affection and concern. "But please, let *me* say when. On second thought, I think we'll both know when. Of course we'll keep the phone lines humming, and you'll know everything as it happens. Then you'll come when it's time to say good-bye, and we'll make every precious moment count." Paula could almost feel the touch of her friend's generous lips against the receiver. "Am I making any sense at all?"

"I'm afraid so," Paula admitted, "and I'll respect your decision. But you will call, any time, day or night, if you need me?"

"I promise," Karti agreed with a sigh of relief. "Cross my heart."

"Then I'll hold you to it. Extraordinary people like you don't come into my life every day, you know. Or go out of it." Paula felt the words etched in pain on her own heart.

"My sister, my friend," Karti murmured with quiet intensity. "We'll get through this together."

"Yes, of course," Paula said, her voice liquid. "Together." *Except when this is all over, we'll be anything but together.* The thought sent tears flowing unchecked down her flushed cheeks. How had she come to care so deeply about another human being in so short a time? And how could she possibly let her go? *As if I have a choice.* Shaking her head, she squeezed her eyes tightly shut. *Like I had a choice with TJ.* Memories of her young son's violent and untimely death only a few months earlier burned into her mind like salt being poured into a fresh wound. *The Lord giveth and the Lord taketh away . . . but why does the taking have to hurt so much?*

"Paula, are you still with me?" Karti asked after several moments of silence.

"Yes . . . sorry. I was just thinking."

"That can be dangerous." Karti's tone was light but filled with compassion, as if she understood perfectly. "Let's just move on from here, shall we?"

Paula grabbed a tissue from her nightstand and wiped her nose. "Okay."

They chatted for a few minutes longer and managed to end the conversation on a lighter note, promising to stay closely in touch. "And don't you *dare* e-mail me," Paula warned. "This is definitely reach-out-and-touch-someone time. I want to *hear* how you're doing, not just see it on an impersonal computer screen, where altogether too much is left to the imagination."

"Yes, Mother," Karti laughed. They spoke a few more words of friendship and encouragement, then hung up. Paula carefully replaced the receiver in its cradle, then lay back against the floral chintz-covered pillows on her bed to contemplate this latest wrinkle in her life. She couldn't bear to tell anyone just yet; she had to come to terms with it herself first. But how?

Instinctively, she slipped to her knees beside the bed. *He'll tell me how to handle this,* she told herself. *He's given Karti the strength she needs, and probably the rest of the family, too; surely He'll do the same for me.* "Heavenly Father," she whispered, "please, please . . ." As words failed, so did her composure, and fresh sobs wracked her slender body until exhaustion dulled her mind and enveloped her in a thick, impenetrable shroud of lethargy. "Later, Lord," she finally mumbled as she laboriously swung her leaden arms, legs, and torso onto the bed. "I'll ask later . . . but please be thinking about it." Her eyes fluttered shut, and she sank into a black hole of insensibility.

❤ ❤ ❤

"You look awful," Ted observed as he stood in the doorway of Paula's office on Monday morning. She didn't respond, only stared at him drearily from beneath swollen lids. His gaze traveled from her barely combed hair to the deep blotches beneath her red-tinged eyes, and he decided to lighten his approach. "Didn't go on a weekend-long bender, did you?"

It took exactly three tenths of a second for huge tears to well in her eyes and trickle down her pale cheeks. "Uh-oh," he said quickly, closing the office door and moving to a chair next to her desk. "Bad joke. Sorry." He reached out to touch her arm, but pulled his hand back at the last moment. "I can tell something's happened . . . you want to talk about it?" He rested an elbow on the desk.

Paula closed her eyes and dabbed at them with a pale green tissue. "Why not?" she said, her voice parched and crackly. "I've already told Millie, Scott, my visiting teaching partner, the bishop—and I've known you longer than any of them. Well, maybe not longer than I've known Scotty." He thought he detected the trace of a smile at one corner of her mouth. "Besides, I'm probably going to need your help over the next little while."

"At your disposal, chief," he said, lowering his voice to match her solemn tone. His eyes were fixed on hers, waiting.

For the fifth time in three days, Paula told Karti's story; and for at least the tenth time, she wept inconsolably. "I feel so utterly, completely helpless," she admitted to Ted, who seemed, at the moment, with his kind blue eyes and sympathetic ear, like her best friend in the world. "I've prayed, but so far I've felt nothing that even resembles peace or comfort." She smiled lamely. "Maybe God is only listening to people in Idaho these days."

"You're probably right," Ted observed with a straight face. "His Mondays, Wednesdays, Fridays, and weekends are all tied up in Idaho; Tuesdays and Thursdays He takes care of the rest of the world. Maybe you'll hear something tomorrow. First thing in the morning."

She grinned in spite of herself and punched him lightly on the shoulder. "You're a big help."

"Anything for the boss," he declared, clearly relieved to see a faint, intangible glimmer of something—was it hope? faith? determination?—return to her eyes. At least it was a start. "Now, in the Big Man's absence, what can I do to help today?"

"You've already done a lot by just listening. Thanks." She patted his arm gratefully. "I have no way of knowing when I'll be needed in Idaho; if I had my way, it would be sometime in the year 2050. In any case, needless to say, between now and when the time comes I'm not likely to be my usual hands-on, obsessive self about much of anything. I'll try to stay focused, but I can't help feeling like I'm heading into a replay of what happened when I lost TJ." She pressed her lips together for a few long moments, then continued. "Only in some ways, this will be even worse. TJ was gone in an instant, without warning; but I know this death is coming, and there's nothing I can do but wait for it. Then afterwards, there's the grieving to get through. Double jeopardy." She shook her head. "You're going to have to keep me on track, Ted. At least don't let me do anything stupid. I don't want to lose business for the company because I'm so distracted that I can't see things clearly. On the other hand, I can't shut myself off from Karti simply because there are deals to make and ad campaigns to run. Just be my brains and common sense for a while, would you? Be my"—a mental image flashed through her mind, and her heart reached out to it instinctively—"my iron rod."

Ted's eyebrows shot up, then he looked at her intently. "What, you mean the one they put in my leg after that high school linebacker twisted it like a pretzel? Or do you mean I actually get to hold on to you," he gripped her hand and squeezed tightly, "and protect you from all those raving lunatics pacing the floor in that funky large and spacious building?" His face split into a broad grin. "No problem."

"So," she smiled back, "you remember the story." *The Book of Mormon comes to life on the twenty-third floor of a Los Angeles skyscraper.*

"Are you kidding? It was one of my favorites when I was a kid." A light flush rose to his cheeks. "Still is."

"I see," Paula replied evenly. "So, will you do it? Help me, I mean."

"As I said . . . anything for the boss." Ted stood and placed his hand gallantly over his heart. "Iron rod and all."

"Get out of here," she laughed. "We've got work to do." For the first time in days, she felt like she might be able to make it through this.

Two weeks passed, then three, and each time Paula spoke with Karti, she noticed no appreciable change in her friend's condition. "I'm sort of tired, and my insides feel a bit unsettled," she would say, "but I seem to be doing all right." She even mentioned something about Christmas, and Paula's heart soared.

Likewise, Sam and the children sounded optimistic. "We're very hopeful that she'll be with us for a long time yet," Sam insisted, and his calm, reassuring manner buoyed Paula's spirits. He was giving his wife frequent priesthood blessings, and they seemed to be helping. Or at least, Paula thought, keeping the disease at bay. Her own prayers mingled with theirs daily, and she began to relax and focus more productively on her work. Perhaps, after all, the doctors had only been doomsayers, and things weren't really as dismal as they had seemed at first.

Ruthie's weekly package of cookies arrived without fail, usually with a short, cheery note. "Mom's doing good today," she wrote one Wednesday in May. "She helped me with the cookies, then we watched a video of an old movie—*National Velvet*. Elizabeth Taylor was *so pretty*—like you. Cool!"

Late in the seventh week, Mark called Paula at work. Karti had begun to fail. "They said it might happen like this," he explained. "She goes along really well for quite a while, then starts going downhill almost overnight." His voice quavered, and he cleared his throat. "Now I can see it's happening. Things were going great, and I guess we were all a little bit in denial. Or maybe we were just holding out for—for something better. Like a miracle."

Paula's throat constricted, and her tongue felt twice its normal size. "Should I come?" she rasped.

"I don't think so," he said. "It's not that bad—yet. She says she'll know when it's time, and she'll make sure the two of you have at least . . . a day or two together." A long pause. "I'd keep a bag packed."

"Can I talk to her?" Paula thought if she could just make some kind of a physical connection with her friend, this news would be a little more bearable. A little less devastating.

"She's asleep. The pain has started in earnest, and she's taking some medication. I know she'll call you in the next day or two, when she gets used to the med schedule. I just wanted you to know . . . first."

"I appreciate that, Mark," Paula murmured. "I really do. Give my love to your family." They exchanged a few words of comfort and encouragement, then the call was over.

Paula leaned back in her chair and closed her eyes. Only one thought, one question reverberated through her mind like an echo across the deepest ravine of an ageless canyon. *How do I say good-bye?*

CHAPTER 16

It was three days before Paula saw the Idaho number on her caller ID, and her heart nearly pounded out of her chest as she sat on the edge of her bed, her hand poised above the phone. *Is it Karti? Yes, of course it is, and she's probably feeling better; Mark said she was getting used to the pain medication. Or . . . it could be someone else, calling to tell me it's too late—that she took a sudden downward turn and was gone in the middle of the night, in her sleep, before anyone even knew it. Now all that's left is the funeral, and a brief graveside service committing her elegant body to the earth and releasing her spirit to return to the arms of her Maker. I wish she'd let me come to see her weeks ago. I just wanted to tell her one more time . . .* She stared at the phone, a huge lump of remorse clogging her throat, until it stopped ringing. Her hand dropped heavily into her lap. *I'll call back in a few minutes,* she promised. *When I'm more in control. I need to be strong for the family.* She mentally pictured a grief-stricken husband and children, huddled together for strength against this cruel twist of events, and she longed to be with them.

A sharp knock at her bedroom door dissolved the image, and Paula heard Millie's muffled voice. "Paula? I saw the caller ID and thought you'd want to answer this call, but you didn't, so I picked it up." After a short pause, her tone became more insistent. "Paula, are you there?"

"Yes, yes, I'm here," Paula called out hoarsely. "I was just waiting to . . . um, I just—"

"Well, stop waiting and pick up the phone," Millie ordered crisply. "It's *long distance,* you know. You've kept Karti waiting long enough."

"Karti? *Karti!*" The name tasted like sugar on Paula's tongue, and a surge of pure joy swept over her. *She's still with us! Still alive! Still Karti!* "Thanks, Millie . . . I'll get it!" Two seconds later, Paula lifted the receiver to her ear. "Karti?" she said tentatively.

"What, you were expecting someone else? Hey, I haven't got all day here. What took you so long?" Karti's voice sounded weary and a bit strained, but was still laced with her typical good humor.

"Oh, I was just being an idiot," Paula laughed. "I do that quite regularly, you know. How are you doing, my friend? You sound pretty good." She crossed her fingers, hoping the news would be encouraging.

"I'm not doing too bad, really," Karti said. "This pancreatic tumor is starting to press on a few things inside, so I've been having some discomfort. Fortunately, my doctor isn't among the fanatic few who think terminal patients shouldn't be allowed to become 'dependent' on pain medication. He's promised to keep me as comfortable as possible, and so far the pills he prescribed are working like a charm. I'm only a tiny bit groggy, and it makes the world pleasantly fuzzy." She giggled softly. "Gee, if I'd known what fun it was being a drug addict, I'd have started years ago."

"Wanna share?" Paula joked. "I could use a little stress management these days."

"Oh, no you don't. You've got to stay sharp so you and your son can conquer the world, one karate chop at a time. Trust me . . . there are a couple of black belts out there with your names on them."

"No doubt there's one for Scotty; he's burning up the mats," Paula replied. "As for me, I'll be perfectly content if I just get through one or two classes without breaking something. It's actually a lot of fun, but I'm afraid I'm past my prime when it comes to this Superwoman stuff."

"Paula, to me you will always be Superwoman." Karti's tone was suddenly deep and earnest.

Paula half-laughed, half-coughed as though she was embarrassed. "Aw, shucks, you're just saying that because I've managed to claw my way up to workaholic status, and—"

"No, I'm perfectly serious. You're an exceptional human being, and your life, especially now that you've found the gospel, will be wonderful. I know it. I can *feel* it."

"Well, maybe," Paula responded, "but it would be a whole lot more wonderful if you were going to be around to—" She cut off abruptly and squeezed her eyes shut, biting her lip until it throbbed. "Sorry," she mumbled. "That was totally insensitive. I shouldn't have—"

"No problem," Karti said lightly. "We might as well face the fact that my time, at least in the mortal sense, is winding down. But never forget, my friend, that even when I'm not here . . . *I'll be watching you!*" She laughed ghoulishly and Paula joined her, sharing a warm moment of humor.

"Thanks, I needed that," Paula finally said.

"Me too. I just lie around most of the time, and things get so . . . *deadly* boring around here." They laughed again. "Oh, my," Karti said, catching her breath, "it feels good to be able to joke a little." She spoke more softly now. "It's not always easy, that's for sure. Every day, when I look at Sam, I see the love of my life swimming upstream against a river of grief, struggling to stay afloat, pasting a smile on his face for me and the children. But I can see it in his eyes; he's suffering, and he's knows there's no turning back now. Eventually he'll just have to let go, let the river take him. Hopefully, someone will be there to throw him a lifeline and help him get his feet on solid ground again."

"You have a strong family," Paula reminded her. "They'll help each other."

"I know, and that's a great comfort." Karti let out a little sigh. "You'll stay close to them, won't you? Andrea and Ruthie adore you, and I know Mark's future is important to you. The other boys could use a good friend, too—not to mention Sam, who may be at loose ends for a while. They'd love to have you visit every now and again, if you could manage to break away."

"You know I will," Paula vowed. "Every chance I get."

"Good," Karti declared. "Now, my last pain pill is starting to kick in, and I'm ready for a little nap." She yawned to prove her point. "We'll talk again soon, okay?"

"Any time, day or night. I'll be here."

They visited for a few minutes longer, until Karti's voice slurred. "Hafta go," she murmured. "Take care . . . love you."

"Love you too," Paula said, amazed at how easily the words came, how sweet they sounded. *Perhaps,* she thought as she slowly replaced the receiver, *I'm finally learning what real love is all about.*

Paula nervously tapped a manicured fingernail against her front teeth. *Why am I so edgy?* she wondered as she aimed the Jag onto the interstate and headed for the Vincente Street exit. *It can't be Karti; she's rallied over these past three weeks, and she seemed comfortable and happy when I talked with her two days ago. I must be feeling sympathetic pins and needles for Scotty.*

It was Friday, seven P.M., and she was due at the Ninja Academy in exactly half an hour to observe her son's competitive exhibition and "graduation" to a more advanced level of training in the martial arts. Bonnie Solomon had praised him as one of her best students ever— quite aside from the fact that he had single-handedly doubled her enrollment by strong-arming his entire gang of Crawlers into the karate/kick boxing fold. In fact, they now had an entire class to themselves.

This should be a real show, she thought, smiling to herself. *All those long-haired, baggy-pants, beer-drinking, ear-nose-and-tongue-pierced borderline juvenile delinquents, now dressed impeccably in spotless white, their faces spit-shined to a high polish, hair neatly banded into stylish ponytails, all studs and rings and wires carefully removed and stored in the locker room for this auspicious occasion.* "Like a Sunday School choir," she chuckled. "But holier."

As the group assembled, Paula noticed that several of the Crawlers' parents were in the audience, seated on benches around the perimeters of the studio. *They look like perfectly normal people,* she mused, *proud of their kids, anxious to see them succeed. Maybe Scotty's taste in friends isn't so raunchy, after all.* She smiled shyly at one of the couples, who raised their hands in greeting. *With any luck, they're looking at me and thinking the same thing about their own boy.*

The evening couldn't have been more enjoyable. Of course there was a lot of twisting and throwing and kicking and mat-slapping going on, but in the end, eighteen grinning adolescents had scrambled up another rung on the ladder of proficiency. And, while club tradition would ordinarily dictate a celebratory beer brawl on such a night of victory, the boys seemed content to wolf down platters of Bonnie's rich double-chocolate brownies and guzzle gallons of red fruit punch. "I tell you, if I get many more groups like this," Bonnie confided as the last of the chewy brown squares disappeared, "I'm gonna have to increase tuition to cover the cost of refreshments." Paula had never seen such a wide, gleaming smile on her new friend's face.

"I'm awfully proud of you. I hope you know that," Paula shouted. A warm wind whipped in energetic circles around the Jag's windshield as they sped toward home on the interstate. Even the dark night sky seemed to have shed its customary mantle of smog, and a panorama of flickering stars danced above them.

"Yeah, I know," Scott replied. "But did ya hafta go do the huggy-kissy thing in front of all the guys? Sheesh!" He wiped at his cheek in mock disgust.

"You bet," she grinned. "I'm your mom; it's in the job description. Besides, it's not every day my little boy kick boxes his way into the Ninja hall of fame. You did take top honors in tonight's competition, after all."

"I did, didn't I?" He sank back in his seat, folded his arms, and rested his Nike-clad feet on the dashboard. "Cool, huh?"

"Not *that* cool," Paula shot back, slapping the side of his leg. "Feet down, Karate Kid."

"Just checking." He grinned and lowered his Nikes to the floor. Closing his eyes, he seemed to drink in the air swirling at him from all sides of the car. "Guess I'll sleep in tomorrow. Miz Solomon says we get the day off."

"A well-deserved reward." *For Bonnie especially,* Paula thought. "Maybe we could go out for brunch or something." She'd go to the office later.

"Excellent," he agreed.

They had traveled a few miles when Paula's cell phone interrupted their comfortable silence. "Sweetie, would you dig that out of my purse, please?" she asked. "It's probably Ted; he wanted to ask me something earlier, but I was on my way to a very important event."

She winked at Scott and glanced at her watch: ten-fifteen P.M. *Come on, Ted. It's un-American to be doing business at this hour. Make a mental note, Donroe: Tell Mr. Barstow to get a life.*

Scott handed her the phone, and she hurriedly pressed it to her ear. "Yes?" she said brusquely.

"Paula. It's Mark Richland."

Instantly, her tone warmed. "Oh, hi, Mark. I thought you were someone else—a minor annoyance. But it's always good to hear your voice. What's up? Scotty and I have just had a wonderful evening, and we're . . . out on the freeway . . . and . . ." A knot of apprehension tightened in her stomach. "This isn't a social call, is it?"

"I'd give anything if it were," Mark replied.

"Tell me."

As Paula listened, the color drained from her face and rendered her complexion eerily luminescent in the pale moonlight. Her knuckles faded to white against the steering wheel, and Scott could see her body begin to tremble. When her muscles seemed to lose their strength and her foot slipped off the gas pedal, he reached over and grabbed her shoulder. "Mom, what's going on? We're stopping in the middle of the freeway!"

The intrusion of his voice seemed to shock her back to alertness. Still crushing the phone to her ear, she quickly steered through traffic to an outside lane, then off the highway to an emergency pullout area. Scott let out a long, slow breath as she shifted into park and crumbled against the seat, her attention riveted on Mark's words.

An eternity of minutes passed, interrupted only by an occasional "I see," "What does that mean?" or "Dear Lord" falling from Paula's lips like small, moist lumps of clay. Finally her shoulders sagged as if an enormous weight had just settled on them. "So it's time." A few more seconds ticked by in silence. "Yes, of course. Tomorrow. I'll let you know the flight." Her eyes closed, and Scott could see heavy tears glistening on her lashes. "Thanks, Mark . . . see you soon." She pressed a button and released her grip on the phone, letting it fall unnoticed to the floor. A low moan escaped her throat as she pressed a hand to her chest, but she said nothing.

Scott touched her arm and felt her flesh still quivering. "Mom . . . it's your friend Karti, isn't it?"

She nodded, then began to speak slowly, as though she wasn't exactly sure how to form the words. "Some kind of emergency happened yesterday—a seizure or something, I don't know. They rushed her to the hospital. She's stable now, but the cancer has done too much damage, and she can't hang on more than a few days. So they're sending her home to . . . to . . ." Paula couldn't say it. Couldn't even think it. "She asked for me . . . have to go as soon as I can. Right away."

"Okay, we'll make it happen," Scott said calmly, a bit surprised at his own mature response. "But first, we need to go home." He glanced beyond her to the steady stream of vehicles whizzing by. "And you're in no shape to get us there."

Even in her state of shock, she recognized the wisdom of his words; but she couldn't quite figure out how to solve the problem. She stared at him blankly.

"C'mon," Scott said firmly. "I'm taking you home."

"But . . . ," she protested feebly.

"No options." He hopped over the passenger door and sprinted around to her side, where he yanked open the door and grasped her elbow in his large hand. "That's right," he murmured, guiding her out of the car and around to the passenger side. When she was securely belted in, he returned to the driver's side and slid behind the wheel. "Okay now, just relax," he ordered, turning toward her. "This may not be the coolest time for me to take a spin in the Jag, but the way I see it, we don't have much of a choice. And it's not like I still need training wheels, ya know; I've been a licensed driver for three months now, remember?" She nodded docilely. He turned the key, and the engine vroomed to life. "So here we go." There was a small grin on his face as he set his jaw and pulled out into traffic.

The drive home was uneventful, but the back of Scott's shirt was drenched by the time he guided the sports car carefully into their garage and shut off the motor. "Whew!" he exclaimed as the door clunked shut behind them. "That was awesome. Scary, but awesome!" He glanced sideways at his mother, who still appeared pale and distracted. "Need a ride to the airport tomorrow?"

Paula nudged her lips into a smile. "Don't push your luck, big guy," she teased, grateful for this moment of bantering between them.

Life is too short; it could all be gone in a moment, she reminded herself. *Hold on to him. Keep him close.* "But you were terrific tonight, both on the mat and on the road." She touched his cheek. "Thank you, son."

"No problem," he shrugged. Stepping out of the car, he circled to the passenger side and opened the door. "You okay?"

"I think so." She swung her legs out of the car and tried to push herself to a standing position, but she collapsed back into the seat, even paler than before. "Well, maybe not."

He helped her out of the car and into the house, steadying her with a firm arm around her shoulders, moving it to her waist as she leaned on him to climb the stairs. She hugged him tightly as they said good night. "Millie and I will be up early to help you get ready," he whispered. "Try to get some rest."

"I will," she said, looking up at him gratefully.

"I'm sorry about your friend," he added.

"Me too. We'll get through this. Heavenly Father will help."

"I hope so." He pressed a quick kiss to her forehead, then turned and disappeared into his room.

Far into the night, Paula lay on her bed, fully clothed, trying to imagine what it would be like to see Karti for the last time. *What will she look like? Will she be bedfast, in terrible pain, wasted away like some pitiful Holocaust victim? Will we talk, cry, laugh, make promises we can't keep, pray together, try to make sense of it, come to terms, have one last dessert "for the road"?* "I've never done this before, Father," she murmured aloud. "Never said this final good-bye to a living, breathing part of my life. Of course there was TJ, but it wasn't the same; he was already gone, and I could only hold him and hope that some part of him could hear me. Please help me; I can't do this alone. None of us can do it alone—not Karti, not Sam, not the children, not me. Dear Lord, help us all." She fell asleep, and dreamed that it was all a dream.

At three o'clock the next afternoon, a lumbering Delta jet touched down on the Idaho Falls runway. As Paula walked resolutely into the gate area, she saw Mark standing near a row of empty seats, hands stuffed into the pockets of his jeans, his brown eyes searching the crowd. He looked as strong and handsome as ever, but weariness cloaked his features—a bone-sucking exhaustion that one rarely saw except in the faces of those who had met with catastrophe. They fell into each other's arms, and he held her hand tightly until they were snugly belted into the Suburban.

"It was good of you to come," Mark said as they began the drive to Roberts.

"I promised her," Paula replied. "I wouldn't be anywhere else." She gulped. "It's just that it's come . . . so soon."

"We were all hoping for more time," he said. "But I think she's ready."

"What makes you say that? I can't imagine ever being ready to . . . to die." She shivered involuntarily.

"I think you'll understand when you spend some time with her. As I've always told you, she's—"

"An extraordinary woman," they said in unison, then smiled.

"This is beautiful country," Paula observed after they had traveled several miles in silence. "Everything is so alive and fresh-looking this time of year." She gazed out the window at verdant pastures, trees with lush foliage bending over lazy streams, stands of long-bladed grasses and vivid wildflowers rippling in the light breeze. A distant range of mountains still sported a few snow-capped peaks, but its predominant hue was definitely forest green. "Quite different from when I was here in early March. I believe it was—what did you say?—thirty below and holding. Not quite balmy enough for a Sunday picnic." She smiled, remembering. "Still, it had its own kind of beauty—stark and pure and absolutely dazzling when the sun came out."

"I can't argue with that," Mark said. "But now it's the first week of summer, and, as the old song goes, 'the livin' is easy.' New life everywhere, and it never gets too warm for a walk along the creek." He looked over at her with a thoughtful, melancholy expression. "Mom loves this time of year. Up until a couple of days ago, she would sit out on the porch for a little while every morning, watching the grass grow, filling her lungs with the sweet air. 'Heaven is Idaho when the valley's in bloom,' she said to me last week. 'And if where I'm going doesn't bear a striking resemblance to this place, then all bets are off. I'm coming right back.'" He chuckled lightly. "Knowing Mom, she'd do it, too."

Ten minutes later they turned into the long, tree-lined driveway leading to the house. Paula rubbed her hands together nervously, and Mark did his best to put her at ease. "The girls are awfully excited to see you," he said. "I do believe there's a fresh batch of peanut butter chocolate chip cookies waiting for you on the kitchen table. Andrea helped Ruthie mix them up this morning. Andi's not usually the cookie-baking type—always has her nose in a book or her face in a makeup mirror. But today is, well, special. And I think they actually had fun together instead of the usual bickering."

"Fun is good," Paula smiled. "Especially when it results in something exquisitely edible."

As the Suburban pulled up behind the house, Paula noticed a window curtain lift and then fall back into place. Within seconds the mud-room door flew open, and two girls scrambled down the steps at the same moment Paula alighted from the vehicle. She spread her arms instinctively, and Ruthie ran eagerly into her embrace. "Oooh, I'm so glad you came," she cried, pressing her cheek against Paula's. "Now our whole family's together." The child's innocent declaration sent a current of warmth coursing through Paula's body.

Andrea hung back a few steps, waiting her turn. When Ruthie skipped away to help with the luggage, the teenager put her long, delicate arms around Paula and clung to her for a few brief, fragile seconds. "Thank you for coming," she whispered. "Mom will love it that you're here." She pulled away, and Paula saw the beginnings of tears in her deep-green eyes. *She knows. She knows I've come to say good-bye; that means we'll all be saying good-bye. Her life will never be the same again . . . nothing will ever be the same.* The sun glinted on Andrea's thick chestnut hair as she smiled shyly, then turned and quickly disappeared into the house.

Sam was waiting in the living room, sitting alone on the sofa where Paula had first seen him with Karti. He stood when Mark ushered Paula into the room, and she was struck anew by the size and commanding presence of this unique man. Yet she somehow remembered his face as being a little fuller, his shoulders a little squarer, his gray-green eyes a little merrier. He was dressed in immaculately pressed brown Dockers and a crisp oxford shirt, but they seemed to rest haphazardly on his body.

He smiled and extended his hand in greeting. Paula took it demurely. "Hello, Sam," she said. "It's wonderful to see you again." She cleared her throat. "I—I know this is a very difficult time, and I'm sorry if I'm intruding on—"

Suddenly his grasp tightened, and she felt herself being pulled into a crushing bear hug. His massive arms around her made her feel small and vulnerable, like a young schoolgirl, but at the same time safe and at ease. She returned the hug, resting her cheek lightly against his chest for a few moments. The top of her head didn't even come close to touching his chin. *Like my father,* she thought. *He was so tall.* But she couldn't remember ever feeling his arms around her.

Sam stepped back, clasped her shoulders in his strong hands, and looked down into her eyes with a sad, kind intensity that stirred her deepest emotions. "Don't you even think of apologizing," he said firmly. "You could never intrude on this family; we love you too much. Especially Karti. When I told her you were coming, her eyes lit up like it was Christmas morning. She hasn't talked about anything else, and I . . ." His voice faded, then came back again. "I haven't seen her so animated in weeks. In spite of the pain."

Paula grimaced. "Is it bad?"

"Not so bad since we brought her home from the hospital. They've hooked her up to a morphine pump; it's a lot better than the pills. She can increase the dosage when she starts hurting. Still, she tries not to use too much of the stuff; it makes her pretty groggy, and she wants to be as alert as possible right up until . . ." He quickly rubbed a hand across his forehead. "Anyway, she can hardly wait to see you."

She smiled weakly. "I want to see her, too. I'll just get settled first, if that's all right."

"You bet," Mark said. "I've already put your bags in the guest room. Do you remember the way?" He pointed to a wide stairwell off one side of the entryway.

Paula put a finger to her lips. "Uh, let's see . . . second floor, big oak door at the end of the hall. Am I close?"

"Exactly right," Mark confirmed. "Let me know when you're ready, and I'll take you to see Mom. Or, if you'd rather, just go find her yourself. She's in their bedroom."

"I know where it is," Paula said.

"Good; you can let yourself in. She sleeps quite a bit, but she might only be resting with her eyes closed. You'll know what to do." Mark bent to kiss her quickly on the cheek. "It's great having you here."

"Thanks. I'll see you all later, then." The men nodded as she turned and made her way slowly up the elegant spiral staircase.

Paula brushed her teeth and ran a comb through her dark, wavy hair, then sank into a large overstuffed chair next to the bed. She gazed out the window for several minutes, taking in a majestic view of the Grand Teton mountain range, now cloaked in deep-green foliage at its lower elevations but still crowned with pristine snow fields on nearly every peak. It was almost impossible for her to comprehend, on this tranquil summer afternoon, that she had come to Idaho on a heartbreaking mission of farewell; that while all around them new life was pushing up through the rich dark soil, birds' eggs were hatching, and sheep were nuzzling their new little lambs, Karti Richland was preparing to give her husband one final, loving kiss, hold her children tenderly to her heart for the last time, and then leave it all behind. What solace could there possibly be in such a separation? Even the gospel's promise of eternal life, for all its hope and consolation, seemed a pathetic second when compared with the reality of a living, breathing, loving wife, mother, sister, and friend.

She slipped to her knees beside the bed and spent a long time pleading for strength, understanding, whatever it took to come to terms. Then, just as the late afternoon sun was beginning to cast long shadows across the mountaintops, she closed her door softly and tiptoed down the hall to Karti's room.

CHAPTER 17

The door was slightly ajar. Paula ventured a tentative push, and it swung open far enough for her to steal noiselessly into the room. Holding her breath for fear of making a sound, she approached the large bed where Karti lay. From a few feet away, in the muted light coming from the partially shaded window, her friend appeared to be asleep. Her face was dreadfully pale, but her features seemed relaxed and composed as she lay on her back beneath a soft mauve and cream-colored afghan. She'd grown some hair over the past few months; a halo of short dark locks framed her fine-boned silhouette. One arm was flung casually out to her side, and Paula noticed she was wearing a soft, lightweight silver-blue velour jogging suit—the one Paula had sent for her birthday a month earlier. *It looks larger on her than I would have thought . . .* She tried to swallow the growing lump in her throat, and resisted an impulse to gather the frail body into her arms. *She's resting so peacefully . . . I can't disturb her now,* she told herself. *I'll just leave and come back later.*

She was moving toward the door when Mark's words rushed back to her. *"She might only be resting with her eyes closed. You'll know what to do."* She stopped and turned back to the bed. Karti had not moved. *I'll only stay a minute. If she's sleeping I won't wake her, but maybe somehow I can let her know I'm here.*

Tensing every muscle to keep from making any jarring movement, Paula lowered herself slowly, carefully to the bed. Long moments passed as she watched her friend intently, but Karti seemed oblivious as she lay still, her breathing even and undisturbed. Finally, Paula reached out and rested her hand gently on top of Karti's, smoothly curling her thumb under the other woman's fingers. She was intrigued by the unique texture of Karti's skin. It felt like elegant pressed tissue paper from an expensive gift shop—the kind one caresses simply for the experience of touching something translucent and refined. It was neither warm nor cool to Paula's touch, but about the same temperature as the air in this comfortable room—almost as if Karti was beginning to edge toward another dimension, already becoming part of a more rarified atmosphere. For some reason it seemed a rather natural progression, and Paula tenderly squeezed her friend's hand.

A tiny movement shifted her attention to Karti's face, where a delicate smile was just beginning to quicken her full lips. Without opening her eyes, she slowly turned her head toward Paula. "Hey." Her whisper seemed to animate the air as her fingers closed around Paula's thumb.

"Hey. You've got quite a thumb-lock there."

"They won't let me lift weights, so I have to settle for finger exercises." Karti's eyes opened and her smile widened. "Welcome back to Idaho, my friend. I knew you'd come."

"It's the least I could do," Paula said, her gaze taking in the deep shadows under Karti's eyes, her sunken cheeks, the IV stand next to her bed. "A promise is a promise, after all. Besides," she added, "Mark said they kicked you out of the hospital, and I had to come and personally check out the facilities here at the Richland Family Fun Center. I hear the food is good."

"No complaints there," Karti reported. "The Relief Society is taking care of everything. If it were up to Sam and the kids, we'd have pizza and Big Macs every morning, noon, and night." She sighed. "Not that I eat that much anyway. This diet is"—she smirked endearingly—"a real killer."

Paula had to laugh in spite of herself. "So it's true," she observed, still giggling. "The sense of humor is one of the last things to go."

"I certainly hope so." Karti's voice lowered, and a sudden glint of steely determination flashed in her dark eyes. "It would make all of this a whole lot easier."

"Then I'm sure the Lord will provide," Paula said kindly.

"That would be much appreciated . . . I wouldn't be caught *dead* without Him on my side." Karti tried to squelch an impish smile.

"Oooh, you're bad, girl," Paula clucked, shaking her head.

"See? It's working already." They both laughed easily and it seemed to buoy them, strengthening their spirits for what lay ahead.

The two women chatted quietly for half an hour, until Karti's strength waned. "I'm not exactly the Energizer bunny these days, in case you hadn't noticed," she admitted. "I'd jump up and fix you a cup of my favorite herbal tea, but those tea bags are just so darn heavy . . ."

"I understand," Paula said, patting her hand. "Can I get you anything?" She glanced around the room as though looking for something. "I thought I heard someone mention herbal tea. Want some?"

"Maybe later. But thanks." Paula noticed a thin sheen of perspiration on her friend's pale forehead. "Right now I think I'll crank up the happy juice and rest for a bit, if that's all right." She reached toward a square box mounted on the IV stand and pressed a button. "There, that should do it. One trip to la-la land, coming up." She sighed and shifted her head carefully on the pillow. "Sorry to be such a party pooper, but I need my beauty sleep."

"Well, it must be doing some good," Paula smiled. "You're still beautiful."

Karti closed her eyes contentedly. "I knew there was some reason why I invited you here. It must be because you're such a good liar. And believe me, I appreciate it. You're a woman of many talents." She paused for several seconds, and Paula thought she was asleep. Finally she spoke again, this time in a whisper. "You'll stay for a while, won't you?"

"As long as I'm needed," Paula replied softly.

"Good. We'll talk some . . . more . . . want to . . . ask you . . ." Karti's voice faded, and within seconds her breathing became even and relaxed.

"Later, then . . . we'll talk." Paula gently tucked the afghan around Karti's shoulders, then sat with her for a few moments longer, studying the thin, porcelain-like features of her pallid face. *It's true, you know*, she said wordlessly. *You're still beautiful.* She thought she saw the trace of a smile settle on her friend's lips.

The evening passed enjoyably, although this was clearly not the energetic, light-hearted family that Paula had visited in early March. Something overwhelming hung in the air—not hand-wringing grief or anger or even grim acceptance, but rather a kind of benign resignation tinged with sorrow, everyone waiting for events to unfold. It was like an orchestra playing exquisite music at half tempo with muted instruments. Even Ruthie, who rarely stopped moving or chattering, seemed to tire easily and often sought her father's comforting arms. When he brought Karti's untouched dinner downstairs, she slowly reached out to touch the peanut butter chocolate chip cookie she had so lovingly wrapped in a cheerful yellow napkin and placed on the tray. "Mommy's not doing very well, is she?" Her eyes met Sam's. "She always loved my cookies."

"Not very well, sweetheart," he confirmed in a voice strained with exhaustion. He looked at Paula. "Karti sends her apologies; she'd hoped to visit with you for a little while tonight, but she's not up to it." He ran a hand through his thick chestnut hair. "Maybe tomorrow."

"No problem," Paula said. "I'll just help the girls in the kitchen." She stood and began to gather a few dinner dishes from the table. Andrea and Ruthie joined her without protest.

"Thanks," Sam murmured. "She'll be stronger in the morning." He said it almost as if it was a question. "I think I'll go back up and make sure she's okay." He nodded solemnly to the family, and as he turned to go, Paula knew she wouldn't see him again until the next day.

"Well," Mark said lightly, trying to dispel a little of the gloom, "we've still got some daylight left. Anyone up for a little basketball?" He glanced hopefully at Alex, then at Jake. They stared at him without expression. "Aw, come on," he prodded. "You've both been bustin' your chops fixing fences all day; you need to relax, and there's nothing like a little hoop-tossing to take the kinks out. Whaddya say?" He grinned disarmingly, though Paula could tell he was struggling to keep up appearances.

"Sure, okay," Alex said, and Jake followed his lead. Mark scooped up a basketball from the mud-room floor, and a few seconds later the back door slammed shut behind the three brothers. They played until after dark.

Later, they all watched videos, but they might as well have been staring at a blank screen. When Paula offered to fix popcorn, no one seemed interested. One by one the boys excused themselves before the end of the last movie, then Andrea stood and stretched. "Church is at nine in the morning, and I'm a real dork if I don't get enough sleep." She tugged on a thick strand of Ruthie's hair. "C'mon, little sister; time for bed."

"All right already," the younger girl grumped. "I'll be up in a couple minutes." When Andrea had disappeared up the stairs, she reached out tentatively and rested her small hand on Paula's knee. "My mom's going to live with Heavenly Father pretty soon, isn't she?" Her eyes searched Paula's with perfect, innocent trust.

"Well, uh, gee," Paula stammered, "maybe you'd better talk to your father about—"

"He doesn't want to talk," the girl interrupted. "Not about that. I think he knows, but it's like he's afraid if he says it, it'll come true." Her eyes glowed with intensity. "Please, Sister Paula. I need to know. Nobody else'll talk to me." She ran one small finger along a seam on the leather couch. "Like I was a little kid or something."

"I'm sure your dad doesn't think you're a little kid," Paula said. "It's just that he's going through a really hard time right now, and—"

"He's not the only one." Ruthie's face was a study in maturity beyond her years as she folded her slender arms across her chest. "Please. I *have* to know."

Paula took in a huge breath and blew it out slowly through pursed lips. "All right, then." She blinked several times and swallowed hard before looking at Ruthie directly. "Yes, I believe your mom will go to be with Heavenly Father before too long. No one knows for sure, of course, but it seems likely. She's very sick, you know."

"Yes, I know," Ruthie said, huge tears welling up from the depths of her black eyes. "But Heavenly Father will take care of her." She took a quick breath and bit her lip. "I just hope He'll take care of us when she's gone."

"He will, sweetheart," Paula said, pulling her close and burying her face in the little girl's dark, fragrant hair. "I know He will." In her heart, she felt the truth of her own words. *But how?*

"I love her so much," Ruthie sobbed against Paula's chest.

"We all do."

"She keeps telling me we'll be a family forever, and I really, really believe her. But it's so far away. I mean, if she goes away now, it'll be like a *hundred years* before I see her again." She pulled back a little and looked up at Paula, her face streaked with tears. "How can I wait that long?"

Paula opened her mouth, and the words came. "You just keep loving her, all your life. You grow up into a beautiful young woman, probably get married and have a great family, and always try to live the way she'd want you to. Then, before you know it, you'll be with her again—this time forever. You'll be surprised how fast it goes." As she stroked Ruthie's hair, another thought came to her, and she knew it would help. "That's exactly what I'm trying to do for TJ, you know—live a good life so I can spend the rest of forever with him. But I know what you mean; it seems like a very long time until I'll actually be able to hug him again and tell him I love him, face to face." She paused as her own emotion began to surface. "All we can do is hang on, sweetie. And pray we'll be able to do things right."

"Do you miss him?" Ruthie asked.

"TJ? Oh, my. Oh, yes. With every breath I take. Every breath." A few tears trickled down Paula's cheeks as she again pulled Ruthie to her and cradled the youngster in her arms. "He was a lot like you in many ways . . . so bright and funny and energetic and full of life. The two of you would have been great friends."

"Maybe we would've gotten married," Ruthie giggled.

"Maybe," Paula smiled, grateful their conversation had taken a lighter turn. "But right now we ought to be thinking of more practical things." She gave Ruthie a tight squeeze. "Like bedtime. Church comes early in the morning, so what do you say we call it a night?"

"Okay," Ruthie agreed, rising from the sofa. She hesitated briefly, shuffling her feet against the thick carpet, then spoke uncertainly. "Do you . . . do you think you could tuck me in? I mean, I know I'm pretty big an' all, but my mom usually . . ." Her voice trailed off, and she curled a lock of auburn hair around her finger.

"I'd be honored," Paula said, coming to her feet and taking hold of her young friend's hand. "Let's go." They walked together up the stairs, each lost in her own private thoughts of loved ones near and far away.

❤ ❤ ❤

"Bad night," Sam murmured when Paula cast him a questioning glance the next morning. She had awakened early, dressed in comfortable slacks and a light cotton shirt, and gone down to the family room, where she'd found him staring into an empty, cheerless stone fireplace. "Pain," he added. "Lots of it." She wasn't quite sure whether he was referring to Karti or himself. Probably both.

"I could stay with her during church if you like," Paula offered. "A few hours away might be a nice—"

"No way," he broke in sharply, then paused. "I'm sorry; I didn't mean to snap at you." He took a deep breath. "Mark can drive the family to church; I won't leave Karti. If you'd like to stay, I know she'd enjoy visiting with you."

"Yes, I'd like that."

"All right. Morning is usually her best time; she's more alert then. She fell asleep around four A.M., so I expect she'll be stirring before long. The Relief Society president and a registered nurse from our ward are coming in a while to help me get her ready for the day. I'll let you know when she's presentable."

"Thanks, Sam," Paula said. "In the meantime, would you mind if I took a little walk around outside? When I was here before, there were four feet of snow on the ground. I'd kind of like to see what was hiding underneath all that white stuff."

"Be my guest. Whatever's ours is yours. And help yourself to anything you can find for breakfast." He checked his watch. "I think I'll go upstairs and make sure everyone's getting their act together for church. I promised Karti they'd be on time."

Left alone, Paula went to the kitchen and ate half a bowl of cereal and a piece of toast, then slid her chair back and stood. *Wish I had Rudy to walk with me,* she thought. *He'd love the feel of cool mud on his feet down by the ol' irrigation ditch.* She smiled at her own preconceived notion of what a farm was like. *Assuming, of course, that there's an irrigation ditch somewhere. If there wasn't, Rudy would dig one.* On this bright summer morning, she somehow missed the comfortable familiarity of his long, golden body.

Opening the back door, she quickly moved down the three cement steps to a wide area of hard-packed earth where four vehicles—the Suburban, a dusty pickup truck, a Subaru station wagon, and a Chevy Malibu—were parked. A few chickens clucked melodiously and scratched in the dust around the softer perimeter. In the near distance an immaculate white barn towered over a small cluster of other scrupulously clean buildings, and beyond them lay acre after acre of recently planted potato fields. *This is nice*, she thought, breathing deeply to fill her lungs with fresh, unpolluted air. The orange-yellow sun seemed to be carefully balancing itself on the highest points of a mountain range to the east. *Peaceful. A far cry from life in an L.A. skyscraper.*

She decided to stay close to home. *No use taking the risk of stepping in something I couldn't identify*, she reasoned. Turning to her right, she circled around to one side of the house. There she came across a broad expanse of newly mown, meticulously groomed lawn of a deeper green color than she had ever seen, even in her own professionally landscaped yard in California. Not a solitary dandelion marred the lush natural carpet beneath her feet. *Must be the fertilizer*, she mused. *They've got the real thing here, after all.* She bent down to run her hands across the rich, springy turf, and ended up sitting for a few minutes while the harmony of a nearby sparrow symphony lulled her into a feeling of tranquility.

The muted sounds of car doors opening and closing, then a motor starting, reminded her that for the children of Samuel and Jakarta Richland, this Sabbath was like any other: a day of worship, rest, and quiet family activities. Except, of course, that on this Sabbath, their mother was dying. Closing her eyes, Paula lifted her face to the sun and felt its warmth caressing her cheek like the fingers of a tender parent. *Be with us, dear Father*, she pleaded silently.

Several minutes later, the cool dew seeping through her slacks encouraged her to continue her exploration. She followed the lawn around to the front of the house and past a stand of several huge evergreens, where she found a profusion of rose bushes in full bloom— red, pink, yellow, peach, white, and multi-colored—lining a wide cement walk to the circular drive. The glorious flowers also nestled closely against all three sides of a spacious but charming screened-in porch, where a white gliding swing and an antique oak rocker sat together like old companions. *This is where Karti has been spending her mornings*, Paula thought, breathing in the fragrant air. *No wonder she thought it was heaven.*

She quickly realized that the rose bushes were too close together to allow her to slip between them, too tall and thorny to jump over. So she strolled a few dozen yards out to the drive, then back toward the house on the other side of the walk and around to the mud-room door.

Sam was leaning against the counter, staring at the microwave when Paula sauntered into the kitchen. He spoke without looking up. "I'm heating a little oatmeal. She said she'd eat something."

"Well, then, that's good," Paula declared brightly. "At least she's hungry."

"I didn't say she was hungry," he replied tonelessly. "She just said she'd eat something. For me."

"Oh," Paula said. She watched as Sam poured milk onto the tiny portion of cereal and stirred it into a thin gruel. "How's she doing this morning?"

"Weak, but wide awake and not in too much pain," he reported. "She asked for you, and I told her you'd be up right after she ate her breakfast." He smiled weakly. "Whatever it takes to get her to swallow a few spoonfuls."

"Hey, I'm honored to serve as an incentive. A good old-fashioned bribe is worth its weight in gold—or calories, as the case may be," Paula joked.

Sam carefully placed a small glass of milk, half a piece of toast, and a blue and white cloth napkin on a tray beside the cereal. Then he nodded to her without a word and left the room. In less than ten minutes he was back, and Paula could tell by a glance at the tray that Karti had consumed almost nothing. "My mistake," he shrugged. "She reminded me she'd promised to eat *something*, not *everything*. 'Besides,' she pointed out, 'a visit with Paula will be the best medicine. Next to time spent with my ever-loving husband, that is.'"

"She's lucky to have you," Paula said fervently.

"I'm the lucky one," he murmured. "I've had the prettiest, smartest, funniest, most loving woman in the world by my side for more than thirty years. A guy couldn't get any luckier than that. Except maybe," his voice cracked, "if he could've had her for another thirty." He looked at Paula with pain-filled eyes. "Or even one more. Just one." His shoulders sagged, and he leaned heavily against the counter.

"I'm sorry," she murmured. "So very sorry."

He cleared his throat. "I need some fresh air; think I'll take a little walk. She's waiting for you."

"Okay, thanks," Paula said, and the two went their separate ways.

Karti was propped up in bed against a mound of crisp white pillows, looking composed and steady. She was wearing a deep-pink robe that seemed to lend some of its vivid color to her sallow cheeks, and her short dark hair, now flecked with a little gray, had been freshly shampooed and blow-dried in soft curls around her face. If not for the deepening shadows of pain beneath her eyes, the too-sharply-defined facial bones, and the slightly clouded expression, she might have resembled a regal queen holding court from her bedchamber.

"My, aren't we looking lovely this morning," Paula observed, depositing herself on the bed and reaching for Karti's hand. It felt cool to her touch.

"Marie and Lois prettied me up; I told them I wanted it to be a special day, so they really went to town . . . did a little makeup and everything." She grinned and batted her eyelashes coquettishly.

"I hope this means you're feeling better," Paula smiled. "We were pretty worried about you last night."

"I'm all right," Karti said, squeezing Paula's hand. "In fact, this is exactly the way I wanted it—warm and cozy, you know? A lovely visit."

"And it is," Paula agreed. A slight uneasiness tugged at her, but she promptly tucked it away in some deep corner of her mind and gazed affectionately at her friend.

They spent the next hour and a half in light conversation, laughing over the experiences of two lifetimes, poring over old photo albums, finally settling down to a deep sharing of testimony and spiritual insights. "You know," Paula observed, "I've been a member of the Church for about half a year now, but in many ways it seems like forever." She gave a little chuckle. "And I mean that in a good way, of course."

"Well, I think it *has* been forever," Karti said as she readjusted her body against the pillows, trying to find a more comfortable position. Her voice was beginning to sound dry and strained, as if she couldn't quite catch her breath.

"Excuse me?" Paula cast her a puzzled look.

"I think we all knew about the gospel a long, long time before we were . . . ever called up for active duty in mortality," Karti wheezed.

"Makes sense. I've been reading about that war in heaven stuff." She touched Karti's arm. "Are you okay?"

"I think so. Just tired, that's all. As I was saying, I also believe we were . . . foreordained to be either born into the Church or accept it later. So it doesn't come as any surprise to me that you would feel so . . . familiar with it. The gospel has . . . just been dormant . . . inside your spirit for most of your life."

Paula nodded. "I could believe that. You want a drink of water or something?"

"No . . . but a little hit of that morphine would be good right about now. Would you do the honors? I can't reach." Karti tried to raise her hand to touch the pump, but it fell limply back to the bed.

She's weaker than she's been letting on, Paula surmised. Without hesitation she punched the designated button.

"Thanks, I needed that," Karti said with a wan smile.

"Anything for a rush, eh?" Paula watched her friend closely as she sank into the pillows and lay quietly for a full five minutes, her face drained of color.

"You know what else I believe?" Karti's eyes were still closed, but her voice was a little stronger.

"What?" Paula was rubbing Karti's arm, trying to coax some vigor back into it.

"I think we were friends . . . long before now. Maybe a million, even a billion years ago. I think we grew up together as sisters in the premortal world." She smiled dreamily. "Maybe even flipped a coin over who would have the baby and who would raise him. Who would find the man of her dreams and who would be the hotshot working girl. Who would live to be older and wiser, and who would . . ." She opened her eyes slowly and met Paula's gaze. "Who would be called home first. I think we worked it all out. And now we're *living* it all out. There was a plan, Paula. I know it."

"Yes, I'd be willing to buy all that," Paula said solemnly, "except for one minor point."

"Hmm?" Karti's eyes were losing their focus slightly.

"It's that part about only *one* of us finding the man of her dreams.

Cut me a little slack here, will you? Granted, Richard Donroe wasn't any great prize, but I'd like to think I still have a shot at finding Mr. Right. I'm only forty, after all; let's just say I prefer to think of this mystery man as 'currently unavailable.'"

"Fair enough," Karti murmured. "I'm sure there was a contingency plan. It'll all work out. Besides which, I—" She suddenly grimaced and pressed a hand to her midsection.

"Oboy . . . you're hurting, and I've worn you out," Paula said quickly, remorse rising like bile in her throat. "Can I do anything for you, besides getting out of here and letting you rest?"

Karti looked at her with shining eyes. "You've done so much already . . . just by being here. Means . . . so much . . . to all of us." She swallowed with difficulty. "Guess I'd better take a little nap . . . maybe see you later this afternoon."

"Count on it." Paula came to her feet beside the bed, then leaned over and pressed a light kiss to Karti's forehead. "Rest well, my friend." As she left the room, she heard Karti moan softly. The small, pitiful sound wrenched her heart.

Downstairs, Sam was sitting at the kitchen table, reading the Sunday paper. He set it aside when Paula entered the room. "I think I stayed too long," she said, responding to the question in his eyes. "She took some medication, but the pain . . . I hope she'll be able to sleep a little."

He pushed his chair back and stood. "I'll sit with her until the morphine kicks in." A deep, impenetrable sadness rose in his eyes. "I'd sit with her forever if it would help." He walked a few steps toward the entryway, then turned back. "Please, make yourself at home. The kids will be back from church soon, and dinner will be here about two, courtesy of the Relief Society. If someone could bring a tray up for Karti, I'd be grateful."

"We'll send up a couple of plates," Paula said lightly. "You'll have a nice romantic little meal—just the two of you."

"Nothing for me, thanks."

"But you have to eat," she protested. "You need to keep up your—"

"Not today," he interjected mildly. "I'm fasting."

"Oh, I see," Paula murmured as he shuffled from the room. She wondered how many meals he'd sacrificed over the past few weeks. Dozens, from the looks of him.

She was nearly finished setting the dining room table when she heard the Subaru pull into the yard. *This will be a nice surprise for them,* she thought, surveying the fresh white tablecloth, blue-and-white-flowered stoneware, and gleaming long-stemmed glasses. A small cluster of yellow and white roses, snipped just minutes earlier from a bush beside the porch, floated in a shallow dish at the center of the table. *They deserve something out of the ordinary for this Sunday dinner.*

Mark was first into the house, and she greeted him eagerly. "How was church?" she asked.

"Good. A lot of people asked about Mom; she'll probably have some visitors this afternoon." He set his scriptures down on the kitchen counter.

"Your father's with her now," Paula reported as the rest of the family filed through the door. "He said someone from the ward is bringing dinner at two, so you'll all have a little while to get comfortable before we eat. I've set the dining-room table, and I thought we'd have a special—"

"Maybe later tonight for me," Mark said. "I'm fasting."

"Well . . . okay," Paula replied with a little smile. *Like father, like son.* "You can eat later, and we'll save you some."

"Uh, same for me," Alex added. "I'm fasting, too."

"Uh-huh." Paula was beginning to see a pattern. "And the rest of you?" She looked from one to the other.

"Me too," Andrea said. "It makes me crabby, but this is Mom's day."

"Same here," Jake declared. "Except for the crabby part."

"An' I'm the bestest faster of all—not a sceck of food or a drop of water since supper last night," Ruthie announced proudly.

"A sceck? I don't believe I've heard that one before," Paula said.

"It's a family thing," Alex explained. "Jake tripped over his tongue when he was a little guy . . . couldn't decide whether he wanted to say 'scrap' or 'speck,' and it came out 'sceck.' We've added it to the Richland unabridged dictionary."

"I'll have to remember that," Paula laughed. "Meanwhile, I guess we can find room in the fridge for dinner when it comes, and we can heat it up again at, uh . . . what time would you say, guys?"

"Six o'clock," they said in unison.

"Right. Then we'll have a meal to remember. And the table will be all set." She looked around her at five shining young faces. "You're quite a bunch, you know that? This isn't even fast Sunday."

"It's what we wanted to do—for Mom," Alex said quietly. "Dad doesn't know."

"Then you probably don't know that he's fasting, too." Paula watched their eyes widen.

"Figures," Mark said. "I think he's been fasting for the past two months straight."

"I must say, it's certainly a tribute to you—and to your mother— that all of you would make this effort." Paula put an arm around Andrea's shoulders and felt the girl lean against her.

"Are you fasting too, Sister Paula?"

Ruthie's question took her by surprise. "W–well," she stammered, vividly recalling the cereal and toast she had gulped down earlier, "I hadn't really . . . then again, I couldn't have known . . . and I, uh, I didn't think . . ." She sucked in a major breath. "But, yes, if you must know, at this very moment, I'm fasting. I am definitely fasting." *Father, forgive me. I'll make it up to You, I swear. Sorry, poor choice of words. I* promise.

"Yippee!" Ruthie exulted. "That makes it one hundred percent. Mommy can't help feeling better now." She gave Paula a quick hug. "I'll go up and see how she's doing." Within seconds she had hurried from the room, followed more slowly by everyone but Mark and Paula.

"Ah, the faith of a child," Mark sighed, loosening his tie and slumping down on a chair by the table. "How can she possibly comprehend what's happening?" He shook his head sadly.

"I think she understands more than you give her credit for," Paula said. "She and I had a little heart-to-heart after the rest of you went to bed last night, and I'm quite sure she knows what's going to happen— maybe not the precise timing of it, but none of us knows that. And as you'll recall, just now she talked about her mommy *feeling* better, not *getting* better. I can't believe that was a casual choice of words."

"Maybe not," he conceded, rubbing the back of his neck. "I just feel so bad for her and Andrea. The rest of us are pretty well grown; it'll be tough on us, but nothing like what they'll have to cope with. And Dad . . . I can't even imagine what Dad will do without her. Those two are joined at the heart."

"I know." *And I'm losing my best friend.* Paula moved behind him to massage the knotted muscles in his shoulders. She rubbed and kneaded for a few minutes until she realized he was crying. Then she wrapped her arms around him and kissed his damp cheek. "We'll get through this," she whispered. "Heaven will help."

The warm afternoon drifted into early evening, and Paula watched in amazement as a steady stream of visitors appeared at the Richlands' door. They were young, middle-aged, and elderly; some brought food or flowers, others came with small gifts like a handkerchief or a current copy of *Reader's Digest.* Each, it seemed, had come on this final pilgrimage to spend time with someone they considered a special friend. One stooped-over, white-haired gentleman spoke for them all when he clasped Sam's hand at the door. "Everybody loves Karti," he said.

It was past seven o'clock when the last visitor said good-bye and hurried down the rose-lined walk. Paula and Ruthie had warmed up dinner and laid most of it out on the table. They were putting the final touches on a green salad when Sam walked into the kitchen. His eyes looked tired, but he was smiling. "Mark told me you were all fasting," he said. "I guess it's about time for us to eat."

"I certainly hope so," Ruthie sighed loudly. She glanced at a clock on the wall. "It's been *way long*—twenty-five hours and eleven minutes. I think I'm gonna pass out." She rolled her eyes and clutched at her stomach.

"Just hang tight, princess," Sam chuckled, enfolding her in his huge arms. He kissed the top of her head. "Your mother loves you for doing this, you know. And so do I."

"Then I guess it's worth it." She grinned up at him. "Yeah, I *know* it's worth it. Can we eat now?"

"By all means." He bowed solicitously and took her arm. "Here, let me help you to the table."

"Silly!" she giggled, pushing him away. "I'm not *that* wimpy." She marched over to the counter, took the large glass salad bowl in both hands, and walked briskly toward the door. "I'll be in the dining room," she called over her shoulder.

Sam leaned against the counter and stuffed his hands into his pockets. "That felt good," he said.

"How so?" Paula asked absently, opening the oven to take out a robust chicken-and-vegetable casserole.

"The joking. We haven't done very much of that around here lately. It was always so easy when Karti was . . . up and around. She was the first one to tease or make some funny crack. We had a great time." He stared, unseeing, at a small spider making its way up one side of the porcelain sink.

Paula quickly washed the insect down the drain. "She must be totally wiped out after all those visitors. I've been worried for her."

"On the contrary," he responded. "She's actually more alert than I've seen her for several days. She drinks it in, you know—the love of people around her. Through the afternoon, I've watched her absolutely come alive as each of these folks, one by one, has touched her in some way with an expression of friendship and concern." He paused. "And she's given it back, too; they've all come away nourished by her faith, feeling better than when they arrived. It's been a miraculous day." He looked at her, an indescribable depth of emotion in his eyes. "A day to remember."

"I've felt it," Paula agreed softly. "I just didn't know quite what it was."

"Well, now you do," he said almost cheerfully. "And I figure the best thing we can do at this point is to try to keep her strength up. To that end, my dear Sister Donroe, would you mind fixing us a couple of dinner plates? I'll take a tray up as soon as we've said the blessing."

"It would be my pleasure," Paula smiled. "While I'm doing that, why don't you round up the family? I'm not sure your youngest daughter can wait much longer; with any luck at all, there'll still be a green salad—not just an empty bowl—on the table when we sit down to eat."

She had barely arranged two small dinner plates on a tray when a plaintive eleven-year-old voice echoed across the entryway and floated into the kitchen. "Sister Paula, we're all here. Could you come—and bring the casserole?"

"On my way," she called. Within moments, the large white oval baking dish had been given a place of honor—right in front of Ruthie—on the dining-room table.

Sam bowed his head and offered a simple prayer of gratitude and supplication. "Bless this food," he said finally, "that it will nourish, strengthen, and . . . sustain life for those who partake of it. For all of us who love each other so much . . . please, Father . . . *sustain life.*" When he closed the prayer and looked up, his eyes were glistening. "I'll just run the tray up to your mother," he murmured.

"I'm awfully glad we fasted," Ruthie said after he left. "It'll help Mom . . . and besides," she spooned a large portion of chicken and vegetables onto her plate, "everything tastes so much better on a *really* empty stomach."

When Sam came downstairs an hour and a half later, Paula was sitting in the living room, an *Ensign* open on her lap. "Andrea and Ruthie cleaned up," she reported as he sank into a chair and stretched out his long legs. "I think they're in the family room, watching a Church video. Alex went to a stake fireside, and the other boys said something about turning in early." He stared straight ahead and nodded, but did not speak. "Is everything all right?"

"I suppose. Long day." His gaze moved to one of the eight-foot beveled window panes, and he stared out into the deepening night sky. "She ate a little. Not much."

"Maybe tomorrow. Leftovers always taste good."

"Maybe." He rubbed a hand across his eyes. "She wants to see you."

"That's wonderful!" Paula exclaimed. "I thought she'd be too tired."

"She seems okay. I gave her some morphine; she wouldn't take any while people were here, but she needs it now to sleep."

"Then I'll go right up." Paula stood. "I'll only stay a minute. Well, maybe five. Or ten."

"That'll be fine. I'll go see what the girls are up to," he said. "If you'd like to—" But she was already gone.

Karti's room was dark and still, illuminated only by a small crystal lamp on her nightstand. Paula stole quietly to the bed and sat down carefully. Her friend's eyes were closed, but she smiled as she felt Paula's hand covering hers. "I've missed you today," she whispered.

"Yeah, right," Paula teased. "Like you didn't have enough company."

"No one quite like my best friend."

"Oh, I'll bet you say that to all your houseguests."

Karti opened her eyes, and Paula could see they were deeply sunken, beginning to edge back behind the thin ridges of her cheekbones. Still, they were alert and expressive. "Not a chance," she said, her voice stronger now. "We go way, way back, remember?"

Paula nodded. "I've been thinking about what you said—the notion of a premortal friendship, maybe even a little heavenly string-pulling to make sure we found each other—and I believe every word of it. A connection like this is truly extraordinary. The only thing is, I just wish we had more time to enjoy it right now."

"I know," Karti breathed. "The bad news is that we have so little of the 'here and now' left. But the good news is that we have *all* of the 'then and there' ahead of us. It'll be great fun."

"Okay, I'll take your word on it," Paula said. "So, you had a good time today?"

"Glorious," Karti replied, her eyes shining. "So many lovely people—friends from the ward, neighbors, even the pretty young girl who cuts my hair. For months, she came to see me when I had no hair to cut—gave me scalp massages. They were heavenly. And so many flowers; can you smell them?"

Paula took a deep breath. "Mmm. Delightful." She looked around the room, and for the first time noticed vases and small, fragrant bouquets everywhere—on the dresser, next to the lamp, tucked into the corner of a chair, even a single deep-pink rose on Karti's pillow.

With a concentrated effort, Karti raised her hand and gently folded it around the flower, pressed its petals to her nose briefly, then lowered it to rest just beneath her chin. "There's a saying my mother loved . . . 'A rose to the living is more sumptuous than a wreath to the dead.' I never gave it much thought, but now it makes perfect sense. So much beauty in the world . . . need to enjoy it while I'm able."

"Your mother sounds like a wise woman," Paula said. "Do you speak with her often?"

Karti shook her head. "She died three years ago, and Daddy followed her less than a year later. Two of my older brothers have passed on, as well."

"Oh, I'm sorry," Paula murmured.

"Don't be. They're all over there . . . waiting. Sometimes I can almost feel them, here in this room, beckoning to me. But they know I won't go until I'm ready . . . I was always the stubborn one in the family." She tried to smile, but it seemed to be a great effort.

Paula forced a little laugh, but she wanted to cry. She squeezed Karti's hand and stood after a few seconds. "I can tell you're awfully tired, so I'll let you get some rest. Sam will be up soon."

"And the children? I'd like to say good night." Karti's voice sounded soft and papery. "Even if I'm asleep, please have them come. Somehow, I'll know they're here."

"We'll round them up," Paula vowed. She leaned over to brush her fingers against Karti's cheek. It was warm to her touch. "I'll see you tomorrow, then."

"Bless you," Karti whispered, her lips barely moving.

When she retired, Paula left the door of her room open a crack. Past midnight, lying awake in the dark, she heard Sam's slow footsteps shuffling up and down, up and down the hall. When sleep finally took her sometime after two, he was still pacing.

CHAPTER 18

Sam shook his head as he and Paula shared an early breakfast the next morning. "She's much weaker. I've been keeping the boys busy on a fence-repairing project, but I'm going to ask them to stay home today. We all need to be here." His gravelly voice and heavy-lidded eyes told Paula what she didn't want to know.

"What can I do?" she asked.

"If you could just . . . stay with the girls, keep them occupied, it would help a lot."

"Of course." She watched him stir his cereal once, twice, then push the bowl aside.

"I've asked the nurse to come earlier than usual," he said, coming to his feet abruptly. "I'll speak with the boys now, then I'll be with Karti if anyone needs me."

"We'll manage." Paula rose and tentatively pressed her fingers against his arm, needing to make some connection with this good man who was suffering so much. "Give her my love, will you?"

His burly hand reached out to cover hers, and he looked down at her with desolate eyes. "You know I will. And thanks." As quickly as he had said it, he turned and walked from the room.

The Richland household came to life slowly, dolefully over the next two hours. Ruthie and Andrea moved about quietly, helping Paula fix breakfast for the family—blueberry waffles, crisp bacon, fresh strawberries and cream. No one ate very much, but sitting together, joking a little, sharing a family prayer and a blessing on the food seemed to give them an anchor for the day.

Afterward, the boys went outside to shoot baskets. Ruthie insisted on baking cookies—"For family home evening tonight," she announced, although a dozen from her last batch still languished in the rooster-shaped ceramic cookie jar on the counter. "Mom likes 'em fresh," she explained. Andrea went to the porch and practiced her flute for over an hour, its clear, sweet melodies floating on the mild summer air like fragrant lilies on a still pond. Later, she played the piano while Ruthie and Paula sang Primary songs. Paula couldn't read music and didn't know the words, but the two girls soon had her singing "Popcorn Popping on the Apricot Tree" with gusto.

At one-thirty, just as they were finishing a light lunch of sandwiches and fresh fruit, Sam came downstairs and shuffled into the kitchen. Ruthie ran to him, and he wrapped his arms around her. Still holding her to him, he looked up and smiled wearily at the rest of the family.

"I have an announcement," he said, and felt their eyes riveted on him. "As you know, this is Monday, and we always have family home evening at about seven o'clock." They all nodded. "However, your mother is really . . . uh . . . tired today, and has requested that we have it a bit earlier. She says she has a very special message for us, and she wants to give the lesson herself. So . . . it looks like we'll be having a family home *afternoon,* if that's all right." He made eye contact with each of them, and they nodded solemnly.

"Oooh, perfect!" Ruthie exclaimed, pulling back and grinning up at her father. "Now my cookies will *really* be fresh!"

"That's wonderful, sweetheart," Sam said gently, ruffling her hair.

Mark looked from Jake to Alex, then down at his own sweat-stained shirt. "Just give us guys time for a quick shower, would you? We've been hooping it up."

"Fine. Let's do it about two, up in our room. Mark, could you bring a couple of folding chairs?"

"Sure thing."

"Good. We'll see you all in a little while." He kissed the top of Ruthie's head, then disappeared into the entryway.

A few minutes past two, they gathered around Karti. Her face was ashen, her eyes heavy with pain and fatigue, yet she smiled and held out her arms to each of them. The effort seemed to exhaust her, but as she lay back against the pillows, her countenance was bathed in love. Ruthie plopped down on the bed at her mother's side; Sam and Paula took the folding chairs Mark had provided; and the three boys and Andrea sat cross-legged on the thick beige carpet. They sang "I Am a Child of God," and Jake offered an opening prayer. Then everyone turned expectantly toward Karti, anxious to hear her message.

"My darlings," she began slowly, her rich voice soft and low, "I'm so grateful we could all be together today. I wanted to show you something very special; your father helped me make it this morning, and I hope it'll help us all understand a little more about . . . Heavenly Father's wonderful plan for us."

She glanced at Sam, nodding almost imperceptibly. He rose from his chair and approached the nightstand, where he opened a small drawer and pulled out something that looked like a length of white string. Moving to a corner of the room nearest the bed, he took a small roll of tape from his pocket. He secured an end of the string to one wall, trailed it about three feet kitty-corner across the seam where the walls joined, and taped the other end of the string to the opposite wall. Then he quickly kissed his wife's forehead and returned to his chair.

"Thank you, sweetheart," Karti said. "Now, everybody, what do you see?"

"Just an old string across the corner of the room," Ruthie answered. "What's it for?"

"Look a little closer, dear," her mother advised.

Andrea had been studying the string from her side of the bed. "Hey, I can see it. A little knot, right there near the middle of the string." She pointed, and all eyes fixed on the tiny irregularity.

"Exactly," Karti smiled. "Now, I'd like each one of you to think of this string as your life—all of it. The length on the left side of the knot is your premortal life before you came here, when you were born as a spirit child and lived with Heavenly Father for a very, very long time. The right side is your life after you leave this earth, when you return to your heavenly home to live forever—also a very, very long time. That leaves the little knot, which represents your time on this earth."

"Kind of like the 'You Are Here' sign on the directory at the mall," Jake observed.

"That's right, son," she said. "And as you can see, compared to before and after, our time here is just a tiny little . . . sceck." Her dark eyes were twinkling.

"Boy, it sure *seems* like a long time," Ruthie observed.

"I know," her mother agreed, "and it's a very special time. This life is where we've become a family—where we've learned to love each other and keep Heavenly Father's commandments so that . . . after this life, we can all be together again. Forever and ever. So . . ." Karti's breathing seemed labored, and her eyes sought Sam's.

"So," he continued, "it's very important to understand that even though we go home to Heavenly Father at different times . . . some of us will go sooner, some of us will live to a ripe old age . . . we'll all be together again quite soon. Then, when we look back on earth life, it will all just seem like . . . a teensy knot in a very long string. And the best part is that we'll never, ever be apart again."

A deep silence fell over the room as seven pairs of eyes stared at the minuscule lump perched on a Lilliputian tightrope between two walls. *It's all relative,* Paula mused. *Still seems like a mighty long time.* She thought of TJ. *There have been moments when I'd have traded eternity to have had him back in my life for these past eight months.* Her gaze moved back to the small white knot. *Maybe I just haven't learned the lesson yet.*

No one seemed to notice when Ruthie slipped from the room for a few seconds, but now she was back, clutching a thin polished chain with a small silver star attached. She carefully unclasped the chain and fastened it on the string so the star hung an inch or two directly beneath the knot. "There," she said quietly. "That's the Richland star. Wherever we are," she glanced lovingly at her mother, "it'll remind us that we're a family. In a million years, we'll remember where we started."

"Yes . . . my precious family," Karti declared, reaching for Ruthie's hand, pressing it to her lips. "Remember me . . . remember us." She looked around the room at her children, at her husband, at her best friend. "You know, I believe Heavenly Father wants me to come home soon. But my spirit, my heart will never be far from any of you. I promise. Just think of the Richland star, and I'll be there. Okay?"

A chorus of whispered "okays" fell on the warm air like the prayers of lost children. One by one they leaned over the bed to kiss her, to touch her, to murmur words of endearment. She was smiling now through her tears. "Let's have a closing song and prayer, shall we?" They sang "Love One Another" to the accompaniment of Andrea's flute. After Jake offered a brief benediction, they all nibbled politely at Ruthie's cookies.

A few minutes later, Paula led the family downstairs while Sam stayed with Karti. Andrea began leafing absently through a copy of *Teen People,* and Ruthie busied herself cleaning the kitchen and filling the cookie jar. When the boys left to see to their afternoon chores, Paula went out to the porch and sat in the oak rocker for a long while. A playful breeze occasionally fluttered through the screen, reminding her of agreeable summer afternoons spent lounging in the gazebo on her parents' estate in Connecticut. Rocking in time to the smooth cadence of a distant memory, she felt herself drifting far away from this melancholy time and place.

"Paula." Sam's gruff voice startled her and set her heart pounding. She rubbed her eyes and tried to shake the sleep from her brain.

"Sorry," she said. "I must have dozed off."

"None of us has been getting much sleep lately," he conceded, settling himself on the gliding swing.

They sat in silence for several moments, until Paula's mind cleared and she felt compelled to state the obvious. "She must be asleep, or you wouldn't be here." *Or else she's* . . . Her senses recoiled at the possibility, and she decided to be quiet and let him say whatever he'd come to tell her.

"No, it's not that," he said evenly.

Oh, dear Lord, it's over. She closed her eyes against the sudden, stabbing pain somewhere in the vicinity of her heart.

Sam seemed not to notice her distress. "She's asking for you," he went on.

"Me? Asking for—" A wave of relief washed over her. "Asking for me?" She took a deep breath and let it out quickly.

"Yes, and she seems quite insistent about it. You know Karti— when she gets something into her mind, there's no way you can . . ." He stared out over the broad expanse of front lawn. "You don't want to keep her waiting. I think I'll just sit here for a while."

Karti's face was flushed, her skin quite warm as Paula sat on the bed and cradled her friend's hand in both of hers. "We've got to stop meeting like this," Paula whispered.

A fragile smile animated Karti's lips, and she opened her eyes. "Glad you're here," she said in a thin voice. "I need to ask you something."

"Anything but my bra size. You know how word gets around."

Karti didn't respond, but her eyes lit up with mirth for a few seconds. *I'd do anything*, Paula thought, *to keep that smile around for another, say, fifty or sixty years. We could have such fun.*

Finally Karti found her voice, though her speech was slow and labored. "You think it went all right this afternoon with the children? I wanted them to understand . . . how everything will work out."

"The string was a brilliant idea—no, an *inspired* idea," Paula replied. "Even *I* understood it; and believe it or not, it helped me put TJ's death into some kind of perspective. I don't know . . . in some small way, it doesn't seem so *permanent* now."

"Good. I hope my children figure it out—especially the girls. They're so young; I worry for them."

"Mark said pretty much the same thing to me yesterday. He'll look out for them. He loves them a lot, you know."

Karti nodded weakly. "I still need to ask you something."

"Ask away," Paula said, this time more seriously.

"It's about TJ." Karti looked directly at Paula, her expression intent.

A brief shadow flashed across Paula's face, and her brows knit together in puzzlement. "TJ? What about TJ?"

"Well," Karti smiled, her voice a little stronger now, "it's no secret that I'll be, uh, taking my leave before long, and I . . . I can't imagine getting over there and not looking up your wonderful son. In a roundabout way, you see, he brought us together—you and Mark and me. I just want to put my arms around him and give him a huge hug."

"That makes two of us," Paula murmured, blinking back a sudden rush of emotion.

"I'm sorry . . . didn't mean to upset you," Karti said.

Paula wiped at her eyes. "No problem—just threw me a little off guard, that's all. I guess it never really occurred to me that you'd actually see him before I would."

"I've been thinking about it quite a bit—spending some time looking at the picture you gave me a few months ago," Karti continued. "I'm looking forward to meeting him."

"Mind if I come along?" Paula joked. "I'd be happy to introduce you."

"I wish," Karti sighed. She looked deeply into Paula's eyes. "But if there's a message . . . I'd be honored to give it to him."

Her implication stunned Paula into silence, and long moments passed before she could reply. "Tell him . . . tell him I'm *so sorry* I didn't listen when he tried to tell me about the Church, but I'm doing my best to get my act together now. Tell him Scott and Millie and Rudy and I are okay . . . Rudy's getting older and misses him desperately, so he might have some four-legged company before too long. Tell him I hope there's basketball in heaven. And tell him," her eyes filled with tears, "that with the possible exception of Heavenly Father, no one loves him more than I do." She looked closely at Karti, who appeared weary and slightly overwhelmed. "And if you don't remember any of the rest of it, just tell him I love him. So much."

"I can do that," Karti breathed. "At least the last part."

"Fair enough," Paula agreed. "I'd like to say I'd return the favor, but—"

"Forget it. This one's on me. We'll catch up when we both get . . . over there." Karti's voice was sounding weaker now, more distant.

"Deal," Paula said. "Now, is there anything—anything at all I can do for you?"

"I don't think so." Karti smiled at her friend with a radiance that shone in her eyes, lit up her countenance, and seemed to warm the air around them. "You've been wonderful through all of this—so kind, so dear. Sam and I . . . and the children . . . we love you for it."

"The feeling is mutual, I assure you." Paula smoothed a lock of Karti's hair back from her damp forehead. "You're all very easy to love."

"Then one day . . . we'll pick up this conversation where we left off. But right now, I need to talk to Sam—would you please send him up?"

"Of course." Paula gently squeezed her friend's frail hand, then bent to kiss her lightly on the cheek. "Rest well; I'll see you soon."

Karti closed her eyes and nodded, a remnant of that transcendent smile still lingering on her lips.

Sam had been with Karti for just over an hour when Paula, sitting at the kitchen table thumbing through an old magazine, heard brisk footsteps in the entryway. Within seconds Sam entered the kitchen; Paula could see the distracted look in his eyes and the grim set of his jaw, but he didn't seem to notice her. His heavy shoes made hard, hollow sounds against the floor as he strode quickly through the kitchen and into the mud room. Lunging for the door, he jerked it open, then slammed it behind him as he charged down the cement steps and into the yard.

Paula hurried to the window. She watched as Sam lurched toward a decorative log fence at the far corner of the lawn and leaned heavily against it, his back to the house. He rested his elbows on the top log and let his forearms dangle over the fence, his head hanging so low that she could see only the outline of his broad shoulders. "What in the world," she mumbled. "Something's happened. I should go to him."

As she reached for the doorknob, a figure came into her peripheral vision and moved steadily toward Sam. A second glance told her it was Mark, and she decided to stay where she was for the moment.

Mark approached his father and touched him on the shoulder. Sam lifted his head, and for several minutes the two men engaged in deep, earnest conversation. At the end, Sam hung his head again, and his torso began to shake so violently that Paula could see the tremors from across the yard. Mark grasped the man's shoulders firmly and turned him so they were face to face. Then he wrapped his long arms around his father, and Sam clung to him fiercely. Long minutes passed, and finally they pulled apart. After a few more words and another brief embrace, Mark left him alone at the fence and headed for the house.

Paula met him at the door. His face was ashen, and he seemed unsteady on his feet. "Good grief," she said, "you look like you've been to hell and back—maybe not even quite all the way back. I saw you with Sam; what's going on? Is it Karti? Is she—"

"I'd like to sit down," he said.

She grabbed his hand and led him to the kitchen table. When they were both seated, she asked again. "What happened out there?"

"There's . . . no easy way to say this," he admitted. "She's asked him to release her."

Paula stared at him, her expression blank. "Release her? Release her from what? I don't understand."

He returned her stare glumly. "Release her from life."

It took an agonizing moment for the words to sink in. *No, I don't believe it. Not Sam . . . not Karti. How could they even think of such a thing?* Her response was hoarse and incredulous. "Mark, do you mean to tell me that she actually wants to end it all—and she wants Sam to help her do it? That's murder!" She jumped up and began wringing her hands. "Knowing the gospel as she does, surely you can't think she would *ever* want to—"

"Now, hold on there just a second, Sister Donroe." Mark's deep voice was slicing through the haze of her paralyzing disbelief, his strong hands holding her arms firmly. "See if you can take a few deep breaths." She obeyed, and he let go of her arms. "Better now?"

She nodded. "But I'll still never understand how—"

"You'll never understand *anything* if you don't let me explain it to you," he said firmly.

"Oh, . . . sorry." Her shoulders slumped disconsolately. *I still can't believe it. Karti couldn't . . . wouldn't do something like that.*

Mark leaned back in his chair. When Paula looked at him, he was actually smiling, and there was a subtle glint of humor in his eyes. "What's so funny?" she snapped. "Or don't you remember five minutes ago, when you—"

"Of course I remember; but in the light of the present misunderstanding, I figure all things are relative. Now, do you want me to clear this up, or what?"

"Go ahead." She folded her arms across her chest.

"All right." He glanced out the window for a moment, as if deciding how to begin. "You know, Paula," he finally said, "I think we've all gotten so attached to you, and you've become so much a member of the family, that sometimes we forget how new you are to the Church. New to the terminology, new to the ordinances, new to the culture. New to the whole idea of the gospel and how it works."

"Sometimes I forget that myself," she admitted. "I'm still figuring out how to be a Mormon." She grinned shyly. "I think I've got visiting teaching down pretty well, but there's still a lot to learn."

"Exactly," Mark agreed. "And when I told you that Mom had asked Dad to 'release' her, I guess I just assumed you knew what I was talking about. But from your reaction, it's clear that you didn't."

"Sounded pretty straightforward to me." Paula felt her sense of despair returning.

"Well, let me put your mind at ease—at least about the 'murder' part," he said.

"I wish you would." Her dark eyes were pleading for some resolution.

"It's like this." Mark leaned toward her and spoke with quiet intensity. "The priesthood, as you know, is the power and authority to act in the name of God. Those who hold the Melchizedek Priesthood have authority to bless babies, confirm new members, participate in Church administration and temple ordinances, bless the sick and give special priesthood blessings, preside over their families, and do a whole bunch of other things within the framework of the gospel. The priesthood is a very real power; it's what separates The Church of Jesus Christ of Latter-day Saints from all other churches on the earth." He paused, looking at Paula expectantly.

"Yes, I believe I understand what the priesthood is," she stated.

"Then you can imagine that when a righteous man of deep faith uses this power, he can accomplish extraordinary things."

"I'm sure that's true," she acknowledged.

"Well, let me see if I can explain a very sacred concept. When someone is extremely ill, and close to death . . . under certain circumstances and as a result of great faith exercised by both parties, it is possible for a man to use his priesthood power to release that individual's spirit to return to God."

Paula took in a sharp breath as she realized the significance of his statement. "And what might those 'certain circumstances' be?" she asked cautiously.

"It could happen when the person is truly 'nigh unto death,' as the scriptures say, and only if it is absolutely the Lord's will that the death occur."

"So . . . you're saying if the time is right, and if there is divine agreement in the matter, Sam could actually . . . *release* Karti from this life."

"That's exactly what I'm saying . . . and that's exactly what Mom asked of him."

"Whoa." Paula's eyes searched his. "And do you . . . do you think he has the faith to do it?"

"I believe he does," Mark answered calmly. "I've known him for over twenty-two years now, warts and all—except there just aren't any warts. If anyone could call down the powers of heaven on behalf of another human being, he could do it. He's done it before."

Her eyes grew wide. "You mean he's *released* someone?"

"No, not that. But I've seen him virtually bring people back from certain death by the sheer power of his faith and priesthood authority. If he makes up his mind, and if the Lord wills it, he could do this for my mother. I just don't know . . ." He paused and stared down at his hands.

". . . if he's up to it emotionally," Paula said, completing his sentence.

"Right. She's been in a lot more pain and for much longer than anybody realizes, and now she feels like she's said her good-byes and wants—needs—to move on. But he loves her *so much*—how can he possibly lay his hands on her head and willingly let her go? All he lives for is another day, another hour, another minute with her. Yet she's asked for this final act of love from him . . . that's what he's out there wrestling with now."

"Unbelievable," she murmured, slowly shaking her head. "How do you feel about it?"

"Terrible," Mark confessed. "She's been the biggest part of my soul for all these years, and I'd do anything—give my own life, even—to keep her with us. But she's at the end of her journey; we all know that. She can linger through another few days of profound suffering—or she can go now, peacefully, under the loving hands of her personal ministering angel and eternal companion. Either way, she'll leave behind a whole lot of broken hearts. Including mine." He quickly wiped at his cheeks. "It's Dad's decision; no one else can make it." He gave her a small, sad smile. "And if I know him, she'll get her way. He could never say no to his best girl." He rose from the table and patted her shoulder. "If you'll excuse me, I think I'll go see how she's doing."

Left alone, Paula felt her head pounding with the enormity of this new revelation. She returned to the window, where she could see Sam still slumped against the fence, his fingers pulling at his hair as he struggled with a host of private demons. It was a heartbreaking scene, and she couldn't bear to let him endure it alone. Opening the door without a sound, she moved down the steps and across the lawn, stopping a few feet away from where he stood. His back was to her, and he didn't seem to know she was there.

"Mark told me," she said just loudly enough to be heard. He gave no response. "What Karti has asked of you," she added. Still no response. "I can't imagine what you must be going through."

He turned slowly to face her then, his massive shoulders sagging under some invisible burden, his arms hanging limp at his sides. *He's aged ten years in the past hour*, Paula thought as she noticed the deep, ragged lines creasing his forehead, circling his red-rimmed eyes, dividing his cheeks and chin into leathery fragments. *This is agony personified.*

His voice was barely audible when he spoke. "I never thought I'd have to do something like this. She's my life, and now . . . now she wants me to . . ." A low moan erupted from deep in his chest. *"How can I do this?"*

He suddenly clutched his midsection and doubled over as though he'd been shot. Paula rushed to him and tried to steady his large body by grasping his shoulder with one hand and spreading her free arm across his wide back. "Just breathe deeply," she whispered into his ear. Instead, he collapsed to his knees. She knelt beside him, rubbing the taut muscles in his neck and shoulders as he sobbed.

Finally the tide of emotion ebbed, and Sam sank down heavily on the grass. "Whew," he said, wiping his face on the sleeve of his shirt. "I guess that had to come out, sooner or later." He looked up at Paula, who was still kneeling. "Sorry."

"Don't be," she said, touching his shoulder lightly. "You're entitled."

"I'm also facing the hardest thing I've ever done in my life," he declared grimly.

Paula regarded him with mixed sympathy and admiration. "Then you've made up your mind?"

"There was never any question, really. When Karti asked, I knew it was right; I trust her enough to know that she's placed herself in God's care. Now I just need to figure out how I can possibly bring myself to put my hands on her head and . . ." He pulled a crumpled handkerchief from his back pocket and rubbed at his eyes. "No matter how convinced I am, at this moment it seems utterly impossible."

Paula felt the words rise to her lips. "You won't be alone, you know. If it's the right thing to do, if you're sure it's the Lord's will, He'll be with you all the way. Mark tells me you're a man of incomparable faith, and I believe it. That faith is what will get you through this—and it's what will get Karti safely to her final destination. Let Him help you, Sam. Let Him help Karti."

The hint of a melancholy smile tugged at his mouth as he studied her earnest expression. "You're pretty wise for a brand-new Mormon, you know that? Thank you, Paula; I believe what you said." He stared at his hands for a full minute. "Now I suppose I just need to get myself together and prepare for . . . a very special blessing. A once-in-a-lifetime blessing." He came stiffly to his feet, all the while shaking his head as though he couldn't quite comprehend it himself. "Tell Karti I'll be back in a couple of hours, would you please? There's a place on the mountain where I sometimes go to pray."

"I understand. And I'll tell her." Paula rose on her tiptoes and pressed a kiss to Sam's cheek. "We'll be here." Then she turned away from him and walked slowly back to the house.

Deep into the evening, a solitary cricket chirped outside the window as Sam Richland blessed his wife, tenderly wiped the tears from both of their faces, then lay down beside her and cradled her in his arms. Karti died peacefully less than three hours later.

CHAPTER 19

Downtown Los Angeles was slowly choking under a bleak September sky. Smog had settled in thick layers over the city by six o'clock every morning, blotting out the sun but still letting in its oppressive heat. "Take me back to Idaho," Paula moaned as she watched the spectacle from her high-rise office. "On second thought, take my top half back to Idaho, and leave the rest right here." Grimacing in pain, she swung her leather chair around when she heard a knock at the door.

Ted let himself in. "Morning, chief," he said breezily, planting himself in a chair next to the desk. "How was your long, relaxing Labor Day week—" He stared at her drawn face. "Uh-oh; I'd say it was less than idyllic."

"On the contrary," Paula rejoined, forcing her face into a porcelain smile, "I had a *wonderful* time." She gingerly shifted her position and grunted genteelly. "Except for the horseback riding."

"I see . . . a little saddle sore, are we?" His blue eyes twinkled, and she couldn't help smiling through her clenched teeth. "Poor baby."

"Well, I've only got myself to blame. Sam was trying to teach me. He thinks anyone born west of the Mississippi ought to be a natural-born cowpoke, and I wasn't about to prove him wrong, so we went riding for three hours yesterday. That was about two hours and fifty-nine minutes too long. The girls laughed until they could hardly stay on their horses." She groaned again and reached for a bottle of Tylenol on her desk. "My head is splitting, too. I don't know why I even came in this morning."

"So you could tell me about all the fun you had," Ted suggested.

"Yeah, that must be it," she grimaced. "Now, is there a reason for this visit, or can I get back to my suffering in peace?"

"In a minute. I just need you to sign these purchase orders for photo equipment." He pushed a thin manila folder across the desk. "The digital cameras we want are a little on the pricey side, but they'll make the art department's job a lot easier."

Paula studied the forms. "That's a lot of money for a couple of little black boxes." She scrawled her signature across the papers and handed him the folder. "You tell Jennifer and Troy they'd better make me proud."

"Will do. Now I'll let you indulge your pain behind closed doors." He rose and moved toward the door, then turned back. "So how are Sam and the kids doing, anyway?" It was a question he seemed to ask after each of her weekend visits to Idaho.

"Pretty well, I think. Mark and Alex are away at school; Jake will leave on his mission later this fall, after the potato harvest. The girls seem to be adjusting to life without their mother, although they're very protective of Sam, and Ruthie sticks to him like strapping tape. Sam is . . . well, he never says much, spends a lot of time looking through old photo albums, occasionally stays a night up in Karti's studio. This weekend was the first I've seen him smile in a long time; it seems that I must look pretty funny clinging to a saddle horn for dear life. So it guess it was worth it." She tried to cross her legs and winced. "Almost."

"He sounds like quite a guy," Ted murmured.

"I've never known a finer man. Sam is more than just smart; he's kind and good, and he loves his children more than anything. He's highly respected in the community, too—and the people in his ward think he'll be the next General Authority. It wouldn't surprise me a bit."

"That's, uh . . . great. Really great." Ted raised the folder to his temple in a salute. "I'll be on my way now. You know where to find me . . . in case you need a donut or anything." He clicked his tongue once and strode quickly from the office, closing the door behind him.

Paula swiveled her chair around to gaze out the window again. *I really did have a wonderful time,* she mused. Since Karti's death in June, she'd spent a good share of her weekends with the Richland family. It had begun with a promise she'd made the day after the funeral, as she was packing for the trip home. Ruthie stood glumly next to the bed, her eyes still puffy from crying. "When will I see you again?" she asked plaintively, her entire face threatening to dissolve into another deluge of tears.

"Soon, sweetie. I promise." Paula stopped what she was doing and folded the girl into a close hug. "You all just need time to be together now, okay? Your daddy's folks will be here for a week or two; they'll be a big help, I'm sure."

Ruthie pulled away and pursed her lips in a pout. "They're old fuddy-duddies. I mean they're nice and everything, but they're not . . . Mom. And they're not you." She sniffed loudly. "They don't even like my cookies."

"Some people have no taste," said a voice from the hall. Paula turned around to see Andrea sauntering into the room. She was dressed in worn Levi's and a pale yellow T-shirt, and her hair was pulled back into a loose ponytail. Her blanched face looked much older than its sixteen years, and her high cheekbones seemed to accentuate the dramatic, somber look in her eyes. For a moment, Paula couldn't help thinking how closely this young beauty resembled Karti. *I'll bet she's already turning heads and hearts. Just like her mother did.* She felt a knot of fresh grief in her throat.

"Look, squirt," Andrea continued, curling a protective arm around the younger girl's shoulders, "Grandma and Grandpa Richland are doing the best they can, trying to help Dad out for a while. It's not their fault they're so . . . *old.*" She tried to suppress a giggle.

"Yeah, I know," Ruthie chimed in. "Last night Grandma was warming up a casserole, and she forgot to turn the oven on. If Sister Paula hadn't noticed it, we woulda been eating supper at midnight!" The girls broke into restrained laughter, and Paula joined them. It seemed a welcome respite from the downhearted mood of the past several days.

"The point is," Andrea said, "we've *all* got to do our best around here, now that things are so . . . weird. I think Dad likes having his parents around; it's kind of like he's a little boy again, you know? He just needs to be taken care of until he can figure out how to get along without . . . without the whole family here. Grandma and Grandpa can do it for a few days, and the boys can help till Mark and Alex go away to school and Jake goes on his mission. But they're just guys, so it's mostly up to us." She yanked her sister's hair affectionately. "We need to make things cool for Dad, okay?" Paula was astonished at the teenager's mature perception of the challenge at hand.

"Okay," Ruthie allowed. "But Sister Paula has to help, too."

"Me?" Paula's eyebrows arched. "I don't know what I could do to—"

"You and my dad are friends, right?" Andrea was looking at her intently.

"Yes, of course. He and your mother and I have been very close since we met last March."

"And you and the rest of us are friends, right?"

Paula smiled warmly. "No doubt about that. I love you guys; you're my second family."

"Well, we need a friend. Dad needs a friend." She shrugged. "You're it."

Paula chuckled at Andrea's forthright declaration. "I know that," she responded. "I'll always be your friend. It's a done deal."

"She already promised she'll come to visit," Ruthie interjected with a sly grin. "Every weekend."

"Whoa, there!" Paula laughed, holding up her hands. "I still have a company to run in California, remember? But I'll come as often as I can."

"That's cool," Andrea said, her voice suddenly uneven as her lower lip began to quiver. "Because I . . . we . . . we really, *really* need a friend." When tears welled in her deep-green eyes and spilled down her cheeks, she quickly hugged her arms to her chest and stared at the floor.

Paula's lighthearted facade dissolved. *Just a frightened little girl, lost without her mother, trying to put on a brave front. I should have known.* She gathered Andrea into her arms and held her until the tears subsided. "I'll be here for you," she whispered, stroking her hair. "I promise."

And Paula had kept her promise. A pattern of Friday-night-to-Sunday-afternoon visits was quickly established, and virtually every other weekend she would find herself winging toward Idaho. She'd taken Millie with her once, Scott three times; and although her son at first protested being separated from his kick boxing buddies, she noticed that he seemed rather charmed by the beautiful Idaho countryside. And by the beautiful Andrea.

Paula relished her time with the Richland family. She saw little of the boys, who seemed happy enough and were always working on the farm, attending Church dances, playing basketball, or going on splits with the full-time missionaries. But her bond with Andrea and Ruthie grew stronger as the weeks passed, and she began to think of them as the daughters she'd never had. They baked, read to each other, took leisurely outings to a nearby reservoir, visited Karti's grave, hiked near a small river and bathed their tired feet in its icy waters. Once they even tried sewing a little. Just once. "Anybody for computer games?" Paula chirped sweetly as she tossed a piece of mutilated fabric into the trash.

Sam joined them when he could—sweet, affable, melancholy Sam, the gentle mountain of a man who only rarely seemed to move beyond the grief of spending his days and nights without Karti. Not that he was temperamental, or even moody—he had no moods at all, only fragments of himself hung out to dry on a line stretching from his heart to the Roberts city cemetery. He was indulgent with his daughters and seemed glad to see Paula when she came; in fact, as the weeks passed he made a point of spending more time with "my three girls," as he called them. Once he even took Paula's hand as the four of them crossed the street after attending an outdoor band concert; but he quickly pulled away when she smiled up at him. As if drawn to Sam by some undeniable connection, she began to feel protective, even tender toward him. Yet she could somehow never bridge the gulf of unrelenting sorrow that separated them.

"Until yesterday," Paula mused aloud, clicking a pen against her teeth. "He was actually laughing when he saw me bouncing around on that horse. I swear it, he was *laughing!* Barely cracked a smile for months, and now this." She leaned back in her chair, causing her to flinch in pain, but she ignored it and enjoyed the sensation of a broad grin spreading across her face. "Go ahead and gloat, Donroe. No doubt about it—you've had a major breakthrough here!" The realization carried her happily through the week.

Early Friday afternoon, Paula summoned Ted to review the next week's schedule. "I'll be leaving in a couple of hours—out of town till Monday," she explained. "I thought you could fill me in on the accounts you're working with and any meetings I'll need to attend." She checked her watch. "Could you make it fast? I still need to get home and pack."

"Sure thing," he said. "If you don't mind my asking, is this business or . . . Idaho?"

"Not that it *is* any of your concern," she replied brusquely, "but I'll be spending some time with the Richlands." She began shuffling a small pile of papers on her desk.

"Surprise, surprise. Two weekends in a row," he said, his voice edged with sarcasm. "I hear they're setting up the Paula Donroe Memorial Guest Room in the east wing."

She shot him a dark look. "What, I can't take a break and enjoy a little time with friends?"

"Whatever," he shrugged. "I was just making an observation, that's all." He shifted his tone to an obnoxious twang. "Ah heer tell awl them haystacks is powerful inter'sting. Eachun with its own pers'-nalitee, an' awl."

Paula huffed in exasperation and chose to ignore his comment. "If you must know, Sam called. He wants the girls and me to go with him to some big computer exposition or something in Pocatello tomorrow."

"A likely story," Ted smirked. "And what will it be next weekend—a gun show at the mall? I can hardly wait to hear—"

"You know what? This meeting is over," Paula cut in bluntly. "If I wanted your critique of my weekend activities, I would've asked for it. But since I don't, I'd appreciate your keeping it to yourself. Now, if you'll excuse me." She stood and cocked her head toward the door.

He raised his hands in surrender. "Fine, fine. I'll see you on Monday, then . . . uh, would that be A.M. or P.M.?"

"Go *away,*" she hissed. "You're way over the line on this, Ted."

"Sorry, boss," he said without contrition. "I guess we'll see you when we see you. Have a good one." He gestured as though tipping his hat to her, then ambled from the office.

When the door closed, Paula sat down heavily, shaking her head. "What in the blue heavens was that all about?" she mumbled. "We've been friends for nearly a decade, and I've never seen him so utterly disrespectful—almost like he was trying to hurt me." She tapped her nails on the glass desk top and stared at the chair he had just vacated. *Hmm . . . if I didn't know better, I'd almost think he was . . .* "Naw," she declared. "Not a chance. He's just stressed. I'll give him a day off next week; maybe it'll put him in a better mood." The decision made, she hurried to tie up the loose ends of her day.

Before three o'clock, Paula was sitting in the airport, waiting for her Delta flight. She tried to immerse herself in a news magazine, but her brief, unsettling encounter with Ted kept hovering in her mind like an unwelcome mosquito on a sultry August afternoon. Didn't he see how stretched she was? Couldn't he just help her hold everything together, without passing judgment on her life and acting like a spoiled teenager? There was business to be taken care of, after all—new accounts to pursue, ad campaigns to build, a million details to oversee. Besides that, she was juggling time for an occasional martial arts class, visiting teaching and other Church activities, frequent phone calls to Idaho, and keeping track of Scott, who had just started his senior year and was spending most of his time either kick boxing with the Crawlers or dreaming of a new Dodge Viper. She certainly couldn't give up her visits to the Richland home, either—not yet, anyway, until the girls were more stable. But she had to admit that life would be simpler when things calmed down a little. How in the world, she wondered, did men and women ever find time to have relationships?

She dismissed this unproductive train of thought, and was just settling down to read the current issue of *Time* when her cell phone rang. Dropping the magazine on an empty seat next to her, she rummaged in her purse and finally pulled the phone out in time to answer on the fifth ring. *I'm gone from the office for two hours, and somebody already needs me.* "Yes?" she said curtly into the small black Nokia phone.

"Paula . . . big-mouth Barstow here. Calling to beg and grovel— around the block, if I have to."

She couldn't help smiling at the image, but made sure her voice was severe when she responded. "Try to the L.A. county line and back, on your hands and knees."

"Wow, you really know how to hurt a guy. Would dinner at a fancy restaurant be an appropriate substitution?"

"For me or you?" She was beginning to enjoy this little game.

"Well, I was kind of thinking . . . for both of us. My treat."

"Ah, two for the price of one. I'm not sure the punishment fits the crime."

There was a long pause, and Paula thought she heard a faint groan on the line. "You got me there," he finally conceded, "seeing as how it wouldn't be much of a punishment—except maybe for you, having to spend time with a thankless degenerate like yours truly." Another pause. "I'm really sorry, Paula. What I did was totally unwarranted, unprofessional, and . . . and definitely un-nice. I hope some day, even if it's in the distant eternities, you'll be able to forgive me." He sounded like a street urchin begging for a crust of bread.

"Hmm . . . in the distant eternities." She pictured his intense blue eyes brimming with remorse, and the remains of her annoyance melted away. "That sounds like a pretty long time. Why don't we just make it next Tuesday?"

"Would that be for, uh, dinner or forgiveness?" he asked cautiously.

"Both," she declared. "A punishment is a punishment."

"And this criminal must *pay,*" he vowed—a bit enthusiastically, she thought.

"Okay, okay," Paula said. "But tell me, Ted—whatever happened a few hours ago to make you so crazy? I can't imagine why you'd act so—"

"Sarcastic? Belligerent? Insensitive? Moronic? That's no relation to Moroni, by the way." A short pause. "I guess I just lost it for a minute there. See, a—a bunch of stuff is going on with a couple of our new accounts, and I'd hoped to go over some of it with you this weekend. We used to spend occasional Saturdays together at the office, as you may recall."

"I know. And now that I think about it, maybe I should be the one to apol—"

"*Flight 3547 to Salt Lake City is now boarding,*" a loudspeaker suddenly blared.

"Uh-oh, my flight has just been called. Can we talk about this over the condemned man's meal on Tuesday?" Paula stood and started to gather her purse and carry-on luggage.

"Sure thing. I'll look forward to it." Ted's voice sounded lighter now, more relaxed. "Have a fantastic weekend."

"That's the plan," she replied. "See you later." Quickly punching the "end" button, she tossed the phone into her purse and hurried toward the Delta gate where her jet was waiting.

Their Tuesday dinner never materialized. Paula begged off, saying she'd forgotten a visiting teaching appointment. Ted didn't mention it again, but over the next two months he seemed to fall into a pattern of observing her comings and goings from a calculated distance, carefully tracking her almost weekly visits to the Richlands' home. She seemed preoccupied, and when they met to discuss business matters she was courteous but aloof. "Weather's changing; it's getting a lot colder up there. Sam and the girls are getting by" became her customary response to his inquiries about her trips to Idaho. Finally, he stopped asking.

For Paula, the tall frame house in Roberts had become a magnet that drew her back at every opportunity—away from the breakneck speed of a high-pressure, tooth-and-nail business climate to a milder, more unpretentious approach to life. With Mark and Alex away at school, Jake off on his mission to Australia, and snow piling up for a long winter, she relished these halcyon days spent with Sam and his daughters. Together they explored ski and snowmobile trails, visited a museum commemorating the Teton Flood that had devastated the area in the mid-1970s, got snowed in and played board games in front of a roaring fire, stared in awe at a shimmering white moon casting slivers of crystalline light on a mote of gigantic snowdrifts circling the farmhouse. These weekends were appealing breaks from Paula's madcap California life.

When Scott accompanied his mother, the girls found him endlessly entertaining. He taught them a few simple kick boxing moves, and Andrea asked him to show her the basics of sketching with a charcoal pencil. "I've always wanted to learn to draw, along with my music lessons," she explained, flashing him a luminous smile. Then her countenance dimmed a little. "Mom said she'd teach me, but there wasn't enough time before she . . . left." Scott cheered her up by declaring that she had enormous talent, and the two spent hours together drawing, re-drawing, and papering the kitchen table with their creations.

Sam was smiling more these days, too. He was reserved, as usual, and his eyes still bore the melancholy traces of grief. But his laughter, when it came, was deep and easy, his step more buoyant, his shoulders squarer than Paula had remembered. When the children had activities of their own, he would take her to lunch, to a Saturday matinee, or sometimes bowling at the Ace Lanes downtown. During these times he would reminisce about his life with Karti, his concern for his family, his future plans for the small accounting business he had built over the years. The talking seemed to do him good, and Paula loved the sound of his solid baritone voice. Without fail, their evenings would end before nine P.M., when he would excuse himself and go up to the room he had shared with his wife for more than thirty years. "He likes to look at old pictures and things," Ruthie whispered one night when Paula seemed disappointed to be left alone with the girls. She nodded gamely and helped her young friend microwave a huge bowl of popcorn.

Paula, Scott, and Millie spent Thanksgiving with the Richlands. Mark and Alex came home on Wednesday afternoon, and the house was ignited with energy and laughter. Sam and the girls had gone shopping for dinner, and Millie insisted on putting it all together. The result, fashioned under her experienced hands, was spectacular. "A feast for kings," Mark declared. "Just like I remembered."

"Has it really been a whole year since you young missionaries had Thanksgiving with us in California?" Millie asked incredulously. "That was just before you found each other," she beamed, squeezing Paula's hand, then Mark's. "A long-lost son comes back to teach his mother the gospel. Like a fairy tale."

"Only better," Mark interjected, catching Paula's eye and smiling warmly. "This happened in real life."

"Such a miracle," the older woman clucked. "And now we're all together again—and then some." She glanced approvingly at each face around the large table. "Such a miracle."

"I wish my mom could be here," a small voice said next to Sam. All eyes turned toward Ruthie. "She would've loved this." A single delicate tear trailed down her cheek.

"I know she would, sweetheart," Sam said gently, circling her narrow shoulders with his big arm. "And you know what? I'm sure she *is* here. Right now. Enjoying this time with all of us." His statement caused a reverent hush to fall over the group.

After a moment, Mark cleared his throat and raised his water glass. "A toast," he said earnestly. "To Jakarta Lillian deClerq Richland—or, as she preferred to be called, Mom—the light of our lives. Till we meet again." They touched glasses all around.

"She must've been a cool lady," Scott said, his voice tinged with respect.

"You would've loved her," Andrea replied, leaning lightly against his shoulder. "And she would've gone crazy over your drawings. Just like me." She smiled winsomely, and Scott's complexion flushed a deep red.

"So, it looks like we're almost finished here," Mark said quickly. "We'll have dessert later in the family room. Scott, want to shoot some baskets out in the yard? It's pretty cold, but we can wear gloves and ski masks. I cleared the snow away earlier."

"Yeah, great!" the teenager responded, his still-red face a study in relief. "I'll get my jacket." He bounded from the room without a backward glance at the chuckling company.

"Count me in, too!" Alex insisted. It wasn't long before the three had a lively game going, their warm breaths hanging like icicles in the frosty late-afternoon air. Later, sipping hot cider and eating pumpkin pie in front of a crackling fire, they chatted like old friends. Alex and Mark were fascinated by Scott's martial arts expertise, and made him promise to teach them some moves before the weekend was over.

Saturday evening came, and with it a heavy snowfall. Millie and Ruthie had made blueberry muffins, and by eight-thirty most of the family had gathered downstairs in the family room to watch videos, eat muffins, drink hot chocolate, and enjoy the warmth of the fire. It seemed a pleasant, relaxing conclusion to the long holiday weekend before Paula and her family flew back to California the next morning. As usual, Sam had disappeared upstairs.

Shortly after ten, Paula licked the last remaining morsels of butter and muffin crumbs off her fingers and stretched languidly. "Guess I'll turn in," she said, smiling at the contented faces around her. "This has been a delicious weekend, but it's back to the real world tomorrow." She gave Ruthie's ponytail an affectionate tug, then made her way leisurely upstairs to the second floor.

Passing Sam's room on the way to her own, she noticed that his door was open. *Unusual—especially for this time of night,* she mused, peering into the room. A small bedside lamp cast somber shadows on the walls; the bed was made, and she saw no evidence of Sam. *Where could he be? Maybe he went to the kitchen for a snack, or*—Suddenly she knew, and a small, tremulous smile played across her lips. *Of course he'd want to be there . . . I've seen the longing in his eyes all weekend.* Without hesitation, she returned to the stairwell and moved noiselessly up to the third floor.

At the far end of the thickly carpeted hallway, Paula stopped in front of the majestic sliding oak doors that she remembered so well: Karti's studio. The doors were open a few inches, and she could see the soft glow of a light in one corner. Carefully pushing the doors open a bit more, she saw a large figure standing near the window, his back to her. "Sam?" she called out tentatively.

"Come," he said softly, still facing the window. She slipped through the doors and pulled them closed behind her.

The room had not changed appreciably since Paula had last seen it eight months earlier. Huge snowflakes fell indolently in a flood of moonlight outside the floor-to-ceiling window, and their reflection on the opposite mirrored wall created a sensation of being part of the swirling landscape. She moved to the center of the room and stood transfixed for a moment. "It's amazing—so beautiful," she whispered reverently.

He nodded and turned toward her. "This will always be Karti's special place," he said. "I feel her spirit sometimes . . . when I come here to think." He gazed out the window, his shoulders hunched slightly, his hands nestled deep inside his pockets.

Paula hesitated to intrude upon the ambience of this exquisite room, but she had to know. "What does it feel like—her spirit, I mean?" Her voice was barely audible.

"Like . . . like a thin veil of love all around me. Like if I focused my eyes in just the right way, I'd be able to see through the veil . . . I'd see her. One day I think I will—when the time is right. In the meantime, I can sense the warmth of her smile, almost feel the touch of her hand, smell the fresh, clean fragrance of her. It's a great comfort to me."

"I'm sure it is," Paula said. They stood side by side, staring into the white mists beyond the window.

"I don't come here all that often," he continued after they had shared several minutes of contemplative silence. "It's almost as if . . . as if I need to stay away for days or weeks at a time, just to let her spirit build up so I can feel it more intensely the next time I'm here." He moved one shoe in a small circle against the polished wood floor. "Or maybe I'm afraid to come, for fear she won't be here. Sounds a little silly, doesn't it?"

"Not at all," Paula replied. "I've had similar feelings about TJ's room. Sometimes I believe I can sense his presence there; other times, I'm not really sure. Being around his things is a consolation, though." Tears threatened as she felt a sudden longing to curl up on her son's empty bed and bury her face in his pillow. *Tomorrow, TJ*, she vowed. *I'll be there tomorrow.*

"Shall we relax for a few minutes?" Sam asked. He took her elbow and guided her toward a slightly lopsided white sofa in one corner of the room. He motioned for her to sit, then settled himself beside her.

"This is nice," Paula said after a few moments. "Very nice."

"Yes, it is," he agreed. "Peaceful." He leaned back against the sofa and stared out the window for several minutes, then ran a hand across his broad forehead. "So many memories," he murmured. "Thanksgiving, Christmas . . . they were Karti's all-time favorites. She lived for the joy of roasting a turkey to perfection, then watching me and the children pick its bones clean. And on Christmas morning, she was more excited than all the rest of us put together. I never saw her eyes shine brighter than last year, when Mark and Alex were home from their missions and the whole family was together again. She was awfully sick, but that didn't stop her from having the time of her life or making it a Christmas to remember. Maybe she sensed it would be the last . . ." His voice broke, and Paula saw the moisture brimming in his eyes.

"I'm sorry," she said, reaching out to squeeze his hand. "This must be a terribly difficult time for you."

"You know," he finally began again, his voice less than steady, "when Karti died, I was completely at loose ends. I wasn't sure I could survive losing her."

Paula nodded. "In some small way, I understand. I felt like I'd lost my best friend."

"Then you do understand. I'd lost not only my best friend, but my soul mate, my lover, my counselor, the mother of my children—an irreplaceable part of me. For months, it seemed my life had no meaning or purpose—except, of course, for the children. But it wasn't the same."

"Like ripping a piece of your heart away," Paula said quietly. "It happened to me even before I—we—lost Karti. When TJ was killed, my world came to a screeching halt. More of a dead end, really—no place to go, no one to comfort me. Until I found the gospel, that is. And the son I thought I'd never see again."

Sam smiled through his resurgent grief. "Amazing, isn't it? Twenty-three years ago, it was a miracle that Karti and I found Mark and were able to adopt him; and as the years went by and our other children arrived, we felt infinitely blessed. Never in a million years did we expect or even hope to make contact with our eldest son's natural mother. Then another miracle happened: Mark went to California on his mission, endured the agony of watching his young friend die, baptized TJ's mom, and in the end discovered that this extraordinary woman was his very own birth mother—Sister Paula Donroe."

Paula couldn't help smiling. "Sounds like something straight out of a prime-time soap opera, doesn't it?"

"Yes . . . if we hadn't lived it, we wouldn't have believed it," Sam replied. "But then it got even better when we actually met you. I think Karti loved you the instant she heard your name." He paused. "No, that's not right. I'm sure she loved you from the moment she first held your newborn son in her arms."

"Or, according to her theory," Paula added, "from the time we knew each other in the premortal world." She felt a sudden longing to feel her friend's arms around her, to look into those incredibly deep, compassionate eyes, to hear her musical laughter again.

"I can certainly believe that," he said. "And you were a tremendous strength and comfort to her—to all of us—when she was so ill." He stared at the floor for a long moment, then looked up. "To her last breath, she loved having you near."

"The feeling was mutual," Paula said quietly. "I just wish I could have done more."

"You did more than you realized. Besides which, you've been our family's salvation these past few months. Andrea and Ruthie could never have made it without you. Neither could I. We've needed you, Paula—and we still do. We always will."

His earnest voice touched her, and she felt a warm flush rise to her cheeks. "We've helped each other get through this, Sam. And I must admit, I've grown very attached to all of you."

He nodded and gave her a tenuous smile. "I believe Karti would be very pleased to know that." Then his eyes bored into hers with unsettling intensity. "You'll stay close to all of us, won't you, Paula? Won't you?" Without warning his face crumbled, and she saw nearly two hundred days of grief in his eyes as tears spilled down his ruddy cheeks. "Lord, I miss her. I miss her *so much.*"

Her heart breaking for this gentle, tormented man, Paula reached out and pulled Sam toward her, cradling his head gently against her shoulder. "It's all right," she whispered. "I'll stay close—even closer than before. Everything will be all right. I promise."

By the time Paula said good-bye to the Richland family the next morning, she had spent the night reevaluating her life, determined to keep the promise. And changes were in the air.

CHAPTER 20

Once she was back in California, Paula's days seemed to fall on top of each other like dominoes, with almost no space in between for incidentals like eating, sleeping, touching bases with Millie and Scott, or having a personal conversation that lasted more than three minutes. *It's really better this way,* she told herself. *Otherwise, I'd be too tempted to open my big mouth and let the news fall out. Only a little while longer, and I'll have my life back. And this time it'll be a* real *life.* Exhaustion tugged at the limits of her endurance, but she felt driven to tie up as many loose ends at the office as she could.

Two weeks earlier, following her Thanksgiving weekend with Scott, Millie, and the Richland family, she had counted the personal cost of her single-minded commitment to Donroe & Associates, and had determined to pull back and rearrange her priorities. The company, of course, was in her blood; she'd never let it go completely. But she could certainly step away from it more often to enjoy the perks of being a terrific mother, friend, and faithful Latter-day Saint.

With this in mind, she planned to offer Ted a full partnership in the business, with complete liberty to run the operation when she took time away from the office—which she planned to do much more frequently in the future. In the long run, she felt he'd be pleased with this turn of events; he'd been looking exhausted for months, distracted and reclusive, and she couldn't help noticing how he'd even appeared to resent her presence lately. Now, with a new infusion of authority, he'd probably welcome being in charge whenever she was out of the picture. *I'll speak with him tomorrow,* she decided two days before her next scheduled flight to Idaho. *He deserves to know what's going on, have a chance to get used to the idea of being the boss. No doubt about it; I'm sure this news will put him in a better mood.*

At eleven o'clock the next morning, she rang Ted's office. "Hi there, handsome," she said cheerily when he answered. "How are things going? We haven't touched bases for—"

"Is there something you want? I'm trying to work on a project here," he broke in tersely.

"Oh, well, excuse *me,*" she shot back in clipped tones. Then she caught herself and mentally counted to ten by twos, allowing her ruffled feathers to settle. "I mean, sorry to break in on what you're doing . . . but I wanted to invite you to lunch."

She heard him sigh. "In that case," he said more easily, *"I'm* sorry. I just get so involved in writing this promotional stuff that I'm a sub-humanoid half the time."

"I understand," she said lightly. "So, could I tempt the more human side of you to join me for a bite at the Tavish? There's a matter I'd like to discuss."

"You're on. Might I have a clue as to the nature of this discussion?"

Paula laughed. "What, you can't wait for an hour? Poor boy, I'm afraid you'll have to wallow in the mystery of it for a while . . . but I can guarantee you're going to like what I have to say. At the very least, you'll find it intriguing."

"Then I'll look forward to it," he said.

The Tavish Grill was an upscale bar and eatery near their office building where fast-track businesspeople gathered for lunch at noon and cocktails at six. As Ted and Paula made their way to a secluded table behind a cluster of seven-foot ficuses, Ted's wry comment broke the ice between them. "I'll bet these plants aren't the only potted species during happy hour," he observed through one side of his mouth.

"I wouldn't know," she said, feigning haughtiness. "I haven't frequented this watering hole since my taste in liquid refreshment turned to something less potent than double martinis."

His blue eyes deepened as he smiled down at her. "What a difference a year makes."

"Boy, you can certainly say that again," she agreed.

"Okay. What a difference a year—"

"Oh, cut that out," she scolded affably as they sat. Their small table was covered by a deep-green linen cloth; at its center, one delicate yellow rose floated in a shallow crystal bowl. "But you do have a point; a year's worth of time can make a big difference. In fact, that's kind of what I wanted to talk to you about."

"Really." His eyes registered interest, and she knew she had his attention.

They ordered, then she got down to the business at hand. "You know, Ted," she began, "I've seen a lot of changes in my life since I joined the Church a year ago. I've been through the grieving process twice, first with TJ, then Karti, and I'm still dealing with those losses. I've had to cope with Scotty's rage and rebellion, get beyond an intruder's violation of my home and personal security, make tough decisions about what a Latter-day Saint should and shouldn't do in the marketplace, and learn how to be a practicing Mormon in a decidedly non-Mormon world."

"Practice makes perfect," Ted offered, a sly gleam in his eyes.

"Maybe," she conceded, "but the 'perfect' part is still a long, long way down the road. In the meantime, I have learned a few significant concepts. Probably the most important is that whether we're aware of it or not, there's definitely a divine center to things, a place where nothing else matters but the fact that we're all God's children, and He wants us to take care of each other. Help each other make it back home after this life."

"'This is my work and my glory—to bring to pass the immortality and eternal life of man.'" Ted spoke the words quietly, almost reverently.

"I didn't know you knew that," she said in a tone of mild amazement.

"Old scriptures die hard. I learned it way back in Primary."

Paula nodded, then went on. "Anyway, I didn't really mean to get into a gospel discussion here. I guess I just wanted to let you know that my priorities have changed a little over the past year, and I've come to realize that my entire life doesn't—shouldn't—revolve around what's happening at the office. I have other things to consider now, and I've decided to make some changes."

He studied her face closely. "And am I to assume that these 'changes' have something to do with me?"

"Exactly." She paused, smiling, while a waiter served them. He carefully positioned a large Cobb salad in front of Paula, then lowered Ted's Texas bacon cheeseburger and thick homemade fries to the table. When he was gone, Paula continued. "I know I've been gone a lot these last several months. I haven't exactly been on top of things business-wise, and we've had some . . . differences," she admitted. "But you've been there for me every step of the way, Ted, and I've watched you rise magnificently to the occasion again and again. You've saved the day more times than I care to remember."

"Just doing my job, chief," he murmured.

"It's much more than that. *Much* more." She reached across the table to lay her hand on his, and he quickly captured her fingers in a firm squeeze. "You've been such a good friend, Ted. Much more than a friend, really—a support, a confidant, a trusted partner. I don't know what I would have done without you." Her voice was low and filled with subtle meaning as she stared at him forthrightly. "Which is why I'd like to make you an offer you can't refuse."

Ted gulped audibly as he glanced down at their clasped hands, then up into her dark, shining eyes. "You would?" he said in a voice crackling with unspoken longing.

"Yes," she affirmed. "You've been my better half, my greatest source of strength and support for a long time now, and I'd like to do something official to let you know how much I care. How much confidence I have in you."

"You would?" he repeated, squeezing her fingers more tightly, his blue eyes glittering with anticipation. "We've been through a lot together, you and I; we've come to care for each other. I've never said this before, but I've always hoped, even dreamed, that someday—"

"Well, your dreams are about to become reality." A wide, warm smile spread across Paula's face. "I need to ask you something. Something really important."

Ted took in a deep breath and forgot to exhale. "So, ask," he finally replied. "You know there's nothing you can't say to me."

"Precisely, my friend. And that's why I'm asking you . . ." She hesitated.

"Yes?" He was practicing saying the word.

"I'm asking you to become a full partner in the business."

Time stopped, and Ted stared at her without comprehension. After a minute or two, he cleared his throat. "Come again?"

"I'm offering you full partnership in Donroe & Associates, starting right away. As soon as we can make the arrangements."

"I see." Ted released her hand and slipped a thick slice of red, juicy tomato beneath the top half of his burger bun. "And just what has prompted you to make such an offer?"

"It's simple, really," she replied. "I've been quite preoccupied with the Richland family over these past several months, and—"

"Tell me something I didn't already know," he muttered.

Paula looked at him and smiled tensely. "As I was saying, I've been away a lot, and I realize the business has suffered somewhat because of it. But I've grown very close to that little family in Idaho, and now I don't see myself ever settling back into the eighty-hour work week I was once accustomed to. I've decided to free up my schedule so I can spend more time with the Richlands and not feel guilty when I take a four-day weekend now and then. There are other important things to consider, too—and Scotty is at the top of my list. We've been on much better terms recently, but it could all slip away if I don't keep him close to me."

Ted chuckled without humor. "And you feel that by spending more time in Idaho, you'll be keeping him close to you."

Paula's eyes flashed. "No, of course not. I just want to make sure that I have time to do both." Her expression relaxed a little. "Besides, I wouldn't be surprised if he wants to join me at the Richlands' almost every weekend. He and Sam's boys have become quite good friends, you know—not to mention his growing fondness for Andrea."

"Are you sure?" Ted's eyes met hers, then shifted quickly to his water glass.

"No doubt about it. I think that girl has got him wrapped around her—"

"I mean, are you sure this is what you want to do—move away from a great career that has claimed nearly every ounce of your blood, sweat, and tears for more than a decade?"

"That's just the point," Paula said earnestly. "I've been trying to look at things from more of an *eternal* perspective lately. This partnership arrangement would still provide me with a comfortable income, and it would allow me the time to be of service to more than just the consuming masses. Think about it: what good would being a member of the Church do me if I persisted in focusing every shred of my time and energy on building an advertising dynasty—at the expense of nurturing those I care about most? Life is too short, Ted; losing both TJ and Karti has taught me that."

Ted looked at her pointedly. "And those you care about most, I presume, would include Sam Richland."

"Absolutely," she affirmed. "Sam is one of the best things that's happened to me in a long time. He's a good, caring man, an outstanding father, strong in the Church, ready to do anything to serve the Lord. He's a wonderful friend."

"Uh-huh," Ted murmured, his eyes glued to the sliver of onion he had been nudging around his plate with a fork. Then he reached slowly across the table to pat her hand, barely seeing it through the mist that had risen in his eyes. "And no one deserves a wonderful friend more than you, Paula. I mean that."

"Thank you, Ted," she responded warmly. "Now, what do you say to my little proposal?"

"Some proposal," he muttered grimly, shaking his head.

She looked at him with a quizzical expression. "But I thought you'd enjoy the idea of being more in charge. Having full decision-making authority would relieve your stress when I'm away, and I know you'd be able to keep the company brilliantly on track. We'll hire a new copywriter so you can concentrate on management— although I hope you'll still give us some creative input, as well. I have the feeling this could work out quite—"

He waved his hand to silence her. "It's not that. It's . . . well, never mind. I'm, uh, flattered that you'd even think of making me a partner, and it's certainly a tempting offer. Let me think about it for a couple of days, would you?" He laid his napkin across his untouched meal and pushed his chair back. "Right now, I need to get back to work."

"No problem," Paula smiled. "I'm flying to Idaho tomorrow, but we'll talk about this next week, and we can make our plans a little more concrete."

"Yeah . . . concrete," Ted mumbled. He stood abruptly. "I'll see you later." She nodded and attacked her salad with vigor as he walked from the restaurant with a slight shuffle to his step.

Ted worked behind closed doors through the afternoon and into the evening. The next morning, Paula asked Carmine to deliver some papers to him. "Can't," she said, running the tip of a pencil through her tightly permed red hair. "He called in sick an hour ago, and his office is locked."

"Just slide them under his door, then," Paula directed. "I'm sure he'll be in before I get back on Monday afternoon."

"Another big weekend with your missionary boy and his family, eh?" Carmine grinned.

"Exactly," Paula replied. "Things will be calming down before long, though."

"I hope so," her assistant said. "Ted has been swamped; no wonder he's sick. I saw him in the break room for just a minute yesterday afternoon, and he looked awful. I'll bet it's the flu."

"Could be," Paula said absently. "You did book me on the three-o'clock flight today, didn't you?"

"Yeah—same time, same place."

"Good. I'll be leaving here around noon, so I'd better get some work done." She flashed the young woman a grateful smile as she disappeared into her office. "Thanks, Carmine. See you next week."

Paula arrived at the Delta gate half an hour before boarding time. She found a cluster of vacant seats and settled herself in the middle of them, where she opened a newspaper and thumbed through its pages until an article caught her attention. Immersing herself in a finance piece about the vagaries of day trading, she was pleasantly oblivious to the continual ebb and flow of activity around her. This was her way of relaxing before a flight. *Maybe I'd better start reading scriptures at times like these,* she mused. *If something happened on a flight, better to be ushered to the throne with a triple combination in one's hand than with a* Wall Street Journal. She smiled discreetly, then turned back to the article she'd been reading. When someone sat down heavily beside her, she barely noticed the slight jarring sensation it caused. *A dozen empty seats all around me,* she thought idly, *and this person has to sit right—*

"Must be interesting reading." The voice sounded oddly familiar, but gruff and willful. She looked up into the bluest eyes she had ever seen. Except she *had* seen them before—just yesterday.

"Ted, what in the world are you doing here?" Her surprised glance took in his rumpled blonde hair and feverish red-veined eyes, the two days' stubble on his face, the disheveled slacks and T-shirt that seemed to sag against his body like a set of ill-fitting underwear. "Carmine said you were sick, and by the looks of you, I'd say she was right. You ought to be home in—"

"But I'm not home. I'm here, all right?" he interrupted, his gaze raking her face with its intensity. "I've got something to say."

"All right," she shrugged, folding the paper in her lap. "What's up?"

"What's up," he said in low, grinding tones, "is that you're on your way to Idaho for a long, leisurely weekend, having asked me to hold down the fort while you're gone, both now and in the future. You're going to have a terrific time with Sam Richland and his family; then you're going to fly home, have a lovely little reunion with Scott, take in a karate class or two, spend a few days at the office, then head right back to Idaho. You're putting first things first."

Paula chuckled tensely. "Yes, I think you've got it just about right. Is there a problem?"

"Well, I won't be here to see it. I'm resigning, effective immediately." His eyes glinted in the dim airport light, and his jaw muscles worked furiously. "I've thought about it, and under the circumstances, I just can't stay."

Her eyes grew wide, and she stared at him blankly. "What do you mean? What 'circumstances'? What are you telling me, Ted? I thought you'd want this partnership."

He leaned close to her face, his lips almost brushing her cheek. "Wrong. I wanted *you.*"

"Excuse me?" she breathed, her hand pressed to her heart.

Ted leaned back in his seat and closed his eyes as though struggling with deep fatigue. A few moments later, he looked at her and sighed mournfully. "The truth is, I love you, Paula. I've always loved you; I can't remember when I *didn't* love you."

"But you've been a married man until . . ." Her voice trailed off.

"I know; until a year ago. It was a bad marriage, but I stuck it out until Janice made things impossible. I was never unfaithful to her, Paula; but that didn't mean I couldn't have feelings for you. We worked together for eight years, side by side, every day, for heaven's sake. I guess I was just hoping, once my marriage was over, that we'd eventually get beyond the 'good friends' stage." He cleared his throat and smiled grimly. "But obviously that isn't going to happen now; you'll be moving on to other things, and I can't—no, I *refuse* to be left behind, day after day, week after week, waiting for you, licking my wounds. So I think I'll just cut my losses and move on."

"Ted, I—I don't know what to say," she stammered. "We've been friends for so long, and I can't . . . I can't imagine not having you in my life."

"You'll get used to it," he said evenly, staring out the airport window at a huge Delta jet. "Sam Richland will make sure of that. I can see it coming."

Paula sat in stunned silence, gazing at her hands folded calmly in her lap, tears welling in her eyes at the thought of never seeing Ted Barstow again.

His deep voice broke into her wistful reverie. "I do have something to thank you for, however."

"Oh? And what would that be?" she sniffed.

"You brought the gospel and the Church back into my life, and I will be eternally grateful for that. Even though," he smiled ruefully, "it now appears that I'll have to look elsewhere to find someone to spend my eternity with."

Paula's gaze shot to his face. "But Ted, I thought you didn't . . . I didn't know you were . . . it never occurred to me that . . ."

"That I might actually get my act together? I know; it seems almost unbelievable. But after your baptism, as I watched the changes in your life—the happiness that seemed to bubble up in those incredible eyes of yours, even in spite of Scott's problems, Karti's illness, and all the other challenges you were facing—even though I resisted for a while, I finally decided there must be something to this Mormon thing, after all. So I read the Book of Mormon six times and most of the other scriptures more than once, met with the missionaries, got acquainted with my bishop, started spending less time on the golf course and more at church. Playing basketball with the guys in the ward didn't hurt any, either. I'd already been baptized when I was a kid, of course, and I hadn't done anything majorly stupid in the meantime that would require a repeat of that ordinance, so I pretty much started out as an Aaronic Priesthood holder. Last month, I was ordained an elder."

She gaped at him. "You read the Book of Mormon *six times?*"

"Well, it wasn't like I had a social life," he said quietly. "You were in Idaho most of the time."

Paula touched his hand and felt his muscles tense. "I had no idea, Ted. What can I say? I'm so sorry I wasn't . . . sorry I'm not . . ."

"Hey, no regrets, okay?" He covered her hand with his and forced a smile to his lips. "The gospel is true, you know. That counts for a lot. Besides, you could always . . ." He hesitated, and his deep blue eyes bored into hers with the intensity of a white-hot flame.

"I could always what?" she prompted. In the background, she heard the final boarding call for her flight.

"You could always change your mind. Give us a shot. Stay here with me."

Paula snatched her hand away as though she'd been stung, then stood abruptly. "Come on, Ted," she laughed nervously, "this is . . . this is just *crazy.* I have to go." She reached down to pick up her carry-on bag, and when she straightened up he was standing very close to her, his fists clenched loosely at his sides.

"Oh, yeah?" he said hoarsely. "Let me show you just how *crazy* it is." This time he didn't hesitate, but gathered her into his arms and kissed her impetuously, passionately, desperately, as though it would be the last thing he would ever do on earth. In his imagination, she responded by pressing her willing lips firmly against his.

He finally pulled away and leaned close to her ear, his eyes still closed. "Good-bye, Paula," he whispered. "Be happy, and God bless." Then he turned and quickly disappeared into the airport's milling crowds.

Paula didn't quite understand the tears that kept seeping from her eyes during the flight. *Get a grip, Donroe,* she scolded herself. *Times change; circumstances change. Ted needs to get on with his life, and so do you. He was there when you needed him, always willing to help, the best friend anyone could ask for. And those eyes . . .* She shook her head forcefully, as though trying to clear her mind of lingering memories. Had Ted really loved her all this time? Looking back, she realized it was true. Was that why it had been so easy for him to make her laugh, to inspire her to be better, more creative than she was, to encourage her when Scott was at his worst, to comfort her when TJ died and despair seemed to be getting the upper hand? Or was it because she had feelings for him, too? Yes, she supposed she did. In fact, after his divorce and her conversion, she might even have allowed herself to love him, if only he'd been willing to . . .

"But he was. He *is!*" The words fell from her lips in a breathless whisper. "He's come back to the Church, hasn't he? He's an *elder,* for goodness' sake! If only he'd told me earlier, let me know his feelings, things might have been . . ." Her throat constricted, and she dabbed furiously at her eyes with a soggy tissue. *No. Ted's made his choice; he's gone, out of my life, a love that only might have been. Perhaps it could have worked, but it's out of the question now. Too many things are pulling us in opposite directions. Besides, maybe in time Sam and I will . . . or maybe not. A love like his and Karti's only comes once in a lifetime— probably once in a thousand lifetimes. But the least I can do is help him and his family through some of the lonely times. Karti would have wanted that; I'll stay close to them—for her. And even more than the Richlands, Scotty needs me. And I need him, too. I'll spend whatever time, do whatever it takes to keep my family together. I know TJ's rooting for us on the other side. I can almost see his huge grin, hear his war whoop as he cheers me on. "Way to go, Mom! You can do it—you can bring Scotty around! We'll all be together one day, and it'll be forever. Count on it!" I won't let you down, son.*

Paula sighed as everything slowly shifted back into proper perspective. She would do it right this time—concentrate less on business, more on the things that really mattered. Along the way, love might find her, but it couldn't be forced—only welcomed if it proved to be the real thing. In the meantime, she would fashion a gospel-centered life for herself and her family as she grew spiritually and learned to serve in new and marvelous ways. A warm spring of faith and gratitude welled in her heart as she considered the possibilities. By the time the big Delta jet touched down in Idaho Falls, she had dried her tears and was ready to greet and embrace whatever the future might bring.

CHAPTER 21

"Where are the girls?" Paula wondered out loud when Sam met her at the gate with a firm hug and a light kiss to her forehead. "They usually tag along."

"We came a little early, and I dropped them off at the Grand Teton Mall," he reported. "They begged for an hour or two of uninterrupted Christmas shopping."

"Something I could use myself," she said. "The folks on my list will be lucky to get a pretty smile and a tin of Almond Roca this year. With all I have to do at the office, I can see Christmas slipping right out from under me." She put her arm through his to steady herself as they walked through the airport doors and onto the icy sidewalk.

"I'll bet you'd get no complaints if you just went for the pretty smile," Sam declared, gazing down at her benevolently.

They walked in comfortable silence to the Suburban, where he opened the passenger door for her. "Let's go pick up the kids," he said, "then we'll find a quiet place to have dinner."

"Sounds good." Paula fastened her seat belt and settled back for the short ride to the mall. *Yes,* she thought as the vehicle's heavy snow tires crunched merrily against hard-packed snow, *this is exactly where I want to be. With Sam and those two adorable girls.*

The next thought jolted her like a mild shock of electricity. *And what about Ted? Where does* he *want to be?* She pressed two fingers carefully to her lips, as if reluctant to brush away the lingering memory of his kiss. Then she blinked hard. *It doesn't make any difference, Donroe. Forget it. He's gone.*

She glanced sideways at Sam, who was concentrating on the slick road ahead. He seemed weary and preoccupied, and her heart ached as she considered what he must be going through. *This is his first Christmas without Karti. It can't be easy, even if he's trying to get on with his life.* As they pulled into the mall's parking lot, she shook off the dismal thought and waved gaily to the girls, who were waiting outside near the entrance.

They found a small Chinese restaurant a few blocks away, and for almost two hours Andrea and Ruthie chatted nonstop, pulling small treasures from their shopping bags and displaying the gifts they'd purchased. "Wait'll you see what I got for *you,*" Ruthie whispered into Paula's ear, her eyes dancing. "Only two more weeks left 'til Christmas!" Sam appeared to be absorbed in his daughters' excitement, and he observed them with satisfaction. Occasionally his gaze met Paula's over the table and they exchanged a warm smile, though his seemed small and sad. *He really is having a tough time,* she reflected.

"We'd better go," Sam announced as a Chinese gong-clock somewhere in the restaurant struck eight-thirty. They all piled into the Suburban, and half an hour later they were pulling up in front of the Richland residence, where Sam brought the vehicle to a stop for a few moments. He gestured toward the house, but Paula had already been spellbound at the sight since they had turned into the circular drive. "It's beautiful—absolutely stunning," she breathed.

Through the tall, prismed panes of the front window, a ten-foot flocked tree shimmered with hundreds of tiny white lights and burgundy fabric-covered ornaments tied with silver and gold ribbons. A porcelain angel in flowing plum-colored robes and a glittering sapphire crown hovered at the very top of the tree, her welcoming arms outstretched, it seemed, to gather all the comfortless urchins of the world to her bosom and infuse them with peace, joy, and good will. The window glass had been artfully frosted to frame the tree, and the elegant image shone out into the icy night like a single perfect message of hope and loveliness.

"Karti's tree," Sam murmured. "Mark and Alex were home last weekend, and we put it up. Just like she would have wanted. Christmas was her favorite time."

"It's amazing," Paula said. "I've never seen anything like it."

"We always have another tree in the family room," Ruthie chimed in from the backseat. "It's got all our favorite stuff on it. You can help us decorate it this year."

Paula turned in her seat to smile at the girl. "I'd like that," she said.

Sam punched the gas pedal, and in a minute or two the group was making its way through the mud room and into the warm kitchen. "Okay, cherubs," he announced, "you can watch TV or videos for an hour, then it's time for bed." The girls dutifully disappeared downstairs, leaving Sam and Paula alone. "I'll carry your things upstairs," he offered.

She nodded her thanks. "I'll wait for you in the living room," she said, shrugging off her jacket and draping it on a kitchen chair. "I can't wait to see that tree up close." He left, and she made her way to the spacious oval-shaped room on the other side of the entryway. In its subdued light, she sank gracefully onto a small sofa and began to relax as the peaceful aura of Karti's tree enveloped her. *This is like aromatherapy for the soul,* she thought, drinking in the scene's tranquil colors and soothing ambience. Her eyes closed, and she sniffed appreciatively at the delicate pine fragrance in the air. The first line of an old pop song tugged at the corners of her mind. *Make the world go away . . .*

"Lovely, isn't it?"

Sam's voice startled her, and her eyes flew open as he sat down beside her. But the tree instantly worked its gentle magic, and she leaned back against the sofa with a sigh. "Mmm . . . more beautiful than I could ever have imagined."

They sat together for the better part of an hour, each lost in thoughts too tender to share. Once or twice, they might have slept for a few moments as the cares of the day drained slowly from their bodies.

"Sam?" Paula spoke his name softly, affectionately.

Hmm?" He turned his head and looked down at her.

"At the risk of sounding corny, I'll say it . . . a penny for your thoughts." She smiled a little. "Or, taking inflation into account, maybe I should offer at least a quarter."

"Cheap at the price," he chuckled, then his expression sobered. "My thoughts? I'm not sure you want to know; I wouldn't exactly say they're all sugarplums and fairies."

She squeezed his arm gently. "I think I already *do* know; I've seen it in your eyes all evening."

"Really." He smiled pensively. "And what have you seen?"

"Over thirty years' worth of love, shining like the golden halo on that angel up there." Paula shifted her gaze to the top of the tree, then back to Sam, who nodded wistfully. "And heartache, and longing, and endless wishing that things could be different. That Karti could be here with you now, wrapping her beautiful arms around you and kissing you and whispering 'Merry Christmas, my love' into your ear." She paused when she saw tears glistening in his eyes. "I'm sorry, Sam. I shouldn't have—"

"No, it's all right," he insisted, wiping at his cheeks. "You know me too well; I couldn't have described it better myself." He rested a hand on his chest. "So much of Karti is with me here—all the love and laughter, the joys and heartbreaks, the funny and tender moments that made our life together so complete and satisfying. I feel nothing but love and gratitude when I remember all of that. But still, we didn't have nearly long enough. When I think of all the hopes and dreams cut short, now relegated to the eternities, I . . ." He shook his head. "Well, it seems like a mighty long time to wait. Especially when I think of how many Christmases I'll have to get through without her." His shoulders slumped a little, and he stared at the floor.

"You'll make it, Sam," Paula whispered, her voice warm with emotion. "I know you will. Karti's love will see you through."

A few moments passed in silence, then Sam raised his head to look at the tree. "She told me she wanted me to be happy," he murmured. "Said she wouldn't mind if I remarried, as long as my new wife wasn't *too* pretty. And as long as I remembered that she would *always* be #2." He chuckled softly. "I told her I had no problem with that."

"You're an awfully good man, Sam Richland," Paula said. "I can imagine there are a lot of women out there who would love to be a part of your life—even as #2."

He smiled sadly. "Maybe. But for the time being, the most I can do is try to stay close to the Lord, gather my family around me, and have faith that good things will come. If I do marry again, it'll be a while. I'm not in any hurry."

Paula nodded. "I understand. A marriage like yours and Karti's is a rare and precious thing. Like a gift from heaven. And, having seen it firsthand, I can't help hoping that one day I'll find someone who . . ." Her voice trailed off as a small wave of loneliness washed over her heart.

Sam patted her hand. "You will, Paula," he said in a fatherly tone. "He might even arrive on the scene when you least expect it. But . . ." He paused, not quite sure of how to continue.

"But . . . ?" Paula was listening carefully.

"But—and I hope you don't mind if I dispense a little advice here—you may never recognize him if you're running in so many different directions that you can't give him time or attention enough to let the wonder of his love sink into your soul."

Paula stared at him in disbelief. "Well, I would certainly hope that if someone like that came along, I'd be willing to—"

"Give him a Friday night once a month?" Sam's voice was infinitely kind, but firm. "I've seen the way you live, Paula. You're bright, beautiful, successful—and driven. Fast-track all the way. It's been great for your business, and I admire you *so much* for the incredible things you've accomplished. But right now, while you're trying to run your company, look after your family, visit us nearly every weekend, grow and serve in the Church, and do a thousand other things, I can't help wondering if a good man would be able to find a place in your life. Even if he were madly in love with you, he might not be willing to wait."

Paula bit down on her lip as the words she'd heard earlier in the day flashed back into her mind. *"You'll be moving on to other things, and I refuse to be left behind, day after day, week after week, waiting for you, licking my wounds. So I think I'll just cut my losses and move on."* A fleeting image of the speaker's azure eyes and slightly crooked smile appeared at one corner of her consciousness. She looked up at Sam and smiled self-consciously. "Ouch."

He rushed to apologize, grabbing her hand and squeezing it tightly. "Hey, I'm awfully sorry; I didn't mean to offend you. You're such an amazing woman, and—"

"Don't, Sam," she interjected quickly. "The truth is, what you said was exactly what I needed to hear; in fact, I've been giving the matter some serious thought myself lately. It just might be the right thing to slow down a little and take some time to smell the . . . pheromones, or something."

"That's one way of looking at it," he laughed.

"But seriously," she continued, "even if I found someone, how could I ever . . . how could I be sure we'd have a relationship like yours?" She thought of her nasty marriage to Richard Donroe, and a bitter taste rose to her tongue. "I'm not exactly an expert in that area, you know."

"None of us has much expertise to begin with," Sam conceded, "and there are never any guarantees. I can tell you this much, though: You're looking for someone who will be your best friend—someone you can work, laugh, argue, dream, pray, and talk with. It sounds idealistic, I know; but being friends is the best way to start. Everything else—all the love, the passion, the magic, the completion—will follow. When you find a man who's willing to be your friend, and who shares a spiritual foundation in the gospel with you, I'd suggest you move heaven and earth to keep him by your side."

"Uh-huh. Seems reasonable," Paula observed. "But on the other hand, Karti told me the story of your mission-field romance—love at first sight, and all that. Sounded like more than friendship to me."

"You're right about that," he admitted. "But the plain truth of the matter is that we were awfully lucky. Chemistry first brought us together, but we had to learn how to be friends, too." He chuckled. "The mission rules took care of that. Later, after we were married, some of the other couples we knew thought all they needed was their passion, and they never bothered to build deeper relationships. Their marriages didn't make it."

"I see," Paula said thoughtfully. She leaned back against the sofa and nodded slowly as her own words of the day before rose like beacon lights in her brain. *You've been such a good friend, Ted. Much more than a friend, really—a support, a confidant, a trusted partner. I don't know what I would have done without you. . . . You've been my better half, my greatest source of strength and support for a long time now.* She closed her eyes and pressed her fingers to her forehead. "Oboy," she murmured, her voice barely audible. "I've been the queen of fools."

"Excuse me?" Sam asked carefully. "I didn't quite catch what you said."

She waited long moments before responding, then opened her eyes and looked up at him, her radiant expression nearly eclipsing the glow of Karti's tree. "Doesn't matter," she smiled. "The important thing is that I caught what *you* were trying to say. Loud and clear. Thank you, Sam." She leaned toward him and pressed her lips firmly against his cheek.

"You're welcome," he said with a puzzled grin. "I hope it helped."

"More than you know. Although I'm afraid it's going to cut our weekend short. Sam, trust me on this: there's something I really, *really* need to do—as soon as possible. Can you help me?"

"I'll do whatever I can . . . but are you going to tell me what this is all about?"

"Soon—but I'd rather do it first and tell you later. If it works out, I know you'll be happy for me. Let's just leave it at that for the moment, shall we?"

"Fair enough," he agreed, eyeing her with a mixture of intrigue and amusement. "What can I do?"

"I need to fly home in the morning," Paula explained. "What's the first plane I can get to Salt Lake City?"

"There's a Delta flight at nine, but you'd have a two-hour wait in Salt Lake. The one at ten-thirty would get you there just in time to connect with a flight to LAX, and you'd be home a little before noon."

"Perfect. Could we take the girls out to breakfast before I go? I'd love to spend a little more time with them, and it'll give me a chance to explain that I have some unexpected business to take care of."

"Of course," Sam said. "But . . . would you mind my asking what the big hurry is?"

Paula's eyes gleamed in the dim light from the tree. "Let's just say that I've suddenly become aware of some very important loose ends that need to be tied up . . . right away." She winked at him playfully. "Mergers and acquisitions . . . that sort of thing."

"I see. Then you'll keep us informed?"

"Absolutely. Cross your fingers for me." She yawned, stretched, and glanced at her watch. "Gee, I guess we'll have to be up early, so maybe we'd better call it a night." She stood and held out her hand. "Walk me upstairs?"

He took her hand, but remained seated and looked up at her with a weary half-smile. "If you don't mind, I think I'll stay down here for a little while. I feel closer to Karti in this room than anywhere else at the moment, and we just need to . . . spend a little time alone together."

"I understand perfectly," Paula said with a warm smile. "I'll see you in the morning, then." She squeezed his hand, then disappeared into the entryway and moved silently up the stairs, leaving him to commune with the love of his life.

Paula picked up a rental car at LAX and drove to a secluded stretch of beach along the coast. She kicked off her shoes, rolled up her pant legs, and strolled for a mile or so, reflecting on the curious turn her life had taken in less than twenty-four hours. Slushing through the cool, wet sand, she felt a smile rise from her lips, bathe her face with an airy light, and settle in her eyes. How had Sam put it? Something about letting the wonder of a good man's love sink into your soul. "Yes," she said aloud to the mild breeze ruffling her hair, "I almost missed it, but now it's time. And I can hardly wait." Returning to the hard-packed earth of the parking area, she hurriedly stepped into her shoes and slipped behind the wheel of the car. "Take me downtown," she murmured as she patted the dash, "and I'll make it worth your while."

The glass doors to the Donroe offices were locked, and Paula's key opened them without a sound. Once inside, she heard the lively strains of Mozart's "Eine Kleine Nachtmusik" spiraling down the hall. *Just as I suspected,* she thought with a smile. *He can't live without Wolfgang.* She moved noiselessly to the office from which the music emanated and peered in through the open door.

Ted stood with his back to her, sorting through a large box of files and memorabilia. The office was a mess; obviously he was making good on his promise to be gone when Paula returned. But he was moving slowly, ponderously, as though swimming through a gargantuan bowl of gelatin. He'd never get it all done by Monday. *Maybe I'll give him a little help,* she thought, a wicked smile playing on her lips. She quickly bent down, reached inside the door, and pushed the "pause" button on his CD player. Then she leaned against the door frame and folded her arms across her chest.

Cold silence enveloped the room. Ted's back straightened, and she could see the muscles tighten under his navy T-shirt. He didn't turn around immediately, so she took advantage of the opportunity to make her presence known. "Going somewhere, Mr. Barstow?"

He slowly pivoted to face her. His face was drawn and hollow-eyed, and he stared at her listlessly. "Gone, Ms. Donroe," he said dully. "Already gone. Just picking up the pieces." He glanced around the office.

"So I see," Paula said. "Lots of memories here." She pointed to a five-pointed solid silver paperweight on his desk. "I gave that to you three years ago, when your brilliant campaign for Tumbleweed Computers shot us into the national limelight. And that," she nodded toward a small brass and crystal clock perched beside his phone, "was your five-year anniversary gift from the company. You were growing a beard at the time." She smiled, recalling the coarse feel of his cheek against her lips as she had kissed him on that occasion. "And I remember—"

"Thanks for the little trip down memory lane," Ted interrupted, his voice unusually subdued, "but I need to get all of this done today, before you get . . ." He almost grinned, and looked a little sheepish. "Oh, I guess you're already . . . back." A puzzled expression flickered briefly across his weary features, then he shrugged and turned back to his sorting.

Paula cleared a few boxes from his leather couch and sat down. "I suppose you're wondering why I'm here."

Ted stuffed his hands into the back pockets of his jeans. "Let me guess . . . you've decided to make a new fashion statement, and you wanted to run it by your faithful ex-employee. I'd say it has all the elements of a smash hit." His gaze moved to the legs of her slacks, which were still tightly rolled up almost to her knees.

Her face reddened as she quickly moved to restore the pant legs to their full-length status. "Oh, I was, uh, walking on the beach, and I guess I forgot these."

Ted's eyes met hers. "So, why *are* you here?"

She gave her manicure several seconds of undivided attention, then cleared her throat and gazed at one of the few pictures still hanging on the wall—a photo of Ted standing in front of a Stealth bomber. "Well, I just wanted to see if maybe we could renegotiate the partnership agreement."

Lowering himself deliberately to sit on the edge of his desk, Ted folded his arms and studied Paula's face, his brows knit closely together. "Renegotiate."

"That's right," she confirmed. "Make it a bit more . . . *substantial.*"

The muscles along his jaw tightened. "I thought I had made myself perfectly clear yesterday. It's not about money."

She looked at him with an innocent, wide-eyed expression. "Who said anything about money?"

He snorted. "This is business. It's *always* about money."

Paula's whole body seemed to relax as she sank back, spread one arm full-length across the back of the couch, and crossed her legs demurely. "Well, then, who said anything about *business?*"

His eyes narrowed, and he rubbed his chin for a moment as though lost in deep concentration. "Am I missing something here?" he finally asked. "If you'd like to explain it to me, fine; otherwise, I've got packing to do." He picked up a book from his desk and tossed it into the box.

"Fine," Paula declared. "But if you go, you'll be missing out on the biggest deal of your life. I'm prepared to offer you not only full partnership in the company, with every perk known to mortal man, but I'll also toss in—"

"Save it, Paula," he said with a long, drawn-out sigh. "Whatever it is, I'm not interested." His gaze fell, and he scuffed one shoe into the carpet. "You know how I feel about you, and I just can't—"

"As I was saying, I'll toss in eternity."

Ted's blonde head shot up, and he stared at her without any sign of comprehension.

"Marry me," she said softly.

Every molecule in his body froze for a split second, then he cocked his head to one side and tugged on his earlobe. "Excuse me . . . I'm sure I was terribly mistaken, but it seemed to me that someone in this room just said—"

"Marry me." Paula's voice was low and bubbling with mirth.

"There it goes again," he said, shaking his head. "I could've sworn I heard someone—"

"Third time's a charm. Marry me, Ted."

Suddenly the teasing evaporated, and his eyes, now a more intense blue than she had ever seen, were riveted on hers. "What are you saying, Paula?"

She laughed aloud at his bemused expression. "I'm saying I love you, Ted. I'm saying I want to marry you and be your wife forever. If you hadn't confronted me with your feelings at the airport yesterday, I might never have realized it—and if Sam hadn't given me some straight talk last night on what it really means to love someone, I probably would never have acted on it. No matter what happens at the office, you're the one I want to come home to every night. For the next gazillion years or so." She felt the burning truth of her own words, and waited for him to speak.

He pushed away from the desk and sat beside her on the couch. "I'm not sure you know what this means," he said, taking her hand carefully, almost timidly in his.

"Why don't you explain it to me." Her eyes shone.

Ted's gaze played over her face. "Well, there are things to consider."

"Like what?"

"Like . . . you'd be marrying a younger man, twice divorced, who—"

"The enthusiasm of youth coupled with the wisdom of experience. Who's complaining?" Her tone challenged him to continue.

"And I'd be marrying my boss," he added. "Unless, of course, your recent offer still stands, and it's a partnership deal."

"We'll run the company together, fifty-fifty. We can take turns being the boss. It'll be fun." She smoothed a wayward lock of short blonde hair at his temple. "And I'd promise to spend weekends at home—with you."

"Not in Idaho?" His tone became more serious.

"Only if you and Scott came along. I can't deny that the Richlands and I will always be close; we're connected in ways that transcend time and distance. But there's a wonderful opportunity here for *all* of us to be friends. You already know Mark, and the rest of the family will love you, too. I think you and Sam would have a lot in common." She smiled disarmingly. "You both like *me*, for example."

Ted rubbed the back of his neck. "Sounds interesting. Where would we live?"

"My place is bigger than yours. Or we could always buy another one, maybe build a new house. While one of us is being the boss, the other one can superintend the construction." She giggled. "I'd love to see you in one of those cute little hard hats."

"You wouldn't look so bad in one yourself," he grinned. "Let's see, now . . . where was I?"

"Getting ready to say yes, I hope." Paula looked at him expectantly.

He sighed and leaned back against the couch. "We wouldn't have a traditional Mormon marriage, you know."

Her eyes registered surprise. "I thought you were an elder now, and we could be married in the temple."

"Oh, sure," he said quickly. "I didn't mean the *wedding* marriage; I made up my mind months ago that my third time around would be done the right way. But from there on out, you have to admit we'll be pretty much playing it by ear, learning how it works as we go. I've still got a lot of baggage from my childhood to work through, and . . ."

"And I'm still learning what it really means to be a Latter-day Saint," Paula interjected. "Milk before meat, that sort of thing. It doesn't come all at once, and we may never quite fit the customary mold. But we'll be a family, and we'll have the gospel. And each other. For better or worse, we'll figure it out."

Ted's brows drew together in worried concentration. "Still, there is one thing that concerns me deeply."

Her expression sobered, and she searched his face for an explanation. "What, Ted? You can tell me anything."

He bit his lip. "The thing is, if I agree to this . . ." He paused for a long, excruciating moment. "If we do this, I'm afraid you'll just have to get used to the fact that . . . well, that you'll never be married to a General Authority."

Paula's countenance lit up as she laughed. "Oh, I wouldn't be so sure of that, my dear. Besides, it's not really for us to decide, is it? On the other hand, I see every bit as much potential in you as—"

"Believe me. I'm sure of it."

She lifted her chin and regarded him quizzically. "And just what makes you so sure?"

"It's quite simple, really. I don't have a middle initial."

Paula's mouth fell open. "What in the—"

"Think about it. Everybody who's anybody over there in Salt Lake has one: Gordon *B.* Hinckley, Boyd *K.* Packer, Dallin *H.* Oaks, Jeffrey *R.* Holland. Even Sam Richland has one, and you said yourself he's GA material. Then there's me: Theodore Nothing Barstow. Period. It's a curse, I tell you. A curse." He stared at her, poker-faced.

"Well, then," she sighed dramatically, "I suppose we'll just have to accept this heavy burden in our lives. I know it's tough to bear, but perhaps one day we'll understand." She tried to match his straight face, but her mouth rearranged itself into a delectable little smile. "In the meantime, see these?" She ran an index finger slowly across her lips, her eyes never leaving his face. "You know the question. If the answer is correct, they're all yours."

He raised an eyebrow. "Hmm. You realize, of course, that in all the years we've known each other, we've never actually gone out on a *date.*"

"You're right about that," she conceded. "I suppose we really should have one—just so we can tell the grandchildren we *dated* before doing anything impetuous. Let's see now . . . ah, I know! It'll be perfect: dinner and the temple, with a reception following."

Ted swallowed loudly and cleared his throat. "Well, okay then. The answer is yes."

"And you, Mr. Barstow, may now collect the prize." Paula's smile widened as he gathered her into his arms to claim what was rightfully his.

PHOTO BY RYAN PEARSON

ABOUT THE AUTHOR

JoAnn Jolley, a graduate of Brigham Young University, has enjoyed a successful career as a writer and editor. She has worked as a publications manager for two international corporations, as an editor at the *Ensign*, as managing editor of Covenant Communications, Inc., and has published dozens of feature articles and personal essays in national and regional markets. *Promises of the Heart* is her second novel.

Among JoAnn's favorite pastimes are music, animals, spending time with friends and family, basketball, reading, writing, and ironing. She lives in Orem, Utah, where she teaches the gospel doctrine class in her ward. She also chairs a general Church writing committee.

JoAnn welcomes readers' comments. You can write to her in care of Covenant Communications, P.O. Box 416, American Fork, Utah 84003-0416, or at her e-mail address: joannj@trufriends.com.